east

Book 3 of the Morningstar series

LJ Farrow

ISBN: 9798987058268

For my amazing, smart, strong, and lovely daughters, I hope these books will convince you that you can turn any dream into a direction.

Contents

Azuma regained consciousness in her two-legged form, and blinked her eyes slowly, trying to piece together the most recent memories she could summon. The blood she tasted on her tongue was her own, so she lay quite still, taking better inventory of her physical state. The left side of her face was wet and gritty from the pavement, indeed, the remaining moisture from the evening's earlier rains had chilled her to the bone.

She rolled onto her back, less distressed about her nudity than the excruciating pain along her left side beneath and behind her shoulder. Rolling from her left arm only served to restore tingling blood flow as the limb awakened. She lifted her hand with great difficulty and shook it, as unsure as a human whether that would speed the recovery from the numbness in such a body part, yet performing the ritual anyway. It was habitual, ingrained, involuntary.

She blinked up at the sky; she was thankful that she had time to think as this lesser Tokyo alleyway was unusually deserted at this hour. Was it something she had done? Not feeling like this, surely.

The tower to her right was familiar, and the memories seeped slowly back to her. The roof. She had been on the roof. But what of her guard? All twelve had been present, leaping into the dark sky ahead of her, windwalking, their black *karategi* giving them the appearance of a flock of birds drifting into the perpetual glow of the megalopolis. She recalled sending them ahead, but something had happened before she could follow.

Sitting up was a minor struggle, as something was still very wrong on that left side, and she noticed that some of the dampness she had felt was in fact blood that had come from a wound on her left flank. Something else stood out in stark contrast to the transitioning shades of grey that marked the foot of the tower where it met the concrete sidewalk, its bright vermilion color revealed it to be the remains of her own *gi,* shed during her hasty transformation.

The answer to her predicament suddenly came to mind, putting all the missing pieces of the past hour into place. It was the human soldier. The one who had been watching, following. Azuma had assumed that their most recent encounter had frightened him, and she'd left him alive only because she admired his incredible courage. He hadn't been afraid of her, even though he'd had some idea (misdirected a bit by modern fiction) about what she was.

When she had realized she was not alone on the roof, and that her guard was gone, she had decided not to engage the soldier after he revealed himself. He had incorrectly assumed that she had no escape from the roof – at least that had been her best guess at that moment, but she knew now that he had returned to finish whatever mission he'd been given.

She had allowed him to chase her to the edge of the roof and then turned to face him before diving backwards off the ledge, spiraling into the ribbon-like form of her other-self as she drifted downward. She remembered her surprise and horror when she was followed; the soldier was wearing no base-jump pack or any other lifesaving equipment. There was another detail as well, but this was still out of reach of her recall. Something about the soldier's face that she had not noticed before, something that had surprised her.

Whatever the revelation, it had been less of a shock than the fact that he merely threw himself after her. But he had horribly miscalculated or mistimed the jump. It appeared that his initial intent had been for her to break his own fall, but she could see that he had not completely understood what she was, thus had aimed for a target that had arms and legs to grasp and not the smooth slippery scales she wore that afforded no purchase.

Against her better judgement, she *had* twisted to break his fall, again admiring the determination and self-sacrifice of her would-be assassin. Her initial instinct had been to let him pay for the mistake and plunge to his certain death.

The vestigial limbs of the dragon were not evolved to catch the weight of a falling body, and the impact had nearly separated her left foreleg from her torso. The pain had been excruciating, but she had somehow managed to constrict her elongated body and tail around the added weight and survive the ground. She did not remember anything beyond the few brief moments after their bodies collided, so the shock must have caused the loss of consciousness and perhaps had startled her into reverse transformation as well.

She could tell that she was already well into her regenerative process, her injuries beginning to heal, but this was slowed by the magnitude of the insult, and in this, her lesser form, the hurts were more grievous. She rolled to her feet and realized that she was not going to get much use from that left arm, and the alarming numbness that she had attributed to recovery from compression was more likely the herald of a significant physical insult.

A weak sound reached her ear and she froze in place, all senses at the alert. The unacknowledged question in her mind was answered. The soldier lay prone, half in and half out of the mouth of a small alleyway several yards away, where his own body must have come to rest. Astonishingly, he was trying to drag himself upright, but she watched as these attempts failed miserably. His sluggish, discoordinate movements suggested concussion, and he gave up further efforts to sit, slumping down onto the pavement once more.

She approached with caution, admonishing herself that she was *Dor-a-gon* and need have no fear of this human. The events of the fall had shaken her. Blood loss had amplified the rawness of her feelings, and his rescue had cost her. Well, this pathetic creature would pay for the injuries it had caused.

She crouched beside him, noticing that the opening between the two buildings was a shallow space too small to be an alley. Azuma's acute eyes saw a recessed platform and she realized it was a loading dock off the street, probably a discreet way to supply the hotel that fronted on the parallel block to the east.

His arm was accessible to her, and she bit down more savagely than she needed to in order to feed, but some small and petty part of her wanted to punish this interloper for her own hurts. She was somewhat surprised that her command and her resolve were so poor; fear made human blood taste all the richer. This was hot and strong, pumped from a stubborn and unyielding heart, but Azuma tasted none of the fear she expected. It was made no less delicious, however, by the strong emotion that she did taste. Anger. She smiled, her lips curving against the salt of its skin; she knew that sentiment well. But the blood told her something else, something surprising, and she remembered what she had seen on the roof. This discovery did not impair her rage.

As she continued to drink, rather than drift into a stupor, the soldier struggled, but Azuma held on, refusing to stop, no longer caring about the outcome. She had no reserve for control.

The sense of fury swelled as she held on, until the soldier dared to punch her, connecting a vicious roundhouse to her face which disrupted her feeding. This one had no quit. She had to smile again, a carmine grin that was even more terrifying than the rage that lit her eyes. But the soldier slumped back to the ground, having spent every ounce of strength it had left. Consciousness departed, and Azuma could see that survival was not certain.

For the lower half of the body was bent at an unnatural angle, the breathing irregular and labored, harbingers that death would have taken this one anyway. She could not initially categorize what she felt; finally, she identified her shame and regret. This was a true warrior, much like the samurai of her earliest days, and something about this one touched her.

She made a split-second decision, and found that once it was made, there was no turning from it. She stood up, grasping the complicated straps on the soldier's vest to get purchase to turn the body over. Its uniform was some sort of light technical armor over a dark jumpsuit of ripstop fabric, and she was surprised to discover more weight than expected, with a muscular density she hadn't predicted. While neither excessively tall nor particularly short, she could see the soldier was of compact build, with spiky short dark hair that stuck out stubbornly in all directions.

With her mangled arm, it took longer than expected to gain enough purchase on the shoulder straps to pull the body backwards, deeper into the alcove. Consciousness had departed her adversary, and

Azuma's shock was blunted by her recall of the discovery on the roof and what the soldier's blood had told her when the head rolled back on the shoulders, revealing a strong attractive face with an angular jaw and prominent cheekbones that was absent any beard. The soldier was a woman.

Hazel eyes fluttered open with difficulty and did not appear to be capable of focus. The woman finally spoke in impeccable Japanese, with a heavy accent that Azuma struggled to identify. "There is a gun…on my left hip. Do me the honor, one soldier to another," she rasped, in a depthless pragmatic tone. Those eyes burned with a dying fire, and still there was no fear that Azuma could detect. When Azuma did not comply, the woman managed to reach the weapon and draw it, weakly trying to lift the muzzle toward her own skull.

Before the soldier could position her finger on the trigger, Azuma disarmed her in one neat movement, ejecting the magazine and chambered shell with practiced ease before replacing the gun on the soldier's belt. She tossed the ammunition away, the brass winking like coins in the air, and clinking onto the pavement in a random scatter, some of it dropping off the sidewalk and bouncing into the roadway that intersected the mouth of the alleyway.

Ignoring the pain in her side as she reversed direction, Azuma pulled the woman up onto the loading platform. The rolling door went up with some difficulty, but she was able to drag herself and her unlikely companion inside. She did not bother to close the entrance to the load bay behind them, simply hefted the soldier onto her shoulders. Azuma was surprised that she did not cry out; she was probably too weak to do so. Azuma crept onward into the darkened depths of the building, aware that with the injury, her lack of clothing, and her human cargo, it was a stretch to hope that she could somehow get them both to the relative safety of her own dwelling without detection.

azuma

Dragon's name was _______.

Never mind that she was first Dor-a-gon, chiwosuu akuma, born with a taste for blood; she was also Nekekube, and to some, Kyuketsuki, the demon who sucks the blood of the living.

When the pseudologues came, those minor deceptive demons who fell to Earth with Akenomyosei, the Morningstar, and told her of its imminent arrival, she was already resigned to her fate. She knew that the glorious afterlife had been taken from her before her very conception, but it remained to the Enlightened Ones, the powerful kami that had allowed Akenomyosei some rule within this realm. She was naturally a pragmatic creature but was also surprisingly religious. She knew that there must be a reckoning for one such as she – although part of creation, her existence and survival were crimes against those created in a divine image.

Akenomyosei had to reconcile anomalies to secure its rule. She had little doubt of its eventual triumph, yet still she plotted. It could be delayed. Perhaps for millennia. It intended her to believe that she was superior to humans, and for a time, she did.

Dragon's sin was bloodlust.

To fend off boredom over the centuries, she had cultivated various means of prolonging her feeding gratification. She had never been human, but she felt she had achieved a certain ability to maintain almost human relationships, to the smallest of degrees. Humans were food, but they fascinated her, nonetheless. Dragon was too singular in her purpose and too isolated in her existence to know much of the broader world.

Dragon's curse was dazzling physical beauty.

While it should have been attractive to her human counterparts, it was so extreme that it was an immediate warning of her intrinsic inhumanity. It served to frighten as much as it beguiled. She discovered that by manipulating a carefully determined combination of human fear and human desire, she could build a wholly human construct – loyalty.

Those humans with whom Dragon engaged in congress slowly lost the rapidity of human decay. This occurred even without the blood sacrifice, and the amplification of lifespan was increased with subsequent encounters. Dragon learned that her lovers could survive a handful of centuries following an interlude of a few months. Their survival inevitably exhausted their blind loyalty, and jealousy ruled them. Some were foolish enough to make attempts on her life. But this created nothing more than nuisance as the disenchanted were easily dispatched, easily replaced.

A single drop of her blood contaminated human judgement even further, and conferred inhuman strength, speed, and appetites. This provided Dragon the means to create a protective army. After centuries of improvisation, she had perfected a blood ritual used to engineer an elite guard. These were called the Akai hogo-sha, born of trysts that lasted for days and culminated in blood exchange, trading their birthright for a number, the privilege of becoming one of the twelve.

Over time, they lost all human interest in food, and robbed of Dragon's perfection, declared their power by succumbing to crueler appetites, although no human could ever satisfy them. This resulted in a state of devotion, understanding, and philosophy that was monk-like in its fervor.

But these were deadly priests.

1

WHEN IETSUNE SAW THAT HIS younger brother, Tsunayoshi, was the favored son in their father's eyes, he was filled with anger, knowing that the Shogun's riches could pass over him. Worse was the disgrace he would suffer. His loss of standing in society, his ability to achieve the most favorable match in marriage…he could hardly bear the shame.

Warrior training had brought him strength and cunning, and he had learned all the old stories of greatness and fame. He had listened well to his many teachers as a boy, and even more closely to those military advisors who attended him as soldier and samurai.

Ietsune had proven useful to his father during the Rebellion, helping to cleanse the land of those who had no origin there. His cruelty was creative and absolute, ensuring the purity of their people and securing the Tokugawa rule. This quieted many who criticized Ietsune's ability to rule because as samurai he led with strength and finality. While he did not have the prized diplomacy that made Tsunayoshi so adept among the nobility and for which he was much admired by their father's advisors, Ietsune's military prowess was undeniable. Yet nothing he did distracted the father's eye from his younger son.

Ietsune knew of the legends of power, those sacred and profane, and had observed that those who overstepped the bounds of honor reaped the greatest rewards. This conceit, this flaw in his reasoning, made him reckless for the acquisition of fame and notoriety, and he all but forgot his humanity, and turned his back on anything that had ever been good in his life.

He sent runners to the four corners of the world to seek talismans that would increase his influence, wanting to ensure his legacy and prolong his own life. He ignored the warnings of caution that were bestowed with good intent, and any who displeased him were fatally dispatched. The perceived slights of his contemporaries were made larger by his emotional weaknesses, and he became ever more violent and insular.

He turned away from the Shinto and Buddhist teachings that had once been sources of strength and wisdom, and this freed his conscience to unleash even more ruthless rule over the lands he had once sworn to protect. He converted the family shrine to his own profane use, shameless following his mother's death. And when again he heard a most famous legend of his boyhood, he placed all his belief in it, for it suited his plans for the domination and annihilation of his enemies.

He seduced the dark *kami* in order to learn the location of *Onigashima*, the island that many believed only existed in legend, and fearful that others might learn what he knew, spent a year trying to find it. Rowing out from his own great island he offered many blood sacrifices to the sea. And when, finally, *Onigashima* rose up from the mist, he approached, with the awful understanding that he would find what he had come for but unable to turn back.

He fasted during his climb up the endless mountain. The island was possessed of a terrible enchantment, and he had heard of those who never reached the top. But Ietsune, steeped in the way of the samurai, was ever prepared to give his life if such were the will of the gods. If he proved himself worthy, the island would reveal its secrets.

Ietsune eventually lost track of time, and his doubts worsened when he reached the cloud bank that embraced the peak he hoped he would reach. But his hair and his beard grew long before his footsteps led him out of the clouds. Once again, when he was able to see the sunshine on the waves that seemed impossibly far below him, he left the rocky rim of the mountain and entered the quiet of a dense overgrown plateau. He made his way through the trees to a clearing that revealed a lake which appeared suspended from the sky itself. Its color was not solely a reflection of the heavenly blue above it, rather the pool was clear to some depth, revealing that what appeared to be a magical illusion was in fact reality. That impossible color was due to some great and powerful force outside of the natural order.

As Ietsune approached the pool, he was met by a sentry. The being had the appearance of an exalted samurai of breeding and prestige, as he wore the dragon armor accorded a rare few of those warriors who had achieved great success in battle. Indeed, this armor was of such elaborate craftsmanship that Ietsune wondered at the identity of its wearer; surely this was a unique and powerful lord. The mask it wore allowed for no identification of any human facial feature, and Ietsune had a moment of fear when his exhausted imagination worried that the armor was hiding something much more terrible than a man. He had honed sharp instincts, and they told him now that he was in the presence of a very dangerous and dark *kami*.

The soldier stood attentively at the water's edge, his *sashimono* prominently displaying the dragon in gold. It hung motionless, as there was no wind, but the warrior's hair seemed to move of its own accord despite the still air. The creature did not speak, but Ietsune heard voices he could not understand, a cacophony that coalesced into something deep and ominous. The language was not of *Nihon*, yet Ietsune understood it, a gathering of many into one, coming from this being; it was inside Ietsune's mind, and around him, and everywhere.

"What you seek here will bring you a legacy of power that cannot belong to you, can only belong to itself, and if you wish to proceed you must survive its terrible test of courage and desire," it told him. Ietsune held his tongue in deference; he was rewarded when the being continued.

"Ietsune, son of Iemitsu, next in line to be Shogun, rare indeed are the rulers of your line. But not so rare as the koi who travel in hordes and are able to traverse waterfalls in a lifelong quest to reach this sacred pool. One in a million of these remarkable creatures can achieve the ultimate transformation, becoming the exalted and mythical dragon. Yet only one in a million million will walk the earth as guardian of this sacred pool and its enchanted inhabitants, protecting a magic as old as the world itself."

The creature gestured toward the pool that had previously appeared empty to Ietsune, but he could now see was teeming with the familiar graceful turns of many koi, their orange and gold patterns rhythmically reflecting sunlight off their iridescent scales. With a movement so quick as to give away its inhumanity, the warrior plucked one of them from the pool, and Ietsune could see that this one was very special, and very rare. It bore no markings on its sky-blue scales; indeed, he would not have known it was there among its companions, as its color matched the strange and wonderful blue of the lake. This koi was somewhat larger than its fellows, and it struggled vigorously to escape its captor.

The mysterious soldier turned to Ietsune and whispered something in an ancient language not to be understood by any human. Ietsune felt the cold touch of fear, an emotion strongly encouraged by his samurai training, an emotion to be embraced, listened to, and ultimately mastered. But whatever this power was, it was not to be overcome by tradition or discipline; this test would determine his fate. He had a fleeting moment of unease, wondering if he would see the shores of Japan again in this life.

Almost immediately, Ietsune noticed that his limbs were immobilized, and the dragon warrior presented the koi to him. Without any conscious effort, Ietsune opened his mouth, and the koi was pressed into it. Ietsune began to panic because the creature's hand and arm followed, pushing the fish deeper into his throat, stretching him open. Just when Ietsune felt his flesh must give way or he must perish, the warrior stopped pushing, but that brought no relief, because the koi wriggled in the depths of his throat, and he remained unable to breathe, the koi dominating him, trying either to escape or establish passage.

"All will be well if you pass this test," the voices surrounded him, but Ietsune could no longer see. The darkness was closing in, he had no air, and death would find him here, on the shores of this lake. He tried not to struggle, wanting to face this on his own terms. Death was not to be feared, as each samurai must face each day with death, and when he realized that the world was slipping away, he abandoned his efforts of control and resigned himself to accept whatever fate deemed just. He thought of his father, and of his brother, and contented himself with the knowledge he would never be Shogun, never contribute to the bloodline of the Tokugawa, and this was the path he had chosen over honor. He closed his eyes for what he thought was the last time, hoping they would open again in the next life.

2

IETSUNE REGAINED CONSCIOUSNESS ON THE rocky shore of the island; his rowboat bobbed rhythmically just beyond the water's edge. The gritty sand of the beach abraded his cheek, and he pushed himself up, looking around. The mountainous peak of the island loomed above him, wreathed in grey clouds that obscured the sunlight.

His hands reflexively went to his belt, but his own swords were gone, perhaps a sacrifice to the dark gods of *Onigashima*. In their place he discovered two new long swords at his waist, and a short sword at his back. He was surprised to find he now wore the elaborate armor of the dragon warrior; the mask stared up at him from the shoreline. The golden standard was beside him, fluttering in the breeze coming off the water.

There was a new heaviness at the center of his chest, and a fluttering there that was foreign, but other than these changes, he felt better than he had even as a younger man. Leaning forward to retrieve the mask, he was startled at his own reflection in its lacquered surface. The eyes that stared back at him were the cerulean blue of the mountaintop pool, reminding him of the blasted blighting that came with the cataracts of the ancient. He was transformed, and it did not displease him that the warmth and humanity of his former countenance were entirely eradicated by the cold depths of these orbs.

3

SEVERAL YEARS PASSED FOLLOWING IETSUNE'S disappearance, and word came from the corners of the earth that he had sacrificed his own men to the dark *kami* of the mountains and the rivers, and even to the sea. The old Shogun grew feeble, and sent messengers following on the four winds to implore Lord Ietsune's return to his father's deathbed.

He obliged. But the man who returned from the far lands had set aside the remains of his nobility, had extinguished his capacity for humanity, indeed had traded his soul for a power even he could not control. And unbeknownst to those who lived in the old Shogun's province, the demon that rode his back committed unspeakable acts.

Those who looked upon him opined that other suns had bleached the very color from his eyes and blasted any love from his heart. He saw much more than he had before and knew that Tsunayoshi had nearly been elevated to the seat that was rightly his.

At Iemitsu's bedside, Lord Ietsune waited. He was patient and stoic, seemingly enduring the suffering of his father. Tsunayoshi had a strange suspicion that he enjoyed it, a pricking insult he could not shake, and he was angered anew at all his undeserving brother would enjoy when it ended. But neither could Tsunayoshi disgrace himself by opposing Iemitsu's desire to elevate Ietsune, no matter how unworthy and ill-equipped he might be.

Ietsune had long disdained social company; Tsunayoshi assumed he sought the pleasures of concubines but had never been personally close to his elder brother. They were born of different elements, Ietsune more like a distant uncle even during Tsunayoshi's boyhood. Since his return from long absence he was even more unfathomable and held no private audiences with his brother.

Although personally distinct, they had fought side by side on campaigns in support of many of his father's most powerful *daimyos*. Tsunayoshi and Ietsune had often prevailed by fighting back to back, each driving threats from the other, cementing their filial love through enforcement of the Shogun's policies, providing leadership to the many samurai who had sacrificed everything to put down rebel Ronin, Dutch rogues, and would-be Christian colonizers. But when battles ended, and skirmishes were suppressed, Ietsune always withdrew, taking with him whatever minor intimacy the brothers had briefly shared. In the years following Shimabara, feeling their father's displeasure with him and unable to ignore Iemitsu's deep affection for Tsunayoshi, he had abandoned the Shogun's court and seemed to have quashed whatever small regard he had ever had for his younger brother.

Tsunayoshi was relatively naïve about Iemitsu's relationship with Ietsune. He had a younger son's carefree path through the world; the greater burdens fell to Ietsune as the firstborn, but the younger would never understand the weight of a father's expectations in the way Ietsune must have. He couldn't know how Ietsune had chafed at his role, hating ceremony and lacking the cultivated and often contrived manners necessary for statesmanship, he was best suited for the field strategies of a soldier. He lived on campaign and refused to learn the lessons of the nobility, preferring to solve disputes with terrorism and bloodshed. He was a ruthless and successful samurai, strangely disciplined within that culture. He had never been able to tolerate the elaborates of politics and had insulted and angered many of his father's most eminent allies. Chief among these was Lord Mashaito, a powerful and influential *daimyo* whose daughter, Onishi, was touted as the most beautiful maiden in all of Japan. It was widely believed that the two men sought to unite their houses by arranging the marriage of

Onishi to one of the Tokugawa heirs. Unlike Tsunayoshi, who saw Onishi as an honorable and intelligent woman who would make a useful ally in marriage, and with whom he could share a companionable fondness, Ietsune rarely received her with more than cold contempt, seemingly unable to recognize her value in any measurable way.

In contrast, Ietsune's men received all the fealty and brotherly regard that Tsunayoshi had experienced from his brother while on shared campaign. Until there were no more enemies to fight, and Ietsune turned on them, murdering them for power. This was all the substance of accusation and rumor, none of it substantiated, but those samurai who had left the province in his company to a one had not returned when Ietsune returned, and to a man he spoke of none of them. He was transformed, and not for better. He had always understood how to exercise power, but apparently not restraint, and in the forgetting of it, he had found a strange freedom of conscience.

But his tardy return had pleased Iemitsu. The old man had forgiven – largely forgotten – Ietsune's transgressions, but the Shogun was much changed from the powerful warlord who had cleansed the country of those who wished to change the old ways. Tsunayoshi observed that Iemitsu's best qualities as soldier and ambassador to the ruling class had been divided between his brother and himself, and they were not marriageable to any great degree in either. He also knew that Iemitsu would have been incensed to be told that his eldest son behaved much like his father when making the most draconian of decisions. This late in life, sickness and infirmity coupled with the threat of his own mortality had made Iemitsu sentimental. He saw Ietsune's return as the ultimate honor to a failing father.

But it was Tsunayoshi who heard the untoward whispers of the townsfolk, Tsunayoshi who paid for the silence of the fathers of debauched daughters, Tsunayoshi to whom they came with grievances, imploring his confidence because they did not want to offend the Shogun, and ultimately because they were afraid of Ietsune. Tsunayoshi buried all ugliness to allow their father some lasting peace in his final days, but saw disaster foreshadowed.

His departure had displeased Iemitsu greatly enough, and Ietsune's absence was so prolonged, that Tsunayoshi could tell that he was being groomed to assume leadership of the shogunate should Ietsune fail to return.

Whatever grudges Ietsune bore him before were renewed ten thousand-fold on his return, because the provincial gossip told of the generally held belief that Tsunayoshi would ascend as Shogun and take all the power and privileges the position enjoyed. It was true that Iemitsu's advisors had pressed him to make it official in all haste, and had not curtailed these supplications upon Ietsune's return, rather renewed them with all due urgency, if greater secrecy.

And Ietsune had an uncanny knowledge of these things. He seemed to see through all that went on around him, seemed to have an insidious understanding of the hearts and minds of his father's men. He refused to hear their counsel or their concerns about what was expected of him in succession – indeed, he spent his days in quiet contemplation at their father's bedside, cementing for Iemitsu his devotion and loyalty. He spent his nights in the decrepit shrine that he had fouled with his dark dealings after the war, and soon after his return it was populated again with priests of some ill repute, the supposed spiritual advisors of their master, slaves to an ancient and dark religion.

And Tsunayoshi was largely banished from the old man's side, partly out of the deference that was expected of him, but admittedly because he too was unable to stomach hours in Ietsune's presence, was repelled by some unnamed dread of his company.

So Tsunayoshi unwittingly reinforced his brother's enmity and mistrust. The seeds of discord were thus sown and cultivated. Unbeknownst to Tsunayoshi, in his final days, Iemitsu, in senile and febrile discourse, spoke to Ietsune in whispered confidences, called him by his brother's name, and the flowers of hate bloomed and thrived in Ietsune's heart, ahead of an inevitable bloody harvest. The father spoke of Lord Mashaito's shared fondness for Tsunayoshi, and their plan that Onishi should be his bride, noting that another favorable match could be found elsewhere for Ietsune. These unwitting poisons were poured into the depths of Ietsune's ears, confidences meant for another, but these were secrets he swallowed with destructive delight, patiently awaiting his inevitable inheritance.

4

ONISHI WAS INDEED A BEAUTY of legend, and the tales told of her did not do her justice. She was pure of heart, understanding that she was to become the bride of one of the Shogun's heirs. Ietsune knew well that her father had pledged her to the Shogun as a bride for his successor. She preferred Tsunayoshi, but she held her tongue on such important matters, knowing that her place dictated she avoid bringing dishonor to her father's house by refusing the elder brother. Just as Onishi would not defy her father's wishes, Tsunayoshi also was honor-bound to submit to the determinations of Iemitsu in such a decision.

But Ietsune made her fearful. Even as a child, he had been indifferent and cruel. It was uncertain whether he would ever succeed his father, as he was impulsive and lacked the proper judgement and decorum to rule. He had none of the polished statesmanship of Tsunayoshi. His lengthy disappearance had given Onishi hope; his strange return had crushed it anew.

Neither Tsunayoshi nor Onishi were aware that Ietsune knew that his brother coveted the bride he had been promised. Worse, Onishi's countenance betrayed her own feelings for her lover, and neither knew that Lord Ietsune had a new heart. One that had no room to forgive betrayal, imagined or not.

Thus, all were at an impasse as Iemitsu faded and passed on to the next world. Ietsune observed a silence that lasted throughout the *Sōtō* ritual. Many nobles and feudal lords came to pay their respects; they were allowed by custom to mourn the Shogun during his consecration and await the funereal blessings of the circumambulation with the family. While the Zen monks prepared the funeral pyre, Tsunayoshi took his leave to wander through the grounds of his father's extensive gardens, trying to decide what Ietsune would ask of him, and fearful that it would not be to his liking.

He was both surprised and delighted upon encountering the Lady Onishi and her attendants admiring the decorative pond at the center of the grounds. When they spotted him in the distance, many of her entourage absented themselves, bowing gracefully to him before withdrawing to the lavish guest house afforded Onishi's father, Lord Mashaito, and his household.

Only Isako, her nursery mate and handmaiden, remained behind to attend her lady, who graciously agreed to allow him to provide her with a tour of the grounds. Isako cleverly fell further and further behind them as they wandered aimlessly; she maintained her lady's honor as chaperone while affording them the privacy of lovers. It was a mistake that did not go unnoticed, the first of the perceived slights committed by a doomed brother.

In the ornamental garden, a smaller monument had been erected by their ancestors, where Iemitsu had prayed for strength as a samurai and soldier during the time of *his* father. Tsunayoshi had often accompanied him in later years, as speaking to and paying respects to the ancestors was a tradition that Iemitsu honored.

Adjacent to this monument was a decorative pond, in which a rare dragon lotus grew. It bloomed but once a year, and one could not predict its color. Most often it belied its name, and while beautiful, the petals were the color of the snowy crane, with no hint of blush. But rarely, perhaps twice in Tsunayoshi's three decades of life, it had bloomed a crimson hue as deep as fresh blood. Iemitsu would have deemed it an omen that the flower was now a brilliant red standard, a beacon, a message to the living. Tsunayoshi thought it proper that his father had received such a tribute from nature.

Onishi gasped at its loveliness and lamented that such a bloom could be enjoyed for so short a time. She acknowledged aloud what Tsunayoshi thought silently, remarking that the gods smiled on his father's memory. He thanked her for her kindness, marveling that her beauty did not disappoint its legend, and her graceful manners and artful speech made her a unique prize, a bride of rare renown. He rebuked himself for such thoughts, knowing that it was her father's place to determine her match, but still assuming he had a chance due to his high birth, and his father's assurances that another could be found for Ietsune.

She surprised him by asking him all manner of questions about his vocation, his aspirations, and his interests. He wondered that she knew so much of him, as they had only interacted at arm's length at ceremonial functions, but was gently reminded that she had spent much time in the company of both their fathers in her own home, and had heard a great deal about his usefulness to the Shogun. Because her mother, like his own, was long deceased, she was hostess there, and naturally expected to provide hospitality.

"He was especially fond of you, as well," she offered in condolence, shyly, as if she wanted him to know it in case Iemitsu had not been inclined to demonstrations of his affection for his sons.

Tsunayoshi found it of interest that she did not mention Ietsune at all. He wondered that he had not seen this warmth in her outside of his company, and it gave him much hope. When he considered the several occasions in which the families had been in contact together, he had not known Onishi to show Ietsune any more than the deferent politeness expected of her.

Hope made him blind, because he was not the strategist that a military man necessarily becomes. His faith rested in his father's words that there would be another bride for Ietsune, one that would provide him an heir. Hope made him bold, because after the sun set on that evening, he plucked the dragon lotus from its home and made a gift of the bloom to Onishi.

Hope got him killed.

5

FOLLOWING THE LIGHTING OF THE funeral pyre, Lord Mashaito received Ietsune in the guest quarters.

He made all due deference to his new Shogun, and although it was irregular, he agreed to leave behind his daughter and her handmaiden when he returned to his *daimyo*.

It was expected that Onishi would require some orientation to her new home, and announcing her as mistress of the household would ease the transition for her when she formally became the Shogun's wife, Ietsune argued.

Lord Mashaito agreed, with a heavy heart, realizing that while his relationship with his Shogun would now be secured in a way that it could not be had Onishi wed Tsunayoshi, the path that he and his old friend Iemitsu had devised was no longer viable. Tsunayoshi was the favored son-in-law, and Mashaito did have the power to refuse the match, but his honor and admittedly his fear made him succumb to Ietsune's demands. He was all but turned out of the Tokugawa household in swift fashion, with promises that he would be welcomed again in a month for the wedding ceremonies.

He took his leave of his beautiful Onishi, holding up a restraining finger to the tear that threatened to fall from her eye. "Daughter, you will proudly do your duty to your family. I wish you the blessing of many sons."

His hands shook as she parted from him with a small bow of obedience, and he was momentarily sad for her. He gave Isako unnecessary instructions regarding protection of Onishi's honor, and then mounted his horse ahead of his own samurai and turned homeward.

Onishi's nighttime weeping persisted for days, and Isako tried to console her mistress in her grief. She was also fearful of what Ietsune might do if he heard these laments; they were unbecoming for one who was expected to act dutifully and honorably.

Surprisingly, the dragon lotus floated in the ceremonial bowl near the night lanterns, as crimson and pristine as it was the day that Tsunayoshi plucked it. Onishi focused on it during her prayers, consoled that no matter what her marriage would bring, she had once been loved tenderly and given such a gift.

When, on the fifth night, having refused to leave her room, Onishi readied herself for bed, Ietsune entered unannounced, carrying with him a small concealed bundle. Isako and Onishi scrambled to receive him, but he waved away their efforts, saying only, "I see that my wedding gift has been stolen by my brother."

"My Lord Ietsune, I do not understand -" Onishi began, confused by his calm demeanor. Her senses were heightened, and she was immediately afraid. Her fear was reflected in Isako's eyes.

"Am I not master here? Are these lands and all upon them and within them not my own, including the dragon lotus? In plucking the flower, Tsunayoshi ensured that it shall never bloom again, a theft of beauty against his Shogun. But worst of all is that by gifting it to you, he has insulted my honor and made of you his whore."

Onishi started to speak, but Isako pulled her down, and the two women kneeled before Ietsune in supplication. Bowing before him, she shook with shame to hear his cruel words. Isako, too, was shaking, because the accusation he had leveled at Onishi was true; she had accepted the gift of another man when promised to this one. It was of no import that he was a monster.

"No matter, I have brought you another gift, one more in keeping with my own sentiments," he said softly, dropping the parcel that had accompanied him. It hit the floor and rolled slightly, its coverings bloody, and with awful certainty, Onishi guessed its contents.

"My dear Tsunayoshi realized that he had forfeit his honor and committed *seppuku*," Ietsune told her. "I served as his second. Now my honor is restored."

"Unfortunately," he continued, turning his attention to Onishi, "Yours shall not be. Isako, prepare your lady for my bed." Seeing Isako's distress, he said, "No one expects the Shogun to marry a woman without honor. I have dispatched a rider to your father with the news of your disgrace, and suggested to him that he may similarly restore his own family's honor by forfeiting his life. You shall still serve my desires."

And correctly reading something proud and obstinate in Onishi's posture, he concluded, "Refuse me and I use Isako first, while you watch."

6

ONISHI MADE HER WAY CAREFULLY through the trees, balancing her swollen belly as best she could over the uneven ground. The recent rains had turned the forest floor to a soft mud that she sank into with each step. She kept watch of Isako's back in the trees ahead, realizing that her maid was moving too fast for her. Onishi could hardly blame her – they were both afraid, and fear was driving Isako onward, subconsciously moving away from her lady as they made their way to the shrine.

Onishi was unsure she could make it, the fast-growing baby inside her was disturbingly agile. Although she was not in any pain, there was something ominous about its movements that made her worry that there would be agony enough to come, agony to match the cruelty of the Shogun's assaults. She hoped that the priests that sheltered there could help her; they were certainly important to Ietsune, but their secretiveness both intrigued and repelled her.

The movements came again, and this time were accompanied by an overwhelming nausea, and she was forced to her knees as surely as if the ground pulled her downward. She sank further into the ordure and involuntarily threw a hand into the muck to steady herself. Irrationally, she wondered if the earth would swallow her whole, and the child be born from its bosom. She sat still for a moment, realizing that in her great anguish, she could not quite bring herself to bemoan her fate, wanting only an end to this endless suffering. When she looked up, she could no longer see Isako ahead, and she had no strength to call out.

The movements inside her were increasing, almost a rushing, rhythmic motion that was nothing like her attendants had described. There had been no abrupt or even occasional kicking. This sensation was never so discrete, rather it had the quality of moving water and seemed to flow from one side of her body to the other.

Onishi knew she was also losing time to vague fugues and distractions. She slept more than was warranted for a healthy young mother, and when awake, was subject to disturbing daydreams and loss of time. Her mind wandered often, and an entire afternoon would disappear. Her sleeping dreams were dark but unspecific; she ran for her life from a nameless dread, neither escaping nor being caught.

"Lady! Lady, are you alright?!" Onishi suddenly heard Isako's voice somewhere to her left, and she knew by the quality of the light that she had been drifting in place, as had become so common.

"I am here," Onishi whispered, surprised that she barely had the strength to do so. But Isako persisted, and eventually discovered her charge, kneeling mired in the churned mud.

"Oh, lady, *no!*" Isako exclaimed, mirroring Onishi's kneeling pose. "It is too soon." She shook her head sadly, and accepted Onishi's weight as her mistress slumped sideways.

Onishi looked at her blankly, grimacing as blood flowed back into her legs, the pain merciless. The movements in her belly were relentless now, never ceasing, and she realized that Isako's statement was in response to something else. Her kimono was soiled with mud, surely, but this was now accompanied by the dark blood of womanhood that soaked through her garments and now blemished the snowy gown of her handmaiden.

Isako did not recoil in horror, as she felt she must, but instead felt piteous sadness for Onishi. They had lived parallel lives, and her beautiful mistress would now depart this life without her. Isako had failed to deliver her safely to the shrine, but looking at Onishi now, she was certain that there was nothing that even the priests there could do to save her.

Isako placed her hands on Onishi's swollen belly and was alarmed at what she felt – ripples of movement that could not be normal. The signs had not been incorrect; there was something otherworldly about this birth, and Isako's dread about Ietsune and the dark gods he had courted were confirmed.

Onishi placed her hands over Isako's, and the latter was distressed at the coolness of her touch. She drew in a sharp gasp of surprise, and turned her eyes to her friend, only to discover that she was leaving this world for the next. The movements beneath their hands shifted, down and away, and Isako realized that the child had been expelled from Onishi's body.

Isako could not bring herself to disrobe Onishi and investigate. A shudder overcame her, and she struggled, panicky, to her feet. She watched in horror the feeble, tentative movements under Onishi's garments and turned away. She began to run, the soft earth holding onto her feet with each step.

True night followed her from the eastern sky, but the moon had not risen, and the western horizon remained a crimson smear. She made her way toward the shrine, hoping to find assistance there even though such priests were creatures of the terrible Lord of this place, pushing desperately onward, slowed by fatigue and the growing realization that she may have been imperiling herself unnecessarily. She thought of Onishi and the infant she had deserted out of fear. If Ietsune discovered that she had abandoned his child, he would have her head.

Reluctantly, she turned back toward her friend, following the marks in the ground that she had disturbed in her flight. She made her way back into the trees, admonishing herself for ever leaving Onishi so alone.

She reached the place where she was certain she had abandoned her companion, the ground still marked and the blood black in the soil as the night came on, but Onishi was gone. A few paces away was an opaque object that stood out in the shadowy clearing, and Isako approached it cautiously. It had the appearance of a flattened sac, egg-like, and before she could stay her hand, she reached out, curious. It had a slippery, leathery texture, and her fingers were suddenly slimy, but the substance felt *living* and warm. Her recoil was delayed slightly, but unnecessary. The thing was empty. Her fingers smelled faintly like standing water, both natural, of things living, and yet with a foulness, of other things ancient and long dead.

It took a moment for her to realize that not all the sounds she heard were native to the night trees, and she investigated further, unable to keep herself from following them into the bamboo to her left. She was momentarily relieved to have found Onishi, thinking that she had simply miscalculated her friend's location.

But then she felt the presence of something else, just before her weak night sight betrayed furtive movements near the body. The frustrated scratching and pulling of a hungry animal. Smallish, perhaps the size of a fox, but luminescent, its body was long and sinuous, serpentine, graceful, but moving like a land beast on legs impossibly small, with an elongated head and eyes that reflected the light like the surface of a moving stream.

When it saw her, that head tilted predatorily, and she saw that it had been attempting to feed on Onishi. Isako was suddenly certain that its frustration was due to Onishi's dead flesh, and she carried herself away, moving even faster and more desperately than before.

She fought through the mud, pressing onward breathlessly as the ground held her more with each step. She lost her shoes, but continued, knowing that her own life hung in the balance. She felt as though she dragged half the forest floor on the hem of her *kimono*, but persisted onward, the younger bamboo shoots snagging and tearing her sleeves and piercing her feet.

She knew the shrine was somewhere ahead, and she had to be close. She could see a vigil lamp piercing the darkness in front of her, but the distance was unclear. She could smell her own fear and moved faster. The ground was firmer, and she struggled to go even more quickly, still sure her pursuer came behind her.

She passed several miniature shrines for the night demons, and their unexpected placement distracted her enough that she fell headlong to the ground, feeling another sharp bamboo shoot pierce her side as she collided with it on her way down. She could not help but cry out in pain and fear, but then noticed the sentry who stood a few paces away.

He wore elaborate armor that recalled Ietsune's complicated accoutrements, and his mask and helmet, like her master's, were dragon-like. He held no standard to identify his allegiance, but she was comforted by the swords he carried and implored him to help her.

Isako sobbed in relief and reached out to him in supplication. "Good samurai, I have come from the forest. A beast is about and has attacked my mistress and her baby. I must get help."

The man maintained his silence, but removed both his helmet and mask, revealing a darkly handsome face, and a full head of long dark hair which was moving independent of the evening breeze, as disturbing as it was beautiful. He made no move to assist her, rather lifted his eyes to the trees beyond them, and smiled an awful smile. He tilted his head, listening to something she could not hear, but soon enough, she knew. Her reckoning had arrived; she would find no solace here.

Tears of sorrow gave way to fear. When the beast arrived, it was more beautiful and terrible than she had appreciated. More disturbing was its accelerated growth — it was now nearly the size of a man. The soldier seemed pleased, and finally spoke, but not to her.

"*San'ninshō, dragon-born, child of blood,*" it crooned, bowing deeply, and the beast seemed to understand. "With this sacrifice, the blood of the pureflesh for sustenance, I welcome you, on behalf of the great and terrible Akenomyosei."

Isako glimpsed the flash of steel as it drew the sword, the impossible sparks of the blade as it emerged, and soon felt the sting of its bite across her shoulders. Her blood was warm on her back and neck, and as the Dragon turned to its feast, she witnessed her ending in its depthless eyes.

7

WHEN THE STRANGER ARRIVED, THE guards could not recall from which direction he had come, only that he was a striking figure in expensive armor who rode a tall dark horse and asked to see the Shogun. Under other circumstances, the security of their master would have precluded honoring such a request without further assurances and some knowledge of the identity of an unannounced visitor; in the present case, if questioned they would have admitted that the man's imperiousness made it impossible to turn him away. In reality, they were responding out of a deep fear that they could not bring themselves to name. There was something about this stranger that motivated their celerity in presenting him to the main house.

The guards there, perhaps because they were more numerous or because more steeped in protocol, nevertheless insisted that he surrender both short and long swords as was their usual precaution for all visitors, not just those who were unknown to them. It would be a loss of all honor to endanger the Shogun in this sanctuary. He was thus presented to Ietsune after only a brief delay.

As he was shown into a small library overlooking the central garden, where Ietsune was in counsel with his advisors, he noted with satisfaction their general boredom and inertia. This was likely a combination of the stifling weather and their complacency of position.

"I bring greetings, Great Shogun, from the shores of *Onigashima*." The stranger bowed with all ceremony. "My master, Akenomyosei, extends congratulations on the birth of your daughter and hopes you will extend your hospitality so that gifts may be bestowed, and respects paid to her when it arrives."

Ietsune gestured to his attendants for privacy, and when they had withdrawn, he inclined his head and said, "Let us walk in the gardens awhile, where we may speak most freely." His expression indicated his awareness that one's walls have hearing and memory.

"I am at a disadvantage," Ietsune admitted, when they had crossed the ornamental bridge and put a discreet distance between themselves and the guards. "I received no notice of your visit, you have not given your name, nor do I have any proofs of your fealty." His posture was imposing, his tone gruff, and he rested a deceptively languorous hand on his sword.

"Majesty, if you will allow?" The stranger reached carefully into his robe and produced an ornate scroll, which he handed over with a deferent bow.

Ietsune took it with a start once he noticed the seal — it was the golden dragon that now graced his own battle standard, the very same he had first seen on *Onigashima* on the day of his transformation. The seal disappeared with his touch, and he unrolled the document, impatient with the slight tremor his hands betrayed. He read the perfectly executed characters.

By servant of my own this instrument delivered
The bearer shall be as I with such authority given
To serve the dragon spawn
To forge the steely sword
To staunch it in her blood
And seal it with your word
On that day will I my presence make
To present the child of destiny our legacy and gift

Ietsune was given to understand part of the riddle – that the stranger was to join his household, that he was to forge a weapon of tempered steel, and that the great spirit warrior that had rewarded him with this power would present itself on the morrow for a ceremony to recognize his heir. He did not shy away from the implication that she was to be sacrificed for his greater power, and had unfortunately forgotten the words of caution told to him by the being at the lake. Indeed, he was so pleased at the prospect that he failed to appreciate the knowing look of his companion.

He made as if to return the scroll to the stranger, but it disintegrated in his fingers, its particles dispersed on the breath of the breeze.

"Lord Tokugawa," the stranger bowed once more, as formally as before, and Ietsune realized that he was impatient with the man's manners. Something about his demeanor, although the very picture of propriety, rang false. The samurai trusted his instincts. But Shogun or not, he would not disobey the one who had conferred upon him such power. "I am Tatsuo Tomo, sent to instruct your daughter's development and ready her for the arrival of the great Akenomyosei and the ceremony that will accompany it."

"Then you must meet her straightaway," Ietsune suggested, and he motioned to his guards to follow.

He led Tatsuo Tomo into the bamboo forest. Its trees grew at an angle, leaning sentries created by the persistent southerly winds. After several minutes of silent passage through sun-filtered clearings, the shrine loomed ahead, a stone structure adorned modestly with several new Shinto arches made of green wood leading to the steps that would take them up to the entrance.

Ietsune noted that Tatsuo Tomo showed the proper deference for the dead, but did not otherwise observe any religious formality on entering the temple, disdaining the fountain and ritual cleansing. He followed the Shogun up the broad risers and into its shadowy interior.

The oil lamps revealed the scrolls written by the priests here, displayed with the warnings that this was the house of *Ryū*, the Great

Dragon. Twelve in all, Tatsuo was pleased to see that the traditions his master had put in place centuries ago had been maintained.

They came to an elaborate archway, again in the Shinto tradition, which the two men passed under in silence. This marked the passageway to the innermost chamber.

The vault blazed with a reddish light; four priests arranged themselves in three straight lines to triangulate their charge at the center. They kneeled in meditation before her. All were thin and excessively pale, with eyes that focused only on the creature they revered and protected.

The Dragon slept, bathed in the glow of the many lamps. Her scales were variegated with black on white patterns, with random orange patches that were reflective of the light, it was this iridescence that gave the room and its occupants a bronzed cast. Her modest size and coloration betrayed her immaturity.

At the sound of the approaching footsteps of her father and his guest, she opened one eye and uttered a fearsome, rattling hiss. To a man, her guards were moved from their prayerful trance, and twelve heads moved in synchrony, all eyes directed toward the intruders, their hands producing *usugurai* with practiced efficiency as if from the air.

To Ietsune's surprise, Tatsuo Tomo laughed with abandon. That laugh frightened Ietsune more than he cared to admit, and there was a cold delight in the handsome face. And something else, too – in the flickering lamplight, Ietsune thought the man's face changed, as though his flesh were but a mask to cover a much more terrible reality. But then the moment passed, and the stranger made bold to approach the goddess of the shrine.

Her attendants moved as one to block his path, but as Tatsuo Tomo moved resolutely forward, each of the priests dropped to their knees in reverence, murmuring prayers of thankfulness for his return. These addresses left Ietsune at a loss, as it appeared that these men knew and respected his unusual visitor. When the man reached the Dragon, she let out a prolonged screech, and Tatsuo Tomo laughed again. "Of course, I am the enemy," he told her, gently cradling her beautiful head. "Smart girl. You shall learn quickly."

Turning once again to Ietsune, he inquired, "Have you given her a name?" He stood expectantly, awaiting an answer.

"I call her Himura Azuma," Ietsune replied. "For the east; a crimson dawn that signals the beginning of all things."

8

IT WAS TRUE THAT THE juvenile dragon could instinctually identify her enemies, and it was no surprise to Tatsuo Tomo that she recognized the threat he posed. He had served the great Akenomyosei as a sort of general, and unbeknownst to Ietsune had been for centuries called many names, most common among them was the Death-Bringer. Chaos called him, and the birth of a dragon was a rare event. The birth of this dragon had been foretold, and her instruction had been entrusted him.

Neither was it lost on him that the Dragon recognized her own father among those she identified as enemy, and her reaction to him was so profound that her priests had convinced Ietsune to stay out of the shrine.

Tatsuo Tomo taught her to name the *Akai hogo-sha*, using the ceremonial tradition of the ancients. Each relinquished a given name, and then they were named by number from one to twelve; the most senior and trusted was called *Ichi*, the next *Ni*, the following *San*, and so on, down to *Jūni*, the twelfth. In her earliest days, when she fed, on occasion her bite was fatal, as she had yet to learn control, and the effects of her venom were unpredictable. The loss of *Roku* meant that *Nana* ascended to take his place, and each priest-guard in turn was elevated, necessitating the indoctrination of a new number twelve, carefully chosen from a member of the secret sect that was faithful to this dragon, guardian of an ancient religion devoted to the Master.

But her bite conferred many other things, most importantly devotion, necessarily blind. Each priest was needed to protect and honor her, giving their lives to her and for her. The venom made them clouded, as if they were drugged into acquiescence and love for their charge. She also fed from them, and in exchange, they needed little sustenance to survive, and achieved inhuman longevity and abilities that allowed them to perform their primary directive. Each believed that he was the favorite; each believed in their acquiescence to service and sacrifice.

But the goddess he had come to serve was necessarily a prisoner. Powerful and rare, she was sequestered here with what remained of those faithful to the Great Two-Headed Dragon, Akenomyosei, the Lord of Darkness and Deceit. It was the Master who would return to welcome her, with sacrifice, blood, and death.

Tatsuo Tomo prepared her well. Ignoring her cries of hunger and pain, he tortured her, starved her, enraged her, making her mistrustful and brutal, and, to his eyes, even more beautiful. Her blood meals became rituals to increase her power, and he allowed her to partake of the flesh he had stolen to hold his form. Within the twelve years of their tutelage, she achieved a not inconsiderable wisdom, despite her immaturity in years. Tatsuo Tomo informed Ietsune that the time had come to forge the Dragon's sword.

When the day arrived for her ascension, she was a weapon, stripped of anything unnecessary to Akenomyosei. Neither control, nor humanity, nor mercy marred her, and she was ready to become the beast that had been foretold, and ascend the bloody throne of her religion. All that was wanted was a martyr.

9

IETSUNE PRESENTED HIMSELF TO THE armorer, impatient with the man, impatient with the progress as the iron was forged and tempered to create the finest steel for a blade unlike any other, a blade fit for the gods. He'd thought he would go mad; for twelve days and twelve nights the apprentices had hammered, their rhythmic blows following at the singsong urging of their master.

Just before dawn on the final night, with the forge burning like the mouth of hell, the Dragon was brought from the shrine for her christening. Ietsune waited in the shadow of the stars, listening to her shrieking fury, surprised once more when she came into view, as now her scales were completely black, the juvenile splotches had been swallowed in her growth. Now the size of a Sika deer, her dorsal fin rippled in the glow of the fire and her tail undulated rhythmically, disturbingly marking time in a cadence like that of his stuttering heart.

Into the firelight came a dark figure, a spectre of smoke and ash and dancing ember. A powerful *kami*, whose form coalesced into a humanoid figure of sulfurous stench as if spat from the earth, pulled into this world from the next. Ietsune bowed in reverence, recognizing the profane incarnation of Akenomyosei, the warrior from Onigashima, giver of his own dark gift.

From the glowing forge the smith pulled the sword, ready to be staunched and tempered with dragon's blood.

Tatsuo Tomo stepped forward to greet his Master, and nodded to Ietsune to prepare.   "Brother Twin who was and who is not, I see the result of your toil. Shall she survive?" the Monster asked.

"Brother, Father mine, who was and who remains, you shall judge and I shall be judged," Tatsuo Tomo replied with a deep bow, and for the first time, Ietsune saw the red reflection of the beast in him, something ancient and lizard-like, inhuman, cruel. It confirmed that the shadow he had recognized in the shrine was real. "I have given what was required and shall depart, but the Dragon shall be ever divided, just as you and I."

"*San'ninshō, dragon-born, child of blood*," Akenomyosei called out in that unknown tongue, yet all who heard understood. The Dragon shivered with what appeared to be anticipation, her scales seeming to move with the rhythm of the dancing fire.

"Ietsune, son of Iemitsu, slayer of the sacrificed Tsunayoshi, defiler of Onishi, and father of Azuma, Dragon Goddess and God, step forward to christen your children and finish the Dragon's blade."

Shiny eyes watched as Ietsune stepped forward, his guards and the temple priests gasped as one as he grasped the red-hot metal. And screaming an oath as his skin melted to the raw *tsuka*, he thrust the still-burning blade deep into the Dragon's breast, and the steel was perfected in the blood that poured forth as she screamed out her fury and pain.

Tatsuo Tomo immediately collapsed inward, like a burning house, and vanished. Ietsune wrenched the sword free, feeling a surge of immense power, believing that the Dragon's death was assured, confident her power would be his own. But she lifted herself up with a terrifying cry, followed by several short barks of ear-splitting sounds that were eerily akin to laughter.

A change raced over her form, the black armor turning a blue as deep as a summer sky, each tiny scale transforming in turn like *Riichi* tiles falling over. Her cries subsided, and she doubled over, coiling her tail around herself like a whip, and her back bowed and cracked, those scales shedding like iridescent raindrops. In the next instant, a human girl stood erect where dragon had been, tall enough to be an adult, taller yet than her father, with the sexlessness of a child. Her eyes were still the cold pale blue of the beast but within seconds warmed to brown as she looked for the first time out of her human form.

She leaned forward, face to face with her father, brown eye to blue, and whispered to him one word, the only word she would ever say to him.

"*Teki.*"

Ietsune understood. She identified him as the enemy. He still held the cooling sword in his ruined hands. His guards reached for their swords, ready to defend their Shogun, but twelve zealot priests were faster, twelve ceremonial blades found flesh, and in that terrible moment, Ietsune was alone. Akenomyosei watched, a shadowy wraith beyond the fire.

The smith and his apprentices kneeled before her; Ietsune's rage was further ignited by this treacherous change of fealty. The wind was strangely calm.

Slowly, indeed gently, the child removed her weapon from his hands, and what remained of his palms hung in scorched and ruined tatters. She passed the raw katana to the armorer for perfecting, then held up her own hands, studying the particulars of her new form, awed by this new body. Then, as if satisfied that she could control it, one hand shot out, fingers steepled like an arrow point, into Ietsune's chest. With a swift and decisive movement, she removed her bloody birthright, the enchanted heart he'd carried to her from *Onigashima's* shores.

He was strong, and the remnants of his evil magic sustained him long enough to witness her devour the heart, greedily licking his life from her fingers. All he had done, all he had seen, all he had been was bestowed upon her, an inheritance swallowed whole and complete. Azuma's dry scream of satisfaction reached the starry gate of the heavens, and the time of the Dragon was at hand.

10

THOUGH HER PRIEST-GUARDS WOULD HAVE returned her to her shrine, Azuma saw her time of imprisonment pass with her father's death, and she put on his armor, carried his standard, and took up his bloody causes. She appointed herself Shogun, to the surprise of the lords and nobles that came calling, but none dared argue with Ietsune's heir. Shockingly, she found that they saw what they wanted to see, a beardless youth, an assumed son, with all the ruthless cunning of the father but of a keen, pragmatic intelligence that impressed the most skeptical of them. They pressed advisors upon her, but these she refused, insisting that she would install a council of her own choosing. Her birthright to the respect of the Mashaito clan was also invoked, giving her an impeccable pedigree with which to do great and terrible things. With Tatsuo Tomo's departure, chaos fell away, and some of her reason and balance emerged, a natural inheritance from the mother she had never known, an outcome unforeseen by her evil tutor and his Master.

Ronin from the countryside that had avoided allegiance with the former Shogun came forward, and an army was cultivated to continue the work of her grandfather. Small uprisings were put down, and creative solutions were found for the captured priests whose proselytization had been curtailed during the Rebellion.

One of these was to torture them into renunciation of their faith, then to force them to marry Japanese women and sire children, in complete contradiction of their vows. This subjected them to ridicule and shame, and they were held out as examples of the weakness of Christianity, which supported the ethnic and religious cleansing Iemitsu had desired. Some were sold as slaves to the pirate merchants of the north. Many were simply executed following prolonged torment and ridicule.

Only the Dutch were allowed to remain, as their teaching of ocean navigation and engineering was useful to the ruling class. Even they were restricted to the periphery of the island nation.

She made the rounds of all the allies of the family, noble and feudal, calling upon them personally. It served her purposes to allow them to remain ignorant of her womanhood; indeed, many of them assumed she was Ietsune's son, blinded by the prejudice that no daughter could display such strength and reason. So she lived as a man would live in those earliest years, and even those who might have known that Ietsune had had no son soon forgot, or had their memories obliterated at the point of a sharp *katana*.

None assumed she was not fully grown, and she did not disabuse them of the notion that she had come of age. Not that she could have; she had no memory of her birth and early years, probably lost in the crucible of torture during the time she was physically and mentally shaped by Tatsuo Tomo. What was not lost was his voice, coming from inside her, unwelcome, commenting on many things. She told no one of this, she had no one to tell; the voice was surely an echo, it could do nothing to motivate or command her against her will.

Of the *daimyo* she attended, one of the most powerful was located in the far lands of the north. Hiro Tanagata was a contemporary of her father, perhaps slightly older than Ietsune, born of a land-owning family of great repute. One of Azuma's earliest visits was to his territory to gauge his loyalty to the Tokugawa, for she knew that many who had feared challenging Ietsune would be interested in the strength of the new regime, would be looking for any signs of weakness. She intended to demonstrate her capabilities, crossing the Tsugaru Strait and arriving in Yeso with 10,000 samurai.

Lord Tanagata had been surprised when he received the request for an audience with the new Shogun, and like many of his peers was power-hungry and corrupt. He was too curious to refuse the visit, and assurances were made that he would abide by guesting laws and extend every hospitality.

Tanagata was impressed with the Shogun's forces, and rode out to meet Azuma on the road from the city, at the encampment her forces had established there. He was pleased to see what he believed was a beardless young man, traveling without any apparent advisor or senior counselor to mentor him. He gave the young Shogun and the *Ouban*, her personal Guard, a tour of the island, beautiful in the summer and forbidding in winter. Tanagata hoped that he could exert some influence on this child and exploit it for his own benefit, and while he considered his options, the gods gave him inspiration.

When they reached the gates of the *shoen*, all were welcomed to walk through the gardens to the manor. Inside the entrance hall they removed their footwear and donned slippers. Tanagata noticed that the Shogun did not remove any weapons, but was relieved to see that the guards did so with deference to the safety of the household.

Awaiting them were the servants of the household as well as Lord Tanagata's wife, one unmarried son, and his daughter Megumi. It was not lost on any present that the beautiful Megumi captivated the attention of the young ruler, who gazed upon her with curiosity and interest before following her father into the home.

Tanagata shared details of the estate with Azuma, encouraging her to examine his books, which were delivered to the guest quarters for perusal. He assured the Shogun of his faithfulness and promised quarterly tributes as stipulated by feudal law. He then showed her and her guards every courtesy, treating them to a meal of exquisite quality, with drink and fine entertainment.

Although it was late in the evening when Azuma retired to her room, her guardsmen quartered in an anteroom next door, she kept the candles burning for a few hours more as she reviewed the figures Lord Tanagata had shared. Thus she was still awake when, in the depths of night, a soft rap on the door drew her attention from her studies. She stood next to the desk, and said, "Come."

The screen slid back and the guardsman on duty peered in. "Exalted one, you have a visitor."

"It is late," Azuma replied.

"Yes, Majesty, but I do not wish to offend our host," her samurai was clearly uncomfortable about something, but probably felt his opinion on the matter was improper, although he did betray a small smile.

"Very well," Azuma assented, and her guard stood to, pulling the screen somewhat farther to admit her guest. Azuma was astounded to see Megumi enter, bowing deeply as she stepped out of her slippers. The guard withdrew, softly pulling the screen closed and restoring privacy.

"My lady, I apologize to receive you in this state, but your visit is unexpected," Azuma said, indicating the armor she wore, still dusty from the road. It was her practice to wear her armor for the initial day of any visit with her feudal contemporaries; once their accord was established she would subsequently don her father's ceremonial dress and colors.

Azuma was young, but she knew that it was also highly irregular that an honorable young woman should present herself without a chaperone, but Megumi addressed this as well.

"Lord Tokugawa, my father sent me to attend you," she said in a very small voice, betraying some timidity, and, Azuma thought, something else. There was hesitation in her bearing, but she came forward, still not making eye contact, and said, "Let me help you prepare for sleep."

It was so odd that Azuma made no protest as the young woman approached, and stepping behind her began to undo the fastenings of the *do*, her overcoat. When this was finished, she came around to the front and gently lifted the armor off, setting it neatly aside, next to the helmet, sleeves, and shin guards that Azuma had previously removed. With gentle hands, she reached up, encircling her arms about Azuma's neck to loosen the leather thong that held back her hair, freeing the dark waves that fell around her shoulders.

Under Megumi's nimble fingers, the shirt was loosened, but when she reached for Azuma's pants to remove the *kobakama*, she trembled, and Azuma suddenly saw what was happening. "Stop." She trapped the young woman's hands in her own and held them against her body.

Azuma realized, with dawning certainty, that Tanagata was sacrificing his daughter's honor to what he perceived to be the Shogun's — her — lust. There was a slim hope that such a gamble would result in an alliance between their houses, but rather than offer the daughter in marriage, Tanagata hoped that Megumi would be taken as a consort, with no regard for her wishes, thereby ruining her prospects at an honorable match. She was being given up as a pawn for power, treated as less than nothing. A high-born whore.

Azuma was still too naïve to realize that this was a common practice that she would be exposed to again and again as a samurai noble, but it made her angry. She said softly, releasing Megumi's hands and taking a step back, "You must not remain here. It is not proper. Return to your mother." She was aggrieved that her voice betrayed too much of her ire, guessing correctly that Megumi would interpret the anger was directed at her.

"Please, my Lord," Megumi pleaded, eyes wet with tears. "Do not be angry. My father will be disappointed, and —" Here she stopped, afraid that what she was about to say would disgrace her father. She pressed her body to Azuma's and placed a kiss on her exposed chest, with all the inexperience of a child who has not been taught the arts of seduction. Azuma noticed two things at once, that Megumi did not yet recognize that the Shogun was not a man, and that she was moved by Megumi, not just her unfortunate plight; the young woman's touch and her scent were causing Azuma to respond in a dangerous, unfamiliar way. It was not safe, this type of emotion, because like all strong emotion it stimulated her basest appetite, and she had been long on the road without a blood meal.

Megumi began again, "You must not send me away, or-or…"

"He will punish you." Azuma stated this flatly, knowing that Megumi was in a terrible position. "Very well. I will not send you away. Come, my lady." She led Megumi to the *shikibuton* and untied the fastenings of the young woman's kimono, beneath which she wore a much simpler dressing gown. She slid the outer garment from Megumi's shoulders and encouraged her to lie down. Megumi's eyes widened in surprise when Azuma pulled the covers up and around her. "Take your rest, my lady. I have no designs on your virtue."

Azuma retreated to the desk and tried to continue her assessment of the figures there, admittedly distracted by the young woman in her bed. It did not take long for Megumi to drift off to sleep, and seeing her in repose, Azuma realized that she was even younger than she seemed, probably no more than fourteen, barely a woman, sent to be used up to forward her father's designs.

She waited an hour longer, knowing that her guard would have succumbed to his fatigue, and when she went out into the garden she wore Megumi's kimono, her long hair streaming, unmistakably the young woman she really was.

In this form, she visited Tanagata in what he believed was an elaborate dream, having assumed correctly that he was not the type of man to share a bedchamber with his wife. No matter. It served her plans. He fed her thirst for blood and her thirst for revenge for the distasteful treatment of his daughter, and though he did not know it, nor would he understand his need to please her in the coming days, once she had his blood his fealty was hers to control.

Thus, Azuma spent her nights in Yeso watching the beautiful Megumi asleep in her chambers, and when she returned home it was no great surprise that Lord Tanagata agreed that his daughter could accompany the group as a gift to his Shogun. Azuma let Tanagata believe that it was his decision to send her, and she let him believe that his position was assured within her court because his daughter was now the Shogun's consort. And when Megumi and her attendant had safely reached the shores of the big island, Azuma gave the order to burn Tanagata's holdings to the ground, and bring her Tanagata's head. In turn she sent runners to ensure his heirs could not contest this act, leaving her free to make a gift of the far lands of the north to another to govern.

11

IN THE VILLAGE NEAREST THE Tokugawa home, Iemitsu had relocated and punished the most senior of the Catholic priests that had been captured a generation earlier. Aged and stooped, he had been released from his prison, and faithful samurai had witnessed his forced marriage to one of the farrier's daughters, who wept with the shame of such a husband. And she was kept weeping as those same soldiers, under order of the Shogun, supervised the wedding bed to ensure that acts the man had vowed to abstain from were undertaken. Such intrusions were repeated and in time, the farrier's daughter bore the priest a son.

Universally considered an aberration, this unfortunate creature endured twice the insult of any half-breed born from shame and dishonor. His appearance was enough, as his countenance favored not enough of those from the land of the rising sun. He was marked with the social ugliness of being neither one thing nor another, a walking disgrace.

His mother, too, was ashamed of him, this token of her own misfortune, and left him to his own devices, often abandoning him to the mercy of the elements when she thought her husband was unaware. She refused to give him a name, certain that he had no soul, and prayed the *yokai* would take her burden as a bloody sacrifice. The old priest, for his part, tried to do his son the barest of kindnesses, but was hounded by the townspeople and shamed. They mocked him, accusing him of being as weak as a woman, one who did not know how to teach the boy to be a man.

The child learned to make a way for himself, and spent more and more time ranging abroad in the great bamboo forest, gathering butterflies and flowers, wandering farther and farther from home, even down to the inland sea, where he created tableaus of seashells and stones of elaborate detail. His butterflies he hung from strands of horsehair in the clearings by the hundreds, and these habits bought him a name. The Collector.

He spoke to no one, indeed he was thought to be dumb, stricken with some affliction unnamed and terrible and directly related to the sins of his father. At best, he was ignored, and at worst, kicked, beaten, spat upon, any and all the terrible things that can happen to an unprotected waif in a place where soldiers looked to sate unholy appetites. He was stripped of his personhood by dint of the accident of his birth.

Travelers would encounter him on the road, bearing his ubiquitous marks of violence and neglect, silently contemplating a collection of fern leaves, or in the depths of the wood building his ethereal dioramas. Though he was to remain unlucky, he survived the succession of Ietsune and ultimately, Azuma came to rule.

In secret, his father would let him into the house through a window. He spent these quiet respites listening to the old man read, fascinated by the many scrolls he kept, and intrigued by those writings in another language. Unaware that the boy understood anything of any import, the priest did not notice that his son was learning, absorbing all around him, self-taught, self-sustaining, he knew two languages by his tenth year. Impossibly, the father had secreted a Bible kept for him by those who had embraced this new religion and now still practiced the *Kirishitan* faith in great secrecy. This, too, the Collector devoured, thirsting for knowledge he would not otherwise obtain – it was against the Shogun's laws to formally educate those who were considered outsiders.

In his nineteenth year, the Collector was caught on the Shogun's land, drawn to see the dragonflies that mated by the ceremonial pond in the early summer, he was discovered by a group of drunken samurai in a dangerous state of boredom. He had grown unwary, having long since believed that he had, literally and not just figuratively, disappeared. They stripped him, dragged him into a forest clearing, and staked him to the ground, spread-eagled.

Early bamboo shoots were sprouting there; bamboo grows with deadly purpose, and Azuma's guards knew this. It will grow right through a man, a horrible, slow, pitiable death of gradual impalement that can take many days. Their mistress was away at the wedding of a powerful *daimyo* of the south, so they appointed themselves the arbiters of justice for this trespass. These brutal men made a point of visiting the Collector every day, sure to bring him a flower or a butterfly in mockery, taking pleasure in watching him die.

By the time Azuma returned home, weary from the road and ready for rest, in need of a blood meal, he had been incorporated into that grisly garden for twelve days. Were the gods merciful, he should have been dead, but intermittent rains had provided him water, doing naught but prolong his agony. The largest shoot of bamboo had entered near his spine and exited his chest during an excruciating four-day travail, blindly making its way to the sky, and the pain of the insult was dulled by his waning senses. This mortal spear had missed all organs that might end him quickly. The flies had found his eyes, and he could no longer see out of one of them.

It happened that she traversed the forest on her way to the shrine, and the path brought her to him. She drew up short, mid-stride, coldly assessing the scene before her. Stricken with hunger as she was, the man could not know that his peril was at its greatest, but he welcomed the leniency of death in whatever form it took. He knew someone was there, but he felt it was not one of his tormentors, as they were boisterous in their attentions. This presence did not feel like them; it was something darker, more dangerous. He felt it in his bones, and he knew it was listening. He tried to call out, asking, "Who's there?" but his voice was a cracked ruin like the rest of him, and his question was unintelligible.

Azuma crawled across the clearing as silent as the night, climbing up over him, ready to open him up and drink. But his one good eye tried to focus on her, and met her own, brown eye to brown eye, and her voice speaking into the silence surprised her more than the wretched creature she'd found. *"Teki janai, kare wa tekide wanai."*

Tatsuo Tomo mocked her from his prison inside her. *He is not the enemy? He is human, food, less than nothing, Imōto.*

She ignored this, and taking her dirk from her waist, she set about freeing his limbs from their bonds. She lifted him up, not delaying for his protest, nor his moans of distress as she slid him off the growths that had impaled him. The movement made him cough up blood, some of which spattered onto her. Weakly, he reached for her face, and she thought him delirious as his hand pushed weakly at her, until she realized that he was trying to clean away the soilage there. It amused her, but she had no time to dwell on such things. She licked her lips, and tasted his blood. It showed her much, and some of what she saw angered her, and some surprised her, but she put all of this away from her thoughts, having more important matters to attend to. This was the one her dreams had foretold, a key to her enduring strength, attendant to her power.

She did not see Akenomyosei watching with interest from a safe remove among the trees as she hefted this encumbrance easily and set off again for the shrine.

12

MASTER *KU* GREETED HER AS she entered the shrine, accepting from her the burden she carried. His mouth twisted in distaste; the man reeked of rot and death, and his wounds bled too little. He had begun the journey to the next life.

"Please bathe him and bring him to the sanctuary," Azuma ordered. "Prepare him for the ritual. I must cleanse myself. Send *Jūichi* to me. I must feed." Without waiting for a response she strode onward, leaving *Ku* to obey, never doubting he would.

By the time she reached the inner sanctum, even *Jūichi* was in place, sent ahead to ensure all was in readiness, his glassy expression the only betrayal of his recent sacrifice. The Collector was positioned at the center of the room, cones of incense burned as offerings to the gods. He had been blessed and washed, prepared as sacrifice, which would have been merciful. Azuma had other plans.

Ichi and *Ni* awaited her patiently, one at the man's head and the other at his feet, but there was not the usual danger or threat, as this one had no reserve to fight her.

As Azuma kneeled beside the Collector he could move only his eyes to try to look at her, but all he was asking for was death, and her earlier conviction to save him was affirmed. This one, unlike others, was not pureflesh, and this was through no fault he could claim. As her priests waited expectantly for bloodshed, she paused again, but there was no further advice from Tatsuo Tomo. *Ichi* bowed in reverence and offered her the ceremonial dagger.

She held the dagger high and it caught and reflected the light from the many lamps in the sanctuary. Her twelve priests swayed in their fervor, but they could not have predicted her next act. In one savage downward stroke she opened her own wrist, squeezing her fist she allowed her sacred blood to flow around and through her clenched fingers and into the Collector's mouth.

All twelve attendants gasped in horror. *Ichi* moved as if to restrain her, but she afforded him such a withering look of disdain that he remembered himself and withdrew without daring to touch her and bowed his head in submission. Azuma could see his wavering resolve; she did not know that these men considered the spilling of the Dragon's blood an ill omen that would surely bring the disfavor of the gods.

Azuma held out her arm to demonstrate that her bleeding had stopped, and all observed in awe as her wound closed as they watched. The man on the dais shivered violently once and was still.

At that moment every lamp in the sanctuary went out, extinguished as if by an ill wind. The priests moaned in fear; the Great Two-Headed Dragon was displeased. But Azuma ignored their superstition and got to her feet. Choosing *Jūichi* as he remained enthralled with her following her blood meal, and was at present most malleable to her will, she instructed him to deliver the Collector to the house.

Once her priest had lifted the man into his arms, the Collector spoke. "Little girl, do you know what you have done?"

Azuma remained silent as she led the way out of the shrine, into the world, across the bamboo forest, and home.

13

THE COLLECTOR AWOKE IN A new place. At first, he wondered
if he were dreaming, because he could remember nothing beyond the
pain and the suffering of the clearing. The room he was in was quiet
and well appointed, with many books and articles of great industry.

He sat up slowly, curious that he felt no pain. It was impossible
that he should not require a long period of convalescence to recover
from the hurts he had endured, yet here he was, bathed, dressed,
without bandage or medicaments.

He could hear the lively discussions of the birds outside, the
breeze as it whistled and sighed through the bamboo and curled
around the corners of the house. He inhaled the sweet smell of the
tatami mat that he reclined upon. A large bronze mirror on the far wall
caught his attention, and he climbed slowly to his feet, surprised at his
own nimbleness after suffering such grievous hurts.

He approached the mirror and studied what was reflected there.
A solidly built young man with a large scar on his chest, two clear bright
brown eyes that radiated with determination and intelligence, wearing
a slightly uncertain expression. There was a great deal of his mother in
that face, but it was diluted by the mark of his father's faraway lands,
and for the first time in his life he saw the differences that others saw,
and knew in that instant how little was required to make one an outcast.

Before he could dwell overmuch on this discovery, the screen
doors to the room were pulled back and a young woman entered with

a tray of food and tea. She was visibly startled to find him awake, and bowed deeply. "Treasured guest, please forgive my intrusion. The master bade me to wake you and serve your meal."

The Collector was unused to such courtesy, and her deference surprised him.

He returned her bow. "There must be some mistake. It is not proper for you to serve one such as I. The laws forbid it."

"Good sir, I am Megumi. I am a member of this household. The Tokugawa rule Japan. This is the home of the Shogun," she told him, laying out her logic before concluding her statement. "The Shogun makes the laws. The Shogun rules here, and has said you are our guest." With another deep bow, she backed out of the room. From the threshold, she told him, "I will send the attendants to assist you to bathe and dress." And then she was gone.

He sniffed the food, wary as one of his position should be of any kindnesses, and satisfied himself that it had no taint. He was hungry, ravenously so, and he devoured the rice, seaweed, and quail eggs that had been provided. There was a rich broth, and all was accompanied by strong buckwheat tea. Following his meal, he felt refreshed, but no sooner did he relinquish his cup there was another sound at the door, and two young boys appeared to escort him to his bath.

He was unused to physical attentions and sent the two out of doors while he attended to his bathing in private, enjoying the hot perfumed water and strong soap. Ignoring his protests, they returned to towel his hair and assist him in dressing, which he realized was necessary, as he had no knowledge of the complicated nature of courtly dress; he was grateful as they fastened the frogging at the neck of his kimono and assured he was appropriately attired to meet the Shogun.

They led him to a long low structure across from the main house, which faced away from the gardens and onto a parade ground for the many soldiers who lived and trained on the estate. Both outer and inner screens were drawn apart, allowing the warm breeze to circulate, and he was presented to the Shogun, who was writing industriously at a low table at one end of the room.

The Collector looked around briefly in curiosity, seeing the many pigeonholes containing scrolls far more numerous than what his father's small library had held. But it would be unseemly to stare at another's possessions in this way, and he wanted to avoid offense, so he abandoned the formal bow in favor of a display of submission, kneeling with his head down, completely at a loss as to what was expected of him.

In a moment, he heard sand being poured over the ink on the scroll, and the soft sound of the stones placed to allow it to dry. Determined footsteps approached. "Rise, esteemed guest, and greet me as your friend," the familiar voice spoke with a touch of good humor.

He rose to his feet and met the eyes of his host – *hostess* – surprised to see the girl who had saved him from the forest. Azuma saw the incredulity in his expression and shook her head gently, placing a finger on her lips as she glanced at the attendants and the guard at the door. He observed astutely that she wore the court dress of a nobleman, and had docked her hair at the nape of her neck as any soldier would. What he remembered was true; Ietsune had only produced a daughter, but it appeared she lived as a man and ruled as Shogun here.

She placed a hand on his forearm briefly in reassurance before dismissing his attendants and asking her guard to give them privacy.

"I thank you for your kindness and hospitality, my...*Lord* Tokugawa," he began, but was unsure how to proceed.

"Do not despair," she told him, seeing his uncertainty. "Your coming to me was foretold in my dreams, and your blood has told me of your past. I offer you a future filled with great responsibility, great difficulty, and great reward, if you are willing to be of service to the Dragon. You, like myself, carry the burden of being an outsider, but this relieves you of social strictures, forgiving impropriety where you must commit it, because society will assume you have no honor, as you have been given no status."

"Very pretty," the Collector allowed. "And how shall I be received by the Two-Headed Dragon, the one who shall not be named, the father of all lies?"

"Is it of consequence?" Azuma asked him. "I am a goddess of my own right, imbued with immense power. Must I not surround myself with those who would further my causes, which are ultimately the causes of the Dragon? Your pragmatism confirms your fitness."

"Fitness to serve you? And what direction is this service to take?" he asked her.

"Whatever direction your judgement deems necessary," she replied cryptically, but he could see she was confident about him with a surety that he did not understand. Then she abruptly said, changing tone and posture, "You called me a 'little girl.'"

"Ah. I did not mean to offend; it was the shock of all that had come before, what you did – in the shrine…" he faltered, still off-balance with her.

"Speak freely. Tell me why you would say it, subconsciously or otherwise," she requested, and there was something forlorn in her voice that he could not immediately place, until he realized that she was ignorant of her beginnings, and there was something that he could recall for her, independent of her experience.

For her part, she did not tell him of her surprise that he had learned something from her blood, since none of her priests had the gift of reading the blood. But impossibly, this one did, just as she could, and she recognized that this was an extraordinary ability.

"I was perhaps five years old when the rumors started," he told her. "The townspeople whispered of the birth of a dragon, that Ietsune had returned from the far lands much changed and had brought with him a gift of the dark gods. I noticed there was much more activity about the old shrine in the woods, and because I was abandoned to roam where I might, I saw much without being seen. The rumor was that Ietsune had a daughter, the news brought on the winds, the talk of the lesser *kami* of the forests.

"It was sometime later, when I had barely gained manhood, that the great fire was burned, and all spoke of the ascension of a new Shogun, and Ietsune was seen no more. The Ronin came in from all parts of the kingdom to profess their faithfulness to serve this new master.

"Yet none spoke of the Shogun as being other than a man, so none could confirm this was not a male heir," the Collector told her. "It was when I tasted your blood that I knew you for what you are."

"But this means – how old are you?" Azuma demanded an answer.

"I have nineteen years," he told her.

"Which makes me only –" her eyes betrayed her surprise at the realization.

"A young girl," he concluded with wry humor, continuing quickly into the silence that grew and recognizing her confounded expression. "In human terms only. The dragon's blood confers a greater maturity in fewer years if what the ancient scrolls tell us of the gods is true. You are fully fledged if not yet full grown as a human woman. It is this human immaturity that allows you to continue this subterfuge and present yourself as a young man."

"Then you must help me to ensure that my rule is secure before such time as I would be expected to show signs of more mature manhood," she concluded.

"In the absence of you ever growing a beard," he observed, "I suspect we will have to secure your rule by other means such that your sex is made immaterial in the face of their fear and respect."

With this bit of wisdom he accepted her assignment and became her right hand, her protector, and her blood servant. She elevated him above all others and thus began a sacred covenant that would survive beyond the last of the samurai.

14

DUSK HAD FALLEN, AND THE household had retired to rest for the night, all but the guards on watch headed for their sleep, when Azuma retired to the bathhouse.

Sinking into the fragrant, steaming water, she was grateful to Tomiko, Megumi's handmaiden, for preparing her bath, but had dismissed the young woman prior to shedding her robe, sending her back to her mistress, assuring her that the master of the house was capable of bathing alone, as was her habit, maintaining their belief she was a man. The lanterns surrounding the tub gave off a peaceful glow in the twilight, and she closed her eyes and drifted into a comfortable doze.

She came awake slowly, aware of the soft touch of another. She opened her eyes to find Megumi sitting next to the tub with the sponge, gently soaping her shoulders and neck.

"Megumi." Azuma spoke the name but said nothing more, did not stop these ministrations.

Megumi's dark, dark eyes met her own, but she too remained silent, moving on to Azuma's arms, her back, her chest. Then she tied back the sleeves of her kimono, and plunged her arms into the water to reach other places, but Azuma caught her hands gently, dispossessing her of the sponge and dropping it down on the other side of the tub, out of reach. "I can manage this myself."

Megumi dropped her head, and said, in a small voice, "Do I displease you? Am I not to your liking?"

Azuma was confused by this, not sure from where it was coming, and remained silent.

"I am indebted to you for saving me from my father's house and you do me great honor by making me the mistress of your home," Megumi spoke so softly that Azuma, even with her heightened senses, strained to hear these impassioned whispers. "I slept in your bedchamber all those nights in Yeso, and I thought that surely, by now, you would bring me to your bed, but you have disdained me, and I fear you do not find me desirable."

"I told you I had no wish to rob you of your virtue," Azuma replied with all the gentleness she knew. "Do you not want to save your honor for a husband? You may tell me, freely, with no fear of repercussion."

"You wish to marry me off?" Megumi sounded bewildered and hurt.

"No, Megumi, I wish to know what *you* want. I do not require you to surrender your honor to the whims of foolish men who value you less than they should," Azuma replied, surprised at the truth in her sentiment.

When Megumi remained silent, Azuma turned to look at her. What she saw in the depths of those eyes welcomed her, and she delayed her words only long enough to tuck a stray tendril of hair behind Megumi's ear. "You are everything that is desirable."

Boldly, Megumi leaned forward and opened her mouth on Azuma's. Azuma responded, sliding loving fingers to the back of Megumi's neck and allowing the kiss to deepen, surprised at her own hunger for this, and it was Megumi's moan of pleasure that returned her to her senses, and she pulled away, not ready yet to reveal the biggest secret she had kept.

"*Erm.* Woman, let me finish my bath," Azuma recovered awkwardly, clearing her throat and assuming a tone of authority.

Megumi flushed, lovely in the lanternlight, and touched her fingers to her lips. "Yes, my Lord." She bowed quickly and withdrew, leaving Azuma to duck under the water in a mix of relief and elation, wondering what the Lady Megumi would think of her missing manhood.

15

THE WIND BLEW COLDER OUT of the northern climes and the sun shone without warmth as winter settled on Edo. The Collector was in the library, the room he had occupied since the day he had been welcomed into the household, reading the figures from recent tribute payments and reconciling them. He was interrupted by one of his attendants, who informed him in an oddly nervous voice that the Master requested an audience.

He nodded his assent absently and returned to his figures, noting the sound of the screen being discreetly closed once more. He concentrated at his task some moments longer before he realized he was not alone.

"I hope I am not intruding overmuch," Azuma said softly, the smile he heard in her voice was reassuring, as they were still unused to one another, and he wanted to avoid offense. "It is good to see that you have thrown yourself into your work."

"I appreciate the opportunity to be of some use," he agreed, with an abbreviated but sincere bow. He said nothing further, just stood quietly and attentively, awaiting her words.

"Please," she said, indicating his neglected teapot. "I meant what I said about our friendship. We are blood kindred. Will you sit and share your wisdom?"

"Very kind," the Collector nodded once more and joined her in repose.

"I wonder if you would be so kind as to expand for me on the subject of my father," she asked him earnestly, pouring two cups of hot tea.

"This will not do," he admonished her, taking the tea and shaking his head. "You should not be serving me. Let us agree that it shall be the last time."

"If you insist," she acquiesced. "I simply felt that our discussion here need not be delayed while we send for Tomiko to serve us, wait for her to finish, and hope that we remember all that needs to be said here."

Again, he heard the amusement in her tone, nearly teasing, certainly ironic. She was impatient with tradition and ceremony, and he of all people had to endeavor to maintain it. He could not change his appearance, but his father had taught him that he could alter perceptions — or at least cause others to question them with perfect observance of social custom.

"Of late, I know only rumor. When I was born, the Rebellion was already over, and Ietsune had departed this place," he told her honestly, not wasting time or words on small talk, which she appreciated.

"There is a great deal written about him in your grandfather's histories, as well as in the songs composed during the Rebellion. He was said to be a fierce samurai, talented strategist, pragmatic, cruel, ruthless. I think the proprieties of the court and society interested him not at all. He had a great talent for warcraft. His men were loyal because Ietsune embraced the *Bushido* and operated honorably."

"And the rumors?" Azuma prompted.

"He wanted power, saw the world differently from his father — oh, Iemitsu needed him during the campaigns to ensure most of the critical victories. Ietsune balked at the yoke, did not care for the slightest implication that he should defer to the niceties of court. I gather that your uncle, Tsunayoshi, was a better diplomat, and there was talk that if Ietsune did not return from the far lands he would have succeeded Iemitsu as Shogun. The daimyos would have preferred it, according to Iemitsu's recorded correspondence with them, but you know this. These documents are in the Shogun's library.

"Ietsune probably resented Tsunayoshi. It is universally accepted that he made some bargain with the dark gods to avoid any future need for compromise. It is suspected that he sacrificed his own faithful samurai to these *kami* to open the doors to the *Yomi-no-kuni*, and allow him passage to the land of the dead, realm of Akenomyosei, Star of Morning, the Great Two-Headed Dragon. Despite all of this, he was the logical heir because, notwithstanding his social shortcomings, he had the strength to continue the Tokugawa tradition, secure an enduring legacy. That is why Iemitsu welcomed home his prodigal son, because he understood this. Iemitsu could have named Tsunayoshi at any time during those later years, as no one expected Ietsune to return, but Iemitsu remained hopeful. Patient."

"Prodigal? I am unfamiliar…" she protested.

"It is a fable from faraway lands. From a very old book that belonged to my father. A story of a son who squandered a bountiful inheritance, did not contribute to furthering the family while his brother remained dutiful, yet the father welcomed the wayward child back with all due ceremony, out of familial duty and filial love."

He was thankful that she questioned him no further on this treacherous subject, and instead asked, "What do you know of my mother?"

"Very little, I'm afraid. There is mention of her in your grandfather's correspondence with Lord Mashaito. When Ietsune assumed power, he closed these lands and conducted his affairs privately. It was whispered that after she gave birth she was no longer seen, but her ultimate fate was unknown."

Azuma's forehead wrinkled slightly, then just as quickly she regained her composure. The Collector thought, correctly, that she knew something of her mother's fate, but he remained still and said no more, and she moved on to another subject.

"You suffered great offense at the hands of some of my men," she observed quietly. "You are not my enemy, yet my lands were defiled with your blood. My home is contaminated by this outrage."

"I have no authority to seek revenge within your household," the Collector protested, but she handed him an ornate *katana*. It was old, and well-used.

"My grandfather's sword has the authority to answer an insult to his legacy that has been committed in cowardice and shame on his lands. Take it and have your vengeance."

"My lady," he demurred. "I am the half-breed son of a foreigner. I cannot carry the sword of a Shogun. As your advisor, I must ensure that you understand this. Your actions will be forever accounted. You cannot diminish your rule with such a social misstep. I must refuse. If you find this way of speaking dishonorable, I accept whatever punishment you deem I deserve."

"Then you must have your own steel," Azuma stated with formality, glad of his direct and spare communication. "I will inform the armorer. You may restore your honor by whatever means you determine, and I will trust that you will see to your own satisfaction. We need not speak of this again." Then it was her turn to give a bow of respect before she let herself out of his chambers.

The Collector did not see it as a test, for he knew that she was restoring him to a place of humanity and respect, and he recognized the wrongness of these men in meting out such an undeserved punishment. He would not hesitate to end their lives, and he visited them one by one, each disappearing like ghosts despite their considerable skill as samurai, and he interred them in his butterfly garden, in secret. The irony of this ritual was purposeful and gave him the satisfaction the insult demanded.

From that day onward, he was bound to her by a debt of life, and elevated above the sacred guard, but did not adopt the name designated for that purpose. He would not carry the shackles of a number, would not take the vows of the ancient sect. But the *Akai* did give him a name, *Noroi*, The Curse, which none dared call him to his face. There was never a time that he did not live up to it. And when the armorer was called to make him his own sword, that sword was also given a name, *Hōfuku*, for its vocation was indeed retribution.

16

IN THE DARK OF THAT year, Azuma noticed subtle changes in the contour of her body, a slight fullness of her breasts, a subtle widening of her hips, but nothing that she could not still effectively hide under her masculine clothing; she remained ambiguous in outward appearance.

But inwardly she was also changing, her maturity bringing on broken dreams of approaching the mirror and seeing there not the face that she expected, but one truly masculinized. She wondered if this was an idealization of some subconscious wish that she could embody a corporeal maleness that she falsely claimed.

There were other dreams, in which she startled awake, breathless and disbelieving, after imagining she shifted, not from human to dragon, but from female to male, her hands on a new body confirming the change of her sex. Once, awake but still confused, she had leapt to her feet, pulling off her dressing gown, confirming that she was as she had been before nightfall.

And the voice inside her changed somehow, it was still Tatsuo Tomo, but not as she had known him, rather as another part of herself. In her dreams as a man, her voice was a man's, and over the next several months she could hear the thoughts of this supposed brother alongside hers, as unwelcome and disconcerting as she could imagine. But after a while she put her early concerns about the dreams aside, writing them off as a normal passage to adulthood, because these fancies never touched her waking reality.

Additionally she noticed that with maturity came greater facility to shift into her other form; and she took advantage of this freedom and power, climbing up to the cliffs nearby, and throwing herself off the great heights. She practiced the ritual starting as a human, and using the motion of falling forward as a trigger, taught herself to coil into the dragon, spiraling downward to the cold, cold sea, and shifting back before or after she hit the water, depending on her mood. Just because she could.

Surprisingly, her endurance for breath holding was greater than she expected, and as a dragon was seemingly limitless. She loved the sea, for all its power and complexity, and she enjoyed her augmented abilities. These diversions were for her alone, the solitude she craved knowing no one could follow her.

If she visited the shrine, she would enter the forest on two legs and leap onto a mature stalk of bamboo, stretching out human arms to vault upward and then float between the trees, this windwalking a new kind of freedom, a curling ribbon of blue, camouflaged against the sky, landing on the clay tiles of the roof and sliding to the edge, timing her landing perfectly. Then she would lean over just so, and falling off the edge into nothingness, she found her feet on landing in the snow. Her delighted laughter brought the curious priests no end of speculation, but she refused to acknowledge these acrobatics with them. In the shrine she maintained an authoritative seriousness in keeping with the gravity of what she knew they held as their religion.

Akenomyosei was a frequent visitor, but did not come to the shrine, rather would appear at her side when she was writing at her desk, or in her bedchamber as she brushed her hair. Azuma had always been secretly pleased at its attentiveness, but received the Great Dragon as one would an eccentric mentor. What other being in her life could understand her so well – indeed, it was the only one that could know what she experienced. So she listened to its flattery, and attempted to tolerate its nonsense.

It fascinated her by partaking of the dried seaweed that she favored, then surprised her by telling her, "The taste is of all the ancient dead things in the sea."

"Are you trying to ruin it for me?" she'd asked, secretly pleased that it shared these mundane observations with her.

"We merely suggest perhaps that is the reason you enjoy it so much." Its favorite pastime, it seemed, was to continually remind her that she was a deity, that she was separate from, and superior to, her human counterparts.

In those early days, she failed to notice that the Collector, the most ubiquitous presence in her life, was always absent when the demon came. Neither did it occur to her that Akenomyosei could be avoiding him, and was watching for something, waiting to see if Tatsuo Tomo had made good on his promise, anticipating a specified outcome in which the Collector had no role.

17

AZUMA RECEIVED THE IMPERIAL ENVOY with the uneasiest of grace, knowing that the arrogance of their messengers was legendary; it was as if they had forgotten all that the Tokugawa had done. The ruling class had been allowed to keep their titles, but not their power once feudal law was firmly established. Azuma uncharacteristically greeted them in full armor, aware that the Dragon Warrior's military dress was a pointed reminder of their place. Nevertheless, the Scribe dictated the Emperor's griefs to her, droning on and on, until the only thing that kept her still was the stern look of the Collector. When she knew she could take no more, and had half decided to feed this fool to the beast inside her, she saw her mentor give the briefest of nods.

"...and we *must* insist that Iehiza restore the trade accord with China, and allow taxation once again. King Shō Nei has been exiled to Edo, and this is a shameful example of –"

"I remind the Imperial Scribe that *I* am Shogun. It is my strength that holds the empire, my father, my uncle, and their father cleansed our lands, fortified our rule, and provided the peace in which we all prosper." Azuma left it unsaid that she did not have to obey imperial edict. The daimyos, with their ties to the court, helped maintain relations between the ruling feudal class and the Emperor. "You'd do well to remember that in Nihon, you insist nothing. What is it to me if a savage proclaims himself ruler of one tiny island? Let him have his typhoons and his forty wives.”

“Indeed, my…Lord,” the Scribe stuttered, intimidated by her fierceness, belittled by her extravagant height, fearful of her rumored provenance. “But Lord Shimazu has entreated us to intervene, as these relationships bring trade and information.”

“Lord Shimazu is my daimyo. If there is a loss of prestige or status to him, it redounds to the Tokugawa rule,” Azuma protested. “If what you say is true, he has done me and mine the greatest of insults in assuming that the Emperor was better positioned to help him.” She already knew the reason for this; but was testing the Emperor’s man to see if he had more information, and to find out whether he would tell her the truth.

The Scribe pulled himself up indignantly, and was about to answer with some heat, but the expression on the Collector’s face made him reconsider his position here. Azuma rested her hand on her sword and tried to appear more patient than she felt.

“My Lord Tokugawa,” he began in a tone far more conciliatory than she expected, “I imagine Shimazu is simply ensuring that the Court remains informed. It may be that he is on his way here as we speak to make his entreaties to you himself. I am here because I am an officer of the Imperial Court and was sent to you.”

“To dictate my best course of action,” Azuma observed ironically, then sighed. To the Scribe it sounded like capitulation, but he could not know how wrong he was. In a lighter tone, she added, “Esteemed guest, I am sure that you are exhausted from your hasty travels. Please accept my hospitality. I am sure if you follow my attendants they will furnish you with lodging and ensure that your group is taken to supper. You will excuse my absence at your meal this evening, I hope?” She did not wait for an answer, simply signaled that the emissaries should be removed, and gave the most abbreviated bow she could make without giving insult.

After they had gone, she gestured to the Collector and they stepped out of the main house together. Neither spoke until they had crossed the parade ground and approached the pond.

"Shimazu has made no secret of his relationship with King Shō Nei. I have even heard him, while confused with drink, brag that he has made a vassal of all of China through his trade accords," Azuma observed.

"Indeed. I think him ashamed to have been duped by one of his own disloyal samurai," the Collector agreed. "Although I admit I am unclear about why he hasn't ridden right over the sea to set it right."

"Shimazu is a coward who wishes to take a shortcut to greatness," Azuma told him. "He thinks to curry favor with the ruling class, knowing that the last Tokugawa to rule here was Ietsune, who disdained Imperial power. Both sides conspire to sacrifice me to this ogre, which leaves Shimazu in Imperial graces to rise as Shogun with concessions to restore some power to the aristocracy.

"Well, let's make 'all of China' a vassal to the Tokugawa," she concluded.

"Might I suggest that whatever Iehiza wants can be underwritten by a greater tribute from Shimazu?" The Collector supplied.

"Shimazu's son can pay it directly to Iehiza, with his fealty. We can shift the capital of the daimyo to Ryukyu. If Iehiza is as advertised, he can be easily bought. We can afford to lose the income from that daimyo, if the trade accord means taxes in our coffers," she told him, turning back toward the house.

"Shimazu's son?" the Collector asked, not yet seeing the whole picture.

"Separate the head of the household from its body," she ordered. "Make it known that it is done on my command. The son shall fear us, the Emperor loses an ally, and we bring a wayward province to heel. Also, I am sure that as a fellow soldier, Iehiza will want a more permanent assurance that the deposed King will not pose any difficulties now or in the future."

"I will see to it personally. And the Scribe?" the Collector awaited additional instruction, but Azuma smiled a terrible smile.

"Leave that to me. After all, his entire profession is in the delivery of messages."

18

ONE EVENING, RETURNING FROM A deadly errand, the Collector entered his rooms from the garden and was surprised to find Azuma sitting on the floor, legs folded beneath her, wearing only her bedclothes.

"Are you deliberately trying to be inappropriate?" he asked her. Here she was, unchaperoned and in a relative state of undress, clearly feminine, in this place where she did not ever drop the pretense of manhood. Not to mention that she had given the household enough to discuss when she made him the head of her advisory council. He was not, under the loosest of defined laws, considered Japanese.

Ignoring this, she asked a question of her own. "Have you ever had a lover?"

"Receiving a question in response to a question is never a good omen. I am going to attribute your behavior to a lack of maturity. And possibly modesty, because you think the rules do not apply to you," he said firmly, maintaining his reserve.

"How can they possibly apply to me if no one can enforce them?" she asked archly, having the nerve to be amused by his disapproval.

"And on what premise exactly does this assumption rest?" he inquired.

"Power," she responded without hesitation.

"What you are referring to is chaos," he dared to correct her, still unsure why she listened to him. He was barely a man himself, hardly an authority. "Power without control cannot be sustained. Exercise power without discipline and boundaries and it dissipates. If you would keep your precious power you must be prepared for the work involved."

"Are you deliberately trying to sound old?" she asked, making eye contact. He could see that while she *was* trying to be humorous, there was also something vulnerable about her. Her eyes betrayed an unspoken burden. "Are you going to answer my question?"

"Who is asking? The Shogun or the Goddess?"

"Azuma is asking," she disarmed him with her answer, but he would not relent for that.

"Ah. Then it would be dishonorable to answer your question."

"No one knows I am here. No one has to know," she told him, and something in her voice was lost.

She looked down at the floor, all her bravado gone, her dark hair a shining veil over her shoulders. At that moment, she looked deceptively fragile and small, her usual long-limbed stature compacted by her position at his feet, appearing as young as her handful of years of existence.

He decided to adopt his usual directness with her. "It makes no sense to waste your time on one thing if you truly want another. You cannot hide in here, and I do not think you want to. You don't need to hear any theories nor question your feelings."

"I just…" She began to say something, but her voice was almost too soft to discern, and she trailed off without finishing. Unusual for her, he knew.

"There is nothing wrong with you. Not in this. You love another woman. You could no more change the color of your hair than alter this characteristic which appears to distress you so. When you have no status, as I once did, people forget you are there. With that odd invisibility, one can learn much about the world by observing it. What you feel is not unusual or new. If it is hidden by others and their habits, that does not make it wrong. It simply is. What we love is immaterial; who we love is paramount. You can worry about what it means to everyone else or you can live your life.”

“She thinks I am a man who can provide her an honorable mate and confer societal status,” Azuma protested, throwing up her hands.

“I think you are not giving Megumi enough credit. She has an excellent mind,” he told her. “I see the way she yearns for you. I am reasonably certain that no one anywhere thinks you are a man. Not any longer. We have outlasted the ‘youth absent any beard’ days. Never mind that you lack *nodo Botoke*. They are all either too polite to say anything, or more accurately, afraid to challenge you, as they should be, if I am doing my job correctly and you are making the difficult decisions that need to be made. Your sex will only matter if you allow others to make it so.

“I could waste my breath reminding you that you are Tokugawa, Shogun, *Doragon*, Goddess, but I will not.” The Collector paused as if considering and discarding many variations of his next statement before deciding on the right one.

“I like green tea. You do not. You drink buckwheat tea. This is the same thing. Simple. You do not drink green tea even to be polite. Over the smallest of things you will not budge. So why would you sleep with a man when you want a woman?”

19

SPRINGTIME FOUND HER PREPARING FOR Ryukyu, to discuss terms with Iehiza, the Ronin warlord who had broken with his master, traveled from Satsuma, and overthrown the King.

Azuma had finalized strategic preparations with the Collector, some of which had been initiated months earlier, and they spoke late into the depths of many nights about the advantages and disadvantages they could collectively foresee.

Iehiza surely knew that Shimazu was dead; by now, his advisors and spies in Satsuma had informed him of such news as was to be had on the subject. Thus he had every reason to believe that he had the power and the authority to deal directly with the Shogun, but both he and Azuma knew that he made no concession to her rule, had not recognized himself or those he led as subordinate to feudal law. She knew her journey to be a treacherous one.

On the final evening before their travel, she curtailed her time for counsel to visit the shrine, for sustenance mostly, but also for meditation. Leaving that place, she passed silently into the trees, and climbing as she had as a child, called the Dragon from her bones. She flung her ribbon-like other self on the wind, curling and unfurling through the bamboo. When her feet next touched the earth she was a young woman, and she returned to her bedchamber undetected by her own elite guard, who were hampered by the darkness of the new moon. She lit the paper lanterns that hung on the veranda outside, keeping the screen open to the night, and pulled on her dressing gown before lighting the lamp and sitting down to read.

Nearly an hour later, she was alerted by the softest of sounds in the anteroom, and she left her chair to investigate, but before she could reach the partition, it slid open slowly, and Megumi admitted herself, once more she was surprised to find Azuma awake. She bowed, recovering gracefully, but said nothing.

"To what do I owe the pleasure of your visit, Lady Megumi?" Azuma asked politely, noting that Megumi was modestly attired, with her outer kimono in place over her dressing gown, although her abundant hair was free, spilling over her shoulders and traveling down her back nearly to the floor, an informality that could be interpreted as an intimate gesture.

"I wanted to ask – will you permit me to travel with you?" Megumi asked breathlessly, and Azuma assumed she had been summoning no little courage to do so.

"Ah." Azuma paused, sorting through her own emotions, wanting to engender complete understanding between them. The wise words of the Collector were imprinted on her soul, and she understood that he saw her for who she was, and his kindness had removed a stigma she had tried to place upon herself. She had been censuring her own feelings, not certain that her advisor was entirely correct about Megumi, and what she wanted.

So she stalled a bit, asking a question of her own, wincing slightly because the Collector had taught her it was rude to do so. "Who will run the household? You are mistress here."

"I am only mistress by default, because everyone assumes…" Here Megumi left the words unsaid, because the reality was otherwise. "Tomiko is more than capable of ensuring your household is maintained while you and your army are away."

"You are mistress in fact, because I say it is so," Azuma corrected her gently, knowing she could delay no longer. It bordered on cruelty, as she cared for Megumi she must spare the girl's feelings.

"I have no real standing or rights," Megumi protested.

"Would you feel differently if I bedded you?" Azuma was incredulous, and she tried to remove any trace of challenge or frustration from her tone. "I cannot understand such reasoning. A woman should not have to feel she must be validated by what she does on her back. I rule Japan; is it not enough in my own household that I give you that standing, and those rights with my word?"

"Azuma," Megumi whispered, and hearing her own name from that mouth was Azuma's undoing. Something within her relented, but she refused to have any further pretense with Megumi.

She settled on the mat at Megumi's feet, putting herself in a position of submission. "I cannot provide you the traditional honor of having a husband. I cannot father sons, cannot give you any children. You will not bear the Shogun's heirs. I give you standing in my home so that you recognize your own value, not just to me, but hopefully to yourself. There are many things that I cannot give you that would provide you with societal status. I have only ever wanted you to tell me what it is you want, whether it is contrary to my wishes or not. You have a right to your own life."

"Take me with you," Megumi asked again, placing a warm hand atop Azuma's head.

"That I cannot do," she replied. "The road, the Southern Sea, these are not fit places for a lady, with all manner of rough and murderous men."

Megumi sank down beside Azuma. "But you -"

Azuma laughed bitterly. "I may be a woman, but I am hardly a lady."

"And what of Iehiza?" Megumi ventured to ask, trying to mask her surprise that Azuma had finally admitted to her what she had long known to be true.

"He would kill me if he dared, and may still try to do so. It will be dangerous. I must insist on your safety."

"And what if you do not return?" Megumi began to weep, her tears falling freely into her lap.

"Then you must be brave, and marry well, and honor my memory as you would if I could be your husband," Azuma replied, taking hold of her hands. "I have made arrangements for you should that happen. But more importantly, what shall my lady require of me when I *do* return?" she asked, allowing a bit of humor to creep into her tone.

"I wish to be yours. Not as I am now, but as we are assumed to be," Megumi's voice betrayed her hopefulness for this outcome.

"If you give me your word that you will consider all that I *cannot* provide you, sincerely, in my absence, ensuring your understanding of what you are contemplating and what you are forsaking," Azuma began, stern and serious once more, "I will court you properly on my return."

"And you will…" Megumi started, but then found she was too shy to complete the request.

"It is late," Azuma interjected. "Go back to bed. I will be at your service, Mistress." That promise made, she ensured that Megumi returned to her room before surrendering herself to a dreamless sleep.

20

WORD CAME FROM RYUKYU THAT Iehiza would receive the Shogun as a diplomatic visitor, graciously and warmly, most likely because he felt he had the upper hand.

The crossing of the East China Sea was difficult, as rough waters had slowed their progress and weakened her men. Once they had arrived, Azuma purposely encamped them for a few days, sending the Collector ahead to Shuri to suggest to Iehiza that this was done for quarantine precautions. Iehiza saw the gesture as deferent regard for his position, thinking it a conservative act to prevent sickness from the mainland spreading to his people. Azuma did it so that by the time she marched to Shuri, the *Ouban* and her samurai faithful were both well-rested and completely recovered from the voyage.

They had decided on a smaller force; Iehiza had forbidden they bring more than one thousand troops, but had finally conceded to some twenty-five hundred, which still gave him the advantage in numbers, as a strictly mathematical fact. He had recently welcomed a phalanx of soldiers sent from the *Kangxi* Emperor of China, Xuanye. This was in honor of their trade accord and in respect to the Ryukyu Kingdom as a tributary state of the Qing rule, which added to the warlord's power.

Iehiza himself rode out to greet the delegation, confident in his safety outside the walls of the city. Separating herself from her troops, Azuma met him in the company of the Collector, and respectful of the privacy of their initial meeting, his guards hung back several yards. Both she and the Collector saw this and were surprised at Iehiza's boldness. Although he had archers stationed on the ramparts of the city wall, it would be nothing for the two of them to dispatch him should they be willing to sacrifice their own lives. It told them much about him.

"Well!" Iehiza addressed Azuma without honorific. "So the rumors are true – Ietsune did not father any sons." His tone was mocking, and he eyed her too forwardly, surveying her figure as best he could under the elaborate armor she wore.

Azuma heard the slightest of creaks as the Collector's hand tightened on his horse's reins in response to this rudeness. She flattened her hand on the pommel of her saddle, a silent gesture to calm him. It was not the time for violence. Yet.

"Lord Iehiza," she, in contrast, was all politeness. "I thank you for receiving us in person. You do me a great honor." She relished the look of confusion on Iehiza's face; he had not intended to be seen as doing so. Out of the corner of her eye, she noted the almost imperceptible softening of the Collector's face, when Iehiza's hesitation at her cleverness had again betrayed his lack of intelligence.

Finally, he laughed delightedly, like a child. He was a man of impulses, Azuma could see, and she smiled. He took it as she knew he would, an invitation from a woman he felt had no right to rule, a woman he was sure he could possess, with enough cunning, with enough might, with enough charm.

His manners improved marginally as they rode together into the city. He presented her to his household, and did introduce her as Shogun to his servants and attendants who then scurried to accommodate her and her men. They were received lavishly, but she knew they were watched, and it was safest to believe that Iehiza's spies were everywhere.

At dinner that evening, they were formally presented at Court. Iehiza, already thick with drink, exuberantly babbling away beside Azuma, presented his contemporaries with verbal flourishes and expansive gesturing, while the Collector stood stiffly at her side. After a while, she whispered something to her advisor discreetly, and he made a small bow of relief and departed.

Shortly thereafter, they were approached by a throng of young women, the least distinctive of which was still possessed of a rare beauty, and the most memorable of which defied description. Exotic and mesmerizing, her eyes were unfathomable in their depth, blazing with vivacity and cleverness. Her kimono was of the very finest silk, with frogging of golden thread, and the jade drops suspended from her ears were the size of grapes, capturing the light as she turned her head to laugh at a whispered comment from one of her handmaidens, and in her profile, Azuma recognized the beauty of the Han.

She came toward them and stopped closer to Azuma than propriety might dictate, and looked at her with open curiosity and delight. Azuma bowed politely. Not waiting for Iehiza to introduce her, she addressed Azuma directly in her own language. "My Lord Shogun," she began, her Japanese rudimentary but charming. And bowing her head momentarily before continuing, she gave Azuma a most forward look.

"All is in readiness for your visit here. We will do all we can to ensure that you and your men feel welcome," she promised with a secret smile. And as abruptly as she had come, she departed in the direction of the dining room.

Azuma looked at Iehiza quizzically. "A concubine?"

"*The* Concubine," he replied proudly. "That is Bi Xiaohui. She and the others were sent as gifts to me from Xuanye. She is as talented as she is lovely. She seems fascinated by you."

"The Jade Princess," Azuma replied. "Her beauty exceeds her legend."

"Indeed. She is a marvelous prize, but not half the prize you are." Iehiza was too drunk to notice Azuma stiffening at this statement, then heard the Collector in her ear. *Patience. He shall pay dearly for his insults.*

"You are a lucky man," she observed, knowing that he could not detect the subtlety of her tone.

"In all things," Iehiza agreed, then said, "Do let me accompany you to table. You must be famished. And then you must rest. We will leave diplomacy for another day."

Azuma could not be more relieved to take her leave of Iehiza when the evening was over, asking a servant to direct her to her sleeping quarters, where she began to prepare for bed but was interrupted by the Collector. They were about to compare their respective observations on the day when there was a knock at the door.

Azuma's guard announced, "Bi Xiaohui requests an audience with the Shogun."

"Please extend my sincere apologies. I will be all happiness to meet with her in the morning; I must confer with my advisor at present," Azuma directed him, and he ducked back into the corridor before returning after a short absence. "The Jade Princess conveys her understanding and asked me to inform you that she will await you in the salon of the east wing while you conclude your business affairs."

"It appears I must to bed," the Collector said, feigning a yawn and stretching unconvincingly.

"Do you mock me, my friend?" Azuma asked, not expecting an answer.

"Between myself and the Jade Princess, I can guess where your interest lies," he told her. "Go and learn what you can. I am sure she is a better strategist than I." He allowed a short snort of laughter to escape, by way of reassuring her that he understood her plight.

21

AZUMA FOUND THE SALON EASILY enough. Situated off the main hall of the palace, it was a long room for receiving the guests of those lodged there, which Azuma suspected were Iehiza's concubines. It was comfortable and well-appointed, furnished for the pleasures of leisure and relaxation. She was curious as to Bi Xiaohui's motives.

Azuma admitted herself to that chamber and found the concubine alone. She wore an elaborate gown of peach silk that highlighted her alabaster skin, and her long hair was free of restraint. Azuma bowed deeply. "Princess, I am flattered to be summoned, but would it not be better to include Lord Iehiza in our discussions?" She knew that whatever this was, it was a part of Iehiza's plan, and she was determined to learn what she could from it.

"Lord Iehiza expects me to extend you every courtesy, and he has instructed me to accommodate you in all things," Bi Xiaohui replied. "For that, privacy serves best, does it not?" she asked, pouring Azuma a glass of plum wine. When Azuma hesitated to accept it, she continued, undaunted, "I also have *sake* should you prefer it."

"I find it best to separate business from pleasure," Azuma remarked, ultimately taking the glass that the concubine offered her, but setting it aside on a silver tray without drinking, unmindful of the perceived insult. Bi Xiaohui would understand her wariness; poison was typically a woman's weapon, and in response the Jade Princess poured for herself from the same flask, drinking deeply in an attempt to reassure Azuma of her trustworthiness.

She placed a hand on Azuma's arm and leaned in close enough for any number of small intimacies. Brown eye met brown eye, and it was clear that this one was no enemy.

Bi Xiaohui whispered, in a conspiratorial tone that matched their respective postures, "I am not a welcome gift from Iehiza, I am a tribute for the Shogun from Xuanye, Emperor of the Middle Kingdom. He sent me with a message. I am to tell you that your messenger was successful in reaching Peking, and that Xuanye agrees with your proposal. The *Kangxi* will recognize the Shogun's authority over Ryukyu.

Azuma placed a firm hand against Xiaohui's waist. "Pretty words. Only meaningful if I prevail," she observed wryly.

"Much more than words, my Lord. It may interest you to know that the troops that accompanied the courtiers to Ryukyu remain loyal to Xuanye and will take up arms on your behalf. They are five thousand strong, determined to keep the Emperor's interest in this kingdom undiluted by Iehiza's foolishness.

"I must also tell you that one month ago I appealed to Iehiza on behalf of a thousand peasant women who arrived from the big island seeking asylum from Osaka and Owari. They asked for nothing more than the opportunity to work the land here and agreed to declare their fealty to this kingdom. He agreed to permit passage for these unfortunates. I am sure they are following these diplomatic discussions with interest," Xiaohui suggested, nodding at Azuma's cleverness. "The cities they fled are strongholds of the Tokugawa if I am not mistaken."

Azuma was hesitant to say anything, so she remained silent. All of this could be an elaborate trap, designed to ensnare her. She had been expecting a message from the Chinese Emperor, but was surprised to receive it in this manner. She wasn't sure whether to be as pleased that the Jade Princess had correctly guessed that the refugees from the south had been clandestinely recruited by the Collector. They were loyal to the Shogun, and many of them secreted weapons they had inherited from their mothers, most of whom were widows of samurai who had fought in the Rebellion under her grandfather.

Both women turned toward the door to the hall, having heard approaching footsteps. Azuma turned back to Xiaohui with some concern, but the other woman was calm. With efficiency, she undid the closures on her gown, dropping her garments to the floor in one practiced move. "Kiss me," her request was an urgent whisper, scarcely more than a breath, and she pressed her nakedness forward into Azuma's arms, pliant and warm against her clothing, her mouth soft and mobile. If she was acting, Azuma was impressed, as her attentions were as ardent as any lover. Azuma plunged her hands into Xiaohui's thick black hair, feeling the consort's body respond to her kisses and her touch. When the door opened, and Azuma broke their embrace, Xiaohui gave a soft sigh that sounded genuinely disappointed.

It was, of course, Iehiza who interrupted, intending to disrupt the interlude, expecting them to be further along in their lovemaking. But he recovered quickly, successfully hiding his disappointment at hoping to find Azuma in a more compromised state.

"I do apologize!" Iehiza exclaimed in mock dismay. "I was making my rounds before bed and heard a sound. I hope that Lady Xiaohui is extending to you every possible aspect of her considerable hospitality?"

"She has been most accommodating," allowed Azuma with an irony that was not lost on Xiaohui. "But I fear that your intrusion reminds me of the lateness of the hour, and I must take my leave and get some rest. My lady," she bowed to Xiaohui with a knowing look, then chivalrously folded her back into her robes, ensuring the integrity of the closures with maddening slowness, aware that Iehiza saw this demonstration of respect but doubting he would benefit from it. "Lord Iehiza, I bid you good night."

Azuma found the Collector in his bedchamber, still awake, and wearing an inscrutable smile that she tried unsuccessfully to ignore.

She left the door to the corridor open for propriety's sake, leaving her guard to keep watch there, and spent less than a minute whispering the night's events into his knowing ear before searching out her own bed.

22

IEHIZA WAS MADDENINGLY SLOW TO involve himself in diplomacy, preferring to provide all manner of diversion and delay. He refused to discuss politics on the next day and the next, always with some excuse that Azuma's delegation should extend their stay in his beautiful kingdom. Charming as Ryukyu may have been, at that time of the year it was raining, a near-constant deluge that was demoralizing in its persistence. It encouraged all manner of ennui, and while her samurai could indulge in drink and womanizing, she knew that too much inactivity would make them complacent and slow. She suspected this was the intended consequence of Iehiza's procrastination.

He did, however, encourage the relationship between Xiaohui and Azuma, at times overtly playing matchmaker at court to the endless amusement of the Collector. If her advisor was truly diverted from any purpose, it was his own secret to keep. More and more Azuma watched him withdraw from humanity. How he kept himself fed was a mystery even to her.

The two of them faced the real challenge of where and how to take their blood meals, and it was in situations like the one they now confronted that she felt real guilt about passing this burden to him with the Blood Gift. His blood had told her he was infinitely wise, and his loyalty had not seemed influenced unduly by her sacrifice. Her blood had conferred longevity, strength, and renewal that may have been distasteful to another, ill-begotten as it was, but he seemed to accept these fates with a determined resignation.

He showed no motivation for anything other than protecting Azuma's interests. He was an enigma, intensely private, silent, deadly. He was her equal at martial strategy, and her better at swordplay, and he understood human beings more astutely than she ever would. And she wasn't the only one curious about the situation.

"So why did you do it?" Akenomyosei asked, referring to the Collector, languidly surveying their tile game. Awaiting her one evening in her chambers, the deity had adopted the appearance of a well-dressed, rich nobleman. Azuma suspected that it understood the distraction of appearing to her in other forms, although she always knew it for the dark god it was. This incarnation was pleasing, a handsome man with indiscriminate features, dark hair that defied gravity (whether Akenomyosei affected such a thing on purpose or simply could not hide this trait she did not know), courtly manners, and a seductive sense of humor. It loved games of strategy, and had taught her much about tiles and dice, particularly how to understand the odds of winning at *kitsune bakuchi* and *chō han* and how those odds could be manipulated. In other words, she was taught valuable lessons about the weakness inherent in trust, because its major strategy was to cheat. Although she had said nothing aloud, she had, of late, been thinking much about her trusted advisor, and wondering the same.

"He was dying," she replied, refusing to let Akenomyosei distract her from her tiles. It would deceive at any opportunity, which she supposed was its way of continually reminding her not to expend any faith on the idea of honesty.

"I am aware. I was following the progression of his demise." Akenomyosei waved this away. "What elevates him over any other sack of blood we cannot see. They die. You should have devoured him."

"A waste, my devoted Morningstar," she replied, making her move and refusing to respond to the outrageous categorization. She knew well from her time with Tatsuo Tomo that Akenomyosei despised humankind, and wanted her to do so as well.

She hesitated to explain what the blood told her. Although she suspected that Akenomyosei knew some of her thoughts, she also sensed that there were certain considerations that it could not follow. While she could tell of how the blood of humans spoke to her, she guessed, correctly, that Akenomyosei had not the imagination or desire to try to fathom the importance of it, and something in her kept that knowledge to herself. She hoped someday to discover the secrets of the lifeforce, but she was content in the present with the knowledge her gifts brought.

"I wonder that he accepts his position so pragmatically," she remarked.

"You conveniently forget that creatures like him are the result of your grandfather's belief in a superior race, and he was less than nothing before you gave him a purpose, and if not a status, a title. He hasn't really changed. He just graduated from pulling the wings off butterflies to pulling-"

Azuma held up her hand to indicate that she understood, and frowned down at her tiles, which now looked suspiciously redistributed. But Akenomyosei was not done.

"You have sanctioned him to become something else, to evolve, if you will, as a monster," it observed. "He furthers our cause, so we allow this small act of rebellion, for now." It smiled, and made its kill move on the game board.

"You are distracted, my dear. Perhaps the Jade Princess would provide a more welcome diversion. She seems to like you."

Azuma did not reply, merely counted the tiles again, noting the discrepancy. Akenomyosei was pleased that she could see through its victory to the underlying connivance, and it was another lesson, another reminder to pay close attention to any worthy opponent.

23

AZUMA TOLD NO ONE OF her plans for Iehiza until she was ready to strike. He had finally deigned to discuss trade accords with her, proposing outrageous terms that he thought she could not afford to refuse. He was also relentless in his pursuits of the flesh; completely unskilled at seduction, she was sure he had to take his pleasures by force. He was so repellant to her that her initial plans to feed from him to gain a measure of control over him were insupportable; indeed, the idea was so distasteful that she vowed to accomplish her overthrow of the kingdom without it. Besides, she was confident that Iehiza's downfall was a prize anticipated with no small amount of enthusiasm by the Collector.

Xiaohui wisely observed that Azuma was starting to make arrangements that signaled she would soon return home, and she too, remained vigilant, anticipating developments that would herald that event. She continued to visit Azuma at all hours of the night, but was unaware that the Dragon Goddess had fed from her.

For Azuma, this was necessary, but also problematic, because the Jade Princess's blood was eloquent of her passions, one of which was an infatuation with Azuma. Surely it was mere flattery. Yet her waking dreams during these interludes spoke to Azuma of a frustrated attraction, and while it was impossible that she would remember the acts that gave the Dragon sustenance, their intimacy made it necessary for Azuma to undertake clear actions to rebuff any sexual advances made voluntarily.

"I would love to see Edo someday," Xiaohui remarked wistfully one evening as she served tea.

"I had thought you eager to return to the Emperor," Azuma replied. "I am certain Xuanye misses your company and your wit."

"There are stories that the mistress of the Shogun's house is quite lovely. Your consort is from Edo, then?" Xiaohui asked artfully, but Azuma was no fool. It angered her that any intrigues, any inquiries, could touch Megumi from the outside world.

"No. Her home was originally in Yeso," Azuma said softly, not betraying her distaste for this subject with her neutral tone.

"Ah, yes. A provincial, uninitiated at court," Xiaohui nodded, as if this brought her relief, made her feel less jealous. For jealous she was.

"Princess, some prefer oysters raw and unadorned, finding that those burdened with pearls have more bitter flesh, their shriveled meats less satisfying to a healthy appetite." Azuma's tone conveyed her ire at Xiaohui's slight, but the woman refused to be discouraged.

"My Lord, I meant no offense. It is one thing to love," Xiaohui allowed. "It is another to starve oneself. You are powerful. Does not the world offer you an abundance of oysters? And can you not taste many of them, not giving up the chance to discover other flavors, though you have found one variety you prefer?"

"My preference does not diminish the allure of the other varieties," Azuma offered this reassurance as a concession. Also, it was uncanny how much Xiaohui saw in those around her, and her analogy came too close to the true underpinnings of their relationship.

The Jade Princess acquiesced with a bow. "I shall do as the Shogun suggests and prepare for my return to the Middle Kingdom.

24

WHATEVER THOSE PREPARATIONS INVOLVED, AZUMA assumed they required Xiaohui's undivided attentions, for her nightly visits were abruptly curtailed. This disappearance should have concerned Azuma more than it did, and she would later regret not questioning it.

Azuma made a habit of riding out beyond the city walls daily to survey her men, visiting them in their encampments and ensuring that their alertness was maintained. Their vocation was fighting, not diplomacy, and while this errand offered them a multitude of diversions, they grew bored.

She whispered in the ears of her guard, and they prepared for departure, awaiting only her command for action. She visited the countryside, seeing many farms, a clandestine reminder to the women she had recruited from Osaka and Owari that readiness was required of them. Azuma was careful not to reveal any knowledge of their supposed plight, but she was pleased that these reinforcements had distributed themselves across the island such that no village was beyond the reach of their influence.

She grew hungry again for a blood meal, and not for the first time regretted having left her priests behind. Later, she was jolted out of an evening reverie by the Collector, who observed, "Your samurai are growing fat and you are wasting away."

It was time for another clandestine visitation, but the Jade Princess was not to be found. She had not been seen at court, and Azuma noticed that the other concubines had been more cautious in her presence, their eyes downcast as they passed, their usual flirtations absent, their ubiquitous giggles gone silent. The salon in the east wing was quiet after dark, the sleeping quarters beyond still as graves.

Azuma made bold to call the Dragon, for she would not be deterred in her search. She who had tasted Xiaohui's blood pulled upon that blood tie to find her. What she found was a ruin.

In the corner of a forgotten chamber beneath the walls of the castle, Xiaohui had been chained, stripped, starved, and beaten. Her heavy jade earrings had been torn from her ears, and she was left, broken and bleeding, to die there.

It was the most abject and cruel of reminders that women were of little societal value without the protections of a man. This jewel, once the Emperor's prize, had been given to another man, and on his whim she was destroyed. It was doubtful that her worth to Xuanye was enough to warrant his retaliation; she was chattel, sent to secure the loyalty of a madman, and her beauty, her wit, her charm, and her intelligence would go unappreciated, disappearing with her into the oblivion of the next life.

Xiaohui was beyond her help, beyond the reach of anything she could do, because she was one of the pureflesh, one who reached for life, not for death. But her eyes tried to tell Azuma what she was too weak to say, and Azuma needed to know why. Once again, what she sought to know was within reach. The blood told her the awful truth of it, the utter waste, the story of a man who could not tolerate the idea that Xiaohui might prefer another over him.

The Dragon ensured that Xiaohui would suffer no more; the ignominy of her demise was ended as swiftly as it could yet be accomplished without further undue pain. Azuma wore the beast's scales like the sacred armor they were, but they could neither deflect nor contain the volcanic rage within. She was glad she had never partaken of Iehiza's blood.

Now, she wanted to bathe in it.

25

ALONG THE RAMPARTS OF THE city, in the darkest hour of the night, the archers were first to meet a grisly fate. Once the wall was secured, the *Ouban* swept through first the castle and then the city and took control of the gates. Those of Iehiza's faithful who escaped the walls, hoping to alert the other forces guarding the ports, discovered the refugees from Osaka and their sisters from Owari blocking the escape routes from the city.

At first disbelieving that a group of women armed with farm implements could be a threat, they soon learned of the cunning and strength a woman can call upon to kill a man. Xuanye's men were dispatched to the stronghold at the sea and left a bloody aftermath, and few of those who had taken the kingdom of Ryukyu the year before were left alive in those last hours before dawn.

At the center of this web of destruction was the Collector, waiting in the dark like a deadly spider, at the ready to catch those who tried to escape in secret or simply wanted to retaliate against his Shogun despite defeat. He had followed his mistress's instructions, and all was prepared for their departure.

Just before dawn, he stole away from the throne room in confidence, in order to make one final delivery on her behalf.

Iehiza slept through the overthrow of his stolen kingdom. The Dragon wondered at his apparent peacefulness; not restrained by conscience, he seemed to have no dreams.

But he was unsurprisingly unable to sleep through the first stirrings of restlessness brought on by the addition to his bed – there are some changes to comfortable rest that cannot help but disturb it. Whether the coolness, the moisture, or the stench, he was soon awake, and with Azuma's extranormal vision she could see him blinking in confusion, still thinking, perhaps, that he could be dreaming.

Then came the moment of realization, when he leapt away from the corpse at his side, seeing the Jade Princess's dead eyes staring at him accusingly. He shivered, but then learned he was attended by more than the dead, because Azuma spoke with the Dragon's voice, saying his name.

He jerked about, turning one way and another, trying to see her in the dimness. Finally he glimpsed the coiling, fearful form coalescing above him, the scant light reflecting in frightful patterns off her moving scales, and she rattled like a snake in her fury, hissing down at him.

As he cowered beneath her, she transformed, floating to the ground on human feet, swiftly enfolding him in her arms. She drank in his terror slowly, savoring it as she had almost nothing before it.

"Please," he begged, but then had no more to say, knowing there was nothing he could ask for that she would give.

"Iehiza, you surprise me," she purred, moving her naked body against him suggestively, enjoying his recoil from these attentions. "I thought this was what you wanted." She gestured emphatically at Xiaohui's body, and continued, "Both of us, together, in your bed?"

Inexorably, she pulled him back toward the bed, recommitting to the transformation only enough to wrap a long, scaly tail around him, twisting and trapping him so that he was forced to look again upon the woman he had destroyed. Azuma opened him up skillfully, ensuring that he lived long enough to see her wearing his blood, long enough that he could still scream after she relinquished him to the Collector.

* * * * *

She attended to Xiaohui herself, refusing the assistance of her sister concubines, who she ordered placed on Xuanye's ships and returned to the Emperor. The Chinese troops she installed to restore order to Shuri. Her final instruction was to the Collector, to return to Edo with her men. Despite his protests, she insisted the *Ouban* go with them.

"Mistress, you risk too much," he argued. "You have no allies here."

"Neither does she," Azuma replied, and they both knew to whom she referred, and to ensure she was obeyed, she personally supervised the departure, watching him stand stiffly on the deck of the ship, refusing to turn away from her, silently castigating her. Probably he stood there long after she was out of sight, perhaps yet until they reached the other shore.

When the time of waiting was over, and an honorable period of mourning for Xiaohui was past, Azuma prepared the funeral pyre, on a bluff above the sea, facing west, toward Xiaohui's beloved Middle Kingdom. Azuma made these preparations herself, alone, in the rain. The women from Osaka and Owari were silent sentinels in the field beyond, not daring to approach, keeping the watch.

She had dressed Xiaohui for a grand entrance into the next life, in the peach silks that flattered her so beautifully, and had found her prized earrings, pressing each back into its place, so that the Jade Princess would arrive adorned in all her finery. Azuma tended the fire late into the night, battling with the downpour, entirely unconfounded that in the small hours of morning, the Morningstar kept vigil beside her until her promise was made good.

"*San'ninshō*, do you know that in the beginning, it is said that the gods came to earth because they were tempted by the beauty of maidens such as she," it told her, referring to Xiaohui.

Azuma turned her eyes to it, watching the flames reflected in those oddly shiny eyes. "And was the Star of Morning lured by such maidens?"

Rather than answer her directly, it said, "It appears she was beautiful enough to lure the Dragon. Forget not that you are one of us, and do not enjoy the feel of the earth under your feet overmuch lest you lose what makes you a god. The maidens aren't meant to survive."

With this, it dispersed like smoke, rising with the embers of the blazing pyre into the infinite darkness, and the indifference of the stars felt cold. The rising sun, when it came, failed to warm her, and she knew that the message the Morningstar had delivered was true. She should have recognized the prediction in the prophecy.

26

THE ROAD HOME WAS LONG, and although Azuma did not acknowledge it, perhaps was unaware of it, she had changed. Another year had nearly spent itself, her name day approached, and Azuma dreaded it; no occasion gave her less desire for celebration.

Normally she loved the trees in their autumn finery, the subtle smell of the decay of leaves as the world looked to winter. But she was weary, the pyrrhic outcome of her campaign weighed upon her, and even the prospect of seeing her home and the priests of the shrine could not improve this unusual outlook.

She stopped rarely, traveling cloaked and disguised, making her way in secret, often sleeping in the saddle so she could keep pressing onward. Strange dreams plagued her travel, and she knew that she would need a blood meal soon, or there would be other dangers. She despised losing control.

Often, she knew she rode in company; she would notice Akenomyosei beside her on a dark beast with wild eyes, its hooves striking sparks from the ground, his form at times shapeless like smoke, at other times human-like, more often not. Just the two of them, in companionable silence.

Occasionally, Tatsuo Tomo would appear, his conversations with the Morningstar unintelligible, his tone of voice infuriating to her. He was possessed of a serpentine appearance, scaly, indeterminate, unlike the urbane teacher of her early life, and she suspected that the beast he showed her was not the worst of his guises.

Most disturbing of all were the later visions, increasing in frequency as she closed the distance to her home, when horsemen in her company were spirits, delivering a message she failed to understand.

Four beings rode abreast, and she was unable to fully see the other three, their faces and forms obscured from her, their horses marked as hers, their saddlery and weapons of four distinct times and places, of lands foreign to her. Two riders wore clothing more primitive than hers, and she suspected one of these to be a woman; indeed, at times one horse was bereft a rider, and the woman held a swaddled babe.

The one she sensed was oldest rode slightly in the lead, positioned to her far left. He wore clothing fashioned for the extreme cold, of furs and hides that reminded her of a Mongol warlord she had met in the far lands.

The more feminine was at her near left, wrapped in heavy linens the color of sand, her head and lower face obscured by these same garments. She was wrapped to avoid exposure, allowing only a glimpse of eyes golden as the hawk's.

The third rode to her right, on Akenomyosei's mount, wearing the cowled black habit of the priests that Iemitsu had banished. It was this apparition that came and went, leaving beside her a riderless horse, and the infant carried by the woman in its absence spoke to her with Akenomyosei's voice.

Finally, she rode alone, but in the far distance, on a parallel road, mirroring her progress, came another. A reflection, a spectre with a mount the same size and color as hers, its armor of the Dragon, its standard her own. Its face was hidden in a long cloak akin to the one she wore herself, another god, its only distinction from her the masculine hands that extended from the gauntlets to grip the reins. This one did not speak nor look at her, and when the roads they traveled converged, he continued companionably beside her, closer and closer, until merging with her utterly, body and soul. She could feel him there under her skin, and her thoughts were muddled, and they spoke together inside her mind for a time, although on waking she could never recall what was said.

These erosions of her thoughts and her spirit she knew were the concerted work of Akenomyosei. After all that had transpired, she had neither the patience nor the reserve to unravel this new mystery.

The rain began when she was still one day outside Edo, pouring down from a flat grey expanse that camouflaged storm from calm. It was a deceptive sky, making her feel as though she were not on the road to Tokugawa at all, rather on a road to nowhere. That sky was unchanging from morning to night, as if she had gotten no closer to her destination, but she saw the blaze of many lanterns from the small village near her estate just as twilight took hold.

She stopped at the inn to rest and take a meal, grateful and surprised to see a familiar white horse secured to the post outside the establishment. She stepped inside, and the perils and travails of the road slipped from her shoulders, the disreality of isolation over, as if stepping back into a scene that was alive because other beings made it so.

By coming here, the Collector exposed himself to the prejudices and judgements of the townspeople, although they were now too afraid of him and his mistress to refuse any service. He did not give their covert glances of disgust and indignance any of his attention, silently handing her a cup of warm sake. She removed her helmet and they all looked down, or away, bowing in perfunctory respect for their Shogun.

He had anticipated her, felt her distress tugging at the blood ties. She gulped the sake, appreciating its warm burn at her center perhaps as much as his silence, which was different in both its character and its depth than that of the road.

When she was finished, her cup was refilled, and he said simply, "Your bath and your bed await, my Lord."

They rode together to the crossroads, and the leaning bamboo spires of her forests waited like sentinels along the lane. As they rode through the gates of the estate, they were met by stablehands who relieved them of their horses.

An attendant assisted with her armor and her cloak, and she dismissed him from the bathhouse before shedding the rest of her clothing, grateful for the hot water that carried the grime of her journey away, even though the worst would take more than water to remove it from her soul.

She pulled on her robe, and wandered barefoot through the forest, ignoring the falling temperature, which affected her so little. She was pulled inexorably onward to the shrine, where her faithful priests waited, anticipating the return of their charge. She found them ready to make the sacrifices needed to strengthen her, and when she returned to the house she was much restored.

She lingered on the veranda, opening her rooms up to the night, which was cool, but still temperate for the lateness of the season. The rains had stopped, but the scents they left behind on the breeze were enticing. She left the lanterns unlit, preferring to gaze upon the stars. She could hear the waves racing along the rocks at the base of the sea cliff nearby.

Soft footsteps approached, and she turned to see Megumi waiting just inside the threshold. Although Azuma could not see her face, her posture seemed shy, and Azuma smiled. She felt that shyness, too. The anticipation of a moment long desired to arrive, and then the indecisiveness when it does.

"My lady, you should be abed," she observed, but Megumi did not respond, so Azuma opened her arms in invitation, and Megumi approached, stepping into her embrace.

Her small shoulders shook slightly, and Azuma asked, "Are you weeping? Do not weep, my love."

"You are finally here," Megumi whispered softly. "I feared —"

"Shhh. I am here, that is all that matters now." She noticed that Megumi wore only her dressing robe, and the warmth of her skin through the thin silk was like sustenance for Azuma, a reminder of life and of home. She took the lantern from the hook, and let go of Megumi's hand only long enough to find the lucifer to light it.

She invited Megumi inside, ducking into the room to place this lamp on a low table. She drew the screens to the veranda to close out the night and turned back to see Megumi letting go of her robe, allowing it to slide to the floor. She had no flaw that Azuma could see, a completely lovely form, the embodiment of female perfection. She did not know how she had resisted Megumi's charms.

"I have decided that there is nothing I want more than to be yours," Megumi told her, and Azuma smiled a little, grateful that the advice she had bestowed on her departure had been followed. "But I wonder what you want, now that you have met the Jade Princess, and loved her."

Azuma reached for the *kanzashi* that held Megumi's hair, freeing the dark flows of it, feeling its weight on her hands. "Ah. You have heard all the gossip; I suppose it was inevitable. And now we are here, together at last, alone at last, and you wish to speak of someone else?" Azuma was still too exhausted to rein in her frustration, and wondered at Megumi's statement, but she understood it. She was still very young, and her nakedness was less a tool of seduction than a showing of trust. She was making herself completely vulnerable to Azuma, a gesture not to be ignored.

Azuma stepped away from her, saying softly, "The Jade Princess was a friend. It was her job to get close to me, the Emperor sent her to respond to a message I had sent him. She was clever and beautiful. You would have liked her very much. I think she was jealous of *you*."

"Of – of me?" Megumi's dark eyes blinked repeatedly in surprise. "What do I have that the Jade Princess would covet?"

Azuma shook her head slowly, trying not to show her amusement and failing. Women were far more complicated than men, stronger but insecure, more fragile yet more resilient, knowing what they wanted but harder to satisfy. She tugged on Megumi's chin, pulling her face up for a series of open-mouthed kisses. "This. And this. And this. She knew the Shogun wanted you more than her, and she had never experienced such an insult."

Megumi broke the embrace to reach for the lamp, but Azuma stopped her.

"I want to see you," she murmured, exploring with her hands, evoking Megumi's pleasure. She felt Megumi's fingers on the closure of her kimono, pulling it open, making her own discoveries, and the sensations were so overwhelming that when Azuma realized something was wrong, it was too late to turn away, impossible to avoid what was happening to her.

The tingling started in her feet, and there was an odd heaviness low down in her abdomen, and she could no longer keep her balance. She sank to her knees and went onto her outstretched hands, fighting the bile she tasted in her throat. This was not the Dragon, into whose body she could slip quietly and painlessly. Trying to further understand what was happening was not possible because the world was slipping away, she was becoming this pain. It did not relent, causing her body to writhe uncontrollably. Megumi's eyes were wide and afraid, but Azuma had no comfort to give her.

The agony bent her the other direction, backwards again, and she felt a few scales emerge and recede at the base of her spine – a part of the Dragon responding to this new stress. She contorted so painfully, arched back and back as if she would fold in half again upon herself, and she screamed with the Dragon's voice but that was not what emerged.

Megumi watched with horror as Azuma's flesh rippled and changed, muscles enlarging, breasts flattening, face widening and growing more angular, brows thickening, hair sprouting along her jawline and trailing down her abdomen.

The scream deepened as the register of the voice dropped lower, became harder and more roughened. And if not terrible enough, the screams of disbelief that tore through it were suddenly echoed by Megumi's own screams. The eyes paled to blue, the irises flooding back to black before the body collapsed, and was still.

Megumi was immobilized by her fear, and she hesitated because she could not turn away from Azuma. To her great dismay, when the figure began moving again, what climbed up out of the ruined dressing gown was a man, sweaty and shaking.

He was, and was not, Azuma. The general features resembled her, the hair, the spare build, the height. But the eyes that peered out of this newly male face did not know her. Nor did she know him. Her instincts informed her senses, and where Azuma had been safe, this man was not.

His eyes were cold, and they fixed on Megumi with evil intent, and her own nudity, when she remembered it, became an invitation she wanted desperately to revoke.

She hiccupped air into her lungs and screamed again, but this alarmed or infuriated him, and strong hands closed on her throat, choking her, extinguishing these cries. He moved over her and she could feel his arousal, so Megumi, although her vision was darkening, increased her struggles. But his hands tightened; his singular instinct seemed to be to continue the act that she and Azuma had started. Megumi fought beneath his unwanted weight, maneuvering herself to drive her hip into his manhood.

He screamed in rage and pain but released her, so she gathered her garments around her and escaped to the garden, running blindly away into the night.

He stalked her in the darkness, chasing her to the top of the bluff, and Megumi, confused by the foreignness of the nocturnal landscape, turned first one way and then another. Without her shoes, her feet were soon cut open on the rocks and small sharp bamboo shoots, and she thought to hide in the thick vegetation that dotted the bluff. But the being that stalked her had honed preternatural bloodlust, and her bleeding feet and the scratches on her face and arms attracted him. Inexorably, she could sense his approach, and before he reached her she would flee, flushed out of hiding, the quarry to his chase.

Megumi's first screams had awakened the Collector, and in those earliest moments of consciousness, he did not know why he was awake, but he felt a nameless dread. Her subsequent screams explained the interruption of his sleep, and he dressed in haste, following the progression of her panicked cries from the garden to the bluff.

Azuma's blood ties were pulling him onward, into a confused rush of thoughts that were so unlike her that his own fear peaked. There was madness in the voice that came across their bond, a voice that he barely recognized, but it could only be coming from his benefactor.

He followed the garbled jumble of emotions, seeing flashes of Megumi fleeing in panic.

It was a terrible game of chance, a struggle for survival and control. When the naked man rose up from the reeds ahead of the Collector on the plateau of the hill, fighting what it supposed to be a rival for the woman, he was unprepared to fend off such an attack, from a god that did not seem to know the man who grappled with it, did not possess the reason of the goddess whose form it shared. It was from this being that Azuma's garbled thoughts ensued, and the Collector failed utterly to subdue it, so he retreated, hoping for another chance to catch it by surprise.

But it was not to be. It redoubled its efforts to catch its prey, and Megumi, inattentive in her terror, ran off the cliff and was broken on the rocks far below. He arrived to see the Dragon spiraling downward behind her, losing the prize to the black sea.

The waves rose up and he felt and tasted the salt spray, but lost them in the mist, so he stood at the ledge, waiting, watching. Finally, there was movement on the beach below the promontory, but even with his enhanced night vision he could not make sense of what he saw.

He leaned out over the drop and let the wind take him, windwalking the short distance it took him to descend to the beach. It was a gift given him by Azuma's blood, but it separated him so completely from his own humanity that he rarely used it. Yet he had known that it might take him some time to climb down from the high cliffs, and when he reached the sand, he discovered his mistress, weak, shedding the scales of the Dragon behind her as she tried to carry what was left of her beloved Megumi.

27

AZUMA'S LIMBS WERE SCRATCHED AND bloodied, and one of her feet was misshapen, as if the joint were dislocated or the bone had been broken. He tried to take from her the dreadful burden she carried.

"I think I killed her," she whispered to him, only clutching Megumi more tightly. "I simply cannot remember. We were making love, and then — and then -" Her voice broke and devolved into a piteous sob that threatened to rend his heart from his chest. "The Dragon followed her off the high cliff, and I saw her falling, falling ahead of me. I couldn't catch her. I just didn't have enough time."

He said nothing, stopping her and helping her to lay Megumi on the sand. He reached for Azuma, picking her up and gently carrying her back to the house. He set her on her bed and went away again.

Much later, the sky lightening in the east, he returned to her. He sat next to her, still not speaking, then turned to study her. He picked up her tattered kimono and smelled it.

"I fear there is something your mentor failed to tell you," he finally said, his grave tone matching the grief she felt. She questioned whether she would have the strength to move from that spot, wanting to hold here, close to what happened, and find a way to unravel the time that had passed since her return and reweave it into something new.

She looked at him questioningly, and then put her head down and wept. He closed the screens, shutting out the day, and sat beside her through the long hours, until the sunlight was no more, and the night had returned. Neither moved, neither spoke.

And when most of the night had been spent in this strange worshipful silence, and he felt himself beginning to drift off, Azuma's voice brought him back.

"The answer is in the blood," she told him, with determined certainty. She offered her arm, and reached for the dirk at his waist. He gripped her hand, afraid of what she might do, but her strength exceeded his own, and her will was not to be denied. She opened her wrist and offered it, and he tasted once more of the life within her. What he saw astonished him and angered him, and he knew it would take all his will to tell her of her other self. And to tell her that she had been right.

But the blood compelled as much as it revealed, and when she commanded him to tell of how she had a dark twin that resembled Tatsuo Tomo, how Megumi had fled the house like a frightened lark, how she had been hounded along the bluff and over the cliff, how the Dragon-change had brought Azuma back too late to save her, he could not refuse. Akenomyosei's terrible plans had been irrevocably set in motion, and Tatsuo Tomo's promise to his master had been fulfilled.

28

AND SO IT CAME TO be that the Dragon withdrew from the world, and releasing her samurai, she bestowed the Blood Gift on the twelve, and that priestly order left behind the shrine that hid among the bamboo trees east of Edo. They became her new guard, passing into legend like the Goddess they served.

A lesser Tokugawa heir was installed as Shogun, but the strength of the feudal dictators of that distinguished line waned, the daimyos growing in power and allying themselves with the Emperor, trading their political support for tax exemptions, and by the time of the Meiji Restoration, feudal power was extinguished. Imperial edict outlawed the way of the samurai, and a new Japan emerged from the old.

29

Text of a scroll stolen from the Imperial Archive during its relocation to Edo, ensuring that it was not available for study by anyone who sought its contents following the Shimabara Rebellion, including any of the Tokugawa that came after Iemitsu.

When the *hitorogami* brought about the formation of Heaven, and thus separated the light from the darkness, five great gods, three and two, were brought forth in that place, though the earth remained dense and dark below the lightness of the *Takamagahara.* These were the *Kotoamatsukami*, imperfect in number, and unbalanced in power, spontaneously created, from which all others arose. Creation, then, in concert with destruction, and the cycle began, and of these gods more has been forgotten than was ever known, as they escaped into hiding thereafter. Some remained divine and begat the high elemental *kami*, and others involved themselves with the darkness below. From the darkness came two more gods, the *kamiyoyanayo,* begat of the fifth of the *kotoamatsukami,* from oddity and asymmetry were two. But the second was an aberration to the other four great gods, and seeking to restore their number, they reclaimed the first, and returned to anonymity.

The second stole its name from the Creator for the insult, and was known as *Akenomyosei*, the Star of Morning, worshipped in perpetuity by the Dragon Sect. It was said to be of two parts, two forms, had no definite sex, and hid after birth. This secrecy and duplicity have allowed it to cause mischief beyond the realms of the rising sun, and it wrote its own mythology.

Ten deities were then born, *Ani* and *Imoto,* each twins of which sister was also wife, and the last of these pairs of gods and goddesses created the eight islands of Japan. Thus came *Izanagi,* brother-husband to *Izanami,* sister-wife, with their enchanted staff which stirred the jeweled seas to form the great archipelago…

30

THE WAVES THAT RUSH AGAINST the rocks near the old Tokugawa stronghold make a sound like the cries of a lonely maiden. Many people travel to that lonely beach to bring flowers and other tributes to the beautiful Megumi of legend, and hear her forever weeping for her lost lover, for whom, it is said, she still waits in the next life.

iara ayana isabel otoño-nuñez

michael bithiah israel bat-aharon

31

MICHAEL ISRAEL LOOKED OUT OVER the vast brown expanse of the desert floor below her, grateful that she was primary pilot on the day's mission, not having to be the 'outside eyes' for this mission east of Tikrit, heading toward the interior of the country. The monotony made it too easy to miss critical details, and a break from looking for power lines and other rare obstacles was much needed. True, flying a helicopter was a whole-body endeavor, but having one hand on the cyclic, both feet on the pedals, and the other hand occupied with the collective was merely an exercise in muscle memory for her, and she could let her thoughts drift while she listened to her radio operator communicate with the American Kiowa behind them.

This joint exercise was for general intel, not routine ground support as most of the locals on the ground would suspect, and they were running down a tip from an American reserve officer given before his C-19 transport plane swallowed him up in the drawdown. He hadn't made the connection to the larger picture; he passed it on during a debrief and that had triggered a chain of events that stretched back to Jerusalem. It was late September, still feeling every bit like summer, although the calendar had pushed them officially into autumn a few days earlier.

The crew of the Kiowa that now accompanied them was carrying their PC for the mission, a senior U.S. army warrant officer with a negligible security clearance. The PC's copilot was a fellow Israeli, and the PC's status meant that while she was command pilot, and assumed that the mission was directed by American orders, she was unaware that both Israelis had left behind regular military service and had long since been recruited to Mossad.

Her copilot kept up a steady chatter on the comms, talking to the other Kiowa and giving her updates from his surveillance. His eyes kept coming back to the extra patch she wore on the shoulder of her uniform, a small four-centimeter Hello Kitty that was entirely non-regulation, but by now was the stuff of legend among her fellow Israeli pilots. He was too intimidated by her to ask about it.

She had certainly not been the first woman pilot, nor even close to being one of the first wave. The Israelis had embraced the reality of women in combat longer than any other Western military power. But she had been the first to be allowed into her elite combat unit, and she was rated for most planes, including the heavy transports, as well as almost any helo.

Not a single progressive movement had penetrated that sacred place, and her commanding officer had greeted her that first day with a hearty "Hello, kitty!" It was *not* a term of endearment, rather, it referred blatantly yet blandly to an anatomic structure heretofore unknown within that crew, and was every bit meant to reduce her to less than the sum of her parts. She had swallowed the insult whole and without comment, but had embraced the nickname, ironing the tiny patch onto her combat uniforms where it remained unremarked upon by the immediate members of the team and their superior officers. It was not unusual for special forces eccentricities to be overlooked by whatever Mother Country to which you swore allegiance. Until, to the horror of those same smug superiors, the IDF Middle East Commander had noticed it, and asked about its significance, whereupon she told him matter-of-factly that she had earned it by having the only pussy in the group. His ears remained bright red for the remainder of the inspection, but there hadn't been any blowback — at least none that came to her attention.

Shortly after that, her executive officer had returned from leave with an opaque adhesive cut to fit the inside of her full-face helmet visor. It was perforated, so that from her visual perspective, it was akin to the usual opaque face shield, but from the outside, to anyone on the ground, it looked like Hello Kitty was flying the rig. It was less apology than tribute, because by then she had earned the respect of her flight team and they had largely stopped treating her as if everyone in their unit required a Y-chromosome to function.

When their coordinates confirmed they had reached the location of interest, she brought the nose of the helicopter down and hovered, examining the sand pattern and deciding that the intel had been solid. She gave the machine more power and let the rotor blades disrupt the desert floor beneath them, before climbing again to let the dust drift away. In a few moments, the cloud had cleared enough to show her what the maneuver had revealed.

The marker was there, but Michael Israel knew that only she and her fellow Israeli understood its significance; the clock on their clandestine mission had started.

32

AZUMA GROANED WHEN THE ALARM sounded, but rolled over and looked at the clock. She was still jet-lagged from her short trip to Los Angeles to present a lecture on differential and variable immunofluorescent gene (DVIG) product bioassays. The conference had been scheduled right up against the start of her second foray into graduate studies at the University of Tokyo. It took her several moments to discern whether it was six in the morning or six in the evening, and she sat up slowly to consider this conundrum. She had intended to be awakened in the evening, to do some lab prep ahead of the class she taught the next morning, but the quality of the light was tricky. She decided to get up despite her body screaming for more sleep. She was hungry, too, but her blood meal would have to wait.

She took the coldest of showers and settled for bitter green juice, drinking it standing naked at the kitchen island. The granite countertop was cold against her thighs, and she noted that the sun was indeed going down.

She foraged in her open suitcase, irritated at her level of disorganization, but she kept no permanent staff here and had been in no condition to properly unpack when she'd arrived. Her guard was deployed at RSI and would be rotating as her personal detail when the Collector deemed it necessary. It was no secret she preferred this independence.

Satisfied that her return to student life allowed for a more relaxed wardrobe, she settled for skinny jeans, not bothering with underwear (she didn't have the patience to dig for it). She pulled on a *Tokyo Ghoul* t-shirt that had been washed to silky softness, haphazardly braided her hair, and wrestled her arms into a well-worn vintage moto jacket. She grabbed up her knapsack and her helmet and took the elevator down to the garage.

By the time her Ducati superbike bumped off the ramp and onto the street she was wide awake with exhilaration. The powerful machine did not command her total concentration, but she gave it anyway; it was needed for the manner in which she had always ridden. It ate up the road, and she pushed it through gaps which allowed for no margin of error – supremely confident in her enhanced reflexes and arrogant in her indestructibility.

She loved this city most at night, when it sparkled like a jewel but was no less bustling than in daylight. It could be surprisingly brutal in its darkest corners, and less surprisingly welcoming. She buzzed past modern stores, and marketplaces, beer gardens and nightclubs. She squealed through a busy intersection and was enticed by the umami scents coming from her favorite ramen stand, so she drove the bike right up onto the promenade and parked it. She didn't want to take the time to eat, but she knew with her exhaustion and no immediate prospects for her sacred meal it was the best safeguard against loss of control and an unwanted shift.

She didn't even have to say a word; she was such a frequent guest that the old gentleman merely nodded when she joined the evening's group of strangers sitting around his cart. He set to work on her food while she drank buckwheat tea, finally blessing her with his masterpiece. The perfect cut of *tonkatsu* garnished with green onions and a rich, silky broth that held perfect noodles. Heaven.

33

BY THE TIME AZUMA COASTED the cycle onto the Hongo campus, most of the faculty had gone home. She went in through the Akamon Gate, and walked past Sanshirō Pond before veering east to the Academy of Sciences. She carried a faculty designation despite being enrolled in a graduate program. Her previous degrees afforded her the status, and the department heads had been both thankful to her for agreeing to teach while she finished this final (and possibly unnecessary) degree, and prideful of her short tenure there. Her presence added prestige to their program, they were delighted to put her name forward in connection with the university. They were also interested in the possibility that she would endow a chair in her name after she completed her studies – while these things might happen after one died, it was better to secure the money while the benefactor still lived.

She understood these politics well, and exploited them. Her ancestry could be traced back to the Tokugawa and the Mashaito clans, one branch feudal and the other industrial/ruling. She was also the founder and CEO of Rising Sun Industries, a multinational genetic research and development giant. She had funded laboratory upgrades the year prior to matriculating, and she had her own closed room installed so that she could continue her most sensitive biologic work seamlessly without having to shuttle between RSI headquarters and school. These improvements signaled the beginning of a long partnership, and a direct recognition of the value of Japanese higher education, whose thought leaders felt she had shunned her birthplace in favor of a Western education. Never mind that without her Harvard and Oxford degrees, Tokyo might not have accepted her.

It didn't hurt that she remained a ubiquitous presence in each of her labs, and it was agreed that she was still one of the most prolific bench scientists at RSI. It was a refuge to her; she handled her executive duties efficiently, but her first love was the science. Genetics was the language of life; understanding it was her pilgrimage. It spoke to her in her sleep, and she kept asking questions of it, unraveling its answers. It was a language that not many cared to understand, but universal was the desire to exploit its secrets.

She used her ID to gain entrance to her building and took the stairs in threes to the third floor. Her office was in the corner, and she was surprised to see that it was marked by a plate that said *Azuma Himura, MD. Ph.D.* Before she had left, it had still been an empty slot, just another office temporarily inhabited but not really claimed. They had wasted no time. Japanese efficiency. In her years at Harvard, the office signage had never seemed to catch up with the changing occupants of its buildings.

Post-It notes crowded her desk like colorful butterflies, covered in a shorthand unintelligible to anyone but her. They might contain state secrets or a particularly clever recipe for seaweed salad. She slid into her desk chair and dashed off a few email replies, including one to a doctoral student for whom she had agreed to act as an advisor. There was a request for a meeting with her own advisor, the formidable Dr. Sumāto Shirogorō, a Nobel Prize winner in Science and Professor Emeritus in Genetics. He was the reason she had decided to complete her trifecta of doctorates; she wanted his keen mind and critical eye overseeing her thesis and thus was extending her scholarly instruction to include one of her own countrymen.

She glanced through her lesson plans for the next several days, not wanting any surprises now that her schedule would be tighter than ever. She counted students, noting that the graduate student who was supposed to be her teaching assistant for the lab sessions the following day had not yet reached out to her. She sighed, but was not overly concerned, expecting that they would slide into the lab at the very last second, having made last minute schedule changes and likely just arriving to campus on the first day of term.

No matter, she was as deft as any grad student at preparing gels, and in her jet-lagged state, sleep was unlikely to find her anytime soon. Let her TA enjoy reuniting at one of the local bars with their comrades for *Kirin Ichiban* and karaoke.

She let herself into the lab and started preparations, ensuring each of the bench stations was properly equipped, checking burners, scales, beaker and flask inventories, and electricity. The individual computer workstations looked sleek and beautiful, subsidized by the first grant she had made to the university. She poured gels and retreated to the front of the room. She stepped out of her motorcycle boots, put her feet up on the chair rail, and signed into her private VPN to access her work at RSI. All quiet on that front; not even the most faithful of her geeks was up this late.

She checked dates on reagents, maintenance logs, even the refrigerator temp logs were perused in her insomniac mania. She made a brief list of questions she would have to answer to start her own investigations, and was just tucking this back into the pocket of her lab coat when an unwelcome tingling started in her feet.

"No, no, no…" she whispered, hoping against hope that it was just a side-effect of sleep deprivation and jet lag, but when her hands began to shake, she knew it was inevitable. *He* was coming through. She wasted precious seconds on despair, then realized something that she should have thought of before.

Moving as quickly as she was able, she slid into the supply room between the labs, grateful her socks and the slippery floor made her marginally quicker in her gracelessness. She was barely able to unlock it with her card, nearly giving up when, on her fourth attempt, holding her left hand steady with her right, the light beeped green and she heard the electronic click as the lock disengaged.

She grabbed a syringe and vacutainer kit and raced to the bench beside the sink, twisting her sleeve viciously and pulling on it with her teeth to create a makeshift tourniquet. She grimaced as she slammed the needle into the vein without her usual finesse, pulling the stylet and cursing when her blood poured out as she fumbled the vacutainer into place. It filled in a heartbeat, and she pulled everything out as one, bending her arm to keep from further blood loss as she disengaged the needle from the tube.

She swiped at the spilled blood on the workbench with the tail of her shirt and popped the top off a Sharpie with her teeth, quickly marking the tube with her last name. Her field of vision was getting fuzzy, particularly in the periphery, and she tilted her head like a predatory bird to concentrate on the *kanji.*

Keeping her arm bent acutely, she ran for the spec fridge in the closed room, sliding around the corner like a skateboarder.

"Please, please, *please!*" she begged, although there was no one to hear her. She wrenched the door open one-handed and tried to concentrate on the ordered items inside. There was a plastic box marked *New/Save,* and she deposited the vial on its side, slamming the door and hoping she would find it where she left it.

She had to make it out of the building still under her own control, knowing that Tatsuo should not be here alone after hours. She doubled over, nearly dropping to her knees as a deep pain spread through her groin. She clenched her teeth against a moan and ran back to her office, weaving back and forth, feeling as though moving through the cruelest of dreams, where one attempts to run but cannot seem to will their legs to move.

She searched for something on her desk, her mind forgetting what she'd thought she wanted. She shook so violently that she knocked everything off the desk in her impatience and frustration. But this revealed a lone ballpoint pen, which she clasped victoriously, and retracting the nib, with every ounce of waning strength she drove the open tip through her jeans and into her thigh, twisting it cruelly enough to dislodge a small chunk of flesh. It took all her reserve not to scream, but she twisted away, tossing the pen deep into the footwell under the desk, and left the office, just barely managing to lock it behind her.

She used the wall to help her remain upright, and her vision was coming in and out, and she could hear Tatsuo's disordered thoughts overtaking her own. When she reached the outer door, she let herself out, tossing her keys and her ID card back inside before the door locked behind her. Now he couldn't get into the building or wreck her bike.

You don't have shoes or transportation, you bastard, she thought with amusement, saving her last thought for the Collector before she pitched face first onto the grass, feeling the ache of her genital shift like a kick to her newly male groin. She gave the blood tie a weak tug. *Find us.*

34

SHE RETURNED TO HERSELF AS the Dragon, miserable, ill, coiled on the balcony of her apartment. The rain had returned, and she was still groggy, hoping against hope that Tatsuo – she – hadn't done anything stupid. Or illegal, given his proclivities.

As usual, greedy for power, he had tried to shift. Luckily for all concerned he was unable to hold on to their shared form as Dragon, and it brought Azuma back immediately, disoriented, sometimes injured (once with a gunshot wound!), with odd tastes in her mouth and on more than one occasion, substance-intoxicated and needing to suffer detox in her human form. Hungover frequently, but some of those hurts were so similar to the hermaphroditic aftermath that she could not tell where her recovery from alcohol began and her recovery from Tatsuo ended.

It was easier to endure the rain wearing scales rather than skin, so she waited. The Collector was not as efficient in following the blood tie, even after the better part of four centuries, and it was possible he had considerable travel to undertake to reach her, but she felt certain he was coming to her in due haste, so she succumbed to a fitful slumber that brought disjointed dreams and no rest.

She awoke to his warm strong hands on her jaw, cradling the Dragon's head gently to wake her. Neither of them harbored fears any longer that she might attack him in this confused and dangerous state, and he rubbed the scales between her eyes with affection and sympathy. If ever he tried to coddle her in her human guise, she shut him down with a look, but it seemed that he took such an approach with the Dragon, especially when she was particularly fragile. It was possible that he despised Tatsuo more than she did.

And it was dangerous to leave the Dragon vulnerable.

At his urging, she tried to stand, and without assistance managed to move with some grace into the apartment, her limbs weak and her tail heavy. He'd started the fire, and she was relieved to see that *Roku* had accompanied him. *Roku* did not protest when she coiled herself around him, her reptilian gaze on the Collector, who turned away to give them privacy while she fed.

When next she awoke, she was human once more, naked beneath several blankets in the corner of the sectional, and she shivered involuntarily before she was able to recall where she was. The Collector sat across from her in an Eames chair, asleep under the lamp with a copy of Shūsaku Endo's *Silence* open on his lap.

35

TEL AVIV MADE HER NERVOUS. Michael Israel had always been satisfied to be sent away from there, the demands of the IDF and later the Mossad a welcome refuge for her. She had never secured her own place, despite the urgings of her superiors that her vocation required absolute secrecy. It would have created too much of an argument with her parents, or more specifically, with her father, who was in denial about his only child.

He did not think it proper for an unmarried woman to live on her own, and was still praying that she would accept one of the young men he believed would make her life complete. He had been shocked when she had announced her decision to remain in the army following her compulsory service, and incensed when she defied him, after he had forbidden it.

She understood that after the loss of her brother she had become the embodiment of all his disappointments. Yet that didn't alter the fact that his hopes and dreams for the future were wrapped up in her in some twisted way as well, as if her eventual production of a grandson would make up for her survival instead of his son, would replace what he had lost.

And hadn't she, in so many ways, tried to atone for her existence every day since that terrible event? Although only four years old, she had stopped answering to Bithiah and adopted his name, Michael, as though that magic would allow her to hold on to him. She had hidden under her parents bed during the *shiva* with a pair of scissors, hacking off her long curls, wanting to transform, putting on his clothes. The shock of the family when she emerged had been evinced in one collective choking gasp. She realized too late that it made her look just like him, that this act was doubly painful because she reminded them of him already, and the living should not have to look upon the dead.

But she had already hardened her heart to them in so many ways. Because they didn't believe her when she said what happened that night, when she had tried to tell them about the monster. Indeed they had medicated her, silenced her, and when she awoke again her twin was gone. The doctor had called it crib death, unusual but not unheard of at four years of age, but she knew what had really happened, how she couldn't have saved him. The creature wanted *him*, had always wanted him, in an awful parallel to their father.

It seemed the monster knew that her fate was worse as the survivor, that it could feed off her suffering much longer than it had from him, taking him away but leaving no trace of itself. It had been every bit as frightful as the *golem* they were warned of in Grandfather's stories, made not of stone but scales. She had seen it watching Michael as he slept, and it had seen her. When it had attacked, Michael had fought it, trying to protect her as he always had, but it didn't matter. The oddest part was that their parents had slept through their screams, but she understood that was what the monsters could do, their magic was to isolate their victims. Adults did not believe, children carried the burden of fear.

Although the whole thing had the odd disreality of a dream, Michael Israel knew it had happened. No amount of therapy, doctors, or cajoling could dissuade her; she just stopped talking about it. But she never forgot. And when she heard scary stories, she knew the monsters were real. It was a relief of sorts. She never had to question the supernatural, she just had to be vigilant enough to recognize it and guard against it.

On furlough halfway through the Gulf War, she had traveled to Thailand rather than return home to Israel. In lieu of beach time, she spent many hours each day getting an elaborate colorful tattoo. It was a work of art, extending from her left shoulder blade to the curved hollow of her back. It depicted the scaly beast that had stolen her brother, wrapped in the arms of a young woman who appeared to be succumbing to its charms. But the clever girl who placed the ink had artfully fulfilled Michael Israel's instructions. If anyone had ever been intimate enough to get a closer look, they would have seen the weapon in the woman's left hand, concealed until such time as she was ready to use it.

This time, Israel felt as though it was awaiting her, the breeze off the sea tousling her hair like the lover she had never had. She started up the hill from the road where her cab had dropped her, climbing the forty steps to the house. The number was purposeful, and she suspected that her father believed that those steps allowed for meditation and purification before anyone entered his home.

She punched in the gate code and was admitted to the garden, tarrying at the bottom of the yard, overlooking the water. The bougainvillea had been trimmed into a series of trees, the result of her mother's nervous energy, the hillside allowed to flourish with any number of flowers and succulents, terraced and orderly. She leaned on the wall and let her thoughts drift, praying for calm, praying for patience.

Her mother found her there. Slim and spare, Hedda was the stereotypical rabbi's wife, disdaining adornment, but relentlessly beautiful, as if infused with the light of hard-earned patience tempered by the iron of righteous suffering. Her skin was soft and still supple, although the wind and sun had weathered her eyes, which crinkled pleasantly as she beheld her daughter. Her hands found Michael Israel's face, and the young soldier was startled to find that those hands had aged, softening enough to remind her of the feel of her grandmother's touch when she was yet a child.

Michael Israel leaned into her mother's embrace; she smelled of challah, olives, and the lavender soap that was her one indulgence, another habit that she had learned from *Sav'ta*. Her mother had never seemed to have any expectations for her; indeed, if her father had been forever disappointed in losing a son, his wife was grateful to *Elohim* that she still had a child.

"You've lost weight," Hedda observed, and Michael Israel had to laugh.

"*Ima*," she protested, shaking her head. "Can you not take one day off from being a Jewish mother?"

"I have taken too many days off since you joined the army," Hedda answered her with a sharp look. "You look beautiful." She tugged a handful of Michael Israel's hair affectionately, and put an arm around her waist, as if physical propulsion were needed to steer her toward the house.

"He is waiting for you," Hedda said, nodding toward the dwelling. "He will never admit it, but he is glad of you returning." Such was the lie that Hedda told every time, like a mantra, as if repeating it, like a prayer, could make it so.

36

MICHAEL ISRAEL RAN HER FINGERS gently over the Mezuzah at the kitchen door as she crossed the threshold, an observance not just of habit, but perhaps to invoke the tradition of a protection she did not really feel in this place of bad memories.

The home was small, and seemed to get even smaller as the years passed, but it was ever clean and cozy, the scents of clean laundry, bread, and freshly cut flowers filling the rooms. There were always crisp linens and colorful pottery, and her mother's eclectic line drawings, meant to provide a touch of levity, but Michael Israel secretly felt that the only thing they conveyed was her mother's sadness.

Her father was in the galley kitchen, and he greeted her in the usual perfunctory manner.

"Bithiah," he said, and somehow even the way he spoke her name was accusatory. He refused to use any name other than the one he had given her when addressing her, even though her operator's license and other identification papers proclaimed her Michael Israel bat-Aharon.

But he handed her a small glass of wine, rather placed it near her, and when she reached for the water to dilute it, she was careful not to touch him. Life in small spaces with an Orthodox rabbi can require contortions, especially since her father observed the most stringent restrictions on touch, for all persons, including his daughter. Then, wiping his hands on a small towel, he said, "Dinner is nearly ready."

"*Aba,*" she greeted him. "May you live a long life."

He merely grunted at her in response, turning back to his cooking, which had been his secret passion since he was a child. Hedda told her it relaxed him, but Michael Israel couldn't tell the difference. It appeared that this would be an intimate meal, just the three of them. While such dinners could be silent and awkward, she preferred them over the nights where he 'surprised' her by inviting some young man to try to match her with.

She excused herself to drop her bag in the bedroom she had shared with her brother, sinking down on the knotted coverlet of her childhood bed with her wine. She stretched her legs out toward the space where his bed had once been and yawned. Her exhaustion snuck up on her, and she realized that, despite everything, there was some subconscious measure of relief about being here again. Home was home.

She washed her hands and face in the basin in the shared bathroom and then went about setting the table. Going through the familiar ritual of finding the linens in the sideboard, the china and glassware in the hutch, the silver. Her hands shaking a bit, always wanting to set the fourth place, still.

She brought the bread, the carafe of wine. She filled the silver water pitcher and at the last minute, stepped out to the yard with a small silver bowl, twisting the blooms of the waxy camellia from their stems and floating them in the water. They were fragrant and beautiful, and reminded her that her work, and the war, could be forgotten here, for a few hours, a few days. All she had to do was try to forget for a time. It was enough that this was the place where she'd learned of monsters.

Hedda touched her hair gently when she ducked through the door, a silent reminder; she relinquished the flowers to her mother and stepped away to pull a scarf over her head. Her father lived with old tradition, and he insisted on observing certain customs, even at home. They sat at meals with their heads covered, as it was a time of prayer and family communion. Michael Israel had even had to wear a dress at home until the time she left for the military; her ubiquitous trousers and shirts since had been viewed with distaste but uncommented upon.

They prayed together, and ate in a surprisingly companionable silence for a time, then Rabbi ben-Ibrahim startled her by remarking casually, "The clerk of the Rabbinate asked after you." His eyes, however, studied her intently, gauging her reaction, probably looking for guilt.

"Is that true, Aharon? The Rabbinate?" Her mother interjected, unable to disguise her surprise at this revelation.

Her father did not answer his wife, merely continued to examine his daughter carefully, and Michael Israel knew he wondered if the inquiry were born out of some disobedience or offense she had caused. She would not, could not tell him that she was beginning a new assignment; she had been summoned to a meeting with the clerk and her own superiors at Mossad two days hence to discuss her discovery in the desert.

She wondered if the clerk had purposely involved her father; it was most likely because he was a known entity to the officials at the Rabbinate, and she was not. They could not know of the complexities of the relationship between herself and her father. He did not make small talk, or gossip – even if he did, he knew so little about her that any probe for information would be fruitless.

She was curious to know what had transpired, but remained silent, maintaining eye contact with him to show she was ashamed of nothing.

"What could I tell him?" the rabbi asked, as if he were responding to no one in particular. "Bithiah is an enigma. A good soldier, I am to understand, although what does that help her family? She is not a dutiful daughter who seeks her father's counsel or obeys his wishes that she marry and provide a means to continue our line.

"But I expect if he should ask of me this, he must know something of my daughter. Perhaps he knows something that I do not know about my only child, who insists on using a dead man's name, walking about in unsuitable clothing, with an untamed hairstyle. I am sure that what they see is that Rabbi ben-Ibrahim's house is not in order."

Michael Israel had studied his anger for a long time. He was prideful, overly concerned with appearances, and this was expressed through demands that his family exhibit propriety in all things, to bolster his appearance and standing in their community. He had never met a person who was not cowed by him; he had never encountered any situation he could not bring under control, other than this one. She suspected he had gotten his way in all things until Michael had died.

"Aharon," Hedda said softly, putting a hand over his. "Michael Israel is -"

"And you encourage this," her father pulled his hand away angrily. "That is not her name, it has never been her name!"

Michael Israel started to stand up; his attacks on her she could bear quietly, but it was too much that her mother should become a collateral target. Hedda waved her back down.

"Aharon, I hear you at synagogue talking so eloquently about free will, and its sacredness in the covenant between people and God," her mother's soft voice surprised her. It was unusual that she spoke up in this way, she who was unfailingly deferent to her husband. "Michael Israel is not a disappointment nor is she a possession; our child belongs to herself, and to God."

"You conflate disobedience with free will, and that is a sin," her father stated with finality, probably surprised to find himself alone on his side of the argument. Michael Israel wisely said nothing, but she had learned more about her mother in one spoken sentence than she had known of her in the whole of her life.

37

FOLLOWING HER SHOWER, AZUMA DRESSED and went in search of food. On her way through the great room, she plucked one of the blankets she had abandoned from the couch and draped it over the Collector.

She was pleased to see that her keys, phone, and university credentials were arranged neatly on the counter. Although she had witnessed the Collector perform many feats of impossibility, his talent for anticipating problems and solving them in advance was ever surprising.

She checked the laundry room and discovered that he had found her clothes, which meant that Tatsuo had removed them prior to attempting the shift. She was slightly embarrassed that she hadn't been wearing underwear, and briefly wondered what the Collector had made of *that.*

Despite their opposite genders, Tatsuo could wear most of her clothing, as she was tall, and she knew that he was similarly built. Other than a slight stretch through the shoulders of her t-shirts, and the unwashed boy-smell he left behind, there was little evidence of him. She imagined the day when he found himself wearing one of her dresses. She relished these imaginary retaliations.

One of the messages on her phone was from Aiko Akawa, a brilliant biomedical engineer and one of her lead investigators. She confirmed that she had been happy to stand in for Azuma on the first day of classes, reporting that the TA had shown up and had proven to be most capable. Azuma made a mental note to send her a gift, and thank the Collector. He had addressed every detail. She thought, not for the first time, that she did not deserve him.

The date on her phone told her something more disturbing – that Tatsuo had been in her skin for nearly two days. She scrolled through the news feeds on her phone for evidence of any misdeeds. If one knew what to look for, evidence of the supernatural could be found, and the internet had made it ridiculously easy to follow the trail of her misbegotten brother, or any of her wayward priests.

It was the most awful, the most frustrating. Where did he take her body? What did he do with it? The lost time was bad enough; the machinations of her imagination were worse. Sometimes, she would get flashes of what he was doing, and for the briefest of moments, she could see out through his eyes, she scratched the surface of his consciousness. Once, she had found herself looking at him in a mirror, seeing his face reflected in the dim neon lights of some nightclub bathroom. But he knew she was there, and seemed to have some ability to push her back down into the depths of his subconscious, banishing her the way she wanted to banish him.

It appeared his appetites were mostly those of a young human male, one with significant impulse control. On the occasions when the Collector had found him before he shifted back, he had been gambling, fighting, or…

He did have a taste for blood, and could be cruel to members of the opposite sex, which was a devastating revelation for her. History repeated itself; the Collector found he was paying for these excesses, much like Tsunayoshi had done centuries before for Ietsune, having to ensure that these uglinesses were not associated with Azuma.

A slight throbbing from the healing wound on her thigh brought her back from her reverie, and she faced the day with renewed purpose, not a little excitement, and, she was surprised to admit, hope.

In the kitchen, she found a detail that the Collector had apparently overlooked. One of the apples in the bowl on the center island had a single bite taken out of it. It had been strategically replaced, put back with its fellows, perhaps a defiant message to her. She ignored this, cutting out the bite and finishing the fruit in spite, then foraged in the refrigerator for something more to feed her human beast. She ate carefully, if a bit impatiently, anxious to get to the university and into the lab. She didn't want a repeat appearance by her twin. She could not immediately locate her helmet, so she disdained it, still needing the expediency of the motorcycle to get her where she was going without unnecessary delay.

Roku was sitting in an armchair in the private elevator lobby, a casual but effective deterrent to any threat, looking none the worse for wear after providing her blood meal. He asked whether she would prefer if he drove her, noting the keys in her hand. But she waved him off with a shake of her head and continued on alone.

Her office was unrecognizable. Everything she had knocked to the floor had been sorted, stacked, and lined up on the desk. Her Post-It notes had been arranged in neat rows and columns on the front of the cabinet doors over her laptop, her pens stacked neatly in their square cup. She laughed out loud. The Collector loved order, and he had KonMaried her. She wondered whether he did it to amuse her, but after all their time together she still could not reliably identify his attempts at humor. At times, when she laughed about something he said or did, he looked confused, as if she had entirely misjudged the intent of his actions.

She dropped to her knees and peered into the footwell beneath the desk, but he had recovered that pen as well, and she spent a few moments rattling the contents of the cup until she identified it. At the moment, it was her most prized possession. Turning it over, she was relieved that he had not noticed the chunk of tissue lodged in the hollow tip.

Alone in the lab, she took fine forceps and freed the ragged flesh gently, examining it before slipping it into a specimen jar with saline.

It was slightly desiccated, but the tip of the pen had protected it from the worst environmental insults, and she knew it would be rich with DNA and other revealing proteins. Hopefully, the essence of her brother was captured there, written in a code that she was amply equipped to decipher, and she could compare it to her own private assay, specimen *alpha*, the template on which all her special studies were based.

She was pleased to find the Vacutainer where she had left it, with a note from the TA apologizing for not running the blood sample because she couldn't find any instructions for its evaluation. She took the spec tube and the tissue sample back to her office and placed it in the small beverage fridge next to the file cabinet, ensuring its safety until she could take it to RSI for genetic testing under the stringent protocols she had established for high value specimens.

She then turned her attention back to other things that demanded her attention, preparation of her presentation for Shirogorō that would form the framework of their scholarly relationship and outline her proposed thesis. She was excited that her interest in application of the DVIG technology had become both more personal and more urgent, and she was looking forward to getting his advice on how to structure her studies and test her hypotheses.

There were journals to read and seemingly endless emails, frustrating because each one had the potential to contain something of importance that required immediate action or attention, yet frequently didn't. There was an issue with parking at one of the RSI labs, and fully thirty-two emails had cluttered her inbox when everyone on the chain hit *Reply All*. She approved several protocols and looked over contracts for proposed collaborations with industry, private sector investors, and the militaries of an assortment of countries.

As frequently happened when she was working, she lost track of time, and was surprised when she looked up from her reading to find the Collector standing expectantly in her doorway. He was dangling her motorcycle helmet from his fingers and had brought her a jacket, but his expression was neutral, accommodating as ever. She was startled at the dimness of the room beyond the lamplight, and slightly alarmed when she glanced out the window at the full darkness. She didn't bother to ask him how he'd managed to get into the building. Again.

"Thank you, my friend," she murmured, waving him in and gesturing to the orderliness of the office around her. She pulled a stack of books and journals from a chair and gestured for him to sit down, which he did, although it clearly made him uncomfortable. "I swear I do not know why you have been so good to me all these years."

The comment was meant to be an offhand rhetorical observation, but he surprised her by answering.

"Do you not? You saw me when others did not," he said simply, referring to the disgrace of his mixed parentage, his lack of standing or humanity in that confused time of primitive beliefs. Now, his appearance did not occasion comment other than that he was possessed of an exotic handsomeness that was universally appealing. He had no difficulty finding companions, not that she guessed he ever had.

"Although you may not realize it, we are much the same. My oath is in the blood; when you gave me this life I had nothing to offer in return but service."

"Surely that debt has been paid one hundred-fold," she answered quietly.

"Longevity does not eradicate the pact to give of one's life in gratitude," he said, and his tone was one of finality, with a touch of disappointment at her loose relationship with honor as he viewed it.

"I did not mean to diminish your commitment, nor do I wish to offend," she apologized, recognizing that he had always demanded that she observe traditions honorably, not allowing her to ignore propriety just because she could. He wanted her to balance her power with a sense of obligation. It was one of his earliest lessons. He was, essentially, the only one who had ever been a parent to her. "Have you come to take me home?"

He simply nodded in response, as if he had spoken his quota of words for the day.

"Can I prevail upon you to travel with me to RSI?" she asked, hoping he had one more indulgence for her, and she was thankful when he acquiesced. His voice in her mind made her smile. *Shall I ask Roku to return the Ducati?*

"Alright." She took the helmet dutifully and pulled on her jacket. "I will drop off the bike and then we can go." She tucked her specimens into the messenger bag she flung across her back before following him out of the office.

38

We have a job for you.

The note was direct, written in the spare hand of her confessor. It was centered neatly in the post box, as if all the care that had been taken to write it was also expended in placing it for her. Iara, smiling, left it behind, not as she found it, but crumpled into a ball. The instruction was to *move* the message to indicate her acknowledgement, but she couldn't resist taking it a step further. She knew he despised imprecision.

She stepped out to the street and lit a cigarette, then crossed the road, taking her time, enjoying the freedom of walking in the sunshine as she always had, feeling the breeze on her legs and the eyes of the old men playing chess in the park following her progress.

She passed the church, wondering if she was watched here, too, wondering whether he could see her on the street, but she did not linger with these thoughts. She stepped into the coffee shop seemingly as an afterthought, for *café turco* and a newspaper.

She passed her brother's boarding school. She sometimes helped him sneak out at night, acting as though she would be chaperoning him, but really freeing him for some fun on his own. He would go to college soon, their father sending him to Barcelona, and she could hardly stand the idea of being an ocean away from him, unable to see him whenever she wanted. Perhaps it would be a taste of how he felt when she left for photo shoots on location or one of her other assignments.

She stepped into the studio, Marco tracking her with feigned disapproval at her lateness. She challenged his Brazilian-Japanese efficiency with her relaxed Dominican outlook.

"*Pouca deleite*," he scolded, using a Portuguese term of endearment that she believed roughly translated to 'little treat.' "Do you know what it says to be late?" Not waiting for her answer, he took the coffee from her hand and drank some, his face twisting briefly.

He removed the plastic lid and produced a small flask from one of the pockets of his camera bag. Iara smiled as he poured *cachaça* liberally into the coffee, and sampled it again.

"It says, 'I am arrogant, and my time is more important than yours,'" he admonished her, then paused, then kissed his fingers at her in forgiveness, as if recognizing she was incapable of better behavior. "Thank you for remembering the coffee."

"I am nothing if not myself," she told him smartly.

"Like every other one-name fashion model." He shook his head. "You have the brains and talent to distinguish yourself from that lot."

But he was done talking, to her great relief. Her rudeness and outlandishness were the armor she wore to protect whatever was left of who she really was underneath. It was most effective at repelling, obviating the necessity of any real closeness with anyone. She knew well how to protect herself from hurt.

As usual, they spent the next two hours immersed in the process of photographing her in various states of relative undress, his artistic eye capturing the essence of what made her uniquely great. In her absolute confidence, understanding her own allure, she used her trademark disdain and her sneer to seduce.

Iara left behind that version of herself with the final click of the camera, not bothering ever to stay, lingering to hear the inevitable praise of whatever photographer, stylist, or editor was involved. She liked Marco, she found it charming that he tried to hold her accountable, but the other kind of enthusiasm made her uncomfortable, mostly because it rang false. She never forgot that she was a source of income for these people, and their flattery was usually manufactured. The fashion industry was as superficial as a cheap manicure.

She reached the critical destination of her day nearly an hour late, having found any number of ways to waste time getting there. She scrutinized the young men on the street, especially those that did not look at her. They did not know that this casual indifference gave them away as *his* goons, they should have looked at her openly, like everyone else. Even if they were seminarians, as she suspected. Gay men ogled her too. Despite what most people think they know about sexuality, Iara knew desire to be a fluid concept. Human beings recognize attractiveness in other human beings no matter what their preferences.

The dark car in front of the building confirmed that he was there, waiting. She was certain that he had been on time, certain of his frustration, which he did not know fed the rebellion in her that she held onto to maintain some power in the imbalance of their relationship. He had once threatened to reveal her trysts with a married woman to her father, and she had calmly replied that she was sure there were forests in his past compared to the splinters in hers, cleverly but obliquely referring to a passage in the Bible, but mostly she let him believe that he was in charge.

He'd have been surprised to learn that she did what she did for him because she enjoyed the intrigues, the seduction of powerful men for their secrets, amazed at how intrusive and underhanded the Church could be. Such secrets were the seat of its power, that and the blackmail that ensued from them. Catholicism had thrived where other religions had not, by refusing to separate itself from political concerns.

In Germany alone, she had read, the Catholic Church was worth twenty-five billion dollars, shocking that a country not traditionally thought of as a Catholic power was its richest organization, the richest church in the world. Even the Vatican was reportedly only worth a paltry fifteen billion; Iara knew that its specific wealth was published as such, but any church's monetary holdings were controlled by its leadership.

So her modeling career had led them to her, because she was coveted, as an object, by many powerful persons. These individuals wanted to meet her, would try to please her, would allow themselves to be compromised by her, so it made sense that she would be asked to embark on this shadow endeavor. It was far more lucrative than her day job; there were powerful governments that paid dearly for the information she passed to the Church. In turn, the Church received assistance removing inconvenient political roadblocks, probably things involving such nuisance considerations as human rights.

The sexual leverage they had employed had backfired, but they had other threats to make, threats that endangered others, the unspoken threat of her own expendability. So she had done what she was told, but had subverted their messenger, slowly, exploiting his own appetites, eroding his control, until he became her puppet, because he could not live without what he wanted from her.

She entered a complex code to unlock the front gate, and a second one was required to admit her to the house. He was waiting, his impatience almost palpable. He had removed his collar and his spectacles, as if in doing so he could somehow distance himself from his priestly vocation, and she often wondered how he behaved when at the Vatican, in contrast to the way he conducted his life elsewhere.

She maintained a formal physical distance from him while he outlined the particulars of this new request, committing the details to memory. They never left any tangible proof of their dealings. She repeated the instructions back to him, and requested he tell her again what was desired, so he did so, but as she delayed him further, she could see him losing an internal battle.

Desire was one thing, but there was a darkness that followed him, and she never felt that the two of them were truly alone. There was a demon riding him, one that wanted more than just the physical transaction, wanted to consume her. Sometimes he shed his civility, and she knew he was ashamed of this lack of control.

But she made him suffer through the sordid details of her confession, on her knees at his feet, taking her time, torturing him because he was forced to hear what she did with others. It was not until he shook like a junkie that she allowed him to touch her. It bothered her conscience not at all that she drank this suffering, the pleasure that she distilled from the pain that followed.

39

AZUMA READ AND REREAD THE results of the evaluation of Tatsuo's genetic assay with a fascinated interest. Most of the impossibilities that the results presented did not bother her in the least; she had expected certain findings to align with the same impossibilities that her own DNA manifested.

The surprise was the final impossibility, because somehow she had not anticipated that rather than confirm confraternity, it confirmed *identicality*. Boy-girl twins are two-egg twins, dizygotes. They cannot be otherwise logically, they must by definition differ by at least one entire chromosome. She and Tatsuo were, by virtue of the secrets revealed by their DNA, true monozygotic twins, formed from the same egg. But it was another technicality that had allowed such a thing to occur. Azuma had puzzled over this until she had a headache.

They were not really twins, not in the loosest definition, because neither of them was in total possession of the organism they shared, and there was the crux of it — the organism. Physically, there were not two of them. Which satisfied a sort of human loophole for the geneticist confronted with the results.

The third technicality was the most astonishing. Something that made them more in common with certain types of lesser non-mammalian vertebrates. Their condition was undescribed in any of the higher phylogenies.

Azuma had a GIF on her computer that she used when teaching basic Mendelian inheritance to undergraduates. It was silly, but an effective reminder that she had found too cute to resist. There was something about it that appealed to her. It was a six second loop from *The Minion Movie*, where the butler at Windsor castle reminds Bob that *'you CANNOT abdicate the throne. There are LAWS!!!'*

Her students were always so surprised that the seemingly intense-and-serious-and-probably-constipated Dr. Himura would use such a meme to reinforce a lesson that none of them had ever missed the questions on Mendelian inheritance on any subsequent exam. Not one.

Well, she needed a new meme, apparently. This one would have curled Gregor Mendel's hair.

She and Tatsuo – well, Azuma, actually, since she was the index organism, was a *human* hermaphroditic chimera, a 26 XX, XY anomaly, with occasional expression of *both* genders. She had originally been *protogynous*, having made the change from female to male, but she had not remained male, making her a *bidirectional* sequential hermaphrodite.

Azuma attempted to delve into a fascinating study that discussed the environmental factors that created such changes in teleosts, a commonly studied group of fish that were nature's best examples of sequential hermaphroditism, but the paper concerned itself with the structural and humoral effects on the animal. It was all macroscience, except for slides showing pictures of gonadal cell change under the microscope.

She poured herself a generous cup of sake and dug through a junk drawer in the lab where she kept odd Post-Its that had no other home. Most of them contained phone numbers, and there were a few business cards. The organization system was hers alone, and she found what she was looking for almost immediately.

Masaru Nakamura was a marine researcher and conservationist, but when she reached out to him at the most recent contact she had, which was the Oceanarium on Okinawa, she was told that he was on sabbatical at Shedd Aquarium in Chicago for a year. Nakamura was a genius who understood the complexities of sex determination and plasticity in fish, and was well-respected for his work in the Japanese fisheries industry. He had been a thought leader in the field for over forty years.

A movement near the door caught her attention, and when she looked up, Akenomyosei was leaning against the jamb, wearing an inscrutable smile. He looked amused, and this disconcerted her. She looked around, her eye stopping on the clock, and she saw that it was after three in the morning.

"Do you realize that you were just growling?" It made this observation while scrutinizing its fingernails, which at the moment were truly disgusting. This was in stark contrast to the rest of its bespoke finery, the dark suit and white shirt, the perfect pocket square, the leather shoes. The floating dark hair that looked like it had product expertly applied to it, of all ridiculous things. Yet it knew well in any age what might attract its victims best.

"Perhaps just a feral response to an intruder," she reminded the Morningstar that her instincts alerted her to any enemy.

"Are we enemies?" It shook that perfect mane of hair in mock dismay.

"Why are you here?" she asked, knowing it was unlikely to give her any clues about its motives, but sensing that the timing was too conveniently close to her recent discovery of the secrets her own DNA had been keeping.

"Because duality is the essence of what makes you a god," it replied, the most forthrightness she had known the monster to allow. The loss of your brother would diminish you." And like the evil parent it was, it did not understand that such an admission told her that she was on to something, taking a path that displeased it. And like the advice of such a parent, it engendered nothing but defiance.

"I suffer these insults to my person because you want to keep me more like you?" Azuma said, incredulous. "I, who you flatter and cozen to keep me compliant, while you manipulate my reality because *he* entertains you with his misdeeds? I thought you already had a pet for chaos," she spat, referring to Tatsuo Tomo, who of late went by another name, one that she couldn't immediately recall.

"We have many special projects like yourself," it suggested mysteriously. "You certainly are the most interesting."

"Which only means that I am probably the most ill-behaved," she replied darkly.

"Charming, too," Akenomyosei cooed, trying to be amusing. But Azuma grew tired of its games, the endless uncertainties, the lack of answers about why she was here. But it was occasionally overconfident, thinking itself of such superior intellect that its stray comments could not be deciphered. She would play along; she did not let on that it had just admitted she was not the only one of her kind.

40

NAKAMURA WAS SURPRISED WHEN HE moved his eyes over the lecture hall at Loyola University and recognized the striking young woman sitting in the fourth row. While she looked like any other fresh-faced coed in her dark turtleneck and jeans, he knew better. The horn-rimmed eyeglasses she wore did nothing to disguise her.

"Dr. Himura," he greeted her ironically when the lecture was over, and she approached him as the other students filed out of the room. "Were you afraid that I would refuse a meeting with you?"

"Nakamura-san," she said warmly, bowing to him respectfully as befitted his status as her countryman and her elder, even if the latter was perception only. She had centuries on him in chronology. "I was hoping not to intrude overmuch. I was in town for a short visit and hoped you had time for a social call from a fellow Japanese scholar." While it was true that her stay would be short, she did not tell him that she had made the trip specifically to see him. She didn't want anyone asking questions about what interest RSI might have in his work, and guessed, correctly, that that kind of publicity was something he would prefer to avoid. She didn't want Shedd's press liaisons buzzing around him when all he wanted was the cool quiet hum of his fish tanks. Her public profile was too inviting of speculation.

"Intriguing, even if it is bullshit," he answered her in Japanese, and finally smiled.

"May I buy you dinner tonight or tomorrow night?" she asked him, expecting he would capitulate. He was far from home, had no wife to return to in this country, and might welcome the diversion of her company.

"You sat through my lecture to invite me to a meal?" he asked, waving his hand as if asking her forgiveness for his incredulity.

"Professor, I sat through your lecture because it was fascinating and informative, and my love of learning has not been diminished by years of study," Azuma told him honestly.

"I must admit I am intrigued," he told her. "I have a prior commitment this evening, but I am free tomorrow night. Where would you like to meet? I can recommend any number of excellent Japanese -"

"I was thinking of something a bit more private," she interjected gently, not wanting to be rude, but given her jet lag she lacked the patience for the elaborate dance of formality this conversation might otherwise require of her. "May I send a car for you?"

She breezed into the Peninsula the following afternoon, arriving just as high tea was being served off the lobby, following a fruitful meeting with some prospective AZ Defense investors. She was escorted by the concierge to her private lobby. The airy rooms were empty, although buckwheat tea and almond biscuits had been delivered in anticipation of her return.

She took a long bath, and allowed herself the luxury of a short nap. The Collector woke her at seven, bringing with him the long garment bag that had come from the dry cleaner that morning. He hung it carefully in the wardrobe and withdrew.

He hadn't given her a reason for delay, had long since abandoned the perceived courtesy of offering her two different outfits to choose from, having concluded that such decisions agonized her, and interfered with whatever else she was trying to focus upon. She couldn't complain. He had impeccable taste.

He often defaulted to creams or reds for her, depending on the occasion. Black was unusual, but the linen jumpsuit she discovered this time defied description. Modern, sparely tailored, it was almost a combination of a woman's tuxedo and an evening gown, tailored to her slim torso, split at the neck, sleeveless, with flowing pant legs that moved like the gauzy fins of the koi.

It could not be reproached for impropriety yet was in every way designed to seduce. It made a powerful statement but did not lack subtlety. She twisted her hair up behind her head, arranging her chignon more loosely than she usually did. The Collector said nothing when he saw her, but there was a slight movement of his facial muscles that gave him away. She was perhaps the only person in the world who would notice, and he meant her to.

She shook her head gently at the black pearl earrings he offered, so he handed her a glass of plum wine instead, and right on cue, the doorbell rang.

Nakamura was in shirtsleeves and black pants, still handsome in his seventies, with very little gray hair. He looked a bit bewildered by the understated sophistication of the suite of rooms, and even more bewildered when he saw Azuma. He stood for a long time looking out toward the lake; the Peninsula was not a tall building by Chicago standards, but the view was still spectacular, and the safest place for him to direct his eyes.

She offered him *Ramune,* of all things, because she had watched him once at a conference downing several of them each day. He disdained alcohol, which was probably for the best, the carbonation in the Japanese soda was more acidic, better suited to hide the taste of the miniscule amount of her venom that the Collector had put into the drink.

"It's childish of me, isn't it?" he said, accepting the bottle she handed him. "I just never outgrew it, I guess."

"I find such idiosyncrasies to be charming," she told him, and she meant it. "Shall we sit?"

They had an intimate supper of the simplest of pleasures, seaweed salad, quail egg, crispy grouper, and sweet *tamago*. He was surprised at how much reading she had done on the subject of sexual plasticity in vertebrates, and flattered at how much of his research she had absorbed. As they talked, he realized that boundaries were becoming blurred, her leg was against his own, and he found that he was having a bit of an overstated physical reaction to her, something he thought had been largely left behind at his advanced age. He thought guiltily of his wife, but surely this exquisite young woman was not interested in him in such a way.

He felt strangely euphoric, and wondered at that sensation, since it reminded him slightly of the effects of alcohol from the days of his youth. And he had never had this kind of reaction to any woman, ever. He looked around for her valet, but the man had disappeared. Something had to be wrong. But she talked conspiratorially to him about a patent application that had just been approved, and how she believed that her current graduate thesis application would intersect with his work, and she wanted to understand the ways in which they might collaborate in the future.

"But I'm – I'm nearly retired," he protested, flattered at her enthusiasm at the chance to work with him.

"I understand. But do reconsider," she pleaded, placing her hand on his intimately. He was stymied by his feelings. Perhaps her behavior was innocent. Then she said, "You are still so vibrant."

Her eyes were so deep and so dark, her lips slightly parted as she watched him carefully. He could see she was being honest with him, so he addressed her as directly as possible.

"Dr. Himura, are you trying to seduce me?" He was glad that his voice betrayed the surprise he felt, since it seemed suddenly ludicrous.

"Why wouldn't I?" she asked, without a trace of ridicule. "I want us to be very close; I want to hear everything you have to say about all of the incredible research you have done. That kind of dedication and intellect is extremely attractive to me."

"But, young lady, I cannot purport to explain the depths of forty years of study to you in one night," he told her, and she could see that the venom was doing its work on him, his words were beginning to slur and he was beginning to slump against the table.

Out of the corner of her eye she saw the Collector in the doorway, but she waved him away, managing to get Nakamura to his feet long enough to help him to the bed. If he was only going to remember a sensual dream, even the briefest subconscious image of the Collector would be enough to make him question it.

"There's no need to explain it to me," Azuma murmured softly. "Your blood will teach me everything I need to know."

She was particularly gentle with him, leaving no trace of her intrusion, not even undressing him. Afterward, she sat in the armchair under the lamp and read, listening to his even breathing.

"How long until he wakes?" she asked, when the Collector had returned to deliver Nakamura discreetly back to his own housing.

"An hour or two," he guessed. "I gave him less than usual, I assumed he was a bit more fragile."

"Thank you, my friend," Azuma touched the back of his hand briefly. "He deserves our kindness and our respect."

41

MICHAEL ISRAEL REPORTED TO MOSSAD headquarters and followed her commander, David Ziegler, into his offices overlooking the central courtyard. The morning felt cool, it was not yet twenty-five degrees, and the breeze off the water was pleasant.

Ziegler offered her a drink, but she declined, dropping gratefully into the chair he offered her. She had just come from Jerusalem.

"What did they say?" she asked quietly, knowing that in the fifty minutes it had taken her to make the trip back, it was likely that he had been contacted.

"I think you surprised them," he smiled, knowing she would understand. "They expected more of your father in you."

"I can have been nothing but a disappointment, then," she said, wondering what he wasn't telling her.

"They liked you," David said, shaking his head.

"Then whatever they have planned must be a suicide mission," she replied.

"Did you wear that?" he asked her, taking in her cargo fatigues, IDF-issue boots, and white button-down shirt. Her strong tanned forearms showed because she had rolled up her sleeves. There was a blue and white *keffiyeh* imprinted with the Star of David around her neck. Her short wavy hair was unruly as usual, and her hazel eyes blazed with intelligence.

"I pulled the scarf over my head," she told him, in an ironic tone that from anyone else would have made him laugh. He'd never dared laugh at her. She needed to be convinced of his faith in her abilities, and he needed her to trust him implicitly, especially considering the work they did together. It was hard enough for her here. From anyone else, such a comment would have been spoken in jest, but looking at her, she probably had done just that. Known that they would see the essential paradox of her being; she was unassuming, but one could not question her piety and her faith.

She was unlike anyone he had ever known. Her body was compact and strong, very androgynous for all her training, but most special forces soldiers are smallish anyway. Her face was angular, singularly striking, and completed closed off. She kept whatever she felt to herself. Her dossier was clean, she had no psychological blips whatsoever, save a sealed interview from the time after her brother's death when she was not yet in school. He had been denied access to it, and he assumed this was because it had no bearing on her military fitness.

No intel could confirm any significant personal relationships, and he could have believed she had no vulnerabilities at all. Surprisingly, during her intake interviews, she had volunteered that when her twin brother had died, she had begun using his name, vowing to live her life for both of them. The way she had said it made it seem like she was bent on some sort of revenge.

Her father had complicated things by threatening the recruitment office, trying to stop her from joining. The Rabbi ben-Ibrahim was a formidable man, and some of the senior staff thought that Michael Israel was trying to replace her brother, become a man in her father's eyes, but David thought not. She could care less about what her father needed; there was something she needed more. It just twisted David up that he could not for the life of him figure out what it was.

"They have a special assignment for you," David began, and when she started to protest, trying to tell him that she was going back to the desert, he shut her down. "You're off that project."

"But I chased that down for years," she said, betraying some frustration, but David couldn't know that it was for personal reasons. He incorrectly assumed that she thought that they were pulling her because of her gender.

"And Milos was there, too. He will go to the desert and supervise security for the dig. Besides, you are too valuable to be wasted on a glorified security detail."

"Is that what they told you?" she asked bitterly, unconcerned that she sounded angry and petulant. "I found the *makom,* and I thought they believed us. They sent us to confirm it!"

"And I promise you will be read in on whatever they find," he reassured her. "Every detail. No redactions. No games."

"Do you believe it?" she was earnest now, taking his measure. "Really believe. That the place where they fell to earth has some significant physical monument?"

"I think I always wanted to," he told her. "Just like I tell my wife I believe in God. I hedge my bets, you know? It's part and parcel of what we do, the skepticism. But that report, and then, the marker that you found? I've never seen those old men in J'salem so worked up. Sure, some of it supports the Essenes. But to find the seat of all evil in a shrine that is supposed to be a myth? That would validate the corporal nature of the Opposer?"

David fell silent, and he turned away from her to look down at the people in the courtyard. "I do believe. I have ever since I saw your face when you climbed out of that helicopter in Tikrit."

"Then you know why I have to go back," she told him, making no other argument out of respect for him, he thought.

"It's out of our hands," he replied. "You've been summoned by the Chief Rabbi. Moshe. Even I haven't been read in on this one. The council this morning was probably just an interview. You passed. They're sending you after a high-value target in Asia."

"Korea?" she asked, her curiosity piqued.

"Don't know. Ultra-high level. It feels like an Israeli concern, but bigger than one organization. Sensitive. Something religious."

"But you're my handler," she protested. "I need somebody I trust on something like this one – it's dangerous to go in with a lead operator I don't know."

"This *is* different. You're right. And technically, you could refuse. I tried to on your behalf," he agreed. "Then they shut me down. You're going, or your government service will be cancelled, and you will be officially retired. You want to spend the rest of your life in that cottage on the shore with your parents, just tell them no."

42

...the child relates that her brother did not die in his sleep, but rather was stolen by a creature she described as the *Death-Bringer*. The child used this term but can have had no exposure to it prior to this interview, which casts it in a more truthful light that [*sic*] her statements have been handled to date.

"...not like the *Golem*...it...scales...and-" (taping terminated following the audible deterioration of the child emotionally) ...

Bithiah is convinced that the beast picked her brother over her, that it wanted her to know its intent, that it had watched Michael many times as he slept.

If this is the result of night terror, and abnormal grief, as has been suggested, then these dreams so closely mimic reality as to confuse the child where the one begins and the other ends...

...the retelling of the story has the same result that has not changed over time...

...she has reverted developmentally, and has lost her toilet training, indeed she involuntarily wets herself every time she speaks of the event, the only betrayal of her emotional distress as she has otherwise withdrawn behind a defensive wall of control remarkable for a child her age…

…the disbelief of the adults in her life has not deterred her own assertions, and she does not doubt herself, rather than withdraw in fear, many of her words and drawings suggest she seeks an opportunity to avenge her lost twin…

43

RABBI MOSHE WAS YOUNGER THAN the other Chief Rabbis, his beard only beginning to turn grey, and of a more modest length than she might have expected. His eyes were kind, and his face was open and smiling. It was a face that looked like it had known much joy.

To Michael Israel's surprise, he met with her alone. To reassure her, the separate doors that opened onto his office remained open, but his staff, his clerks, all were sent away, some openly curious about this development. She knew that many in David Ziegler's group believed that conversations here were recorded, but she had nothing to conceal, and nothing she was authorized to reveal.

He offered her tea, and when she refused, he poured his own and invited her to sit with him, at a set of four chairs around a small magazine table. She chose the seat across from his, facing the doors, and found that she could find almost no fault with it, it was comfortable, if a bit low. She suspected it had been chosen mostly for aesthetics, but the soldier in her didn't quite trust a chair that she couldn't get out of efficiently.

"Your father is a holy man," he observed, and just as she was about to decide that she should prepare to be bored, he added, "But he is perhaps also frightened."

She had schooled her face to show nothing of her thoughts, but this was unexpected.

"He praised you warmly," Rabbi Moshe continued, watching her, but he could read nothing in those bright hazel eyes other than polite attentiveness. "And, I should add, he did not qualify any of his statements.

"You may be too young to remember your grandfather. Ibrahim was a resilient man, a Holocaust survivor, and in the ways of those who have lost everything in the most unspeakable ways, when he had a son, here, in the Holy Land, it did not matter that we should all be safe, we Jews know there is no true safety for our people in this world.

"I am sure that Ibrahim and thousands like him questioned bringing a child into such a world. But our resilience as a people is in our willingness to always embrace life. Ibrahim was a beloved rabbi, and an overprotective and conservative father who taught his son the old laws and did not protect him from the uglinesses that he had suffered. Prevention of anything in the future lies in the remembering of the evil that men do.

"I am not sure your father even looked at a woman before he was forty. He was older than that when he met Hedda. To have joy as one never thought one could have, and then to lose a child – it tempts one to hide the other, hold on so tight that all open air and possibility are shrunk down to only the boundaries of protection, and fear.

"He is not sad that you are not a son. It is that to love you as he loved before would be to suffer again the pain of loss. That is why he is proud of you publicly but unable to say to you privately what he should.

"And when his only child does not leave behind the fight, when she returns to it, in the most dangerous and intimate of ways – in a part of the world where a Jew is not just a strategic enemy but a religious enemy, a *personal* enemy, it is too much. She is in contact with the most diabolical of men, she is in a helicopter that could be plucked from the sky, falling, falling, to the earth, perhaps never to be seen again. Oh, your mother, Hedda, she is much younger and more resilient – she regained her footing after the tragedy, and she knows that your flying is a symbol of something else. You are the bird whose wings could not be clipped and in the sky you found your freedom. This is no surprise.

"He talks to you of grandchildren, but in our faith we know that nothing is certain. The shepherd loves and protects the lambs he has, in the here and now, and cannot worry about the lambs yet unborn.

"Finally, he does not understand you. A Rabbi hates a question he cannot answer. It is the nature of our education and our profession, I think – even though our whole life's work deals with unanswered questions, as it must. All holy men must grapple with the mysteries of their faith.

"When your brother died, you stepped forward, not to be him, but to remember him."

Michael Israel stared at Rabbi Moshe but still refused to betray her feelings. That did not matter, because he was weeping for her. She didn't understand that he saw her inability to cry for herself and it was the only thing he could do to help her.

After a time, he wiped these tears away, he began again.

"What you found in the desert is an extraordinary thing. It is a place that we must strive to understand. I fear that there are some whose interest in that place is unwholesome, and it must be secured, protected."

"Hidden?" she asked, not hiding the accusation from her voice.

"I know of your desire to be involved, but you are required elsewhere. You may not know it, but we remain in the business of investigating threats to our faith and our people, and the definition of what is a credible threat has changed much in the last century. Never again will the slightest hint of danger to humanity be ignored.

"There are those in other places, of other faiths, who search out evil, who follow supernatural developments and always have. We have learned to doubt, and that is what The Opposer wishes us to do. That is why certain organizations, certain people, have been excluded from this work. I have faith in your belief of the divine and the profane.

"We send you out in an unofficial capacity to learn what you can of a monster who lives in plain sight, perhaps the monster you have searched for all your life, the monster from a dream that was not a dream. We have credible intelligence that will be provided you. There will be no handlers, no operators, only you. You will be accorded official diplomatic cover, but it would fail to stand up to any scrutiny should you suffer any setbacks." Rabbi Moshe's eyes were as warm as ever, but he knew she heard what was left unspoken. David was out because he was a famous doubter; she was being given a chance to hunt a beast, perhaps the one she had never lost sight of, but she was now armed with the one thing that she had formerly lacked. Someone had been listening to the words of a heartbroken child; she had been believed!

Diplomatic discovery would result in scandal and censure. If she attracted the attention of the beast it would come for her, which was exactly what she wanted. She knew if she failed she'd come home in a box, if at all. But she had signed up for that long before she had joined the IDF.

44

"YOU FAIL TO RECOGNIZE THE dangers of such an application," Shirogorō admonished her.

"I recognize them, but Shirogorō-san, ensuring that I control the economic interest in the technology is the reason for the patent application. It doesn't mean that I would use it," she argued gently. "Or could. The United Nations has put control statements out around the inadvisability of human cloning and neonatal intervention. This would be a therapeutic treatment, for a *mature* organism."

"Why me? You've been corresponding with Nakamura. Kobayashi has shared his findings with you." Shirogorō was frustrated, because he did not know her well enough to understand that her ethical stance on many of these issues aligned with his own. "I cannot back such a proposal with the IRB."

"I don't need you to," Azuma reassured him, and he sighed, knowing that her existing renown in the field of Genetics meant she was right, the board would approve her research parameters without hesitation.

She tried again. "Esteemed Professor, Nakamura and Kobayashi mapped the loci for sexual plasticity. I need you to help me when the DVIG shows us the differential amounts of gene product. You are a Nobel Laureate; you understand selective methylation better than anyone alive, and that is what control of the expression will require. Without your advice, I am performing blind interventions. I would like these fish to *live* so that we may observe the results of controlling the intersex shifts."

"Why did you agree to advise me if you do not trust me?" Azuma asked him. "I tell you what. I want you to look at a patent application I filed ten years ago, after several wealthy Chinese families approached me with an investment proposal. They wanted me to use guided MA cloning to intervene upon frozen embryos to assess them for facial features and select for those with genes tied to a very specific bone structure, that of the Han majority.

"I filed it not because I saw the opening that I could have driven a truck through, perhaps several of them, each loaded with money, all to ensure that a bunch of rich and entitled people had the most desirable genetic outcome. I filed it because I already had the *capability* to apply the technology and wanted to ensure that it could not be used without some ethical controls, to keep it out of the hands of those who want to pay to engineer beauty, intellect, power. The gods have given us the means, but not always the judgement we need, and I wonder whether they are inviting us to self-destruct."

She hastily wrote the patent number on one of the ubiquitous Post-It notes from her backpack and stuck it to the whiteboard next to his office door. "I need you to see me as something less than a corporate mogul and something more than a money-hungry mad scientist. Please. I wouldn't have asked for your help if the responsible application of this technology were of solely financial importance."

"Azuma." His voice stopped her as she was heading out the door. "You told me that your brother was very sick. Does that have anything to do with this?"

She was startled. She had told Shirogorō about Tatsuo in the sketchiest of terms, trying to let him know that he might see her brother around at times, but that he was a disturbed and ill man. She had done so attempting to preempt any difficulty that Tatsuo might cause while she was in residence here, making it seem as if she had to look out for him because they had no parents to do so. She had appealed to the old professor's sympathy, and at the time he had expressed his gratitude that she had been truthful with him, warning her that as long as the situation did not interfere with her studies or disrupt the department he would be understanding.

"It has everything to do with this," she whispered sadly, bowing respectfully and taking her leave.

45

SHE STARTED WITH HERMAPHRODITIC FISH. She subjected them to the standard evolutionary pressures to sex change and used her DVIG to evaluate which genes lit up, and how much protein product each gene produced, to see what was driving the change.

She used only females in the first round, first studying the differences in proteins produced when they were placed in ideal situations with a group of other females, all organisms of mating age. She found that all exhibited genetic change, or readiness, to become males, but until there was enough room or an abundance of food sources within the habitat, none of them produced the gonadal products to make the shift to male, and then it was only the fittest, youngest fish.

She studied the effects of weight gain and growth on several different species, but isolated them this time, keeping each fish away from other fish, wanting to remove the stress of procreation, wanting to observe what size thresholds in the absence of another fish to mate with would do. While she found that there was a point at which, above a certain fin-length measurement or a certain weight, every solitary female began to exhibit genetic readiness in the form of protein building blocks to enable the change, none actually switched her gender, even at extremes of size only known before in males of the species.

But every female above the baseline length and size that was *shown* an average sized female, even one in an adjacent tank, would shift readily from female to male. The male presentation would persist if there was a chance that procreation was a possibility or a need. But if the neighboring female was removed, or replaced with another male, the second, or bidirectional shift took place, and the fish resumed its female state, irrespective of its size.

It was not lost on Azuma that her own emergent event with Tatsuo had occurred under a sort of sexual stress with Megumi. She had faced the stresses of battle and hunger before that horrendous night without any indication that Tatsuo had ever tried to come through, and she was seeing objective evidence that some hormonal signal had triggered her first change.

Subconsciously, she had suspected it, and had maintained an elective celibacy ever since, save for the Dragon's communion, when a member of the *Akai* had to be initiated. At those times, however, all her priests were present, and the blood exchange, by necessity, was the earliest act of the ritual. Her blood meals had not been taken from pureflesh for over three hundred years; she had traded pleasure for necessity and survival.

Her next rounds of study involved abandoning teleosts that could perform these shifts and always had, to other species that had not shown such an ability. Control experiments were done to prove that there was no previously unrecorded sexual latency in these species, specifically, to show that the stresses that had caused sexual plasticity in teleosts could not be reproduced in the new species.

She then used the DVIG data to recreate the physiologic conditions and protein byproducts that were required for sexual change in the new species, with promising results. Because the teleost DVIG data showed how much and what kind of protein shifts were needed to effect change, she could reproduce these prerequisites in a different fish and engineer the evolutionary pressure required to change once the proper stimuli were introduced. What was most promising in those organisms that responded positively to this genetic modification was that they could not go back the other way. Azuma could turn a female carp into a male, but even when she introduced the right genetic conditions and environment, this transformation was not bidirectional.

This gave her a great deal of hope, as the final goal of all this meticulous study was to create a one-way ticket for Tatsuo. She wanted to make it impossible for him to become male, force a full-time genetic expression to female, leaving her in control of her body, not having to worry about the hermaphroditic change, which she could not control, in addition to the emergence of the Dragon, which she wholly controlled.

The problem was that every hypothesis broke down when using males. It was much more difficult to coax a sexually plastic male into a female change, even in the presence of a group of males much larger than the organism being studied. It appeared that such a group was willing to wait longer for a female to appear, and it was true that the DVIG assays revealed that this male-to-female change required more genetic activity and increased protein complexity. And size and weight were problematic because males were less likely to debulk unless they were in a situation of famine, in which case the reproductive gonadal activity in *all* the males decreased, whether there was a female present or not – if there is not enough food, it makes no evolutionary sense to procreate.

Azuma ran concurrent studies to try to control these changes using selective methylation, under the tutelage of Shirogorō, who championed her efforts to build a useful algorithm. Methylation can sometimes turn off a gene, or make it less active, by using a chemical reaction to lock the DNA and prevent it from making certain proteins. But she failed again and again, and she couldn't seem to unravel the source of her failure.

While she managed to control the shift from female to male in the closest phylogenetic fish relative of the Dragon, her koi cousins, the interventions had to be repeated in the presence of sexual stressors but not size stressors. The males could not be forced to female expression without increasing protein levels to dangerous concentrations, many of which were toxic and too many of which were fatal to the organisms.

She tried ablation of certain genetic loci, essentially ridding the animal of the part of the gene responsible for the sexual shift, and this worked variably, sometimes causing the death of an animal due to the unintended consequence of turning off an essential protein that had not been highlighted by the DVIG – especially those proteins in the smallest of quantities which had escaped below the level at which the DVIG protocol could see them.

It was the wise Shirogorō who gently pulled her back from the problem so that she could see the forest for the trees. She had already successfully suppressed male expression in all the species studied by controlling the shift from the female side. If she wanted female expression, she had to intervene in the juveniles. If she wished to exhibit male expression, the application of the correct evolutionary pressure was successful in female-to-male transformation.

To avoid the male shift, she need only focus on the female.

So she developed an intervention focused on herself, rather than Tatsuo, uncertain of her ability to prevail over him, because doing so was thwarting Akenomyosei.

And because this targeted therapy was to be used on herself, she was suddenly grateful for the meticulous ethics of her mentor. He had forced her to perform the work and preserve the organisms, which became personally impactful now that she was the target.

For months, the Collector found her where she had dropped off to sleep, because she would not stop working. She finished her thesis in near-record time for someone running a company in addition to creating ground-breaking scientific technology.

And when it was time for her to take her own cure, she embraced the risk, trying not to regret all that she had already lost to Tatsuo, and saddened that she was essentially using her knowledge to decrease the capabilities of her genetic code rather than enhance them. It felt hypocritical.

Two weeks before graduation, Shirogorō asked her if her brother would be attending the ceremonies.

She was surprised to hear the sadness in her own voice when she answered.

"I'm afraid not. I had to send him away."

46

MILOS SQUINTED THROUGH THE DUST that swirled in the setting sun. It felt as though he had become a creature of this dry place, where sand invaded everything, setting up residence in his nasal passages, his throat, the corners of his eyes. He moved a bit closer to the pit, pleased that the dig was progressing rapidly, and he thought he had heard someone call his name, but after several early false alarms due to the acoustics of the stone, he knew it was only a transmitted echo from the depths of the excavation, where most of the engineers and archaeologists were focused on their work.

He took a cursory walk around the perimeter, noting that his sentries were on point before he approached the hole. It was truly impressive, and intel had confirmed that the structure, which had been betrayed by a simple marked stele only four feet wide, could now be viewed easily by satellite, large enough to be seen from space.

It consisted of two concentric rings, the center opening of indeterminate depth, appearing to be a sun chamber or an oubliette of some sort, its sheer walls going down and down with no evidence that the excavation would reach the bottom anytime soon. The outer ring was formed by a narrow stone staircase that twisted downward, on and on, following the curve of what appeared to be a massive inverted shrine, or tower. The diameter of the rotation got slightly smaller as the team got deeper.

Between the pit and the stairwell were rooms and passageways of infinite and intricate complexity. The ultrasound images and the cartography reminded him of an M.C. Escher drawing. The reality was not so charming. Milos was a religious man, and he trusted his instincts. There was death here, he could feel it. Worse, there was a darkness, as though the thing swallowed all light, and the walls felt alive with suffering.

They had found no evidence of human or other remains, but the group had not reached the bottom of the main structure nor the central opening. He found he was as fascinated now as he had been at the prospect of finding it, but the reality made him long for home, made him wish for ignorance of its existence. He knew that leaving it would be a relief, and he hoped when the initial excavation was finished that the diplomats would arrange a permanent solution for securing it, one that had nothing to do with him or his team.

The security detail had been remarkably easy, and that bothered him almost more than he wanted to admit. He had expected whatever locals could reach the site easily to be drawn in by a natural curiosity, but the nomads who inhabited this desert wasteland had stayed away. It was eerily isolated, as if one would come upon this place and forever after would avoid it.

These introspections were interrupted by a scream from the hole that brought Milos and the sentries on the run. They could hear no distinct cries for help, instead what floated up from the dimness of the staircase had the quality of an excited babble, unintelligible and frightening, but could have been the other team members responding to whatever had caused that first agonized outburst.

He could see his own fear reflected in the faces of the other soldiers, and his bones were cold. He marshaled them by making a circular motion with his hand near his face.

"It's the echoes off the stone that make it sound garbled like that," he said, unsure who he was trying to convince. "Let's get down there. Two of you with me and the rest of you stay topside and keep watch."

The stairs were in darkness after the first several feet, the inner face washed with orange light from the last rays of the setting sun, and the lights mounted on their weapons made eerie cones of glare that seemed to move as the dust motes danced in the warm air, not providing any reassuring visual acuity. It became very cool as the surface receded behind them. The digging had progressed such that they had a long way to go to reach its depths, but Milos was still surprised that they were unable to see the worklights of the crew below them.

It was ominous, and it made him hurry.

Two hundred meters to the east, Forcas watched the frightened group of sentries huddle near the top of the oubliette. It waited, watching the sun slip ever lower, finally sinking away at the edge of the sand before making its way toward them.

Several minutes later, the Death-Bringer slipped down the stairwell, into the chaos it had created below by eliciting the mortal screams of the souls at the surface. It drank the fear it could taste on the air that rose up from the pit, pleased as always to be home.

47

IARA STEPPED OFF THE PLANE into the windy Tokyo evening
and shivered as the cold air found her skin and whipped her short wavy
hair away from her face. Her t-shirt, while fashionable, was thin, and
her ripped jeans admitted too much of the frigid blast. Half a world
away, Santo Domingo had been enjoying its endless cycle of warmth.
She was jet-lagged and wanted to scratch her agent's eyes out for failing
to remind her that Japan was cold in the winter. She doubted the
modeling work would be interesting enough to distract her from the
bad weather, but she needed a new adventure, so she had agreed to
stay in Asia for a few months. It was the best possible cover.

She was blissfully unknown in the Far East, and she enjoyed
traversing the airport without paparazzi trailing in her wake. Not that
she worried about a bad picture after a twenty-three-hour flight; Iara
was gorgeous rolling out of bed, in harsh lighting, and even without a
jot of makeup. It was just nice to be left alone. Relatively, anyway.
The magazine crew had shared the private jet, but she had established
her usual boundary when one of the young stylists tried to speak to
her.

"Stop talking." It was her go-to command. She hated small talk,
and refused to suffer fools that thought they knew her simply because
her face was so ubiquitous in Western advertising. Thus, she had spent
much of the flight instant messaging her younger brother. It fed the
stereotype, but she didn't care. *People* magazine was never going to
gush over her in an article, expressing surprise that she was *so* down-

to-earth. And thank the Lord. It had allowed her to have a career in which she had never been asked to put on anything remotely fluffy. Or pink.

After clearing customs, in the transportation hall, a Uniqlo vending machine sold ultralight down jackets in pouches the size of a jackfruit. She dipped her card, chose a silver one, and pulled it on while she waited for the rest of the group to assemble. She popped out to the curb and had a clove cigarette while the hired cars were loaded. Everyone was situated, but the smoke tasted like a steak would to a starved man, and she had waited so long for it. So she made them wait. They didn't dare complain – they just had to endure the pain of their own exhaustion while their meal ticket finished her damn cigarette.

now

48

AZUMA GUIDED THE RANGE ROVER up the winding mountain road, barely needing to do more in the sharpest turns than nudge the wheel with her fingertips. She loved the performance of the heavy SUV, loved to drive herself, which she did so rarely. Yet she never traded the autonomy of this drive, a challenging road whose construction had been directed by her wishes and paid for by her riches. The contractor had argued strenuously that it could not be done, but had succumbed to her false flattery when she had allowed that such an observation was possibly true, but she was certain that if anyone could accomplish the task, it was him.

He had earned every precious *yen*, and it had taken nearly ten years to complete. His smile of satisfaction had slipped only slightly when she had told him, upon its completion, that his next task was to build her mountain home at the top of it.

She had modeled the approach after the thousand steps up to the Gate of Heaven in the Tianmen Mountains of China. The eleven-kilometer approach to it by road had been made famous when Range Rover had driven one of its archetypal vehicles up to the rock formation. They had called it the Dragon Challenge. It still made her smile.

The sky was the bruised purple of a false dusk, as dark as it ever got in much of Asia, where the light of some megalopolis seemed ever at work to prevent the descent of true darkness. But as she climbed ever higher, and the air thinned, her eyesight would have allowed her to see stars if there were no high clouds on this night.

As she doubled back again and again, the snow began to fall. Softly, slowly, the large flakes drifted downwards in a hypnotic dance that necessitated further concentration on her part. The grade was beyond the legally acceptable limit for passenger cars, but it was a private road, so she had not had to comply with such a regulation. It was of little matter, since only the preternaturally gifted could successfully navigate it, as much a necessity of security as an exclusivity of conceit.

The rare mortal business associates that were allowed access to her private compound arrived by helicopter, but Azuma disdained such travel. She preferred the feat of technical skill it required to reach her aerie by land vehicle.

She cleared the final curve and drove without hesitation onto the bridge that crossed the ravine to the next peak. It was a suspension affair, with reinforced bamboo struts and cables made from the same steel as her samurai sword. It spanned four hundred meters, above a drop three times that distance to the sharp boulder garden below, created in a tectonic shift that had occurred ten thousand years before the connector had been built.

At the exit of the expanse was an unpleasant surprise for the unwary, but Azuma leaned into the sharp curve that hugged the boundary wall to her right. To her left was a sheer drop down the mountainside. She maneuvered a final jog in the pavement, happy to see that her headlights had been spotted. The timing of the gates was flawless, and she did not even slow as she drove in under the row of Shinto arches that graced the entrance to her home. If asked, she would not have remembered that this was the exact reproduction of the entrance to the shrine where she had suffered her earliest and cruelest tests of will.

She alighted skillfully from her elevated seat, leaving the keys in the ignition at the turnaround. She stood still for a moment and turned her face to the sky. Like a child, she loved the sensation of flying upward through the silent flakes as they caromed past her face, or alighted on her collar, their softness and color matching that of her cashmere coat.

She stepped out of her stilettos, unmindful of the cold, and ignoring the inviting lamps on either side of the ornate front entrance, slipped into the shadows by the wall, turning in through a side gate that led to her private garden.

She shed her clothing as she walked, faster along the stones, past the silent bonsai sentries with their frosty mantles, until she reached the large *koi* pond at the bottom of a manmade waterfall, the rocks arranged to create the most rhythmic and beautiful sounds with the water flowing ever over and around them.

Naked now, she committed to the water without hesitation, sinking into the silence, submerging entirely before stretching out her arms and legs and floating to the surface, her face to the sky, her hair trailing behind her in the water. Ever so gently she was buoyed up by the occupants of the pool, each tiny fish iridescent and luminous, genetically modified by hand following germination, each microscopic embryo gifted with the ability to glow. It was a parlor trick she had perfected during her first term as a graduate student, and was probably the most popular preparation that RSI had patented. Surprisingly lucrative, too. What child sees a glowing *koi* and doesn't want one of their own?

For reasons she did not comprehend, this type of fanciful carp was attracted to her very presence. They swarmed her whenever she entered the pool, and she could feel them pressing against her, questing, probing, their motion moving her within the water, as if her wishes animated and motivated them.

It was strangely relaxing, certainly soothing, and she sought these moments of peace as often as she could. Here she was oddly surrounded by beings loosely related to her by phylogeny, and yet as alone as she could ever manage to be. The silence was not absolute; she was able to hear the movement of the waterfall and the disruption of the tiny bubbles on her submerged skin, but it was near enough an absolution of her many sins as she hoped to get.

She noticed a sore spot in the fold beneath one of her breasts, and worried at it with her fingers, gently freeing the tiny scale from the skin that had grown over it since her last transformation. The relief was almost immediate; its cost only a small amount of pus and blood.

All too soon, she sensed the presence of another being, and with an inward sigh she shifted her weight and put her feet down on the bottom of the pool. The Collector waited patiently. Azuma wrung the cold water from her hair and accepted the comb he offered her to secure it. He held her kimono for her as she descended onto the path, and letting go the moment her arms were securely covered, he murmured, "Akiko is here."

She nodded in acknowledgement and thanks and he withdrew in his customary silence. He had left her slippers, but she abandoned them on the path. No matter, that which she left or dropped on these grounds was retrieved without comment or ceremony, and she found it where she expected to, as and when she desired. The household was trained to efficiency and discretion.

A soft glow came from the lamps in the upper hallway leading to her private rooms. She passed from it into the softness of candlelight and started in surprise when she saw the time on the nightstand clock. It explained the stillness of the form that was sleeping peacefully on the deep counterpane.

Akiko's breathing was regular, and Azuma was amazed she could sleep here. She was young, and seemed not to have the sense or the instincts to be afraid. Azuma wondered how terrible one's life would have to be that mortal danger was just another everyday phenomenon. The maiden was a feast for the eyes, but Azuma needed stronger sustenance.

By way of making her presence known, she knelt beside the bed and placed frigid hands on Akiko's thighs.

"Oh, you're cold," Akiko murmured, immediately awake but making no protest. She reached out for Azuma, her dark eyes full of longing. "Let me warm you."

After ensuring Akiko was in the throes of pleasure, Azuma took what she needed, the marks she made skillfully hidden. The blood was untainted by disturbing emotion, its taste sweetened by satisfaction. She let Akiko sleep for a few hours while she reviewed scholarly journals, and just before dawn she stepped out into the anteroom where the Collector awaited instruction.

"Make sure she gets home safely and ensure she receives her usual payment," Azuma told him, not waiting to see his subtle bow of acknowledgement. She showered and when she returned to her bed, it was empty, the linens changed, Akiko's subtle perfume fading from the air. Azuma breathed in, breathed out, and closed her eyes on the day.

49

AZUMA HATED SOCIAL OBLIGATIONS MORE than any other kind. Her calendar was full to overflowing, and she had her father's disdain for political maneuvering, although thankfully this was tempered by sensibilities she had inherited from other relatives who had understood the need for it.

But the Prefect of the Shibuya Prefecture, one of the central Tokyo districts, had been a very purposeful and useful ally, so when his personal invitation to a gallery opening was extended, she accepted. She arrived with *Hachi* in tow, finding it amusing that her fierce young priestess seemed entirely off-balance in her required formal wear.

"Cheer up, my friend," Azuma whispered wickedly. "Tomorrow, it will be *you* that everyone is speculating about."

"With all due respect, *Aijin*, I don't want to be your 'flavor-of-the-month,'" *Hachi* hissed back through clenched teeth.

"I know, you could do much better," Azuma said, trying not to laugh as *Hachi* squirmed, afraid she had caused offense. But at the last moment, she turned to her escort/guard and smiled, showing that she was trying to be funny. "Relax. You're only here because *he* won't let me attend a public function without supervision."

"He's wise. You have enemies," *Hachi* flipped her blond hair with a small movement of her head, unaware how many eyes among those nearby watched her longingly.

"None as interesting or dangerous as those I used to have," Azuma replied, wondering just how long she had to stay to meet the rigorous demands of decorum. "Now get lost. Try to have some fun. That's an order. By all means, if someone offers you a drink, take it."

She turned away, knowing that her bodyguards did not have to be on top of her to be effective, and they knew that she could handle herself well enough under threat. She noticed a familiar face across the room and made her way through the crowd, stopping every few steps to speak to this or that dignitary. It wasn't just her money, wealth, and influence that made her so popular; RSI was a global force, and it was fashionable to be seen with her. She found that type of celebrity ridiculous.

"I guess they'll let just anyone into these parties now," she commented in the Monster's ear when she reached its side. The young man next to it had a petulant expression and was wearing a new face, but she would recognize Tatsuo Tomo anywhere.

"You two remember each other?" Akenomyosei's grin was somewhere shy of mirth, and her old mentor barely glanced at her. Apparently her recent experiments had foiled the promise he had made to his master to bind her in duality like the two of them. "Well, forgive Forcas, he is out of sorts these days."

Forcas. That was it. She hadn't been able to recall the name he was currently using, and she was grateful the Morningstar had volunteered it. She saw the flash of resentment in its eyes. Names carry power. She promised herself she would remember it.

"Surely you're not here for me?" she inquired, looking from one of them to the other.

"Just taking the temperature of the room," Akenomyosei told her. "Your date is transcendent."

"And she'd eat you for breakfast," Azuma laughed politely, to create the illusion that the three of them were enjoying some diversion in case anyone was watching. "Is there a point to this exercise?"

"Can we not follow the goings-on, the ebb and flow of humanity? You used to love having me around."

"Did I?" Since it was of a mind to waste her time, there had to be a reason. She glanced at her watch pointedly, and yawned.

"Humans. Always thinking it is *kismet* when they meet, not wondering about the machinations and purposefulness of that fate, leading them onward, sometimes into traps of their own making."

"How sweet of you to worry."

"You recall what I told you about the motivations of the gods, we hope. That should serve." With that, it strolled away toward the back of the gallery, and she noticed that Forcas had vanished.

She went in search of the Prefect, wanting to ensure she paid her respects and thanked him for his invitation. He was surrounded by his staff, hangers-on, and his own security detail. Of interest was a young soldier in a black uniform that she did not immediately recognize, at parade rest but wary of all who came near. A flash of goldish-green eyes beneath the rim of a jaunty beret. Not Japanese. Some sort of security contractor. Azuma filed the anomaly away in her mind and turned her attention to her host.

They exchanged a few quiet pleasantries, and Azuma made eye contact with *Hachi* across the room, raising an eyebrow and smiling a secret half smile when the old politician placed a hand almost-but-not-quite too low on her back. *Hachi* rolled her eyes, *what can you do?* Her expression was so priceless Azuma had to swallow her laugh.

Thankfully, the man's niece appeared, and she excused herself. She wandered the space, enjoying the art on display, stopping to enjoy one of her favorites, a study in scarlet, the height of a two-story building. It had been suspended from cables anchored in the arching metal rafters, seeming to float in space.

She lost herself in the design, mindful of its simple beauty, when a movement in her peripheral vision caused her to turn. The woman who stood next to her did not attempt to hide her obvious delight in the artwork, and Azuma watched her expression as it moved over the expanse of color and light.

But the fascination did not stop there; the woman was exquisite in every way. And Azuma was not the only one who thought so; she noticed the furtive glances and outright stares of many of the other guests. But there was something about her that did not invite casual approaches, her posture and the set of her face suggested she did not suffer fools.

She had the unselfconscious posture of a fashion model, with chiseled facial features that were not softened at all by her makeup, which emphasized huge dark eyes, their brown color infinitely dark and deep, almost like inkwells infused with sparks of light. Those eyes were haunting, sensual, and dangerous. Her dark hair was short and appeared shapeless, but it was stunning in the carelessness of its style, which suited its wearer perfectly, the loose curls completely untamed. Her mouth was lush, full, and weaponized into a sultry pout that was likely its state of repose.

Her dress, if it could be called a dress, was couture, short enough to be scandalous in this forward-thinking group, and her back was bare, revealing elaborate tattoos of surprising beauty and artistic quality. Her piercings did not diminish her allure, including the two diamonds in her nose and the dainty ring through the middle of her lower lip. Azuma guessed her height at just under six feet, but she wore six-inch heels with the grace of a dancer. She brought to mind a pixie that had caught fire and fallen to earth, scorched and smoking, even more magical for the insults she had suffered.

When she turned her head, instead of the sneer that Azuma anticipated, her eyes widened slightly in surprise. She glided closer and now Azuma could see that she was not Japanese, but was unable to place her provenance with any certainty. A number of far-flung places on the globe could have produced this peerless creature.

They turned toward each other, and Azuma maintained her silence, as was her habit.

"I could stand here for days and still need more of it," the young woman finally spoke. Azuma nodded, thinking the same thing, but not about the painting.

They discussed the painting for some moments, and Azuma did not reveal that she owned it, having put it on loan here where it could be widely enjoyed. She was surprised when the woman moved in close, abandoning personal space in favor of placing a bold hand against Azuma's abdomen, letting it drift slightly downward before she spoke. Azuma surreptitiously signaled to *Hachi*, her hand flattened at waist height, palm down, staying her guard's approach in the nearby crowd. It was her version of *stand down, all is well*. The *Akai* didn't take kindly to breaches to their goddess, perceived or otherwise.

"I can tell you are a person of appetite. So rare here, in my experience." Her accent betrayed her origins, lovely and lilting, the tones of Caribbean Spanish flavoring her Japanese. The Japanese of someone who absorbs languages on the fly. An unusual type of intelligence.

"You mistake our reserve for lack of passion," Azuma countered, dropping her eyes to the woman's body for the briefest of moments to telegraph her appreciation of its attractiveness and not breaking contact by stepping away, rather she leaned in, dark eye to dark eye. The Dragon gave her no clear signal as to whether this being was enemy or not, which she found fascinating. She almost laughed. But she had no more time for pleasant diversions, noticing that the Collector had arrived to accompany her on other errands, so she plucked a drink from the tray of a passing waiter and handed it to her new friend.

"You'll have to settle for this to quench your thirst tonight, I'm afraid," Azuma told her regretfully. "I never mix my business with pleasure."

"A shame," the woman laughed ironically, reluctantly retrieving her hand and breaking contact. "You might discover that such a habit, once cultivated, cannot be easily broken."

50

AZUMA LOOKED UP FROM THE contract she was studying, vaguely aware that the Collector was speaking to her. She looked at him questioningly, and he didn't quite smile, but seemed to want to.

"What have I done to amuse you this time?" she asked.

"You need to feed," he said softly. "You're distracted, and we have business to discuss. Shall I bring Akiko to Tokyo?"

"I like Akiko," Azuma smiled indulgently and then shook her head, sinking back into her chair, and indicating he should take the one opposite. "Mmm. I'll make other arrangements this time."

"I'm sure a more…permanent agreement could be come to with Miss Akiko," he said gently. "You don't have to scavenge."

"Akiko is -" Azuma shivered, and pulled her sweater closer around her shoulders. She shook her head and made a pushing gesture with her hands.

"Is love not a possibility for even you?" It was his turn to push her a bit, knowing exactly what that shiver was signaling.

"Love, wow." She stretched slowly and blew a puff of air out slowly, looking out on the night. "I like Akiko *because* she will never fall in love with me. She is chasing death, or at least flirting with it. Love," she tasted the word and found it wanting. "I had love once. We both know how that ended."

"Megumi, were she here, would tell you that dying for love is the most extraordinary sacrifice," he countered.

"Megumi is not the one that was left behind," Azuma replied. "I would never have asked it of her. We don't ask of others those sacrifices that we are not willing to make ourselves."

"Then you lie to yourself; you, the samurai, for whom death is a journey you must ready yourself for each day, would have died a thousand deaths for the Lady Megumi. And so you have," he reminded her, before mercifully moving on to other concerns. "The Vatican received the decoy we leaked."

"So we should expect spies," Azuma replied. "Doubtlessly unsubtle. Who benefits this time?"

"Shiguro. There are others; I suspended my inquiries when you sent me to Africa. I have taken it up again. It's an organized group. They are prepared to help any outside interests averse to your causes."

"Yakuza?"

"Endlessly. Always. They claim they do not believe in old legends and you are not a threat."

"That and I refused to consider his son as a suitor," she said, in all seriousness, but to her surprise he laughed, a single short bark of mirth that appeared to hurt him. She giggled at this strange predicament, surely her Collector was the only being she knew who could sustain injury from laughter.

"By *Fūjin*, you must not," he protested, wiping tears away.

"I didn't find it funny."

"Sometimes you have a lack of appreciation for the ridiculous," he told her, buttoned up once more.

"Let's get creative," she suggested. "We could get some answers and send a message at the same time. It'll be fun."

51

NIGHTCLUBS BRIDGED THE GAP BETWEEN the legitimate and the profane, daylight and moonlight, the boardrooms where those with powerful interests got in bed with all manner of players with connections from the unsavory to the outright criminal.

Certain promises could be extracted only under specific conditions. Things could be witnessed but unseen. Behind the velvet barriers of a VIP suite, Azuma found that she could conduct business that, while sensitive, required this sort of public privacy.

On one such night, to her surprise, the young woman she had seen at the Prefect's reception approached. She danced in plain view of Azuma and her guests, and then made eye contact with Azuma and tugged on her flimsy crop top, exposing her upper abdomen, which revealed a single phrase.

Anatahadare?

It was written in some dark substance – eyeliner, potentially. Azuma could feel the heightened interest of the members of her party, and smiled. It was some feat to accomplish, upside-down and backward so it could be read by the intended recipient. And in Japanese, no less – *who are you?* Perhaps she had used the dark mirrors of that very establishment. It signaled intelligence that apparently did nothing to temper recklessness. Azuma's assessment of her cleverness had not been incorrect, rather she had perhaps underestimated its potential depth.

Azuma withheld any outward reaction, and went on to pursue discussions with her guests as per her intended purpose. She watched absently as the woman was gently diverted by the *Akai* and encouraged to seek other amusements. When she abandoned the dancefloor, she eventually ended up in the VIP suite directly opposite Azuma's own, surrounded by similarly beautiful people and their many admirers. She seemed to be the center of attention there, but appeared bored. After some time, she took her leave, but not before blowing a kiss in Azuma's direction that Azuma pretended not to see.

At the conclusion of her business she summoned *Ni* and asked her clandestinely to gather information about the woman and report back. For this instruction Azuma received the barest of nods, and satisfied with her other concerns, forgot all about it in favor of finding sustenance.

52

"WHAT DO YOU THINK, OLD friend?"

"Is the juice worth the squeeze?" he replied with a question of his own, despite that long-ago lesson that such a practice was unwise. It was purposeful, suggesting that he was not inclined to comment on such matters.

"Very wise," Azuma allowed, keeping her eyes on the intriguing young woman who danced with such abandon. "Do you think this is a weakness of mine?"

"I've not known you to have weaknesses, my mistress," he murmured, followed by an inscrutable smile to indicate that he knew his ironic tone had hit its mark. "Perhaps a blind spot, an allowance you make for unfortunate young women."

"Unfortunate?" Azuma frowned, knowing that according to her intel, this gamine wunderkind had amassed riches. She was one of the few who had profited from her own exploitation.

"Isn't it clear?" The Collector sat with her quietly, and she knew his assessment of Iara was from the perspective of a conservative male Japanese elitist. Which meant that if you were to engage in sexual congress with a foreigner, it was best if she was blonde, voluptuous, and submissive. History had stamped him, and Azuma knew he saw too little flesh, too many tattoos and piercings, and a lifestyle and attitude that were not deferent in any way. He was not intimidated, however, as many other men would be. She also knew he was likely the only member of her guard that could achieve pleasure from a sexual encounter without cruelty. It was simply that he played a long game, saw the chess moves several turns ahead, anticipated the checkmate.

"She appears to be...a handful," he concluded politely, and Azuma was sure this was his final say. So, she pushed him once more; he probably expected it.

"And I'm not?" she asked archly.

"*Himura-san*," he began, and she could hear the amusement in his voice, the only thing that betrayed his fondness for her. "With certainty. But after all this time, you are an organized and predictable one."

"And you see her as a return to chaos and unpredictability?" she remarked, but he kept his peace. It was answer enough.

She took comfort in the knowledge that the whole thing would likely amount to no more than casual sex. But, entirely aware that she might be lying to herself, she removed her suit jacket and waded out onto the dancefloor.

Under the blacklights, the pattern of her scales was evident on her skin, and many times club denizens had admired what they believed an elaborate tattoo. It frightened away the fainter of heart, and beckoned the recklessly curious. She imagined that such a characteristic functioned just as the gods had meant it to.

53

"I LIKE KITCHENS.

"They really are the heart of every home. I cannot *tell* you how many stupid parties I've been to where the kitchen was the smallest room in the house, but everyone would just cram themselves in there together anyway."

Azuma paused, glancing at the gentleman who owned the house, and smiled softly, placing a finger on her lip and shaking her head, as if she were enjoying a private secret. He, for his part, struggled futilely against his bonds, his eyes blazing with anger.

She wandered about the room, looking at various appliances, picking up interesting objects. "Everyone – and *Shiguro-san*, I do mean everyone – has a drawer with the most amazing things." She idly began opening drawers and examining their contents, choosing those she found promising. "The wife saves a nail that she thinks may be great for hanging a picture one day. But me, I see a great way to get under a tooth, do some amateur dentistry. It's a quirk I have.

"And so many people fancy themselves home chefs, so they purchase specialized tools, cleavers and the like.

"But your wife," Azuma marveled at the thought, but continued with a smile. "Your dear wife is a baker, of all things. And surprise, surprise, she has some very useful equipment here." She rattled a few more drawers, making additional selections.

"A torch! How very French," Azuma exclaimed. "Not that you deserve *brulee*, but it does get marvelously hot, and the flame is compact so that the user can really focus on a delicate task.

"And this – this is magnificent." Azuma held up a small, complicated gadget with a red handle and a shielded, sharp tool. "Shiguro, I am willing to bet that you don't even know what this one is for. No matter, I shall explain. This tool cleverly removes the pit from a cherry. Handy if one is making pie, I'm told.

"It is simple, elegant, and brutal. This tool pushes the stone from the fruit and through the guard there with a gentle squeeze." She straddled a chair across from her audience and held it up in the light. "But do you see how they engineered this? A cherry is not so very firm, but the stone is substantial. This tip here? It isn't all that sharp; really, this part of the tool is quite a lot like a blunt screwdriver. But that is what makes it so effective for my purposes, really. One can place a fingertip here against the guard, the thing is meant to hold the fruit in place and apply pressure, so, even though it isn't quite so keen, with gradual, firm pressure, eventually that end will make its way through the flesh. I imagine there are several soft body parts it would be effective on. It crushes and tears slowly. I like to take my time with these things."

Azuma nodded to *Ku*, and Shiguro's gag was removed. He screamed at her, "You dare come into my home and threaten me – you will die for this!" He was so incensed that his saliva flew onto her cheek. The Collector immediately wiped it away with a handkerchief. Azuma glanced at him gratefully.

"No threats. I don't waste my time with them," she replied. "Promises are more in keeping with my worldview. You stole from me, and you conspired against me with others, who, like you, promised fealty in exchange for the power I could provide. You thought that together you could outflank me."

She deliberately and silently lined up the items she had gathered on the table in front of him. She nodded to *Ku*, who picked up the cherry pitter.

"I'll talk, I will *talk*," Shiguro relented, his eyes wild trying to see what *Ku* was doing out of his field of vision.

When all his secrets were revealed, Azuma realized that her count of the traitors had been incorrect, but her surprise did not register visibly. Rather, she smiled before she spoke. "There, you see? I knew we didn't need all of this." She gestured to the items on the table and swept them to the floor.

Shiguro was sweating and shaking with relief. "Of course not, I –" His words came to a choking halt when the Collector passed Azuma's sword over her shoulder.

She balanced it on the scabbard's toe, passing it thoughtfully from hand to hand, and said, "Now I can make it quick and I doubt you'll feel much pain."

"If you kill me, the Council will retaliate," Shiguro warned, but his voice no longer conveyed anger, or any of the authority he had previously claimed. In fact, he sounded as though the only emotion he had left was doubt.

"On the contrary, I think when they hear what happened to you they will not only acquiesce and tell me everything they know, but they will no longer meddle in my affairs." She swung the blade effortlessly, the steel singing a song of deadly quickness, so rapid the stroke that there was barely a need to clean the blade before sheathing it. She nodded to *Ku* to follow her, but when she paused to pass her sword back to the Collector, he stopped her long enough to dab a spot of blood from her left cheek, just beneath her eye, his fingers gentle on her chin.

She, in turn, conferred upon him a quizzical look, as her ivory dress was splattered with the evidence of her bloody task.

"Not on your face," he murmured. "I never could stand for it, even when you were still a child." Then he turned back to the table, and rolled out his knives, the signal for *Ku* to escort her out.

The Collector stayed behind, painstakingly putting the finishing touches on her message. And when Shiguro's son returned from a night of drinking, what was left of his father was an elaborate display of patience and training; cuts of meat, delicate as the sashimi carved at the hands of a sushi master, were arranged atop the table in the shape of a dragon.

54

"YOU DIDN'T TELL ME YOUR brother was so gorgeous," Iara said from her spot on the bed. She stretched like a cat, her naked skin glowing. She knew she was flawless, and Azuma had to admit that move never failed to get her attention.

This time, though, the young woman's statement distracted her from the flesh on display.

"My brother?" Azuma asked the question as innocently as she could manage. Her many years had taught her to be an expert dissembler. Tatsuo Tomo had long been suppressed, so this could only have been an apparition, a visitation from Akenomyosei's familiar, her old cruel mentor. This was a message for her somehow.

"You didn't even tell me you had a brother," Iara pouted. She was determined to have a conversation her way. Azuma ignored her attempt to elicit guilt and remained silent. It had the effect she desired. Iara talked.

"I saw him at Womb. He approached me, said he had heard that I was working in Japan. Someone had told him I was seeing you. He said he was a fan."

"Oh? That's unsurprising," Azuma remarked indifferently, pulling on her robe and turning away from the bed. Her appetite for companionship was suddenly gone.

"He was very engaging, seemed to be having a good time. He was surrounded by beautiful people, and the women there couldn't get enough of him," Iara went on, and as Azuma had learned, what people say can give away a great deal; Iara was obviously attracted to him. "He asked how you were doing. Are the two of you not close?"

"To the contrary, we're twins. Two sides of the same coin, really. I guess I am just more private," Azuma answered, but could not hide the bitterness of her tone. Iara heard it, and came off the bed, pressing that body into her, tugging the robe open, her warm skin against Azuma's.

"No wonder we clicked," Iara observed with wicked amusement, correctly reading that she was treading in dangerous waters. Azuma kissed her, roughly, and bit down on Iara's plump lower lip hard enough to draw blood, but this was just encouragement to her young paramour, who dug her nails into Azuma's hips. Azuma extricated herself from the embrace abruptly, ashamed that she enjoyed the look of disappointment that flashed in Iara's eyes, there and gone, as she was not one to show others any weakness. It was part of what Azuma liked most about her, but the subject of the discussion had her annoyed and short-tempered. Was she jealous? After all this time? This perceived frailty of her own drove her to crush it; she pushed her feelings away.

"I have to work," Azuma told her curtly, and Iara pouted again. More beautifully than ever. Azuma was certain that pout had always had the same effect on whomever it was directed, but she forced herself to shake her head.

"You really have no time?" Iara pleaded. "You run the world. You could make time. For me."

"Probably. But that would make you worse than you already are." Azuma smiled. "If that's even possible."

Iara's laughter followed her out of the room, and she made a mental note that she needed to remember what she wanted from their relationship was not serious enough to permit too much drama.

55

IARA WANDERED THROUGH THE ROOMS on the ground floor of Azuma's mountain home, idly drifting from one treasure to another, curious about and awed by the immense wealth that must have been required to build the place. The helicopter had delivered her for what she believed was another date.

"So you flew me up here to break up with me? *¿Qué es esta locura?*" In her frustration she reverted to her native tongue, and Azuma had the good grace to swallow her amusement at this outburst.

"Not exactly, but a relationship with me requires sacrifice," Azuma told her, after explaining that she could no longer continue their casual dalliance. It was a calculated risk, to bring a spy into the household, but it was the best way to attempt to unravel the Vatican's intrigues. Only the Collector and *Ni* had knowledge of this confidence.

"You want me to sign an NDA, no problem," Iara, mercurial, adaptive, accommodating what was needed in the moment to avoid delaying gratification. Azuma could certainly admire the woman for what she was. Her capitulation so smooth that Azuma knew that she had apparently entered into many of them.

"I was thinking of something more meaningful; something more pragmatic. If we are to go forward, we need a more formal understanding. My lovers must see me for what I am, must bind themselves to me in blood," Azuma explained quietly, and Iara froze like a startled deer, her big brown eyes not unlike the female doe's when confronted with a predator. But she was very resilient, and she mastered her fear with her natural curiosity, probably wondering how she could turn the situation to her advantage. She now understood that it was pay-to-play from here, without acquiescing to whatever was asked at this junction she would no longer have access to Azuma and her secrets.

"So I ask you again. Shall I put you back on the helicopter and send you down the mountain with well wishes for many more adventures here in our amazing country, and my gratitude for the pleasure we have shared? Or will you stay, to bear witness, to serve, to stand beside me as my consort?"

Iara heard the flowery language and supposed it to be another example of the eccentricity of the super-rich. She had seen it before. She did not know that it was already too late to return to the city, and her life before this moment, because her role in the larger betrayal was already suspected, if yet unproven. Death had cast its shadow over her, and there was only one way forward.

So she nodded, uncertainly, and Azuma took her by the hand and introduced her to the ritual that made her fear that the choices she had made had only one possible ending. And she knew that the church that she loved and despised would find another sacrifice if she failed.

56

"HER HANDLER IS A PRIEST," the Collector told her, passing on a buff-colored folder, and watching quietly as Azuma flipped through it.

"But she hasn't made contact with anyone yet?" Azuma asked, knowing it to be true.

"Not even with the Council who helped her position herself. Not since-" He paused, not wanting to make any connections for her or encourage her to make assumptions she was overly willing to make.

"Are you afraid that I will believe she has been reformed simply because she may have feelings for me?" Azuma asked, pulling out several pictures of her young lover with some of the most despicable and powerful men in South America. "This is what the Catholics have become? Perhaps Iemitsu was on to something, keeping them out. A forward-thinker, ahead of his time," she observed bitterly.

"I know you feel sorry for her," he pointed out.

"I don't know what I feel. If she is as conflicted about her religion as she seems to be, then it is because her church has essentially turned her out, sacrificed her flesh while they barter for power. And don't tell me she has a choice, because I am sure they threaten her even now."

"Do you think she will ask for your help?"

"I don't know if she knows how. At this point, without evidence of betrayal, I don't want to draw conclusions. Let's see if just being far enough away from a bad influence and our blood bond gives her an opportunity to walk away."

"She reminds you of Xiaohui," the Collector was wise, and saw much.

Azuma sighed. "Perhaps so. Only this time the madman is sanctioned by a powerful church."

"All churches are capable of gross abuses, this is not the province of only one of them," he pointed out gently, and she knew he thought still of his own father, by all accounts a good man. "This is so because they are run by human beings who are fallible, driven too often by cruelty and greed. It does not mean that the religions themselves are not valuable safe havens for many who live their lives in observance of the best principles of faith.

"Like Xiaohui, she is a pawn. And the madman is important to the leaders of this church, a frequent guest at the Vatican. It appears he has been given a great deal of latitude in the way he has been allowed to operate." The Collector turned to a section near the back of the file that contained several pages of notes.

"He has been sent all over the world, and seems to apply his vocation in a less than pious manner. She has worked with him longer than any of his other operatives."

"Which simply means that Iara has likely been successful at manipulating her manipulator. No surprise there," Azuma said.

"But this is a priest of a rare sect, one that has existed since the time of the Inquisition," the Collector surmised. "These priests are deployed for the 'glory of God,' the so-called *Dei Gloria*, sanctioned by the Church to commit murder, torture, and all manner of atrocities to advance the reach and influence of Catholicism. The acts are justified by divine discretion. The modern church has apologized publicly for these outrages, but the sect persists to this day."

"Commission of sin for the eradication of it?" Azuma smiled bitterly, understanding well that such hypocrisies were the foundation of power.

"Indeed. But this particular priest has never kept an operative indefinitely. They seem to fall down wells and break their necks, or meet their end strangled in bedsheets. All unconnected to him and his movements, perhaps natural consequences of their work for him."

"Surely she doesn't believe it won't happen to her?" Azuma had difficulty thinking Iara could be that naïve.

"I'm sure they all believed it. Perhaps he is diabolical enough to let her believe he is obsessed with her," he shook his head. "I didn't make any statements about her contact patterns ending when she came to your bed, but let's understand each other clearly. Perhaps she is enamored of you, and has real sentiments of love or attachment. If she proves disloyal, we cannot have any liabilities of that kind."

"I agree. Even if she remains loyal, or asks for our assistance in extricating herself from this web of lies, can we ever stop watching our backs? The Dragon cannot tell whether or not she is *teki*, which suggests to me that even Iara does not know what she will do," Azuma sighed. "I know what you ask of me, my friend. If the time comes, when the time comes, I will tie up the loose ends. I cannot ask you to do such a thing for me, and I will accept that responsibility as I have exposed us to the risk."

"Very honorable. But I think the risk was necessary. Friend or foe, keeping her within reach was the wisest course."

57

IARA WAS INCENSED TO FIND the soldier in Azuma's bed. Her deep brown eyes were ablaze with fury, but she was trying to maintain her carefully cultivated indifference. The points of light in her eyes were like sparks that were ready to ignite at the slightest provocation. She had recovered from her initiation much as Azuma had expected she would, quickly adapting to what she felt was a position of entitlement among those who served the Dragon. She was mumbling under her breath, her Spanish peppered with colorful and unladylike epithets.

She switched to Japanese in deference to Azuma, saying only, "Why?"

Azuma smiled an inscrutable smile. "Because I need to find out why she is here and who sent her. I cannot do that if she dies."

"So, resuscitate her with *your* blood. You don't need me for this." English now, to telegraph her displeasure, and because she assumed in her naivete that Azuma wouldn't understand it.

"My blood will cloud her memories and her judgement. This soldier has been following all of us, and when we left that roof, she followed, blindly. Without any guarantee she would survive it. It's a dangerous nemesis that commands such loyalty, and such sacrifice, that their messenger is ready to die for answers. Whomever is behind this, they are not likely to give up. Ever."

"Then turn her. Send her back to them as an object lesson and she will collect their heads and place them at our feet."

"Our?" Azuma had not bothered to dress, and she pulled Iara into her arms, pressing her body suggestively against the other woman. Iara leaned in for a kiss, but Azuma refused her this intimacy, instead tugging Iara's hair and forcing her head back painfully. "There is no *ours* – there is only mine. You chose to serve, and serve you shall." She increased the pressure until Iara's anger was only a memory replaced by her fear. Azuma was reminding her abjectly that she should worry about a broken neck. Even the *Akai* could not survive such an injury.

"Don't make me prove to you that I have no favorites; you are the Dragon's Consort, but it buys you nothing if you lack loyalty," Azuma hissed, forcing her to her knees. Iara was cold, calculating, ruthless, and fearless, unlike any other companion Azuma had ever had, but she was too much the petulant child when she did not get her way – Azuma had no further patience for her nonsense.

"*Hai, Aijin,*" Iara gasped, and was promptly released. Her use of Japanese signaled her submission was absolute.

She rubbed her neck absently, and then yanked up her sleeve to bare her forearm. She settled on the *shikibuton* next to the sleeping soldier, and even that slight disturbance must have caused pain, as the woman cried out weakly. Iara's anger had returned, and she was too infuriated to look at Azuma; she opened her vein with economy and allowed the drops to flow into the soldier's open mouth.

The woman turned away from this disturbing gift, but Iara was patient, guiding her mouth back toward the blood. She reached for the chain around the woman's neck with her free hand, tugging gently to reveal the tags that were attached to it. She studied them briefly, and raised her eyebrows in surprise, before addressing the soldier by name. "Michael, if you wish to survive this night, you must drink, you must help me."

Iara was both mystery and surprise to Azuma, but she found this act to be less humanity-driven and more in keeping with whatever manipulative skill that her young companion employed to enforce her will on others. Michael complied weakly, and Azuma was relieved that at least the will to live had not been extinguished. She would survive, her strength renewed without any transformative effect that would have been the legacy of Azuma's own blood.

58

WHEN SHE WAS FINISHED, AND the soldier was sleeping comfortably, Iara went in search of Azuma, who had slipped away during the exchange. She stood outside the sliding doors to the balcony of the suite, watching the busy machinations of the nighttime crowds on the street below.

She glanced at Iara, and crossed to the bar, where she poured out a generous measure of spiced rum and held it out like a peace offering. Iara took it gracefully, but said scornfully, "Aren't you worried this might fuel my fire?"

"I can hope," Azuma replied with a sardonic twist of her mouth that did nothing to mar her exquisite beauty. The rum had been one of the first gifts Iara had given her, before Azuma had revealed that she was anything other than a lover, before she had groomed her as a consort, when the *dominicana* had still believed that perhaps for the first time in her life she had met her match and was falling in love. Before Iara had learned that her own nickname, *La Monstrua*, given in response to the misanthropic behavior of a top international model, meant next to nothing when compared with the acts of her ruthless lover.

When Iara looked closely, she could see that Azuma was moving more slowly than usual, and that she appeared to be stiff or favoring her left arm. "They never should have left you," she observed, taking a softer tone.

"I told them to go ahead. It was better that I faced this threat alone, the *Akai* are unsubtle and might have cost me a chance to get answers," Azuma replied.

"You need to feed," Iara stated the obvious. "You didn't take enough from her. Let me help you." She stripped off her thin t-shirt and put her arms around Azuma's neck, this time voluntarily submitting. "Just no marks on my neck, please, I have a shoot tomorrow."

Azuma lifted her onto the granite countertop and leaned over her. She knew how to hide the marks she made, and as skillfully as ever, she elicited pleasure and sustenance enough for the two of them.

59

WHEN SHE FELT SHE HAD convinced them that her only phone conversations were to her younger brother, Iara was confident she could safely reach out to the priest. He immediately offered to meet her in Japan, and she felt strangely triumphant hearing the hunger in his voice.

"There's no need. They suspect nothing. The intel was correct and comprehensive. The group here got me close, and I can get to the information easily. She trusts me."

He told her the Vatican wanted new documents, and told her to look for additional instructions in the usual place. She wondered what power she might exercise over him now that she had been accepted as an insider, with the gift of power she had received.

Ni could make little sense of the exchange but understood its confirmation of an ongoing betrayal, and she passed the transcript on to the Collector.

He reiterated that her instructions were unchanged. She was to follow, observe, and report back about the Dragon's Consort.

She confirmed her understanding and went back to work.

60

ALETA OPENED HER EYES SLOWLY, BUT her most recent memories returned immediately, with consciousness, and her startle reflex went through her like a jolt of electricity, followed by adrenaline. She sat up quickly, ready to fight, but was greeted only by a small quiet room. In the chair under the window sat a very young nun in a white habit, reading a book. The nun set the book aside, her lovely eyes settling on Aleta with a calm kindness and mild curiosity. The snowy color of her garments framed the face of a pixie, and Aleta briefly wondered if she was in heaven, before her rational mind took over and she shook off the remains of her slumber.

She reached subconsciously for her necklace, and only when her fingers closed on the small metal talisman did she become aware of her need for spiritual reassurance. A quick glance around revealed little, other than she was presumably in a place of safety. The bedroom was sparely furnished, monastic even, the only decoration a detailed crucifix, Latinate, with Christ in the throes of His passion. This hung on the wall over the bed and was about the size of a man's hand.

She noted that she had been placed atop the bed fully clothed — not even her shoes had been removed — and the door to the room was open to a hallway, across which she could see a small white bathroom. Her lab coat was draped neatly over the footboard. She was relieved to see that her crutches were within reach, as were her eyeglasses, in a small tray on the table next to the bed. These she put on, and although the details of the room sharpened somewhat, there was nothing additionally revealed by donning them.

The nun regarded her silently, perhaps waiting for Aleta to speak. Sunlight streamed into the windows, and Aleta checked her watch. She was surprised, but not alarmed, to discover that she had lost the entire night and much of the following day to sleep. Shock was unpredictable; the brain shut down as a protective measure, she understood the physiology. She gingerly swiveled to her left and put her feet on the floor. She reached for and secured her crutches, settling them onto her forearms and marveling at the comfort it brought. It was something so familiar and ordinary that it was soothing.

She was grateful that the nun did not offer to help nor move to assist her in any way. She was unsure what such solicitous behavior might unleash. Aleta disdained pity of any kind, and wanted people to recognize her strengths, not her physical weaknesses. She had just begun to register surprise at how well she felt when the nausea hit her like an unwelcome intruder, advancing on her control, and she gagged loudly.

At this, the nun did move, gesturing but not speaking, making herself available to assist, and Aleta nodded gratefully, praying they would make it; she did not want to vomit at all, but the indignity of doing so all over that pristine habit was beyond the pale.

They made it — just — and finally the nun spoke, but only to murmur words of comfort. She held Aleta's hair back, and when it was over, brought a cool cloth for her neck and retrieved a glass of water so she could rinse her mouth. Aleta realized she was hyperventilating, so she slowed her breathing and restored some calm.

The nun had been too small, and Aleta too weak with sickness, to support her weight, so they sat together for a few moments on the tiled floor. The nun gently stroked Aleta's back and waited patiently.

Aleta was surprised and touched. The nuns she remembered from Catholic school were forbidding creatures, probably abused and marginalized in the male hierarchy of the church. They seemed loathe to touch and lacked physical gentleness, probably because they never experienced it. But there was something else much closer to her own experience; most people shy away from illness, subconsciously or otherwise. What sick people lament most is the isolation and the physical withdrawal of those around them.

"I'm sorry," Aleta apologized, pleased that her voice sounded stronger than she expected it to.

"Don't apologize, Dr. Madison. When you're ready, we can try again," was the soft reply. "I am Carter."

"Carter? That's an odd name for a nun." Aleta was used to the Church renaming these women, sometimes even giving them the name of male saints. She didn't bother to ask how the woman knew her name.

"I'm only a novice," Carter replied, with some sadness. "But my last name is Thomas, so I have petitioned to keep it once I have professed my vows and take my vocation."

This time, between the two of them, Aleta was successful in gaining her feet. Carter led her back into the bedroom, but rather than return to the bed, she helped Aleta to the chair. After ensuring that Aleta was comfortable and offering her another glass of water, she asked, "Would you be alright for a moment? I'd like to let Father Weston know you're awake."

"I think I am okay now," Aleta nodded, and watched her disappear through the door. As soon as she was out of sight, the realization that she was alone overcame her, and she felt dizzy and nauseous once more. She leaned forward, putting her head down, leaning her weight against her legs, and waited, successfully, for the moment to pass. She drank some of the water, grateful for its coolness, and let the sunshine warm her shoulders.

About three minutes passed before Carter returned. "Father Weston is on his way."

The name was familiar, and after a few moments, she realized it was the name that Amaoke had given her. But it seemed that he had warned her to be wary of the priest. Was this the priest that had saved her from — her mind refused to think of that now. But the reaction returned, and again it was physical, and she began to shake uncontrollably.

Carter was immediately at her side, kneeling beside the chair. "Is there anything -?"

"No, no." Aleta shook her head slowly. "I suppose it's to be expected. I'm still afraid."

"I know about fear," Carter whispered, and her tone was chilling despite the sunlight. "Is it okay if I pray?"

"Please." Aleta whispered too.

That's how Father Weston found the two women, hunched together in prayer in the bright rectangle of sunshine in his rectory bedroom.

61

THE WOLF RAN THROUGH THE forest, following the familiar trails left by his brethren over many moons as they chased down their prey. The soft thump of the ground beneath his feet, its mossy smell, and the rot of many generations of leaf litter were all part of the rhythm of this run, as comforting to him as his memories. He could smell the meltwater in the trees, and a mingled scent that became part of the great Kuskokwim River somewhere off to his left. A muskrat dodged quickly down its hole; the wolf gave a soft huff of amusement and let his tongue hang out. The bellows roar of his breathing accompanied him, the background noise of his existence. He would have been surprised to know how distinct a sound it was.

Accustomed he was to this solitude. It was as if this pristine wilderness existed to house him, and he alone in it. But in this dream, there had always been a dark presence in the forest, no matter how beautiful or calm appearing. Dangers lurked in these woods, and some of them waited for him.

The Spirit of Bear-Woman was there, awaiting her vengeance for the daughter he had stolen from her to feed his first magic, all those centuries ago. The lost watched silently, those souls for whom he carried no names, indeed no memories, who had been harvested by the berserker who had ruled these snowy woods with awful finality. Pureflesh, their blood spilled over this ground by tooth or claw; he knew not which. His mother, guardian and protector, balancing the retribution desired by nature. His wife, her spirit advocating self-forgiveness for transgressions of the past, refusing to allow his crossing of the Deep River. And Quuran, wisely watching sage and advisor. But the wolf did not reason out the connections, simply knew that the energies were balanced this time, and his interests were well represented.

The Ungalek, just across that flimsy boundary between this world and the next, a boundary that could be crossed too easily for the sake of its evil mischief, enraged. The Morningstar, everywhere and nowhere. Yet even in this vulnerable state, this spiritual limbo between worlds, Amaoke was protected.

But the dream had changed along the way. Two-legged Brother, for whom he searched and searched, was likewise in this place, searching in turn for Wolf. They had never been apart, separated, divided; the wolf looked inward but could not find him there. The cost was their suspension in this, the dream state, and into it came something new. A presence of power greater than his. It had a scent of its own. A goodness of its own.

The trail he followed turned abruptly and began to slope downward, toward the unseen river. He slowed, abruptly dug his claws into the soil to brace himself, and stopped short. A man stood by the river, facing the water, his weathered hands clasped behind him. His sealskin parka was ancient, the pelt worn in patches at his elbows; in place of fur, the hood was lined in the darkly iridescent feathers of a bird. His *mukluqs* were also quite primitive, the handiwork beautiful and time worn. His lifeforce was radiant, less something the wolf could see than feel, and it made his undercoat shake. A whine escaped unbidden, something that had not happened for nearly a millennium, his own involuntary admission of submission, and he planted his belly on the ground and turned his head, exposing his neck.

The man turned at the sound but was unsurprised to find Amaoke there. He smiled, and that smile was arresting as no other in Amaoke's long life had been. It was knowing, and lovely. His face was dark, lined by sun and wind, and carried the knowledge of many moons, many hunts, but was interesting for its lack of any strong gender-identifying features. The wolf's senses signaled male energy, but this was a countenance both grandmotherly and grandfatherly, favoring neither sex. Though aged, his hair flowed over and around his shoulders, vital, dark and shiny as obsidian, and its motion was independent of the air currents that came off the river and whistled through the woods. It undulated, weightless, and Amaoke realized that this was similar to the Morningstar's; interestingly, unlike that being, this movement seemed natural, like the flowing of the river, and was not at all disturbing, as if the great forces of the earth did not control him. Gravity could not touch him. His expression was open and curious, with the delight of a child, and his eyes were bright and animated, though dark and deep without a distinctive color.

The man kneeled a few feet in front of the prostrate wolf and held out his hands. Amaoke, still whining, crawled forward, blasted by the being's power. The man chuckled.

"Amaoke," he intoned in a language of the First People older than Amaoke's own, yet still somehow easily deciphered. "Little Wolf, have you forgotten me?"

And then his hands plunged into Amaoke's fur, the knowing fingers finding all the wonderful spots that loved to be touched, and that touch brought knowledge, and peace, and Amaoke's shivering was banished. Of course, Raven himself.

Amaoke discerned that the all the dark energies of the forest remained, but they were no longer a threat. Raven's presence balanced them all. And the wolf, ever vigilant, ever present in his life, both dreaming and awake, ready to act at a moment's notice, after a thousand years, surrendered and slept.

It was a vision or a dream that he next recalled, for although he floated in darkness, it was an experience of detachment he had never known, a safety he had not felt since the loss of Mother Noki. And into this deep passage came voices, one old to his memory, and one new. The Morningstar and the Raven. What was said one would not have wanted him to hear, and the other most certainly meant him to.

You dare not interfere with my beast. We have an agreement.

We are in agreement about only one thing. I fear you have forgotten your best capabilities, old friend. This marvelous creature has been poorly used.

My plans are not of your concern.

All is of my concern. You are of all, and my arms remain open to you.

Open only to my capitulation. To my deference.

Is it so terrible that you lash out using the suffering of pureflesh? I am here. I will yet bear out your grievances.

It is too late to come home. I enjoy my throne better than your service.

Clever that, although there are doors that remain eternally open, even to you. Poor Milton was manipulated to write that for you.

His love for me was in the words. He breathed life into a philosophy of poetry more captivating than the sacred texts.

Love, oddly that which cannot be defined by the pureflesh. They own it but cannot describe it. They feel it, give it, search for it without articulation. Appropriate that words cannot encompass such a thing. I think you blind to it, and it knows you ill. One cannot rule by autocracy, only by consensus is power conferred.

You say that. You, whose power depends not on exigency but only on existence? More have denied you than I.

Against one is not for *another. Pureflesh must be allowed choice. Take it away, and you strip of them their inherent dignity. Without which, there is naught.*

Your precious pureflesh are not worthy of such regard.

Divinity is in unity. You have an eternity to learn it and you shall. I will never deny you your place. Clever phrasing doesn't change the universe. Reign where you will. If a king serves nothing, and no one, what is the meaning of his rule? Such a king cannot even be his own subject. I am, and always have been. Even you had a beginning, and you understand from whence you came. Your provenance cannot be undone; denied or embraced it has a part in all you do. And that is and shall ever be your limitation.

62

"THERE ARE ALWAYS THOSE WHO seek death," the Collector told her. "That is how I knew."

"How do you recognize them, my friend?" Azuma asked, knowing that he was trying to soften the blow.

"Easily enough, I used to be one of them. You denied me that death, remember?"

"I knew it in your blood, not before," she told him, sadly.

"But such persons don't stop reaching for death after they have found a means to it. They embrace its cold kiss. And woe to those of the living who are near," he shook his head.

So she took Iara to the inlet near the old stronghold, that place on the sea that represented the best and worst of her childhood. They walked up the beach as the gulls screamed in the last of the light, and the low tide whispered over the rocks. Azuma led the way up the bluff to the promontory, recalling the beauty of that heartbreaking view.

They watched the sun sink away to the west, watched the sea, watched the sky in silence, and she put her coat over Iara's shoulders when she shivered in the salt spray.

"I loved someone once – really loved them. This place is important. It is a place I come often. To remember her, although all I want is to forget, because this is the place of her betrayal."

"She betrayed you?" Iara's startled look was like a lance.

"How much simpler the story would be if that were true," Azuma murmured. "But it was my betrayal. I betrayed her as I betrayed myself, and she died here. The locals say you can still hear her crying for me from the next life."

Iara pushed her chin further into the turtleneck sweater she wore, the downy cashmere settling against her cheek. "How long have you known?" she asked.

"I've always known. For a time I believed you wanted to tell me the truth of it, but simply could not."

"I made the choices I made because I enjoyed them. I enjoyed you. But I don't know how to be something I am not. I knew the cost, and I have probably been always willing to pay it. For you, it was worth it," Iara was honest at last.

Azuma turned toward her, and kissed her deeply, neither of them closing their eyes, and finally, the Dragon could see the answer that had eluded her there in the dark depths of her lover's sorrow. And when it was time to take a breath, Iara took that last step on her own, turning away and stepping down gently from that high place into nothingness.

Azuma said a small prayer to Megumi, asking her to help Iara find a higher path in the next life.

63

WHEN AZUMA RETURNED TO THE hotel, she was short and brutal with her staff, and this earned her a chiding grunt from the Collector. This, in turn, infuriated her even more, and she dismissed him curtly, reminding him of her instructions to secure sensitive specimens in the States — one a private concierge evaluation that was to be couriered and handled with RSI's highest priority and pristine chain of custody; the second a batch assessment from a military study that required discretion and secrecy. He shook his head sadly, recognizing that her anger was born of her frustration at what she thought was her own failure. Because Azuma had held out hope that Iara would pick loyalty and blood over betrayal.

Azuma knew that such behavior was shameful, but she refused to show any awareness of her wrongdoing, refused to look back at him at all. Since he knew she was really punishing herself, he took no lasting offense.

Azuma took the private elevators to her suite, where *Hachi* was standing guard. She bid greetings with a small formal bow. *"Doragon."*

This was ignored, and Azuma entered the dwelling, slipping off her shoes and heading down the darkened hallway to turn on the lights. Before she could get to the switch, she paused, hearing a small incongruous noise, and that awareness saved her life. She jerked sideways and dropped to a crouch, and the bullet passed over her head, on into the great room where it ricocheted off the bulletproof glass and finally lodged in the struts of her favorite sofa.

She twisted around and stood up in one fluid motion, immobilizing the soldier's gun hand in her right hand. Michael was strong, but Azuma had healed, and no human was match for her meta-strength and reflexes. Still, they turned together, wrestling for the gun, until Azuma found the catch on the magazine and it dropped. She turned in on herself, pressing her back against Michael's chest so that she had leverage on the woman's trigger finger, and discharged the bullet in the chamber. She then flung her body back out of reach and turned, hoping to distract the soldier, since she didn't think she would let go of her gun. But let go she had, and her left fist was ready to deliver a blow.

Azuma dodged it handily, thinking she had underestimated this opponent and gaining more and more respect for her. But boxing would make no match for the martial arts expertise the Dragon had cultivated, so when Michael settled into her stance, Azuma merely bowed and took her own.

She vaguely heard *Hachi* pounding on the door outside, having heard the gunshot, but she paid it no heed. Her bodyguard would be thwarted by the biometric lock that was armed when Azuma was inside the dwelling anyway. She engaged with the soldier in fierce combat, and what Azuma had thought a boxer's stance was only loosely so, because what Michael brought was a deceptively casual but effective variation of *muy thai* that kept her out of Azuma's grasp for several minutes. She even managed to land a few sharp blows, likely the aftereffects of Iara's blood gift, and that thought gave Azuma a brief pang of sadness that surprised her. The grief of what she had done snuck up on her, distracting her, and this did not go unnoticed by her opponent.

But the Dragon's self-awareness was greater than her grief, and she welcomed Michael's kill blow, stepped into it, and the other woman bounced off of her torso like a wall, her momentum carrying her to the ground so fast she had no chance to break her fall, and her skull bounced violently off the parquet. Azuma fell on her, pinning her to the ground while she was dazed, absorbing punches that had lost effectiveness, letting her tire before putting her in a choke hold, and when Michael lost consciousness, Azuma waited a few beats more and then climbed to her feet, leaving the other woman lying on the floor where she had fallen.

She tossed her head and straightened her clothing as she returned to the main door. She put her thumb in the lock and opened the door. *Hachi* gasped in relief but immediately kneeled at her feet, bowing her head in submission, knowing she had failed.

"Not your fault, *Hachi*." Azuma said tersely. "Resume your post." She did not await a response, as the door closed again behind her she glimpsed the relief in the sentry's posture.

She went back down the hallway, stepping neatly over the body at the boundary of the entryway, and passed into the kitchen. She heated *sake* and considered her next move. When she heard the furtive movements of the soldier regaining consciousness, she grabbed two ceramic cups and went to investigate.

Michael was sitting up, groggy but aware, and her hazel eyes tracked Azuma warily. Azuma stopped short of her reach, poured the warm sake into the cups, and offered one to her guest. "Would you like a drink? It seems to help me after a hard day."

Michael accepted the offering with less reluctance than Azuma might have expected. Azuma took her own drink across to the long couch in front of the windows and sat down, pulling her sword from beneath the central cushion and balancing it between her knees. She briefly glanced at the hole that the bullet had made in the upholstery, then downed her *sake* with practiced efficiency and rested her arms casually against the scabbard, with one thumb against the *tsuba* in readiness, knowing the soldier would read the gesture correctly. "Now we can behave in a more civilized manner."

When Michael remained silent, Azuma said, wonderingly, "I disposed of your ammunition."

Michael's posture was deceptive, and one corner of her mouth betrayed her confidence. She shrugged in a way that only the young can, and replied with satisfaction, "You should have stripped me. I always carry spares. Or taken my gun."

"A primitive weapon. I was taught that honor dictates the preservation of an opponent's defenses. Besides," Azuma continued, "I am to understand that a soldier's weapon is a friend."

"A trusted friend," Michael nodded. "Much like your sword."

"Oh, the sword is not my friend," Azuma corrected her. "It is more than that. It is an extension of my arm. A part of me, the signature of my soul. To call it a friend is an insult. A friend can still betray you."

"Am I a prisoner here?" The question was asked without a hint of concern, merely a request for information.

"Are you?" Azuma considered the question, then relented. "I don't keep prisoners. I need information, and you can either provide it or you cannot. Your value to me is proportional, directly to the former and inversely to the latter."

It was clear that Michael understood; she was expected to talk.

"I can see your reluctance, so I will start. Indicate yes or no," Azuma instructed. "I assume your ultimate directive is to kill me, since your bullet in my brain would have precluded any subtler alternative, such as the retrieval of information."

Michael nodded so Azuma continued. "Now the hard part. First, who do you answer to? I cannot identify your accent, but your Japanese is impeccable, which suggests that you either had exposure to it before, which I doubt, or a great deal was invested in your training."

Michael tilted her head in surprise, but said nothing.

"You have specialty training, originally this was as an enlisted soldier in your home country. But the work you are doing now is to support a private interest, or deep State. Am I right so far?"

Michael's eyebrows indicated that she was, indeed, her surprise and respect registered on her face.

"My first encounter with you was at the Prefect's reception, yes, I noticed you, and no, at that time I did not guess the context. I thought you a ceremonial guard, or extra security," Azuma told her, in response to the expression on the woman's face. "I have lived a long time, and survived many enemies. I prefer to let them believe that I only see what they want me to see.

"But what I missed was that you were making first contact in-country. You were reporting to the official who had to sign off on your movements for you to operate. The Prefect is a busy man; his people likely told your people that the meet needed to occur in public, and your people cleverly disguised it as provision of an escort to divert other parties from suspicion.

"You briefed him in generalities, but he had received instructions to green-light your request, and he didn't know I was the target, or he would have given it away. I am a high-profile citizen, whether I like it or not."

Michael shifted her weight and in one fluid movement came to her feet. She had shaken off any effect of her earlier defeat. She approached cautiously, settling across from Azuma by leaning against the far wall. "Continue," she murmured, confirming Azuma's theories.

"And later, when you directly presented yourself, on that roof, thinking I would believe it was our first encounter, your actions suggested that you were operating under some religious superstition related, if I am not mistaken, to vampires." Azuma said this last with not a little amusement, and added, "Arithmomania is thought to distract and delay them from pursuit of a potential victim. It does affect me, but any enhanced creature would not be slowed by such a stunt. And it is that single action that gives you away. You aren't Catholic, their approach is never subtle. I should know; my earliest days as a warrior were spent unraveling the effects of their early forays into this country, continuing my father's legacy.

"Your accent tells me you are not European or American. Not Oceanic. Not Eastern Asian. That leaves the Middle East, but you are no Muslim. So I ask myself, what else is there? A country so tied to its religion that its soldiers are more like crusaders for the Great Rabbinate of Israel, by way of the *Mossad.* But I must imagine that you started in IDF, and were ultimately recruited to the *Kidon.*"

Michael's eyebrows lifted briefly in response, but she maintained eye contact and her mouth twitched at the corner. Azuma found it strangely charming; an inadvertent tic that betrayed vulnerability. The soldier had not expected her to know so much.

"I am flattered. The assassins of Israel have not bestowed their deadly gifts on the land of the rising sun before. North Korea, of course, but here? Previously unrecorded, if ever."

"If you already have the answers you seek, you no longer need me," Michael spoke directly and quietly.

"I still don't know why, aside from the obvious religious objections to my genetic work," Azuma pointed out. "The Rabbinate is surely uninterested in that — if ever they were other than as a human rights campaign. Surely they wouldn't kill me for it. The Vatican, on the other hand, views me as an apocalyptic threat, although they are more interested in what is contained on my servers than martyring me. And military application of our technology is requested directly, by countries and industry alike."

"Above my pay-grade. No one has read me in on the particulars," Michael studied her fingernails, enough of a tell by the inexperienced youngster. Talented, perhaps, but still new to the part, and unused to failure. Azuma gambled and called her on it.

"Why lie now? *Of course,* you have been read in. The 'tip of the spear' and all that?"

"I know enough that I am comfortable with my mission. Not that I have to be. The weapon need not have the motivation of the arm that sends it to strike."

"I don't see it. You were chosen for a reason. They know their target," Azuma disagreed, guessing that the most outstanding item on her dossier from the perspective of a religious man was her high-profile and unashamed interest in beautiful young women. She suspected that it hadn't occurred to Michael, but she couldn't be sure

– it was probably front and center in the file the soldier had received when she was originally briefed. The old rabbi that had sent her may even have been transparent that she was not only being chosen for her skills but also other assets. "And generally, I don't see an operative of your caliber blindly acquiescing to an assassination request outside your normal theater of operation for anything other than eyes-only. One person sent you, and only you. That person acted alone. I want to know why."

"I cannot help you."

"Then you will have to go home," Azuma told her. "Without fulfilling your directive."

"You'd let me go?"

"Of course," Azuma replied. "You are not the enemy."

"You cannot know that. Perhaps I want you dead as much as the person who asked," Michael warned.

"You should want me dead *more*," Azuma observed. "I imagine the authorities will ship you home without letting you walk free another second here when they hear about your credentials."

Michael shook her head slowly, and Azuma recognized the gesture for what it was – a refusal to provide any more information.

Azuma picked up her phone and looked at the soldier critically. "Feel free to take a shower and have something to eat. It may be the last kindness you receive for a very long time." Michael's eyes were hard, but after a few moments, she turned and left the room.

When Azuma heard the shower running, she called for *Hachi* and set in motion her own arrangements. And when Michael Israel's extradition was assured and its immediacy confirmed, she whispered very specific instructions into *Juichi's* ear before departing the apartment without any subsequent contact with her adversary.

64

MICHAEL ISRAEL SAT CALMLY, ALONE in an interrogation room, waiting for the inevitable questions. She had been briefed as to every possible eventuality, and the information she was authorized to impart could not incriminate her, so she resigned herself to wait. They would keep her here, possibly for hours, with the air conditioner cranked, alone, with no human contact.

It was what she would have done to soften someone for an interrogation if she had a more civilized reason to be asking the questions she asked, immigration, drugs, petty larceny. She smiled. Special forces soldiers are used to privation.

She was surprised when, after only two hours, the door opened and Azuma Himura was escorted inside, accompanied by what could only have been an immigration official. The bureaucrat was clearly deferent to Azuma, perhaps a bit in awe of her severe beauty, but certainly had been instructed to extend her every courtesy.

She was flawless in a black cape dress and heeled leather boots, fastidious, really, wearing smooth black leather kid gloves and jade earrings. The two sat across from her, and Michael Israel glimpsed the mischief in Azuma's eyes when they made eye contact.

"I didn't want to delay your departure," she spoke directly to her. "I came in immediately to give my statement so that we can expedite your return to Israel. Mr.-"

"Muro," he supplied quickly. "Sama Muro. I am at your service, Dr. Himura."

Michael Israel was amused. The man was like a schoolboy.

"Yes, Mr. Muro. I wanted to ensure that Michael Israel has no difficulties leaving the country. My dear friend, Prefect Sato, hired her as a contractor for a special security project of mine. Very sensitive work, but it required certain restrictions on her official paperwork. We need to avoid unnecessary bureaucratic intrusions right now.

"One of her parents is very ill, and she must return home as quickly as possible. I wanted to personally vouch for the great service she has provided our countrymen, and myself, so that her visa could be adjusted to allow her to return at another time."

"Yes, Dr. Himura, but there is an indication here that she tried to attack you in your own home," Muro looked down at his notes, frowning.

"That is why I am here," Azuma said. "I was very distressed when I received your summons to make an official statement. This extraordinary young woman intervened to save my life, I could hardly live with the idea that she was accused and might be mistreated. I came right away."

Ah. Michael Israel recognized the theater for what it was. And Muro, who should have expected this woman, one of the titans of industry, to be far less melodramatic, was eating out of her hand. She had to give credit where it was due, Azuma was giving him what he needed culturally, perhaps personally, deference and submissive femininity in the face of his bureaucratic privilege. Michael Israel restrained herself from rolling her eyes, but only because she saw the twitch at the corner of Azuma's lovely mouth, and because she had her own role to play.

"Well, I will take your statement and see to it that we expedite her request for a new visa," Muro nearly stammered, so eager was he to please his distinguished guest.

"Before we go, could you see to it that she gets some refreshment?" Azuma asked.

"I'll take care of it myself," he offered, standing and opening the door. Looking at Azuma, he said, "Dr. Himura, if you'll come with me?"

"May I just have a moment here privately? I'd like to extend my gratitude, you understand?"

"Well, it is most irregular," he began uncertainly, but looked longingly at her again. He glanced into the corridor. "I suppose I can approve it," he said, like a man who wants such authority but is not sure that he really has it. "I will secure something for her to eat and drink, and then we can finish our discussion, Dr. Himura."

When the door to the hallway closed once more behind him, the two women faced each other. Azuma touched the corner of her eye and tugged on her earlobe gently. It was a message, but Michael Israel found it strangely sensual. She was being reminded that they were being filmed and recorded.

Azuma produced a cellphone from the pocket of her dress, and Michael Israel understood the reason for the gloves. "I wanted to bring you your phone," she said, thinking privately that the Collector would find this amusing. Another of her unfortunate young women.

Michael Israel took it from her but said nothing.

"My private line is in there, should you recall anything of importance," Azuma said. "Or should you find you require my assistance."

"Why?" Michael Israel asked, thinking it the safest response, and one not easily deciphered by anyone outside this conversation.

"I think you know the answer," she replied, and turned away just as Muro returned, disappearing into the corridor.

65

FATHER WESTON STOOD IN THE doorway for some moments before his presence was detected, and he used that time to speak a short prayer of his own. He had questions, but the distress he felt from both women concerned him. The doctor was rightly in shock, but he wondered at Carter's emotional state. Was this causing her to relive her own painful attack? He knew his concern was not the detached love of a confessor, and inwardly he chided himself. He did not expect to escape his sins, but he would not suborn hers.

When they turned their attention to the doorway, he asked, "How are you feeling?"

It was obvious that the question was directed at Aleta, but she didn't answer him right away.

She examined the man in the doorway with not a little trepidation, taking in the dark wavy hair, the eyes, the trim cassock, the silver cross. His height was striking, but he carried it naturally, and there was something reminiscent of Amaoke in his posture. But he was excessively muscular for his chosen profession, built powerfully in contrast to Amaoke's slimness. She kept coming back to his eyes. Behind those thick spectacles, they were persistently human, warm, and kind. But she was reluctant to be reassured. The resemblance to the Morningstar was overwhelming. The two were fundamentally the same. But where the other made her feel only revulsion to her very core, she felt no such response to this man. Carter stood and took a step toward him, putting herself briefly between Aleta and the priest, which Aleta took to be protective of her. But then Carter stopped abruptly and dropped her eyes before moving to the corner nearer the door, and Aleta realized she was carefully schooling her behavior.

Aleta looked from one to the other. Realization dawned that Carter had withdrawn to avoid giving something away. A relationship? Her professional instincts and observation were employed whether the situation called for it or not. Aleta did not sense any impropriety but concluded that the two were in love. Clear enough, both were denying themselves due to constraints of church and professed vows. Perhaps it was an acknowledged prohibition between them, and the thought gave Aleta pain. To love, and continually sacrifice such a thing. It was momentarily too big for the room, and everyone in it felt uncomfortable.

To his credit, Father Weston maintained his composure admirably. Other than a slight wrinkle that appeared between his brows, and disappeared almost immediately, he held his peace, attentive for her response.

"I am…better than I expected to be," she finally answered his question.

In response, he crossed the room slowly, handing her a small card before retreating again to the frame of the doorway. He leaned against it casually, but she suspected his calm demeanor belied what he really felt.

Aleta did not immediately recognize the card; it was soft and furred at the edges, the way paper gets when inadvertently washed. She made out her own name upon it, and suddenly was sure that it was Amaoke's.

"Do you know where he is?" she whispered, suddenly wanting nothing more than to know he was okay. She didn't use his name, just sensed that this priest would know whom she was referring to, since he had the card in his possession.

"What is your relationship to him?" Father Weston asked her.

"I'm not sure that's any concern of yours," she replied crisply, the Catholic girl in her feeling slightly guilty that she dared to speak to a priest this way, but pulling on a lot of practiced doctor authority that was helped along by the advantage she had over him in age. "Where is he?"

"I'm not sure it's any concern of *yours*," he replied darkly, and for the first time she could see it, he was truly as arresting and formidable as the other. Except that he did not make her afraid. At least, not as much.

"He has a — special condition," she allowed, softening her tone. "I haven't been able to reach him for some time, and I am worried that he might not…might not be well." She was very careful with her word choice.

"*Special condition?*" His tone conveyed all the skepticism and sarcasm that could only be warranted if he knew of Amaoke's true nature, and Aleta noticed the sardonic elevation of his eyebrow as he narrowed his eyes. His expression was amused. "Indeed."

"Father, please," she said. "If you know where he is you must tell me where I can find him." She allowed some of her authority to creep back into her tone, but in her heart, she was desperate to know that Amaoke was alright.

"I can do better than that," he told her, indicating that she should follow him. Carter came after her, and the swishing of both gowns, dark ahead, light behind, was a bit disconcerting as she maneuvered her crutches to best support legs that were threatening not to carry her while avoiding the swirling material at her feet.

66

CARTER DROVE. THE HOUSE THEY emerged from was on the grounds of Blessed Sacrament, which Aleta recognized immediately. She had been invited to a Nativity mass here by a schoolmate once. It was a lovely and forbidding place. The house was not the formal rectory; it appeared to be some sort of converted groundman's cottage.

At his urging, she preceded Father Weston through a gap in the wrought iron fence that surrounded the property, while Carter headed toward the church. He waited silently beside her at the curb, and when Carter pulled up in a white minivan, he held the front passenger door for her, waiting until she had stowed her crutches in the front footwell before climbing into the back seat.

They headed east of downtown, past the St. Louis Cemetery No.2. Traffic slowed briefly in the shadow of the Superdome, then they turned onto Galvez and into the quiet dusty neighborhoods beyond the I-10 overpass. They slowed in front of a church that was obviously shuttered, but Carter turned down the street beyond it and parked in a diagonal space across from the alley behind it.

She shut down the motor and sat quietly. She turned to Aleta and said, softly, "This is St. Constantine's. The bishop suppressed the parish last year."

None of this meant anything to Aleta, but when she climbed out of the car, she felt cold despite the relative warmth of the afternoon and was glad for her turtleneck sweater. But it wasn't just cold she was feeling; it was instinctual fear. It was the same emotion she had felt in those first moments with the Morningstar, and it persisted and deepened as they approached the church.

Father Weston seemed unperturbed, but Aleta could see that Carter was uncomfortable as well.

There was a stout chain and padlock in place on the alley door, and Father Weston took a few moments to remove them before unlocking the deadbolt and pin bolt with two separate keys. He let the women in behind him and kept the chain and padlock. Once they were all inside, he relocked the door and led them down a few shallow steps into a standard church cafeteria. The light from the small meshed window in the door didn't penetrate very far, and the corners of the room were shrouded in darkness. Aleta could feel the hairs on her arms and legs standing on end. She swallowed, trying to gather her courage, as it was apparent that the priest was not going to turn on any lights.

"Give me a moment," he murmured, disappearing to their left, where she heard a door open into an adjacent space. More cold air reached her and Carter, and it was then she knew she had not been imagining the young nun's discomfort. Carter was standing as close to Aleta as her crutches would allow.

A light briefly illuminated the area, and she could see that it was a small garage. In the space farthest from where she stood there was an ancient long sedan, black, forbidding. It was not a hearse, but might as well have been; it was like something from a dim memory, and then she had it. It reminded her of the priest's car from *The Exorcist*. She did not recall seeing a garage door when they were in the alley, but it must have been there because the floor sloped upward to ground level to allow egress. The nearer vehicle fascinated her. It looked to be a fully loaded eight-cylinder sportscar. She would have thought it black as well if it had been the only car in the garage, but next to the other automobile, she could see that it was the deepest of blues, the color of midnight. It was beautiful, a thing of vanity, and it was completely incongruous with its surroundings.

Father Weston reached beneath the rear quarter panel and retrieved a small box. It was a key keeper. She wondered if they were going to get into the car, and at that moment she realized that she wanted nothing more than to get away from it. There was something wrong with it. It felt alive, like something prescient, as though it could roar to life at any moment and she could not stop the shudder that overcame her. It passed like a wave to Carter, who threaded her arm through Aleta's. Normally, Aleta would not have permitted such solicitousness, but she realized that they both needed the comfort. Carter was apparently afraid of the car as well.

Abruptly, the priest turned off the light, and Aleta jumped when he clicked open the box to retrieve the key within. The small noise was almost too much for her nervous state.

"Come with me," he said softly, and before she could wonder how she would make her way, she realized that her eyes had adjusted enough to make him out ahead of her in the gloom.

They walked toward the front of the building, and she began to smell the incense and wax from the sanctuary, but Father Weston turned to take a short hallway and led them down a long staircase into an area that smelled of old liniment and sweat, the scents of a gymnasium. He stopped in front of a pair of double-doors and unlocked them with the key he'd retrieved from beneath the car.

Aleta's screaming brain was in overdrive. *Why are you just following along into a dark basement? How many horror movies have you seen, idiot woman?*

This reverie was interrupted by Father Weston's soft voice to her right. "Carter, please stay behind. I brought you because it isn't appropriate for me to be alone with Dr. Madison, but neither is it appropriate for you to come in here."

Aleta wasn't sure which one of them was more fortunate, herself or the nun. At least she wasn't going to be left alone again. It was small comfort.

He led her into the room, and she sensed the space open up around her. Then she realized that it smelled like a gymnasium because it *was* a gymnasium. She was standing on the parquet floor of what appeared to be two basketball courts arranged side to side. There were two windows high on the far wall, probably to the front of the church, and two more at ground level to her left. They let in scant sunlight, and she realized it was not because they were tinted, rather that they were filthy.

There were nebulous shapes along the walls, likely overflow storage for folding chairs and tables, as in any other church gym.

In roughly the center of the room there was a squarish structure, but it did not appear solid. She took a step forward and squinted into the gloom. There was a smell here, too, that reminded her of animals, zoo-like, neither pleasant nor unpleasant. As her eyes further adjusted to the lack of light, she began to better differentiate shades of gray, and she saw that it was a stout iron cage of some sort. She came to this conclusion just moments before she realized that the cage had an occupant.

She felt compelled toward it, and had almost reached the bars before the voice of the priest behind her brought her up short. "Perhaps you shouldn't get too close."

She was about to say something sharp, but then she heard a guttural growl from the cage, and she saw him. "Amaoke?"

The pitiful creature on the floor of the cage had Amaoke's silhouette but was covered from head to foot in downy white fur. It was most prominent atop his skull and along his spine, where it stood up in a longish ridge. Now that she knew what she was looking at, that white fur made him easy to see in the dimness of the room. There was something wrong about the shape of his head, and she thought he was injured until she realized that his ears were rotated and flattened along the sides of his head, exceptionally pointy, and his face was disfigured by even more prominence in the center, his nose flattened somewhat and his canines pronounced, exaggerated, much sharper than she recalled, with his lips stretched thin over them. It looked painful.

He came weakly to his feet, snarling in Weston's direction and pushing himself against the bars. It was then that she realized why she had noticed all the hair. He was wearing no clothing, and he was obviously only partly transformed, still mostly human.

"*Oh,*" she said in surprise, and turned her eyes away from him to preserve his modesty.

"Don't turn your back on him," Father Weston warned. "You're too close to the cage." When he reached for her arm again, Amaoke roared in rage. Aleta could suddenly detect a very sharp smell in the air that she hadn't noticed before. She recognized it immediately. Male musk and aggression.

"Don't touch me," Aleta spoke to the priest in the calmest voice she could muster. "How dare you keep him in a cage like this. He's not an animal!"

The eyebrow again, the silent skepticism.

"Well, he isn't," she insisted over the harsh growls that persisted even though Weston had moved away. She went directly up to the bars until she could see where the door should be. She put her back to it. "Open this."

"Bad idea."

"Open it. Immediately." Weston could see that she was a bit afraid of him, but he admired her strength.

"I can't let him out. I'm acting on *his* wishes, actually. If you'd let me explain-"

"Then let me in," Aleta interrupted.

"What do you think he will do if I open the cage?"

"You'll be lucky if he doesn't kill you. But even out here you aren't safe, and I think you know it." Then Aleta had another thought, and her eyes narrowed. "You put him in here. Why don't you want to open the door? What did you do to him?" Amaoke's breathing was louder than she liked, but at least he'd stopped growling now that she was closer to him than to the priest.

"It's complicated. Initially, I tased him," Weston admitted honestly.

"You – what?!! You *TASED* him?!!" She repeated his words in indignation.

"I thought he was a demon," he said calmly.

"You were wrong!"

"But he isn't human. I knew that. And he'd been following me and my – he'd been following Carter. And he isn't in control of himself. I shouldn't let you go in there." He looked pointedly at her, hoping to intimidate her. "Haven't you been through enough? I don't think you're equipped to deal with him after all you've recently been through." He couldn't help sounding sympathetic, and that was the final straw. She rose from her fear as a phoenix from the flames of her own ire.

"I have a palsy, Father. It does not affect my brain. I am not an idiot," she said through clenched teeth. Turning to the cage, she looked only at Amaoke's face, and added, "Amaoke, I am coming in there with you. Don't dignify this man's ignorance, please."

His tongue lolled out pitifully, but he gave a soft huff in response and moved away from the door, sinking back to the floor of the cage.

She stared Father Weston down until he complied, coming forward like a reprimanded child to unlock the door. He held it open only long enough for her to slip inside, and then closed it gently behind her, locking it immediately. And he was still too close to the bars, and to her, so Amaoke snarled bitterly, which did little for her fear. He stopped immediately, perhaps scenting her distress. Thankfully, the priest took two measured steps away from the cage, but she could see that he was genuinely concerned about her, because he would go no farther.

She lowered herself slowly to the floor, using her crutches for balance, and Amaoke immediately climbed over her protectively with his body, giving Father Weston real distress until she said, "It's a dominance display. He's protecting me from you."

"Could it be it's the other way around?"

"No. You tased *him*. You're definitely the threat," she replied. "Now go get him some pants."

Finally, she saw something she could recognize in the priest's expression. Shame. But she refused to feel guilty for talking to him that way, and in response to the enduring silence, he turned away, leaving the two of them alone.

67

"SUSPICIOUS AS EVER, MY DARLING girl!" Akenomyosei greeted her, ignoring the pages she had tossed in its direction as they landed near its feet, coming instead to embrace her. But it never got the chance, as she turned away abruptly, deliberately, determined not to betray any of her feelings. The predominant one was anger, which she could use, and the Monster would encourage, but she was racked with a stinging grief for her Collector.

"*San'ninshō*, whatever is the matter? Are you not delighted at these new developments?"

"By which you mean that I now have genetic proof of another of your experiments?" she asked, watching its reactions closely. "This is neither gift nor surprise."

"We let you have your pet, until he outlived his usefulness," Akenomyosei observed. "We don't recall being asked whether you could share the gifts of your blood with him. Besides, you were less than kind the last time you saw him."

Azuma felt a pang of grief to be reminded of that transgression, which she regretted even more now. But she refused to let this creature drink of her suffering.

"Am I not a god? Created by you to rule the Dragon Sect in preparation for some diabolical endgame? Do the gods ask permission for anything?!" In her rage, she could feel the scales of the Dragon turning over on the skin of her torso, and she ignored this, not wanting to rein it in. "Was that ever your intention then you should never have wasted your time on me. You should have kept Ietsune. At least admit this is punishment for what I did to Tatsuo, it's far more dignified. But you cannot bring yourself to speak the truth, it is only in your actions that you honor it. That's why you need Forcas. He, at least, is truthful, no matter how brutal."

"I think your 'cure' insulted him," Akenomyosei suggested. "Perhaps you should interrogate him about the fate of missing persons."

"I'm asking *you*," she said quietly, welcoming the change, letting it spread downward, her legs drawn upward as she whipped her elongating tail toward her maker, wrapping its borrowed form in the coiling mass as she pulled it relentlessly closer to her.

"You should kill me now, if you can," the Dragon hissed, blue eyes meeting those shiny, depthless orbs. "Now, and forever, you become *Teki*, enemy of this Dragon and my Sect, apart from me and all of mine, and I shall not revoke this vow even with my dying breath."

Akenomyosei's form dispersed through her limbs like smoke, accompanied by the voices of the cacophony that rang in her ears, as it told her, in that odd language, unknown but understood, "Do not give away the element of surprise. I know the secrets of all of you, better than you know yourselves."

Its departure triggered her shift back to human and she stood tall in the center of her office, and answered it, because she knew it could still hear her. "I want you to know I am coming."

68

ALETA WAITED UNTIL SHE HEARD Father Weston lock the gymnasium door before she spoke.

"Oh, Amaoke, I am so sorry."

Amaoke pushed his head against hers in answer and then proceeded to sniff the air all around her, making sure she was okay. His forced grimace deepened, and she said, "I know. I probably haven't had the best control of my bodily functions. The Morningstar paid me a visit."

He huffed again, softly, for her, and then gave a short growl of what she guessed was frustration. "Father Weston rescued me. I wasn't harmed. He kept me safe." When he seemed satisfied with her words and the truthfulness of her safety, he lay back down beside her, curling his body protectively around hers and looking to her for permission to put his head in her lap.

She nodded gently despite her wariness and stroked his face and upper arm. His fur was so soft, but she did not tell him this, rightly thinking that it was impolite. With that, she stopped petting him, because she realized that she, too, was inadvertently treating him like an animal.

She thought for several moments. She knew that something was off. He had told her that when he transformed, he looked something like an Arctic wolf, and that the Beast was also completely bestial, except for its upright, bipedal posture. This form was grotesque in a way that she felt was unnatural, unfinished, and she asked about it.

He sneezed in disgust, and again she sensed his frustration about something. It occurred to her that this state was entirely out of his control, that it was probable that he was unable to shift back into his human form. "Since he tased you?" she asked, understanding that he was unable to speak to her.

Amaoke nodded. He rocked his body forward and shook his head, and then backward, and again made that small headshake.

"You're stuck, can't change into a wolf, or back into a man?" She correctly interpreted. "How awful. How long have you been here?"

He lifted a hand twisted into a claw-like appendage, the fingers shortened, curled, and locked into position, and brushed one, two, three, four, five of the bars in sequence, then shrugged. Aleta assumed this meant five days that he could remember, possibly longer.

"I need to get you out of here," she said softly, horrified that he had been here, alone, unable to change, locked in a cage. It had to be his worst nightmare come true. But he merely shook his head slowly and put his head back down onto her lap, and curling his body around hers, went to sleep.

Although it was rather cool in the basement, Amaoke was warm, and she was surprised to find that while she was not very comfortable on the hard floor, she once again felt safe, in a way she hadn't since he'd left her office on Christmas Eve. While she took what comfort she could from that thought, it also terrified her, because she could not afford to believe that she was in love. It did not occur to her that Carter and Father Weston's plight was very like her own because the sympathy that she could spare them she could not spare herself.

The warmth, and the rhythmic breathing of her sleeping charge lulled her, and Aleta dozed where she sat. When she opened her eyes, she realized that it was because she heard Father Weston's key in the lock, and the darkness of the room had deepened as afternoon gave way to evening.

She cast about for her crutches, hoping to extricate herself from Amaoke's embrace without disturbing him, but realized that he was awake and likely had been so for a while. He shifted away from her so that she could stand, and she moved to the front of the cage to await the priest.

He materialized from the shadows just beyond the bars, and she saw that he carried only the key in his hand. He had changed his clothes, or perhaps just abandoned the cassock, keeping dark pants and a simple black dress shirt with his white collar in place. His hair was slightly unruly, as if he'd been pushing his hands through it, and it stood up in places. She examined him closely, still unable to trust her eyes where he was concerned – would she ever be able to? He looked human, and wore an expression of both weariness and concern.

"Are you ready for a break?" he asked her, but she had already planned her answer.

"We're both coming out," she said firmly, and was almost surprised at how convincing she sounded.

The priest sighed audibly but said nothing as he unlocked the cage. She wondered if he was deferring to her out of a wish to avoid conflict. Amaoke, for his part, had taken up that low steady growl again, but he did not follow her when she left the confines of what she had believed to be his prison.

"Amaoke?" she queried, encouraging him to follow, but while he refused to turn away, he also refused to come out.

"Come on, Brother," the priest said to Amaoke, surprising Aleta utterly. "A shower will do you some good."

She was shocked when Amaoke responded, slinking out of the cage, half walking, half balanced on his hands. He never stopped growling, but allowed Weston to support his weight enough so that he was able to walk upright, and Aleta could see that his heels were pulled up off the ground by his partial transformation, an *equinus* contracture brought on by the arrested change. Oddly, the two men were exactly the same height, to the centimeter if she was not mistaken.

As they turned to lead the way out of the gym, she was struck again by the uncanny similarities in their posture and gait, despite the differences in their physiques. One had the musculature of a gladiator, the other the lean strength of a marathoner.

Amaoke's growl persisted, at a low register, and Aleta strained to hear, but caught the priest's soft words when they were on the stairs. "Cut me a break, will you? I *know* she's yours, man. I get it." She thought she heard a hint of amusement in his tone, and he gave a small chuckle when Amaoke stopped growling, only for a moment, before starting up again this persistent protest.

At the top of the stairs, instead of turning toward the back of the building, Weston turned right and continued up another flight to the floor above. There was a door open at the end of a short landing, and Aleta could see into a small alcove that had been turned into an office, the shaded desk lamp illuminating the landing and the short hallway beyond. She realized that this was the rectory, and as they entered, she understood why the other place had seemed so spartan. This was the priest's true home.

The rooms smelled of cotton and paper, and it was a scent reminiscent of the library of her childhood, layered with faint incense, bread, pepper, and wine. There were bookshelves lining the walls, loaded with books and religious artifacts. More books were stacked on nearly every free surface, but the place was otherwise orderly, clean, and warm. There was a fireplace, a more than functional kitchen, and surprisingly large, loft-like windows that faced the alley but afforded a view of the twilight city in the near distance.

Carter was seated in a comfortable armchair between the windows, and she stood up when the group came in, taking Aleta by the arm and gently redirecting her to the kitchen. Amaoke and Weston continued, the former ignoring the nun entirely, and the latter merely nodding gently in her direction without stopping.

"Would you like tea?" Carter asked, as if they were old friends, and Aleta were merely a visiting houseguest. Aleta suspected that it was best to go along with it. For now.

"I'd love some," she accepted, not a little surprised to find that tea sounded wonderful.

"Any preference?" Carter asked. She pulled out a wooden box filled with teas that were likely to be forbidden luxuries in the Church's view and gave a small shrug.

Aleta smiled, and chose something without really looking at it, and they sat down together at the reclaimed farm table that occupied the center of the kitchen.

Weston returned sooner than she expected, and her expression must have conveyed all her many questions. He sat down with them and accepted the tea Carter offered him with grateful – loving? – eyes, their fingers touching for a heartbeat longer than decorum might dictate, before turning his attention to Aleta.

He paused a moment, removed his glasses, and setting them aside on the table, leaned back, stretching powerful arms up toward the ceiling before running his hands through his wavy hair. Aleta surmised that it was this habit that made it so unruly. He was ridiculously handsome, and she noticed that he was still very, very young. He trained deep brown eyes on her that were not so very young, and said, "I only have a few minutes. I'll let him warm up in the water, but his hands are still useless. I will have to go back in and help him wash."

While Aleta struggled with her astonishment, he continued, "You see, he has forgiven me for the Taser."

"But he – why the growling?" she stammered, unable to think of anything else to say.

Weston sighed. "You're his lady. You were right that he finds me a threat, just not for the reason you thought. I'm too close to you for his comfort."

Aleta managed to hold his gaze, barely, but could not control the flush that came immediately to her face. "I'm not, I mean we – he – we aren't a couple."

"It's possible that Amaoke the man hasn't claimed you, but the wolf apparently sees things otherwise," he told her gently, his tone attempting, and failing, to undo the awkwardness of the subject. "For the same reason he ignored Carter a moment ago. He is avoiding a challenge. Likely, it's all instinctual, not something conscious at this point."

"Like some sort of dominance issue?" she asked.

"More like a marking issue, I think, based on what I've read," he replied.

"Marking? Like marking territory? And what do you mean, *at this point?*" she asked.

"Well, I don't think it is what you are thinking," he began. "Dominant wolves mark their females by mating with them." At this, she could no longer maintain eye contact and her face felt as though it were on fire. This was not a conversation she would have with her sister, much less this unknown priest. "And if the two of you are not a couple, the wolf in him might be concerned that I could…well…" He cleared his throat and reached to place his hand gently over hers, taking a liberty, but at the last moment his face betrayed a small frown and he pulled away from her, clearly uncomfortable. He was quiet, and that wrinkle had returned to his forehead. "I promise I will tell you everything, but I need to go help him finish up."

Weston started to stand up, but she held out a hand, making a gesture to make him wait a moment more, and said, "I never thanked you for – for before, for saving my life." He nodded and gave her a small sad smile that told her more than she wanted to know; he knew that he may have only delayed her fate, not prevented any ultimate outcome.

Then he excused himself from the table, leaving his tea untouched, and disappeared into the back rooms of the apartment. Aleta looked to Carter, but the nun was pointedly peering into the depths of her own tea, her countenance as pink as Aleta's. Aleta couldn't be sure, but she suspected that it was as much due to the subject matter of the discussion as her own feelings.   "Weston has stayed with him since it happened," she said softly, finally looking up at Aleta. "I think he feels guilty about his mistake, but in the beginning, there was real danger. I know that over the last few days, things have improved."

"Do you know what happened?" Aleta asked, trying not to sound confrontational.

"I do now. It's part of our work. But he told me to stay away. He handled this alone," Carter admitted. "Today is the first day I have been here. He finally told me the details this afternoon, after we brought you here."

"Can you tell me what you know?" Aleta asked her, anticipating the negative response but unable to keep herself from asking.

"It isn't for me to explain. I don't want to confuse the facts, anyway." Carter shook her head. "But I know that the decision to send Weston to your office was mutually agreed upon by the two of them. I was summoned when he had to bring you back to Blessed Sacrament. I don't think he anticipated that."

69

ALETA EAGERLY AWAITED THE RETURN of both men, and she could hear Weston's muffled voice once the sounds of the shower ended. Her expression must have betrayed her disappointment when Weston alone returned to them.

"I think he's still pretty wrecked," he said, and then amended himself. "Exhausted, I mean. He went straight from the shower to the bedroom floor and fell asleep. I think today was pretty stressful, even though it was good for him."

Aleta pushed herself up and headed toward the back room, needing to reassure herself that Amaoke was well. Weston moved aside to let her pass, and when Carter stood up, too, he gestured for her to wait. When he was satisfied that she understood, he turned to follow Aleta, unsurprised at her need to see Amaoke for herself.

Aleta found the room easily enough, off the short corridor to the priest's sleeping quarters. The residence had four small bedrooms off an arched hallway that ended in a bathroom, room for assigned and visiting clergymen. Three were obviously unused, and she discovered Amaoke asleep on the floor in the second room to the left, curled on his left side. The room's windows faced the alley.

While incongruous with his arrested state, she was relieved to see that he wore black warmup pants and a simple white t-shirt that must have been borrowed items of Weston's clothing. Other than the minor rhythmic twitching of his legs and those muddied features, he appeared comfortable.

"This is the easiest rest I have seen him take," Weston's voice came from the doorway behind her.

"May I?" Aleta turned to face him and indicated the bed.

"Please," he gestured warmly, inviting her to sit wherever she liked.

She sat shyly on the end of the bed, and glanced over her shoulder every so often to assure herself that Amaoke was still doing alright, so Weston took the chair near the nightstand and tried to appear relaxed. He could tell she was unsure and still a bit fearful, and suspected that she might still be in a bit of shock from the events of the last two days.

"Is there anyone we should call and let them know…?" he inquired, wanting to get the preliminaries out of the way before he got to her many questions.

"I don't – that is, I live alone, so I'm not expected anywhere," she sighed inadvertently, and he was surprised at the unexpected vulnerability of her tone. When she realized what she might have betrayed, she added, "I have some family in the area. My sister and I touch base every few days, my parents about as frequently. It isn't time for anyone to be worried yet."

He nodded, feeling better.

When he didn't say more, she prompted, in a tone much gentler than before, "You tased him, and…?"

Weston smiled, and Aleta could tell by its lopsided charm that he was letting down his guard. She sensed that perhaps he too was exhausted.

"And as soon as I did, his reaction told me he was not what I assumed he was. Then I touched him, and I knew everything he was feeling – "

"Wait – what do you mean you knew everything he was feeling?" she asked, narrowing her eyes skeptically.

"I know. It sounds crazy," he admitted. "I have always been a bit of an empath, you know, I am sensitive to the emotions of others.

As I've gotten older, I just thought it was a natural extension of my vocation. After my ordination, it seemed to develop further. It always helped me with parishioners.

"But with him, probably because of his *condition*." Here he gave her a pointed look, and she could see it was an attempt at levity. "Well, I can *feel* what he is feeling. It's not exact – I get more of a gestalt about what he's on about in any given moment – but it's like we can communicate through touch.

"He was really out of it, and for a moment there, I thought he was overly sensitive to the electricity – I keep it pretty cranked – but he is a big dude." Weston stopped, realizing he was rambling a bit in the distress of the memory. "Anyway, his heart stopped for a second, and it seemed like he was dreaming or something, but then he was back with me, but he'd passed out. And his form was shifting, there were hairs popping up all over him, and it was like his muscles were moving under my hands, and he started to twitch, and I couldn't hold him.

"I had a pretty good idea from his feelings and what I was getting from him what was happening, just saw the wolf in my mind. But I had to restrain him. Thankfully, he was out long enough that I could get him here.

"I could sense when he was starting to awaken, and all I got was rage. It took all my strength to get him from the car and down to the cage. We almost didn't make it." Weston saw the furious expression blooming on Aleta's fine features, so he stopped talking and unbuttoned the cuffs of his shirt, rolling back the sleeves so that she could see the healing scratches and bites that marked them. He pulled his collar tab and unbuttoned enough for her to see the deep gouges on his upper chest and the side of his neck. She shivered.

"Exactly. I don't want to think what could have happened if I hadn't been able to secure him. His emotional range was flat, homicidal. And his change was more advanced than he is now; he was almost a wolf. He won't recall all of it, but over the past several days, he *has* become more human, but it is slow, and I doubt he has any control. I still don't completely understand the effect on him, but without being able to talk to him…" Weston shrugged.

"His emotions have become more elaborate as he shifts back, but I could feel that he was averse to my letting him out of the cage," he explained. "It was as though he were advising me against it.

"Do I want to know why you just happen to have a *cage* in the church basement?" Aleta couldn't help herself.

"Probably a story for another time," Weston suggested, and then attempted to get them back on subject. "Two days ago, no, maybe even the night before you were visited, he was so distressed and restless that I dared to reach through the bars and touch him — something about direct contact clarifies his feelings from general to specific. He'd been dreaming, and he growled the whole time but let me near him, and I knew it was the Morningstar, and I just got a sense of you, although it wasn't entirely clear. I had discovered your business card in his ruined clothing, so I said your name and he went berserk. He didn't calm in any discernable way until I promised I was going to find you.

"I actually called your office to try to locate you. They were closing for the weekend, and wouldn't tell me more than you were out. They put me through to your call service, but you were not the call physician, so they transferred me to Psychiatry, and the ward clerk told me you had been rounding — sorry, I'm all over the place here. I finally trusted his instincts and drove over to the hospital. Then *my* instincts took over, and I knew the Monster was there. He can't hide from me," Weston's voice dropped to a whisper for the final sentence, and Aleta thought absently that he probably didn't even recognize he was doing it. She also realized she was trembling with fear as he gestured to himself, acknowledging the resemblance but not explaining further. "I almost got lost deciphering the campus directory and then had a moment's difficulty with your security door."

She could sense the frustration in his tone, the distress he must have felt. He didn't continue, didn't need to force her to relive the terror of the actual encounter.

At that moment, a soft growl came from behind the bed.

"That's enough for tonight. Can I get you anything?" Weston asked, moving to the door and extending the distance between them.

Aleta shook her head tearfully, not really wanting him to leave, but knowing somehow that Amaoke needed her trust. She pushed off the edge of the bed with her hands, letting her crutches slide to the floor with a muted clatter as she curled up atop the bedspread. The tears came then, silently, when Weston had retreated fully, and she was wracked with shakes so violent she feared they could be heard. She started in fright and could not help cringing away when she felt the mattress shift as Amaoke slowly climbed up next to her.

He did not make a sound, only turned around slowly, pressing his warmth and bulk reassuringly against her back, placing himself between her and the door. With his vigil over her ensured, he went back to sleep, his rhythmic breathing a ragged lullaby. A very, very long time later, Aleta surrendered to her own exhaustion.

70

IN THE MORNING, SOME OF Aleta's fortitude and equilibrium had returned. She was awake long before the sun, and though she was initially confused about where she was, by the time her mind told her it was Monday, she knew she was in the rectory at Constantine's. Amaoke was no longer beside her, and she looked around briefly, but the room was quiet and empty.

She used the bathroom at the end of the hallway, and splashed cold water on her face. She studied herself in the mirror, and other than looking like she hadn't showered or changed her clothes in three days, she didn't see anything new there. Thus, reassured that she was still mostly intact, and knowing she had patients to care for, she took the hallway back toward the main living space.

It, too, was empty and quiet. She backtracked down the hallway briefly to check the other bedrooms, but no one was about. When she returned to the front hall, a glance into the kitchen gave her tremendous relief. Her lab coat, which had her cell phone, was hanging over the back of one of the chairs. She had been certain she had left it behind at Our Lady but perhaps it had been retrieved on her behalf.

She put it on, since it was easier than trying to carry it while maneuvering in an unfamiliar place with her crutches, hailed an Uber using the app, and let herself out of the apartment. She went down the darkened stairs, noted she was still feeling jumpy when one of them creaked in protest, and retraced the path they had taken to reach the back doors. But when she went up the short flight of steps to the alley, the door was locked.

She hadn't anticipated this obstacle, but remembered the garage off to her right. Reluctantly, feeling her way into the corner, she found the door, and pulled it open. There was weak moonlight filtering through the cross-hatched panes of a side door inset next to the roller doors. She stepped into the garage and turned to close the door to the kitchen. As soon as it closed behind her she heard it lock.

She paused, then shook her head, supposing that it made sense that an exit door would always be accessible as an egress but locked from the exterior. She placed her crutches carefully as she made her way along the narrow space beside the rear panel of the sportscar, feeling her way in the dark, but when the back of her forearm brushed the metal, she recoiled in horror. The car felt *alive*.

Aleta took a deep breath, trying not to panic, but her entire rational life was squarely behind her now. "C'mon, Madison, it's a car, only a *car*, pull yourself together," she muttered softly. She reached out deliberately, and placed her open palm on the trunk lid.

The smooth finish felt like flesh, and she was overcome by the most violent vertigo she had ever experienced. The entire room was moving, no reference point to focus upon, and it made her feel ill. She distinctly felt that her touch was causing a disturbance, because the entire vehicle started to shudder and shake. Worst was the shrieking sound of distressed metal, and then the screams, the voices were all around her, within her, and when they spoke she understood, though the language was unknown to her.

Daughter, sister, doctor, friend
You shall free us in the end
Let us in and let us out
Us within You without
See us here and set us free
Free to feed and free to be

Like a mantra, hypnotic and strange, they implored her, but she was unable to move and unable to answer.

Pureflesh pureflesh come and play
You shall join us yet today
You shall fly and we shall flee
Free to feed and free to be
Should you give to us your bones
We shall make this earth our home

The door to the church flew open behind her, and Weston was at her side. "Put your other hand on the car!" he shouted, and he placed his own hands on the car, and it shuddered and shrieked ever more violently, the voices swarming around them both.

She heard his strong voice, strident and clear through the din, "*You are children of the Lord, your God, and shall not gash yourselves nor cut a forelock for the dead. For you are a people sacred to the Lord, your God, who hath chosen you from all the nations to be a people peculiarly His own.*"

The moment her other hand encountered the metal, the cacophony disappeared, as utterly and completely as if it had been sucked into the vacuum of space. The silence felt like a blanket coming down upon them, and Weston's head dropped forward in relief, his long hair a deeper shadow obscuring the paleness of his face for a moment. He reached behind himself for the light switch and turned on the over-bright fluorescents, one of the bulbs buzzing like an angry wasp.

They gazed at each other in surprise and disbelief, both breathless and trembling. His eyes blinked, owl-like behind those spectacles, as they adjusted to the light.

"Deuteronomy?" she asked softly.

"The very same," he nodded. "What are you doing?"

"I – I was trying to get out without disturbing anyone. I have to go to work."

"I don't suppose you'll reconsider," Weston suggested with a wry smile.

"I'm on call. I have appointments. I need a shower." Aleta's voice shook as she recited the day she faced as if she were clinging to the known. He knew she was purposely avoiding asking about what they had just encountered, a masterful shutdown and display of emotional fortitude.

"I can make tea. I can call Carter, and we can give you a ride. I don't think you should be alone," he said gently, already knowing she would refuse.

She started to say something when her phone pinged softly from her pocket. She squared her shoulders and shook her head. "That will be my Uber. I'm sorry, Father, but right now I am not associating safety with your company."

71

ALETA DIRECTED THE UBER DRIVER to drop her at her office. It was still early, but she knew she could shower and change in the fitness center at the hospital.

She dropped in at the clinic to grab a go bag that she kept around for the occasions when she had time for a workout, turning on every light in the place as she made her way back to her office. The door was open, and the lights came on as always when she crossed the threshold, but she couldn't stop flinching away from that chair even though it was empty now.

Calling on stubbornness and false bravado she turned her back on the room to collect her things. She saw the mail she had dropped placed neatly on the corner of her desk and smiled. She thanked God for Weston and then put on her game face.

It lasted only until she stepped into the shower. Her nakedness made her vulnerable, and the shower room was empty at this hour; the die-hard fitness freaks and the surgeons had not yet arrived. The water echoed on the tiles, and she had difficulty determining which of the noises she heard were from her own movements. Her mind would not let her believe she was alone, and she kept peering out of the shower stall to reassure herself. She dropped the shampoo three times before she gave it up. She did the necessaries, and then got dressed.

A glance at her watch showed her it was too early to round. The patients on the behavioral wards would still be sleeping. She went back over to the clinic in the predawn dark, and realized that she hadn't even asked Weston about Amaoke. And where, exactly, had the priest come from?

The front office staff was starting to arrive when she reached the back door, and she exchanged absentminded greetings with them before making her way back to her office. She lost herself in the completion of medical records, dictated an addendum to a consult, and was just about to return to the hospital for rounds when there was a soft knock at the door. She looked up to see her sister, Alaina, carrying a simple arrangement of hothouse lilacs in a jar. She let herself in and placed it on Aleta's desk with an unreadable expression.

Aleta, for her part, was gobsmacked. Alaina was like one of those expensive supermodels who never graced anyone's presence before noon. It was surprising for a botanist to not be an early riser, but she had made it work. Despite keeping the hours of a club denizen, she and Aleta had had the same work ethic instilled by strict and loving parents, and her dedication had ensured her success.

Aleta's athletically gifted older sister sprawled her lanky frame across the couch, bouncing a bit because she knew it was irksome. "Baby sister, who the *hell* is Father Weston? You did something, didn't you? Confessed some outrageous sin?" Alaina spoke the last question in the same tone she used to use when they were kids and she wanted Aleta to believe she was in trouble with Mom and Dad. *You're gonna get it now.*

Aleta couldn't suppress her laugh. "Blasphemy, sister," she said, and both sisters crossed themselves in synchrony, Aleta touching her necklace before kissing her fingers, and her sister grasping the small gold crucifix that rested in the hollow of her neck before doing the same. An old ritual. Only Alaina could swear and invoke the name of a priest in the same sentence.

But something was bothering Alaina, because her hand returned subconsciously to the crucifix. Unlike Aleta, who had always been a bit afraid of that version of Jesus, Alaina's crucifix was ornately detailed. Both necklaces had been gifts from their parents at First

Communion, Aleta's Mobius loop signifying God as Alpha and Omega, since Christ-on-the-Cross had made her cry since she was very small.

"So, what's up? Papa Westie was in quite the twist. The sun isn't even up, and he kept calling and calling."

"I'm surprised you're awake," Aleta told her, trying to keep her tone light, sure that the sordid details of the weekend remained unknown to her sister, based on her breezy attitude.

"Had to get up to answer the phone," Alaina said sourly. "Lucky for him, Mom wants more of these lilacs for her prayer breakfast, so it's probably just as well. Got me going."

"I do know him. I was talking to him about what happened to me last year." It was as close to the truth as Aleta dared to get.

"He is worried enough that he reached out to me. Isn't that a breach of confidentiality?"

"Only if he tells you what I confessed," Aleta pointed out, wondering how Weston knew she had a sister, then recalling that she had told him about her. She also puzzled about how he had obtained her contact information but was unwilling to dwell on it for long. "What did he say?"

"Darn. You're so buttoned up all the time that I bet your sins are really juicy," Alaina lamented, but when she saw her sister's censuring look, she relented. "He said he felt you were under a great deal of stress. He didn't want you to be alone. He asked me if I thought you would let me stay with you for a while."

Aleta was ready to say it was out of the question, but she thought about her abbreviated shower and surrendered. "It might be nice to have company for a few days."

It was Alaina's turn to be shocked, but she mastered it quickly and bounced up off the couch, saying, in a breathy, dramatic voice, "Okay, Al, I will sacrifice my social calendar for your needs. Slumber party!"

Like the whirlwind she was, she crossed the room in three steps, placed a quick rough kiss on top of Aleta's head, and was out the door before Aleta could open her mouth to respond.

72

WHEN AMAOKE AWAKENED, HE WAS fully human, lying on the bed next to Aleta. He was surprised, but everything about being there with her, like that, felt wrong. Well, almost everything.

He'd found a pair of well-worn grey Converse sneakers in Weston's room and slipped them on, smiling. They fit well. He put his head back in the room to confirm that Aleta was still sleeping peacefully, and thinking that she was as safe as she could be here in the church, he went downstairs.

Weston was asleep in the chair in the church office downstairs, his Bible open under the lamp, and some hastily scribbled notes under his head. He looked very young; his glasses had been set aside, and his face was childlike in sleep. Amaoke was glad; he knew the poor priest did not rest easy nor for long.

He left through the Judas door in the garage, tasting the sweetness of the night air in his lungs and on his skin, relieved to have completed a shift in one direction or the other. He suspected it was the effect of Aleta's nearness. Knowing she was safe and seeing it with his own eyes calmed him.

He'd been so happy to be fully upright on two human legs that he decided to take a walk. Weston's warmups were surprisingly comfortable, but he questioned the cuff on the pants; it made them ride up slightly on his ankles which could not have been a good look. Odd for a guy anyway. It was, however, better than nothing at all.

The moon was down, but he could feel it, and he headed toward the I-10 overpass in the near distance, intending to loop back after a few short blocks, but the air felt good, just being out of the church, out of the trap of an arrested transformation. Before he knew it he was downtown, past the stadium, and the city was waking up around him. Newspaper trucks roared by, carrying papers for all the corner convenience stores, and the ubiquitous coffee bars were waking up to today's brewing wars.

By the time he'd returned to the church, Aleta had gone. Weston reassured him that she had seemed herself, and relayed the story of the encounter in the garage.

"They *spoke* to her?" Amaoke wasn't sure whether to be amazed or concerned. In the end, he was a bit of both. "Where is she now?"

"She went to work. I sent her sister to check on her, and asked her to make sure she wouldn't be alone," Weston said, and seeing Amaoke's look, he added, "Dude, I can't invite myself into her house, and I didn't know what kind of condition you'd be in."

It was still endlessly amusing to Amaoke to hear this priest using Millennial-speak, but he ignored that for the moment. "What about Carter? At least she is more equipped for the worst of them, and more appropriate."

"I can't override the rules that govern Carter's status without jeopardizing my already tenuous standing with the Mother Superior. She is a novice. It is the one thing that guarantees her safety and allows her to assist me with my work. The Catholic Church is serious about its nuns." There was a note of bitterness in Weston's voice that Amaoke hadn't heard before. "We can go over to the hospital if you want to."

Amaoke shook his head. "If she said what you told me she said, she is afraid of you. She's pretty tough. She needs her independence, it helps her feel less afraid. Let's wait and check in with her this evening."

"That's casual. After she made arrangements to have her sister stay there?" Weston's eyebrow twitched sardonically.

"I didn't say show up," Amaoke laughed outright. "Okay, you're right. That *is* what I meant. But a phone call would do it."

They walked to a local diner four blocks away and Amaoke felt as though he could eat his weight in fried food and wondered how Weston could stop after two buckwheat pancakes and a glass of orange juice. He wanted to go home, but he knew Weston was still vigilant about his condition, so after breakfast he walked back to the church. He was surprised to find he was exhausted, and fell asleep easily on the couch in the upstairs apartment, not dreaming.

When he awoke, the late afternoon sun was setting, the last rays of sunlight hitting the buildings downtown, winking off the cars on the overpass. He found Weston dismantling the cage down in the gymnasium. He liked Weston a great deal, finding that the two of them spent a great deal of their time in companionable silence, not needing to talk. The priest's presence was calming to him.

Together, they struck the walls, separating the sections from the floor anchors. Amaoke helped move the heavy segments and store them, concealing the components among the accordioned bleachers and folding chairs, then the two of them swept and mopped the space. The space seemed less dreary with all the lights on in the early evening, as though it hadn't just held a supernatural prisoner and was ready for a youth group to play a few pick-up games.

Weston grabbed a long pole with a hook that he passed to Amaoke, saying, "Let's open those transoms for a bit, air this space out."

They used the hook to turn the latches on the small windows that opened at ground level, and as soon as they were open, a foul and recognizable stench reached Amaoke's nose. The Ungalek, Death-Bringer. And at the same time he noticed it, he saw Weston visibly tense, listening for something. Amaoke strained to hear as well but could detect nothing. The scent signature persisted, and it was unmistakable.

"I assume you know who that is," Amaoke said softly.

"Bad news," Weston confirmed it.

"Is he here for me?"

"Probably not." The young priest reflected for a moment. "I don't know. Those are his friends trapped in the car. I've been expecting him. I don't think the usual approach works with him."

"You want my help?" Amaoke asked, thinking it was not ideal that they were stuck in the basement.

"I'm not convinced he can get into the church," Weston said doubtfully, as though he could not convince himself. He was still studying the ceiling intently, still listening. "I mean, of course, I'd love your help, but I'm thinking, what if he is just here to create a diversion while our worse friend pays another visit where it isn't wanted? I can handle him, and he knows it."

Amaoke just stared at him in disbelief, but it was plausible. It was disturbing enough that he looked like the Morningstar. Apparently he thought like the Morningstar, too.

"Let's get you out, at least," Weston said. "I did feel like she was a little disappointed when I showed up the last time."

"Because you're not me?" Amaoke grinned as he made the joke, but did not like the idea of leaving him alone with Forcas. It couldn't be helped.

"Watch that pride, my friend," Weston responded. "I can give you a hand up to the window."

Amaoke looked at the opening skeptically. "My shoulders would never clear it. But if you crouch, the wolf can push off your back."

"Can you complete the change? And how much do you weigh?" Weston looked worried on both counts.

"Really? Less than you, wolf *and* man. I haven't exactly been gaining weight in here," Amaoke said.

"That breakfast was pretty robust," Weston said in mock defense.

But there was no more time for talk. Amaoke stripped off the borrowed clothing, which seemed to amuse Weston even more, and when he called the wolf, it came, with all its grace and fury.

73

IN HIS FOUR-LEGGED FORM he slithered easily through the transom and out of the basement. He didn't bother to look back, and the scent of the Death-Bringer faded as he left the neighborhood. On a rainy, moonless night, he had little to worry about what people did or didn't see, and in the Crescent City there were always much more fantastical beings walking the streets than he.

The pavement was damp from a persistent drizzle, and as he ran desperately along the route to Aleta's house, the rain came in earnest, drenching the streets and reflecting the traffic and automobile lights off the wet streets. Once he left behind the crowds of the Quarter, he hurtled himself along at more dangerous speeds than caution would have normally allowed, but he didn't care who saw him. He imagined, again, that by the time reports of a stray dog, no matter how unusual, reached the authorities, he would be long gone from the area in question.

He followed Canal Street to the Greenwood Cemetery, and then made his way west on City Park Drive past the country club. He then turned northward on Bellaire, worried about all the spirit activity in the enormous Metairie Cemetery that was now too close to where Aleta lived for his comfort. He took the slight jog in the road as it crossed the railroad track confluence and sprinted for the cross street at Country Club Drive. He saw a break in the traffic and jumped out into the gap, unable to see the midnight blue Jaguar that gunned through the intersection until it was far too late to change course.

His eyes registered the brightness of the impossibly close headlamps just before he was hit squarely by the broad front grille and the wolf's body was immediately flung forward, tumbling several feet in the air before hitting the pavement with a yelp and sliding a few yards before coming to rest. A bubbling whine was all he could manage, and he was bleeding and broken, but he had to get out of the street before he was hit again. He managed to crawl to the edge of the roadway, where he was forced to stop. Breathing and moving were more painful than anything he had suffered in recent memory, and he had a peaceful moment where a groggy daze let him forget he wasn't going to die and escape this agony. He sprawled awkwardly in the gutter, putting his head on the curb, and the rainwater ran under and around his battered body.

Then he remembered Aleta, and slowly he lifted his head and practically dragged himself those last agonizing three blocks, the darkness descending over his vision, listening to himself wheeze around the unbearable pain in his torso, smelling his own blood and wet mangled fur. He managed to make it around the side of her house, and onto the patio, and only when he was satisfied that there were no inhuman scents nearby did he allow himself to surrender to the darkness that was pulling him down and down into nothingness.

He was returned to a hazy half-consciousness by a horrified shrieking, and then he heard hurried footsteps going away and then a voice, shouting, it seemed, calling for Aleta, and did she know there was a bleeding, naked man on the patio? He would have appreciated the irony if he wasn't in such distress.

More footsteps returned, and he smelled her spicy scent, and heard her exclamations of horror, before he felt her warm hands on his neck and his chest. He knew he shouldn't open his eyes, but he couldn't resist, and there she was, beautiful as ever, with her sister, who he recognized from his secret visits of the year before, standing beside her in obvious distress.

"Alaina, get me a clean cloth, and some towels. And bring the comforter from the bed," she instructed her sister briskly, wisely assigning a task to distract her from hysteria and removing her from hearing range.

"Amaoke, what happened to you?" she asked, leaning over him and placing a hand gently on his head. "Don't talk yet, I think you might have a punctured lung. I should call 911." She started to reach for her crutches and rise, but he caught the sleeve of her sweater in one desperate hand.

"No," he tried to protest, but only a wheeze came out and he couldn't catch his breath, so he tried to shake his head and the pain was excruciating, and it felt like some of his limbs were not working very well, so then he lay still, hoping she would understand the importance of keeping him out of the hospital. If he was supposed to die, so be it, he was ready, but heroic measures in the trauma unit at the hospital would raise more questions than answers, and otherwise he was going to heal, his preternatural regenerative abilities were already at work.

Alaina returned with the blanket and the towels, and Aleta instructed her to spread the comforter out on the patio next to Amaoke. "Help me get him onto the blanket, A," she said, but he knew that even together they would be unable to move him, so using his good arm he dragged himself slowly onto it, having the idea that she was going to use it to move him.

He was pleased by her cleverness, and once he was settled after several minutes of struggle, Aleta covered him gently with the towels, which both helped with the cold and covered his nakedness, which did not seem to bother her at all but was causing her sister no end of distress. Then she picked up the end of the blanket nearest his head, by wrapping one of the two corners around each hand before balancing her weight on her crutches and then motioning to her sister to take the end by his feet, and the two of them slowly and painstakingly dragged him across the patio and up over the small threshold into the kitchen, careful not to jar or shift him too much.

"He smells like a wet dog," Alaina observed, wrinkling her nose.

"A!" Aleta scolded, "He can hear you!"

"I'm sorry, Al, but it's true," Alaina persisted, and then added in a whisper, even though she could see he was awake and listening, "And why is he naked?!"

Amaoke could have fully appreciated the humor in the situation had he not been in so much pain.

"A, now that we've got him inside, why don't you go home," Aleta suggested. "I will take care of this and call you tomorrow."

Alaina looked as if she would like nothing better, but there was a shadow of doubt on her face, as if she was reluctant to leave her sister alone with a strange naked bleeding man. Her protective instincts toward her sister made him like her immensely. She said, "If he is…stable, could I just have a word with you?" Then she grabbed Aleta's arm and all but dragged her into another room, which would have been out of earshot if Amaoke had been human.

As was his custom, he tried not to eavesdrop out of a sense of politeness, but he caught a few words here and there. The gist of the conversation was that sister one did not want sister two alone with a maniac in the middle of the night. He caught the word boyfriend but couldn't decipher the rest of the sentence, but he could smell suspicion and fear. Then Aleta's voice murmuring something reassuring and bland, and something about what happened in Japan, but he wasn't sure he heard that part correctly. A few other words were exchanged, and he could smell a mingling of their scents which meant they were probably embracing, and then a heavy door opening and closing. Then he heard movement heading away toward the other end of the house, and finally the sound of Aleta's footsteps approaching once more.

That gentle hand was back on his head as she kneeled next to him, putting her crutches on the floor. She didn't speak, but tenderly removed the towels from his body and surveyed the damage. "Oh, Amaoke, I don't know if -" she finally began, but then abruptly curtailed her statement with a look of determination.

She took a cloth and warm water and cleaned his skin, then placed a thick dressing on the right side of his chest, which was looking slightly bashed in and placed heavy tape over three sides of it, pushing a long strip of gauze into the wound underneath, like a wick. It made him cry out, but his chest felt better as fluid drained out. Then she wrapped his torso loosely and ignoring his protests of pain, rolled him up onto the injured side so the wound could drain, propping him at an angle on some pillows. She treated the minor cuts on his hands and face, and put butterfly tape over a gash on his right thigh after irrigating it thoroughly and dousing it with an antiseptic that burned when she applied it, causing him to cry out a bit. He hadn't wanted her to know how much he was hurting, but when she was done, he was already breathing better.

She checked his pulse regularly and was paying close attention to his breathing. After a couple hours she seemed satisfied, and she brought him some water in a cup with a straw. He drank it down gratefully, desperately needing to sleep, and smelling her fatigue as well.

"What happened to you?" she finally asked, setting the cup down and sitting beside him on the floor.

"Car," he explained, knowing she would understand that he'd been hit.

"But these injuries!" she protested, looking unsure of what to say next. "They aren't quite right for a pedestrian…unless…" Understanding dawned in her eyes, and he could see that she had figured out that the wolf had been hit, not the man. Smart girl. Then she remembered herself, and asked, "Can I get you something to eat?"

"Later," he told her, completely sure that his stomach was not ready for food and knowing that it was nearing the middle of the night. "I need sleep. You do too."

She raised her eyebrows in surprise that he was thinking about her welfare in his state, but she nodded. She brought another pillow for his head, and pulled a soft blanket from the back of one of her living room couches and settled it over him, before settling down on that very couch and closing her eyes.

When the rhythm of her breathing told him she was asleep, he slept too.

74

WHEN HE WOKE AGAIN, LATE morning sunshine was streaming into the kitchen, and he was still in terrible shape, but already improving. He looked around and saw that a cordless phone was next to his head, along with a short note in neat, precise script.

Out on a short errand, call right away with any problem. 504.929.2992. A.

When Aleta returned, she brought with her some of his clothing from the carriage house, along with his few toiletries.

"I called your landlady this morning; I feel like I know her since I have left so many messages with her," she explained, giving him a sharp look. "I told her you'd been hit by a car. She assumed it happened out on the highway, while you were working, and I didn't bother to correct her. She gave me directions to the house, and I brought back a few of your things."

"Thank you," he replied, sincerely relieved that there was such a simple solution to his conundrum about his unexplained absence from the carriage house. How fortunate that Aleta didn't have to lie for him.

"They do think you are in the hospital, though," she remarked, giving him a look. "Frankly, that is where you *should* be, getting proper medical care. It went against everything I was trained to do and everything I believe in keeping you here last night. It is irresponsible of me not to get you to proper care, and I could lose my medical license for what I've done. That leg wound needs proper stitches, and you really needed a chest tube."

"I was awake and alert, and I refused to go to the hospital against your advice for proper medical attention," he responded, smiling, then alarmed her by sitting up slowly, testing his limits. "At least that's my answer if I am ever questioned."

Even though Aleta was trying to be stern, he could see that she couldn't help but be amused. "Can I help you get dressed?" she offered, but he shook his head slowly.

"If I wait another day, I should be able to shower and dress myself," he replied, calculating that timeline based both on how he felt and previous experience with recovery from injury.

"Then let me get you some food," she suggested, making her way behind the counter. He could hear her moving about, and smelled eggs, and smoked salmon. She had strawberries, too; he could hear her cut them up and put them on a plate.

She sat on the floor next to him and leaned against the back of her kitchen island as they ate, and he asked, "How's your sister?"

"How did you-?" she started to ask, but he tapped his nose by way of explanation.

"You have a similar smell, but you also look somewhat alike," he explained, knowing that it was not an ideal time to admit he'd once stalked her, and watched the two of them together. "If you didn't favor each other, I would know from the similarities of your scents."

"I really should thank you for something," she said, getting up to clear their plates. "I have always been close to my sister, but in my heart, I held something against her for a very long time. Meeting you helped me to overcome that." The last part was spoken over the sound of water running into the sink.

"Last night, I got her to leave me here alone with you by telling her you were my boyfriend," Aleta admitted, returning from behind the counter and sinking slowly into a chair at the small table nearby, stowing her crutches absentmindedly. The flush in her cheeks and increase in her heart rate were not due to embarrassment, he realized with surprise. She found him attractive, her scent transmitted that, along with a slight flaring of her nostrils and a mild dilation of her pupils, despite her fear. "I'm just telling you in case she says something about it. I'm certain she didn't believe me anyway," she added, almost as an afterthought.

"I'll play along," he promised, trying very hard not to laugh. "Tell me about this issue with your sister." He forced himself to relax, sinking down against the pillows on the floor.

"The first thing you have to understand is that she was still a baby when I was born. She wasn't yet two years old, and I came along, and my birth defect only added to the amount of attention I took from her. Our parents are great, they worked hard to make sure she got as close to equal time as I did, but by the time we started school, she was resentful of me. I guess she used to tell her teachers and school friends that she didn't have a sister, although everyone knew she did!

"Everyone chalked it up to a special case of sibling rivalry, exacerbated by my disability. She had some issues with lying, really it was more like telling elaborate tales that she was probably using to draw more attention her way. The most interesting part is that even though she wanted to deny my existence, as we got older, she was my closest friend and champion. She protected me from bullies until I learned how to protect myself, she made sure I was chosen early to play kickball and be included, she stayed next to me in the pool until I was proficient at swimming with my assistive devices.

"She turned those tall tales into a gift for storytelling that was unparalleled. She was always the best slumber party and summer campfire companion, because she could weave the scariest bedtime stories you ever heard out of thin air.

"And she became a terrific athlete, training for hours on end in junior high and high school, just driven to perform, as if she was making up for all of the physical things that I was unable to do. I think there were two things driving her. The first was a sincere belief that she would do all the things that I couldn't do on my behalf, you know? That was the loving sister. But there was also a part of her that did those things because she knew, deep down, that it was an arena in which I could never compete with her, never take the attention away from her. That was the other side of her, the vulnerable side.

"When we were in high school, I won a science competition and was invited to Japan to present my project at an international science fair. The whole family was planning to go. Alaina was incensed because it conflicted with her divisional cross-country track meet. Neither my parents nor her track coach could see any reason why she shouldn't come on the trip with us; she had already time-qualified for the state meet during her first cross country event that fall, and would be going to the state meet whether she competed at the divisional meet or not. What she wanted was to get both the divisional and the state title. Technically, she was old enough to stay home. But our parents insisted that my event was a once-in-a-lifetime opportunity, and they fully expected her to be present to support me.

"The night before the science fair, Alaina had a sort of breakdown. She saw something, off the balcony of our hotel suite, and she was hysterical. The story was so fantastic that it defied belief, and her behavior was so bizarre that she had to be hospitalized and sedated."

Aleta abruptly stopped talking, and shivered as if the story was physically affecting her all these years later. Amaoke waited for her to continue, and after a short while, she did.

"She woke me in the middle of the night, and she was terrified. She was more affected by jet lag than I had been and was unable to sleep. She told me that she had stepped out onto the balcony, and she had heard these strange voices, speaking in Japanese, almost like whispers, coming from one of the balconies below and to the left of ours. When she looked over the edge of the balcony, she had seen a beautiful woman in a red *gi*, a *shinobi*, like a ninja, crouched on the railing of the lower balcony, and she flew up into the sky. She was followed by several other men and women dressed in black *shinobi*, who had launched from other balconies, all around ours, one by one, like a swift flock of birds. They disappeared into the night sky, but she said that one of them had seen her, and it had made a frightening face and hissed at her, showing its long fangs, like a vampire.

"She was insistent, screaming and dragging me out onto the balcony, pulling me by my nightshirt because my legs wouldn't carry me, and our parents came running because she was wild by then, and she could see that I didn't believe her. When Mom and Dad made it onto the balcony, she was holding me there, at the railing, and I was lifted off the ground as she raved. I think they thought she had lost it, that she was thinking of throwing me off, and they wrestled her to the ground, and pulled her off me. I knew she was jealous of me, and upset about the trip, but I never believed, then or now, that she ever would have hurt me. She was screaming at me, saying things like *you have to believe me, they saw me* and *what if they come back*, cursing at all of us for behaving as though she had lost her mind, when I now know that she thought she was trying to keep us safe.

"The hotel doctor was summoned, and they sedated her and took her to the hospital for testing. The toxicity test was inconclusive, but at the time, it appeared that she had taken some illicit drug, and was having some sort of a reaction to it. The other possibility was a psychotic episode.

"I missed the science fair, and I never forgave her. I thought she had deliberately sabotaged the trip by taking drugs and having an episode. My parents were extremely concerned because they still thought she could be a danger to herself and a danger to me, so when we returned, they committed her to an inpatient rehabilitation and psychiatric facility.

"She continued getting some sort of therapy off and on, for many years. She suffered from terrible dreams for the rest of that year she was at home, and she went off to college the next year but continued to have problems coping. She was diagnosed with all sorts of things, including borderline personality disorder, which I began to suspect was incorrect when I was in medical school. She had a drug problem of sorts for a time and was unable to finish school.

"She was angry for a long time, and then somewhere along the line she gave up. She became very truthful, to the point of bluntness, as a way to signal to all of us that she was okay, I guess. She hasn't been to therapy or on any medication for about a decade, and she went back to the university and finished her degree in plant biology. She owns and runs her own flower shops and has an enormous greenhouse over in Metairie.

"Our relationship was tainted by that event because even though I forgave her for the outcome of the trip and got over the disappointment of missing the science fair, to this day, she has never, to my knowledge, recanted her story about what happened to her that night. I held on to a great deal of my own anger about that, somehow wanting her to just admit it was a tale.

"I probably went into psychiatry looking for answers to what causes such events, especially after being suspicious of Alaina's psychiatric diagnoses. I was drawn to psychotics, because they have bizarre visions and auditory hallucinations, and I probably thought that by understanding them, I could better understand my sister.

"Then you came along and showed me that there is more to the physical world than the rational mind may want to admit. It opened up a host of possibilities for my patients, for all psychiatric patients. But most importantly, it opened my own mind to the possibility that my sister had been telling the truth, and that I had failed her, because I had left her alone with that frightful event all these years.

"After your appointment, when I woke up with paramedics surrounding me and everyone insisting I go over to the hospital for tests, the first person who came to see me was Alaina. They released me that evening, diagnosed with dehydration, of all things. Alaina insisted on coming home with me, and when she asked me what had happened, while doctor-patient privilege proscribed my telling her what I had witnessed, I took her in my arms and apologized to her for failing to give her the benefit of the doubt all those years ago.

"I told her I could believe her now, and that while I couldn't tell her why, it was important that she know it. I even called our parents in her presence and told them that I had experienced something that made me certain that Alaina had been telling us the truth all those years ago. I think they were confused, and probably frightened that I was overworked and suffering from exhaustion. Whether any of the three truly understood what was happening was unimportant to me; I just wanted Alaina to know how sorry I was.

"Alaina is smart; she made the connection between my epiphany and my little trip to the hospital, and asked me if I had seen something. I admitted I had but was unable to give her the details. I think she was relieved I was alright, more than anything else, but also grateful to finally be believed."

At the conclusion of her story, Aleta slumped a little, as though comforted to have spoken that history out loud. "I will spend the rest of my life making it up to her, if that's what it takes. I will also be a much better listener than ever before, I think. Hopefully it will make me a better doctor."

Amaoke was quiet, absorbing what she had told him. The creatures Alaina had described to her sister did not fit with what he knew of dark spirits, whose actions never appeared to happen in such precise coordination. He thought of the being that he'd encountered at the clinic where he'd gotten his blood drawn. The story also loosely aligned with one of the Morningstar's recent statements about Father Weston, how he was *the most gifted of all of you. All of you.* All of who? Besides, Weston seemed fairly normal to him; especially empathic, perhaps, but that trait seemed to fit with his calling as a member of the clergy.

75

AMAOKE WOKE SOMETIME LATER AND realized that he must have fallen asleep while his mind was wandering. He looked around for Aleta, but she wasn't in the room. His nose told her she was at the other end of the house, and his ears told him she was deeply asleep given the cadence of her breathing. He hoped he hadn't fallen asleep while she was talking, but his body was unpredictable when he was hurt. He suspected she would understand.

It was dark outside, and he could feel that the moon was up by the pull it exerted upon him. He felt stronger, and he tested himself by sitting up. While it was still painful to move, because his muscles were sore from keeping still, and his bones were not fully healed, there was no longer any of the excruciating pain he had felt the night before, and his breathing was back to normal.

Using the edge of the counter that jutted out above his head, he pulled himself up, slowly standing, then stretching his body up to its full height. His stomach rumbled loudly, and he wanted to smile because he was finally ravenous. The return of appetite told more about his state of healing than anything else could.

The bandages on his torso were full of old blood, and they had dried to a crust that was stuck to his skin on the right side, so he left them alone. He was relieved to feel that his chest had assumed its usual convexity, so his ribs were healing well. Aleta's pillows and comforter were essentially ruined, and there was old blood on the kitchen floor underneath his makeshift bed.

He went to the patio door, slid the latch and went out into the night. He stood in the yard and stretched his arms up to the sky, whispering several prayers of thanks to the spirits for this life, longevity, good fortune, and good health. As he always did, Brother *Iraluk* made him feel stronger. He did not sense any unnatural spirit activity in the yard, and to be certain he circled the back of the house, aware that he needed to get back inside before any of Aleta's neighbors saw a naked bloodied man wandering in her yard.

He went back inside and wrapped the soiled pillows and towels into the ruined comforter. He searched under the sink for cleaning materials and was rewarded for his efforts. Aleta's cabinets were extremely organized, and he found what he needed to mop up the mess he had created on the floor in the kitchen. He went back out onto the patio to see if that needed any attention, but the tiles were clean, and he guessed that she had been able to clean out here, but not inside, since she probably hadn't wanted to disturb him.

With a bit of quiet exploration, he found the guest bathroom, and he took a long, hot shower, soaking the bandages enough to get them off. His hair was filthy and matted with dirt and blood, and it required a bit of attention to get it clean. He used the shampoo that was on the shelf in the enclosure, grateful that it smelled of mint and herbs rather than flowers. He dressed in the clothes she had brought from his apartment, smiling about the Converse sneakers Aleta had found in his closet, almost the same color as Weston's. It reminded him that his work boots were likely lost to the confrontation with Weston. The boots were his most common footwear choice out of necessity; the Converse were the closest modern thing to *mukluqs* or moccasins he had found for everyday comfort.

Amaoke carried the bundle in the comforter out to the large trash bin next to the garage, which he located by scenting the air in the breezeway. When he returned to the house, he looked in the refrigerator for something to eat, but there wasn't much to be had, and he didn't want to take what little there was. He glanced at the clock on the stove, and saw that it was still reasonably early, just past nine-thirty, so he wrote a short note to Aleta beneath the one she had left for him earlier.

A, thanks for your care and for sharing yourself. Be safe. Hope to see you soon. AS.

He knew that he couldn't stay, couldn't smother her independence and her strength with his presence. He sensed that it was not what she wanted. Weston was right, keeping her completely safe was impossible, and he knew personally what her autonomy meant to her.

With that, he called Alaina from the house phone, which was conveniently programmed such that he knew which button to push to reach her, and when she answered, he remained silent, putting down the phone so she would not hear his breathing. He knew it was unfair to alarm her, but finally he could hear her say, "I'm coming over now." Undoubtedly she was perplexed that her sister was calling and unable to say why. He refused to be a continued burden, but likewise did not want to leave Aleta on her own. He heard a small chime sound in the bedroom, likely a cell phone to alert her of her sister's imminent arrival, but there was no indication that it had awakened her. He hoped this middle of the night drama wouldn't cause more stress.

In exactly eight minutes, when his hearing picked out the sound of a car in the drive out front, he let himself out the sliding door at the back and was gone before the lights blazed from the bedroom window as Aleta responded to the frantic pounding on her front door.

76

HE WAS HEALTHY ENOUGH TO return to work the week following the full moon, recovered completely and no small thanks to Weston ensuring that his employers had a plausible excuse for his absence. The worst part about it was the shopping trip required to replace the ruined work boots, but it was getting easier to find shoes in his proper size, and he was enjoying being back on his feet, literally and figuratively.

And the dreaded shopping trip had not been all bad, as he had passed a boutique that sold high-end household goods. There was a lovely soft comforter in the window display, and Amaoke had stopped in to buy it and some matching linens and pillowcases for Aleta, replacements for the things he had ruined. He gave the matronly proprietress Aleta's address and paid extra to have the items sent directly to her.

"Will there be a personal note?" the woman asked, and he could tell she was curious about the purchase, but he suspected his appearance made her afraid to ask more.

"She'll know all she needs to know," he replied with mischief in his eyes, and this made the woman blush. She smiled and told him she would take care of everything, and her flustered reaction told him that he had picked out all the right things.

If only everything about the situation with Aleta could be so simple; other than sending her the linens he had no idea how to proceed with her, and his first instinct was to keep her completely safe and stay away from her. But the better part of him knew that he owed her more than just a silent disappearance, and he suspected his leaving without making any further contact since could be hurtful. She probably had a lot of questions, and he hadn't stuck around to answer any of them, even after she had confided in him about her sister, and her own failings. Not very gentlemanly.

Her newly forged alliance with his landlady was confirmed by the note that had been waiting for him on the patio door a few days later. *Aleta called to thank you for the gifts. She is worried about you. Please call and let her know how you are doing.*

He couldn't avoid her entirely, and he didn't want to. It had come to him, too late, that he recognized the car that had struck him that night. Something Aleta had said had triggered the memory. When she had told him that his landlords thought he had been struck at work, it jarred loose the thought that the Morningstar had driven such a car past his worksite. When he put the possibility that the Monster had orchestrated that violence in perspective, he wanted to understand it.

Dark spirit energies remained quiet since his confrontation with Weston and its aftermath, and he knew he still had certain things to discuss with the young priest. He felt a kinship with Weston, but had not been back to see him since they had parted ways at the church the night he was hit. There were questions that still needed answers, and they couldn't be put off indefinitely.

But he wanted to regain some of the relative peace of his independent existence, even though he doubted it was possible. All the recent events he could name heralded trouble to come. Amaoke sensed it, and he suspected that whatever the priest had to tell him would ensnare them both and have far-reaching implications.

77

MICHAEL ISRAEL WENT STRAIGHT to David Ziegler after her flight touched down at Ben Gurion, taking the train from Lod into the city, where she took a short cab ride to Ramat Hasharon. He met her in the lobby, and they took the stairs together to his suite of offices. It was obvious he had been spending a lot of time there. His beard was unkempt, he'd slept in his clothes, and he seemed to have aged a decade in the few months she had been away.

He offered her a drink, which she refused. He looked for a moment as if he wanted to force the alcohol on her and she assumed it was because something had happened, and he needed to send her back out to the field. She had no idea it was because of the desert.

"Tell me about the desert," she said, feeling as though Japan could be pushed aside in favor of problems she could solve, wanting to know what they'd found, wanting to know what she'd missed. It was the way she had always been; clear the slate, clear the conscience, and do it again. That pragmatism had served her in every instance of her existence, and she relied on it again. "Is Milos back?"

"Sit down, please," David said, and the tone he adopted was so formal, so unlike his usual demeanor, that she knew something was very wrong.

"David, stop it, what's wrong? If it's Japan, I can -" she started to explain, but the look in his eyes was so bereft, so aggrieved, that her words caught in her throat. He didn't care about Japan. Japan was forgotten.

"Milos is dead," he told her, those three words dropping on her like bricks. Milos was one of the best of them, and he was dead. After all they had seen and done, the security detail in the desert had killed him.

"Who was it?" she asked quietly, prepared to start planning to hunt insurgents as soon as David would release her. "Locals?"

"Not entirely sure. The profile doesn't fit, but this could be a rogue group. Some extremist arm of one of the existing cells, but our analysts don't buy it. Allied Force commanders want us to use it as an excuse to hunt jihadis, of course, but something is off. I need you to see it."

"Sure. Show me the file. How did he die?" Michael Israel asked.

"Michael. It's bad, maybe the worst I've seen," David told her. "I can share the file with you, but I want you there, on the ground, to walk me through the scene. There are some things I would rather get your impression about without any prior prejudice from the details, but that is impossible."

"The worst you've seen?" she repeated quietly, and started to feel afraid. David's career was as distinguished as any commander, and he had done three times the field work of most.

"Unfortunately, I have to show you the file and read you in before you go anywhere. Because whatever this was, it was personal, and I argued that you should have a choice in the matter." He suspected when she knew it all, she would still demand to be assigned to it.

"Personal, how? Milos didn't have any enemies," Michael Israel protested.

"Not Milos. You," David said softly. He passed her the file, impossibly thick for such a short assignment, and she saw that it contained numerous photos, the telltale thick paper contributing to its weight and substance.

She set the file down on the conference table and said shakily, "I'll take that drink now."

While he busied himself with that task, she sat down at the table and opened the file, sure that whatever he brought her wouldn't be strong enough to make a difference.

The first few photographs were satellite intelligence surveys, and she recognized the flat expanse around the stele from the date of their helicopter mission out of Tikrit. The next several photos showed the initial shots of the dig site, and Michael Israel could make out the sentries and some of the scientists on the magnified views. She came to the first mag view that didn't look right, and was having a hard time making sense of what she was looking at. She had read that sometimes the brain cannot pick out order in a pattern and acknowledge what it is seeing because the disorder is so profound, or the image is so disturbing.

But she didn't have to puzzle over it for very long, since the very next photo was a close-in reproduction of the detail of the previous survey. It showed a hole, a pit of some depth, off to the left of a nearer ring that on closer inspection showed a stairhead going down into the earth. Just to the west of this opening was Milos. He had been turned into an upside-down exclamation point, his feet pointing away from the steps, and his severed head arranged slightly beyond them, eyes open, frozen in horror, seeming to stare right into the lens of the tactical surveillance camera, some 36,000 kilometers above him.

She shuddered, taking the whiskey that David handed her and gulping it down, grimacing at the bitterness but relishing the warmth that spread across her chest. Milos was holding something in one hand, and she flipped through subsequent shots to identify it, but there was no answer to be gleaned from the satellite shots.

She forced herself to keep going, photo after photo of the slain soldiers and scientists, barely noticing that the latter shots had been taken from only a few feet away, by an operative with a camera, down where the satellites had been unable to see. Finally, the close-up of Milos' broken form on the sand, and the filthy doll he clutched. The doll was either torn or broken, folded sideways, its round head lolling on its body, iconic, unmistakable. Hello Kitty.

On and on, she dug through the remainder of the photos. The final one she knew would forever haunt her dreams. Written on the face of one of the smooth walls near the bottom of the excavation, a taunt, written in blood, the final part of the grisly message a smear, like a signature:

HERE KITTY KITTY COME AND PLAY

It *was* personal. The challenge was unmistakable. Her search was over; clues left by the very monster she sought awaited her at the *makom galut,* the place of the fallen.

78

DAVID INSISTED ON ACCOMPANYING HER to the dig site personally. They argued all the way down to Tikrit about how to approach the site, but she was adamant.

"You asked me to take a look. I'm not doing it with an audience," she told him. "Either you get clearance for the two of us to ride out there, or I go home."

He pleaded with her to be reasonable, they needed security forces in the event of a second attack. He didn't tell her he was concerned about her; there was something relentless in her tone and bearing that almost frightened him more than what he feared they would find in the desert.

In the end, the theater commander agreed to send them with a single escort, air support; and they were cleared to take two helicopters out. The mission would be for Michael Israel and David to get another look at the site while the second helo would stay in the air, looking for any threats while the Mossad agents were probing the excavation and vulnerable on the ground.

The commander insisted on all other tactical precautions, and as Michael Israel holstered her weapon and waited for rockets to be loaded before her pre-flight inspection, she thought of Azuma. If she wasn't the enemy, perhaps she could be an ally. At the very least, she would believe in the aspect of this that defied belief, and Michael Israel hated to admit that she was out of her depth. But then she filed such thoughts away, needing to focus on the here and now.

David was no less apprehensive when they left the ground, as he was unfamiliar with these routes and was the lookout for obstacles since Michael Israel had the controls. She was a gifted pilot, but aggressive on the stick that morning; she wasted no time putting the bird nose down and shooting out over the brown expanse of the interior. The trailing helicopter kept up, but it was clear its crew was surprised by the urgency of her approach.

They circled the pit twice from the air before she set the Kiowa on the ground several hundred meters to the east. They waved off their escort, promising to maintain radio contact, and the second crew started their security protocol.

They sat quietly inside the rig for several minutes more, while the dust they'd stirred up settled. Finally, when she unbuckled her harness, the sound seemed loud in the deafening silence that had come after the rotors were turned off.

The quiet felt wrong. The bodies had long been removed, the equipment transported out, but even David felt something that made it harder for him to hold on to his doubt. There were ghosts here.

They made their way across the sand to the hole. It was more impressive from ground perspective, as it gave them a more personal sense of its size relative to a human being. The central pit was huge, seemingly depthless, and they stepped to the small wedge of solid ground adjacent to the top of the stairwell to peer down into it. Satellite depth sounding had revealed a depth of four hundred feet, but the scientists had not reached the bottom.

They kept their radio frequency in sync with the helicopter, to try to catch any chatter from the other crew, but suddenly Michael Israel's voice was loud in his ears. "Avenger Four, we are descending and may lose radio contact. Confirm."

"Avenger Four, we copy. We'll keep things locked up topside."

Her flashlight was attached to her shoulder epaulet, and she switched it on, leading the way down. David shouldered his shotgun, even though she hadn't drawn her weapon, and followed, checking the stairs above them periodically. He couldn't erase the images from the file from his mind, and still did not have a reasonable explanation as to how his tactical experts had been ambushed.

When he estimated they were halfway down, based on the mapping provided by the extraction detail, they began to hear sounds. It was eerie, almost like distorted human voices, what sounded like the crazed babble of a madman, and a few moments later, a scream.

Without stopping, Michael Israel glanced back at him. "It's the desert drafts forced through the walls of the pit and out through these passageways," she explained, gesturing to one of the many dark doorways opening off the staircase. "It's one enormous echo-chamber."

He swallowed, nodding, and they continued their descent, the warmth of the surface far behind them now. The stepped through successive cold spots, and he was reminded of the thermoclines he had traversed in the depths of the ocean when diving.

The noisy chatter got louder as they went deeper, and he thought he would go mad. Any soldier lives with fear, but this was the stuff of nightmares, a horror movie come true. He wondered at Michael Israel's resolve to go chasing this, whatever it was, but he mastered himself and kept going.

They turned a final corner and were confronted with the message on the wall, and at the same time assaulted with a rancid permeating miasma that David knew by only one name: Death. The smell seemed to have seeped into the stones. Michael Israel stepped to the wall and put one shaky hand next to the message, confirming for herself that it was real.

At some point she must have lost control of her bladder, as the seat of her fatigue pants was soaked. She didn't even notice, her face drawn in a grimace of pain and rage as she recognized the stench of the beast that had stolen her brother. Her wail of grief was so piteous that he reached out to her, but she had fallen to her knees at the base of the wall. There was something small and round that had come to rest there.

David peered over her shoulder to see what she had retrieved, watching as tears poured from her eyes as she rocked back and forth, trembling violently, a seizure of remorse, and though he couldn't discern it, relief. It was the first time he had ever seen her show such emotion, and that frightened him more than the sum total of this cursed mission.

In her hands she clutched a filthy *yarmulke* that had once belonged to a very small child.

79

AMAOKE CAME HOME SEVERAL DAYS later to a more direct communication taped to the patio door. He recognized Aleta's own handwriting on his landlady's pink paper.

Dinner at my house. Wednesday, 8 pm. A

He took it down and had to smile. She knew he had no way to decline the invitation, and no way to accept it other than to show up. He was trapped by his own habits. It would be the height of ungentlemanly behavior to stand the lady up.

The following Wednesday he showed up on her doorstep with a bottle of wine, the vintage was one he had seen her drink at some point during his stalking forays. He also brought a bouquet of pink tulips after agonizing about what a woman might read into the type of flower given to her – he felt roses were too forward, but he wanted something that would convey a tentative attraction and telegraph to her that he recognized how special she was. He kept his clothing casual, wearing jeans and a light brown pullover sweater that was soft as a t-shirt, and the Converse sneakers that she had brought to him after the accident. He tugged his hair into two braids, again cutting it close on time, considering he'd still had to detour to pick up the wine and flowers and he hated to be late.

She came to the door in a modification of what he considered her uniform; she had traded her t-shirt for a cream-colored cashmere tunic that hugged her slim curves and complimented her warm skin tone.

She was delighted with the tulips, and exclaimed, "These are so beautiful! My sister would be excited; she is very interested in beautiful flowers out of season."

She leaned into him briefly, her hand against his chest not quite a hug, but more like a reassurance. He knew she was also convincing herself that his body contours had returned to normal. The doctor, making sure the patient was truly well.

"Then you should congratulate her instead," Amaoke smiled. "Her assistant sold me these from her greenhouse."

"You remembered she has a shop nearby," Aleta marveled, giving him a look of appreciation and surprise. "Thank you. It is so thoughtful."

She grilled steaks on the patio, where the fire pit kept the cool evening air at bay for a time, and he was impressed with her cooking. She was as efficient in her daily life as she seemed to be at her work, her movements like a dance, ordered, graceful, with no wasted motion. Before long, what little remained of their dinner was cleared away, and he could see she wanted to talk.

"Shall we go inside?" she asked, shivering a bit, as the fire died down next to them.

He helped her gather the last few items from their meal and followed her into the house. She sat on one side of the counter, so he settled down on a stool opposite. She offered him wine, but he shook his head.

"You don't like it, do you?" she observed, remembering that he had declined to join her in a glass at dinner.

"I never liked the taste of alcohol," he told her. "I also have my concerns about the potential side-effects," he admitted, bringing the subject back to him to make it easier for her, since he suspected that was what she really wanted to talk about.

"You are completely recovered?"

"I was mostly recovered before I left here," he said. "During the time when the moon is approaching full, as it was that week, it has its greatest effect on my restorative abilities. I heal much faster than if the moon were waning."

"And no apparent residual effects," she observed, studying him quietly.

"I am still not entirely recovered," he admitted. "There will be some stiffness and soreness for several months more, I expect. The process gets slightly slower as I get older."

Amaoke paused, and stretched his arms above his head, arching his back. He settled back against the counter and put his feet on the rungs of the stool he was perched on. Aleta mirrored his pose, putting her arms on the countertop and leaning toward him. When she was settled, the tips of their fingers were almost touching.

His hands closed the gap between them, picking up hers and turning them over, examining her delicate palms. He was surprised by the sharp acrid scent of her fear as it spiked, then subsided when he sat very still, just holding on to her, enjoying the human connection. He closed his eyes and relaxed his grip enough that she could free herself if she wanted to, but she didn't move. He wanted to tell her how brave she truly was, and how much he admired that bravery, but he felt that her control and her independence seemed tenuous to her, and he worried that his words would cheapen them. Maybe he could have said something if her apprehension did not persist.

With a sigh, he released her, pulling his hands back to himself, feeling sad that the scent of fear subsided even more when he did so. She had no way to gauge the amount of control he had gained in his centuries of experience, and his showboating in her office at their initial meeting had to have been a jarring experience. He had always regretted that approach; she was not the person he had assumed she would be when he had gone to see her. He still believed that she had a great deal to contribute to his enduring dilemma in terms of theory, and of science, but he had given her enough to absorb.

Add to that event her assistance with his wounds, the appearance of the Morningstar, and her courage through both his suspended transformation and the aftermath of his accident, her fear was to be expected. All those events were connected to him in some way. He had brought all of this into her life. He could hardly expect her to divorce that fear from him.

Just when he thought it was time to take his leave, she asked quietly, "Water, then? Would you like some?" Unlike him, she hadn't moved her hands from the spot where he had held them. They remained on the counter, like a continued offering, a symbol of trust and faith in his goodness. She remained forward on her stool, leaning toward him, hands with palms upward, open to him. It was a hopeful sign.

He stood up without giving her an answer, and she read his discomfort. She stood herself, and turned away, quickly pulling two bottles from the refrigerator. She offered one to him; he hesitated only a moment and then accepted it, grateful that she continued to try to keep things easy between them. She watched him drink and opened the other bottle for herself.

Then, perhaps to move them further from the awkwardness of the moment, she said in a lighter tone, "After all that has transpired, I think you should know where I hide the-" she began, but in two long strides he closed the distance between them and held up a hand to stay the rest of her statement. He met her eyes and shook his head.

"Don't tell me any of those kinds of secrets," he warned her, reaching out to squeeze her shoulder reassuringly. "They might not be safe."

Although he was pretty sure that ignorance about the location of a spare key wasn't enough deter the Morningstar and his petty demons, Amaoke remained in some ways the superstitious man he had always been. He knew that the sharing of secrets was still powerful magic, because of the trust inherent in the act of doing so.

Aleta nodded as though she understood, and he was pleased that the distress of the prior moments did not return. She crossed through the kitchen and sank down onto the couch on the far side of the living room, so he took a seat on the sofa opposite her, realizing that her home furnishings were like those in her office. Everything was modern in appearance, but very comfortable, and he settled against the cushions, feeling her scrutiny.

"Why is this happening to you?" she asked, then seemed to make the first of many connections. "The car accident, that was no accident, was it?"

He admitted that it wasn't, and avoided telling her the worst of it; he was concerned that the event was a message that the Monster was not to be deterred from its plans. If getting Amaoke to comply with its wishes involved causing suffering, so be it. He was far less concerned about his own skin; he knew that Aleta remained in peril. It shamed him to keep these thoughts from her. So he spent some time explaining to her why he thought he was being punished, why the repeated attacks on his person.

As if she could read his mind, Aleta began to shake her head slowly. "I don't believe that you could truly become a mindless, raging monster," she stated with conviction.

"That truth is present in everything you are as a person, as a man," she explained, staying his protest with a small wave of her hand. "I have listened to you speak of your mother and all that she taught you about – what was it – the rules of living? The way you spoke of her, and of what you learned, make it clear to me that you have held on to those teachings for centuries, still valuing them enough to persist in behaving a certain way to respect that tradition, even after such a long life! Many people would diminish the importance of longevity by scorning their connections to humanity, or viewing such a privilege as an excuse to behave inhumanely.

"You embrace your human side and live among people, immersing yourself with us. It is difficult to be mindful of others, and would be so much easier for you to give up on this side of yourself, but you haven't done it. And then there's-"

But there she stopped herself, and looked down at her arms, encircled by the bands of her crutches. Amaoke waited, certain that she was about to say more, shocked by the observations she had made and her sincere belief in his ability to keep the monster within him under control. Simple, small things that he had done each day of his life were important, but did they have enough power to protect him from the unknown?

Without raising her eyes, she said quietly, "When we met, you didn't ask me about my legs." It wasn't a question, but he could tell by what remained unsaid that it required a response.

"In my culture, it is believed that you give others the respect you hope to have. You think well of them, so that others will think well of you. You look for the best in people, because if you do not, the good things and the respect that you seek will not come to you," he replied, hoping that his answer would make sense to her.

"The Golden Rule?" she asked, laughing a little, then seeing with surprise that he did not understand, she explained, "Our tradition states that you should treat others as you wish to be treated."

Rather than say anything, he nodded, considering what she had told him. "It is very similar," he allowed. "But it is also a way of modeling our very best behavior, not necessarily for others, or because anyone is watching, but because it is the right thing to do. If I ask you about your crutches, I am pointing out a potential weakness, and such an act could bring weakness to me, or reveal my own weaknesses to others, do you see? Also, your legs, your crutches – fundamentally, they do not tell me anything about who you really are. They cannot reveal whether you are kind, or cruel, clever or foolish, caring and helpful or reckless and destructive, right?"

Aleta blinked several times, as if she was holding back tears. "This is my point. To approach the world in such a way requires an abundance of care," she stressed. "There is no monster within you that can distort who you really are."

Amaoke had no answer for that, as he could not be sure it was true, even though he could see she wanted him to believe it, as perhaps she believed it. "I do know that my repeated presence here endangers you, as it places you in the path of the very darkest spirits. They could follow me to you." This was the closest he came to acknowledging the peril she faced; he really did not want to give more power to the possibility by speaking of it.

"The Morningstar again? Those — whatever-they-were — in the church garage. Let them come," she whispered, and he knew she could not know what she might invite with such a statement. Weston had told him that they had done everything short of name her; they had invited her to let them inhabit her flesh. Involuntarily, her hand went to the Mobius loop at her neck, which he had correctly identified as her own talisman. "I am prepared for whatever has to happen."

Amaoke silently disagreed with her statement, thinking that no one, not even he, could prepare for the chaos that the Morningstar and his underlings could generate. He thought about her relative youth, and what a tragedy her loss of life would be.

Aleta saw him struggling with thoughts that he wasn't sharing with her, so she asked, "What are you thinking? I may be afraid, but my faith in God is strong."

"I'm thinking that you cannot know what you are saying. I'm thinking about how young you are," he said simply, holding up a hand when he saw she wanted to protest. "I am not saying you are not capable, and smart, and resourceful, only that you are young, and I am thinking about what you would miss if your life were cut short."

"Perhaps they would be things that I am not meant to have," she retorted defiantly, lifting her chin. They were dangerously close to something painful, and although he thought he knew what it was, he kept to what he had learned of her directly over their relatively short relationship.

"But you appear to be determined to sacrifice those things, or forsake them," he told her gently. "There are important things, things which you should believe you deserve, even if you have never experienced them. You should move toward life, not away from it."

"Weren't you the one who told me that you were headed toward your own death?" she asked.

"By way of explaining away the idea of immortality," he clarified. "I believe death is in front of me, as it is for all mortal beings, but I am not looking for it, not trying to hasten it. I may be called upon to martyr myself, but I have lived a long time, and I have loved, and been loved. It is lonely, as you said, being so different from others."

"You don't dwell on your differences," she said softly.

"What would be the point of that — I cannot change who I am. I have tried to make the best of it, to honor my mother's memory."

"I think I have made the best of my own differences," she concluded, but he could hear that she doubted her own statement. "I have worked very hard to be more than what others expected, and I have worked very hard to help others, and make a difference in the world."

"Without asking for anything for yourself," he observed. "It is admirable, even commendable," he told her, and because he could sense that she was angry, he stood up and carried his empty water bottle back to the kitchen. "But there is still something missing, something vital."

"Like what?" she demanded, and he knew she was so defensive because she did not know any other way to manage what was hurting her, deep down.

He settled his bag over his shoulder and moved toward the door, wishing he could stay, wishing he could take away some of her pain, knowing that the time and the circumstances were wrong. He opened the door and stepped out into the night, leaving his words behind, "Love, Aleta. You deserve love."

80

"THE COURIER IS HERE." The guardian put her head briefly into the room, but her mistress was absorbed in the file she was reviewing.

"Send him in, *Ichi*," Azuma advised, saddened that she was going to have to hear what might be the last she ever would of her Collector.

"*Aijin*," the courier bowed in respect.

"Thank you for your time," Azuma indicated the chairs near the window. "Would you take tea with me?" She sent *Ichi* to alert her assistant to serve them.

They sat together, and the courier looked thoughtfully out on the landscape. It was clear that he was very uncomfortable to be in her presence, and perhaps to be received so informally.

"Please be at ease," Azuma tried to help him. "I know you are the bearer of bad news, but I bear you no ill will. What you tell me will help me a great deal, I hope."

"But I have no knowledge of his fate," the man protested, perhaps hoping to forestall any disappointment she might have in response to his tale.

"I understand," she said. "But perhaps what you do know will be of help."

"He met me in San Francisco. It was just like always, we had a drink in the bar, and he passed me the specimen.

"He told me to ensure that it got the highest priority of the samples, and they were to report to you when it was received. He said he'd be getting to Tokyo later than planned, he was delaying his trip by a day to run an errand for you, I thought."

"Did he tell you anything about the specimen?" she asked.

"It happened that he saw the guy who gave the specimen, said the subject was flirting with the tech or something, and that's why they crossed paths. Apparently the subject trailed the Collector and witnessed him windwalk.

"The guy wasn't human, but not like us, something bestial was his best guess. Big guy, dark, with very odd eyes and teeth. But it bothered him that they'd had an encounter."

"Encounter?" Azuma prompted. "Did he suggest that there was an altercation?"

"Not at all," the courier shook his head. "Just that he was seen, and recognized as a supernatural. The guy caught it right away, the Collector could tell that he knew before he took off. It rattled him. He collected all those samples in Africa, and no one even knew we were there, even the Sorceress and her ghoul. This surprised him."

"That's very helpful," Azuma thanked him, not sure what it all meant, but he stopped her.

"But I haven't told you about the woman," the courier said. "Later that night, when I was stepping out to go to the airport, I saw him in the bar, with a woman. That's not so unusual, I guess.

"This one was distinct, beautiful, with maroon hair, very full and thick. She had on some sort of high-fashion outfit, a cape or a jacket with a bunch of purple feathers. I had never seen anything like it before – I thought maybe she was someone famous.

"They were alone together, I think," the courier hesitated. "I don't know if this means anything, but there was a man sitting across the bar from them, had some kind of cute hairstyle, and he made eye contact with me as I went out to the street. Creepy."

"Cute hairstyle?" Azuma repeated the term. "Was it dark, longish, wavy?"

"Nope. Something modern. Long on top. Wearing Armani and darkish glasses. Pale, like a junkie maybe, or a high-class hustler."

Azuma knew exactly what he meant. And who. Forcas. She smiled, and it was such a cold expression that the courier was not reassured that she was pleased with the information he'd brought her.

And he was right. The information brought her no pleasure, but she was satisfied. It was time to pay Dr. Madison a visit.

81

AZUMA REFUSED TO HEAR ANY excuses.

"I want to know where, when, why, and how it happened. Immediately," she demanded in a quiet voice that underscored her anger, and her IT specialists blinked at her tone. She was always direct, but this was rare frustration and disbelief at the seriousness of the event. Everyone at RSI worked very hard to avoid being the target of her displeasure; she was intimidating enough.

"Ma'am?" One of the executive assistants from the administrative pool stepped into the room.

"Not now," Azuma told her without taking her eyes off her staff.

"But-" The woman tried again, although it was clear she wanted nothing more than to disappear when Azuma turned a near-homicidal gaze in her direction. Bravely, before she could be sent away, she stammered out, "It's urgent. The caller says to tell you she is 'The Soldier,' and she needs to speak to you as soon as possible."

"Keep her on the line, please, go," Azuma replied impatiently. To the engineers waiting for further dressing down, she merely said, "Answers to me personally in one hour or I'll know why not."

She pushed through the doors to the conference room and then beyond to the back hallway, taking the stairs three at a time in her heels because she knew it to be quicker than the private elevator.

She nodded to *Jū* as she came into the back suite, and picked up her personal line. "Put her through here."

"I'm sorry, ma'am, she wasn't able to stay on the line. I'm sending you the transcript now," came the hurried apology.

"Perfect."

It came across almost immediately, and Azuma opened the file.

14:26:02<<recording initiated<<

O: Rising Sun Industries.

C: I'm calling for Azuma Himura. It's urgent.

O: Dr. Himura is not immediately available. Is there anything-

C: She asked me to contact her if I discovered any information.

O: I'll be delighted to pass any information along to her as soon as-

C: Not an option. Please put her on the line. Tell her it's the soldier. She will take my call.

O (uncertainly): It may take a moment to locate her. Hold, please.

At 14:28:19 of the recording, Michael Israel spoke again, and Azuma was impressed. She was aware that she was being recorded, and she also knew that when the operator returned, she would see only that the caller had hung up, and not think to check the transcript before she forwarded it.

C: Azuma, we found the shrine of the Opposer in the desert. There was a massacre at the site by a non-human operator, who left a message for me. I have to get on a plane right now. Find me in Tel Aviv.

14:28:33<<call terminated<<

Azuma listened to the recording three times, having a hard time reconciling its contents with what she knew of Michael Israel. She sounded afraid, and she was asking for help.

She stuck her head out the back door and *Jū* leaned in to hear her instructions.

"Let Haneda know that I will need the jet. Call down and have them ready with the helicopter in eight minutes. I'll call ahead with flight plans en route; let them know our destination will be Tel Aviv. I want *Ni* to travel with me this time, tell her pack for three days and meet me at the helipad. And make sure I get my report on that data breach before wheels up from Tokyo."

82

THE JAFFA HOTEL IN TEL Aviv had once been a nineteenth century French hospital. Around those old bones had been built a luxury oasis, coveted for its prime location at the port, near the old flea market, in the most progressive part of the city. Minimalist design accented the rich history of the place, and the staff had been most accommodating to Azuma on arrival after very short notice.

After being assured of management's willingness to deliver on her every possible need, she and *Ni* were shown to their suite of rooms. *Ni*, ever vigilant and thorough, combed the temporary dwelling for any irregularity, and satisfied that it was secure, took her leave to familiarize herself with the property and the particulars of the surrounding neighborhood. Compact and petite, *Ni* combined the allure of a geisha with the ruthlessness of an assassin. Her shark fin haircut made her seem less serious, but her temperament never invited underestimation.

Best of all, she was a marvelous decoy. Most assumed that she was a traveling companion rather than a security guard, which Azuma encouraged. It was best if no one knew which of them was more dangerous. Azuma suspected it might be *Ni*.

She traded her dress for linen slacks and a cotton t-shirt and twisted her hair up behind her head, then took the elevator down to Michael Israel's floor. She found the room easily and knocked on the door. After a significant period of time, she could hear movement on the other side, followed by an ominous silence. Finally, she heard the rattling clicks of the chain being disengaged.

The wraith that stood in the darkened entryway did not seem the same woman that Azuma had known her to be only a few short weeks before. Michael Israel looked haggard, and she pulled the door open slightly, enough to allow Azuma to enter, and then, pressing it shut behind her, brought her left hand up quickly, putting the gun to Azuma's head and cocking it.

"Why did you save my life?" Michael Israel asked, her bright eyes blazing with a challenge.

"I do not know." It was mostly true. Azuma had spent a great deal of time interrogating her own motives on the subject. She refused to admit that she saw much of herself in this remarkable young woman. "If you were going to kill me, you should have pulled the trigger immediately. Don't talk. Do. Now I know you need my help. Put the gun down."

When Michael Israel did not comply, Azuma simultaneously grabbed the woman by the waist and secured her gun hand, pushing it up and away as she swept her legs and took them both to the floor. The struggle for the gun was minor; Azuma tossed it away, but despite being disarmed, still Michael Israel fought her, fast and elusive even on the ground, and Azuma was again impressed with her determination and her training. She was no match for the Dragon, and when Azuma had secured the other woman's arms and pinned her to the floor with her own weight, both of them panting for breath, Azuma caught the scent of anise, and then saw the bottles of *arak* lined up on the small wet bar.

"You cannot prepare for a fight like this," Azuma said. "In Tokyo it was nearly a contest. But you were sober, and well fed. You asked me to come. I'm here. I should think our fighting behind us."

She stood up, grasping Michael Israel's forearms and pulling her to her feet. Once she was certain the soldier had her balance, she kept contact a beat too long, finally breaking away from the awkward embrace. She turned her back and stepped into the room.

The place was close, stuffy, as if the windows hadn't been opened recently and the bedding was stale. The shades were drawn against the daylight, and there was no evidence of any recent meals. Azuma glanced into the bathroom and saw that the towels were in order, untouched. The bed was undisturbed, but there were pillows on the floor next to the side furthest from the door.

"Your mother told me I would find you here," Azuma told her, and Michael's head came up abruptly.

"She is fine. Worried. I had only the information I had already collected about where to find you. Your father was not at home," Azuma said reassuringly. Hedda had been curious about Azuma, but had simply passed along the information about her daughter's whereabouts. Azuma had explained that she was a friend from Japan, and that Michael Israel had asked her to come. Hedda was surprised at this, but said that she had been staying in the city since she'd returned from Iraq, hadn't come out to the house on the sea.

"I should call her," Michael Israel said in a soft voice, slurred with drink. "Just can't. Can't. She would-she would know."

"Mothers do know when something is wrong. She already knows, whether you call or not. I can bring her here if you'd prefer not to go there." Azuma had noticed the discomfort the mention of her visit had caused, and assumed that the young soldier had good reasons for not wanting to be at home.

When she got no answer, she said, "When did you last eat?"

Michael Israel shrugged, and half slumped, half fell into a sitting position on the floor next to the bed. She picked up her gun, and Azuma was concerned because the safety was still off. Once again, she stood the young woman on her feet, took the gun from her as she would take a treasured toy from a child, put the safety on, and set it aside. She wrinkled her nose at the smell of sour sweat and alcohol.

"Clean yourself up. Then come up to my room and we can talk."

Michael Israel turned toward the bathroom, so Azuma pulled the blinds and opened the windows, letting the breeze blow in off the sea, feeling the air circulate, the sunshine cleansing the shadows away. She dumped the remaining *arak* down the drain and put the empty bottles into a small refuse can which she placed outside the door.

She made a cursory examination of the room, looking for other contraband. In the closet, she discovered spare ammunition tucked inside the woman's boots on the floor, but there was also a thick manila file on the shelf above, full of pictures and notes. She pulled it down and took it with her, returning to her suite upstairs, she settled in to read. *Ni* came in some time later, and put her head into Azuma's room.

"*Aijin.* All is secure. No threats."

"Thank you. I can handle things this evening – I will call if I need you. Enjoy yourself," Azuma replied.

"Sleeping. I'll be sleeping," *Ni* reported sourly, and Azuma couldn't suppress her smile. *Ni* had been the closest thing to a protégé that the Collector had ever had, and sometimes her behavior was as inadvertently funny as his had been.

Azuma reviewed the contents of the file carefully. She thought she recognized the handiwork, and sure enough, there it was in the notes, written in an orderly hand, small precise printing reporting the findings in a matter-of-fact tone. The Death-Bringer. Azuma wondered at the use of those words. But she had no context to tie this to Michael Israel, even though she knew these events to be connected to whatever was frightening her so terribly.

When Michael Israel knocked at her door, the sun was down over the sea, and Azuma had ordered food from a local sushi place, *omakase,* she had told them, selfishly picking something she wanted to eat. She assumed it would be acceptable to Michael Israel, who had spent enough time in Japan that she was indoctrinated as to the nature of its foods.

"Thank you," Michael Israel said softly, seeing the food. She wore clean clothes, and respectfully stepped out of her boots in the doorway.

Azuma nodded quietly, and not wasting time on small talk, she said, "I read the file."

"I was afraid that I wouldn't get this chance, to find the Death-Bringer," Michael Israel told her. "And for the last week, I find I am afraid that I won't be able to finish it. That's what I've been hiding from.

"He murdered my brother and wanted me to know. Left me. To suffer the loss – to set me on this path, to suffer, all these years. And now, it taunts me." Michael Israel sat down across from Azuma at the small desk, her bare feet making her seem even younger and more vulnerable than she was.

"But why the 'kitty' reference?" Azuma still could not connect those dots.

"It's an oblique reference to me. It's my call sign," Michael Israel explained, and in response to Azuma's confused expression, she said, "It's a long story, and not really important right now. Essentially, it's a way of calling me out, letting me know that what happened in the desert is a message for me. And I want it like I want nothing else, that chance to make his death mean something, to take back what's mine."

"Vengeance won't bring him back," Azuma shook her head. This child against Forcas. Impossible odds.

"You can't possibly-"

"What? Understand? I understand it completely. I, too, have been a soldier." Azuma gave her a hard look.

"I just thought that you could help me," Michael Israel said, and there was so much longing for release of the burden she was carrying that Azuma's heart hurt.

"Because you assumed what? That another monster could tip the balance?" She shook her head. "This is something that may elude us both. Death itself, with the resources of The Dark God and its immeasurable power. It would take several-"

And that thought brought her up short. The crux of it had come to her, born of conjoined need. Could she use what she knew of the others to stack their side of the imbalance? She stood slowly, and went to the window, looking out to the west as though she could see over the miles, toward a distant continent that held the answer to an urgent question. Another beast. And the Sorceress to the south. Were they enemies? If so, did they share an enemy in the Star of Morning, one that created common cause?

The samurai had known it. Any soldier believes it, and history had borne it out in any number of different ways. The enemy of my enemy is my friend.

"Are you saying there are more of you?" Michael Israel did not miss the implication, correctly grasping what was unsaid.

"At least one that I know of. Another that I have yet to confirm," Azuma admitted. "But don't read that as hope. Monsters only act out of self-interest. Even I may only be here to help myself. You're very lucky that our interests are aligned."

83

ALETA DID NOT BOTHER WITH any more notes, and Amaoke was sad because he feared that perhaps he really had seen her for the last time.

Then, one unseasonably cold evening on the eve of Mardi Gras celebrations, while he sat on his porch listening to NPR News drift out to him from the countertop radio, he looked up to see her letting herself into the yard through the garden gate. The dogs were moved from their places at his feet to amble over to provide her an escort, unable to hide their disappointment that she had brought no food with her. They ignored her crutches, probably because they had thoroughly investigated that mystery on her prior visits to his landlady.

She favored him with a shy smile as she approached, which he returned, abandoning the chair he sat in and offering it to her. She wore jeans, and a lovely blue wool peacoat with a matching scarf, but he could tell she would be a bit cold sitting outside. Once she settled into the chair, he ducked inside the carriage house to retrieve a blanket off the back of one of the couches.

He turned off the radio and went back outside, taking a seat next to her, and noticing the coolness of the cushion he was glad he had given her the chair that was already warmed by his body heat. He tossed the blanket over her legs and put his feet up on the low table in front of them, forcing himself to relax, hoping that she would, too.

They sat for some time in silence, and Amaoke closed his eyes, enjoying the sounds of the streetcar from St. Charles Avenue, children playing a few streets away, and the night traffic in the shops on Magazine Street.

He rocked upright when one of the dogs let out an impressive snore, and said, "Was that the dog, or me?" He was pleased that she laughed at his lame attempt at humor, and it had the effect he hoped it would, because she started talking.

"I got your DNA results today."

Amaoke remained silent, waiting for her to continue. There was something flat in her tone that made him suspect she was upset.

"The report suggests the specimen was contaminated," she finally said, and the exasperation in her tone was obvious. "By a dog."

He almost laughed out loud, but there was no room for mirth in her expression. When she spoke again, her voice was bitter. "But there was no accompanying request to resubmit a second specimen, of course."

He didn't fully understand what she meant, and she saw it in his face, so she explained. "I think they found something extraordinary, but the result they gave me is a classic misdirection. They don't want me to know what they discovered. I can only conclude that whatever information was imparted by your genetic profile, they want to keep it a secret."

"Is it possible that they really think the specimen is contaminated?" he asked, genuinely wondering if her relationship with him and all the strange events of the last two months were making her paranoid.

"Theoretically," she allowed, while slowly shaking her head. "I considered that but rejected it because of the *way* they reported the result. They stopped short of saying that there were two separate species represented in the sample. That made me suspicious. But any respectable lab would be reluctant to return such a result. Especially RSI, with their concierge service and global reputation. I would expect apologies, and a request to submit a replacement specimen, and a refusal to report without a repeat of the test. These labs have to operate with the idea that the test was ordered as part of a treatment plan; they would want to flag this outcome to make sure that the physician of record had some notice that any therapeutics pending a result should be put on hold."

"So why are you angry?" he wondered.

"I don't like to be patronized. They should assume whatever they know I must already suspect. Also, we don't know exactly *what* your DNA result really shows, or what meaning they attach to that result, or how the information will be used." She shivered violently, and he was certain it wasn't from the cold. Her next statement confirmed it. "I sound angry but honestly I'm afraid. I'm not comfortable with the unknown factors."

"I'm afraid you've left me behind a step or two," he apologized, not understanding her.

"You told me that the Beast can pass on its properties, and we discussed the possibility that your unique genetic makeup could be weaponized, that others like you could be created," she reminded him. "That is my fear. I wonder whether they are using the contamination result to buy time to cover up further testing and study of your DNA, and the isolation of the unique biologic factors that have contributed to your meta-human abilities.

"I worry that whoever controls that information gains some sort of additional leverage over you."

"You mean manipulation? I understand your concern, but if that was the Morningstar's aim, then why-"

"Just hear me out," she stopped him there. "What if this being is playing a long game? What if the implication that your father's death had some unnatural contribution to your creation was just the first step in the process? What if it – the Morningstar, I mean – was just biding time until humanity caught up enough to create a race of superhumans? That would be an evolutionary event on a grander scale than most of the sci-fi movies ever even consider. It wouldn't necessarily be a race of helpful beings who just happen to be ultra-gifted and apparently instantly altruistic. Such a thing could be the end of humankind as we know it, because a group of such beings that have your – oh, *condition*," she cringed at the word; it was becoming an ironic joke. She shook her head. "Apex predation. The skills and cleverness of *Homo sapiens sapiens* with the bestial instincts to turn off all governing civility. Truly diabolical."

"*Sci-fi?*" he asked her, as innocently as he could manage even though he grasped the ramifications of what she suggested. It earned him a gentle shove in the shoulder, but it lightened the mood.

"Okay, I won't make a meal of it, but I wanted you to know that things don't add up. What happens if the worst imaginable occurs? What if, in the end, you weren't needed because they had your clones. That's when *you* become expendable. I just feel like..." she paused and Amaoke waited for her to finish her thought, but she never did. He was as pleased and surprised as always that she was once again putting his welfare ahead of everything else.

"Now you've caught up to me," he sighed. "You can say it out loud. Something has been set in motion. But I would argue it was inevitable, with or without my genetic code. I was already on the path toward you, and Weston. I was put on the path long ago, and when I have strayed from it, if my actions threatened the plans of the Monster, it has punished me.

"Weston has asked for my help with a few things," Amaoke told her, abruptly changing the subject. It was not of his nature to fret over things beyond his control. He would face whatever challenges life presented when they materialized.

"What things?" she asked warily.

"Well, I imagine it's a hunting trip of sorts," he said matter-of-factly.

"Do you want to tell me about it?" she asked, as ever shifting back to her professional remove. Weston made her very afraid, his nose told him that.

"I don't have any details," he admitted. "I still owe him a conversation about what has transpired since we last talked. Our parting was rather abrupt."

"Would you like my opinion?" she inquired, ignoring the second part of his statement. Now there was something he couldn't quite read in her tone.

"Always," he said, and he meant it.

"He's going to get you killed. Probably himself, too."

Amaoke sighed. She shivered again, violently and abruptly, and her hand crept upward to her necklace. She looked very young, and he felt very guilty about what he said next, so he took her free hand in his. It felt companionable, except that her fear spiked again when he did it.

"You have excellent instincts. Against all my better judgement, I think you should join us. Just for the talking part. I think you have some unanswered questions of your own," he observed, and they both knew he was referring to her experience in the church garage. "I think the three of us will get a more complete picture from it."

"Oh, Ama." Aleta knew she betrayed too much in those two words, but she no longer cared.

"What will it hurt to talk?" he asked, even more confused by the rapid changes in her scent. Waning fear. Desire. Sadness. Regret.

"You are surprisingly naïve," she sounded defeated. "Weston is already resigned to what he believes is certain. I cannot believe you do not see it. He believes the mythology. He embraces martyrdom. He welcomes the death he sees coming."

after

Official record of DNA analysis of cross-species superhuman chimera alpha, located on private server at Rising Sun Industries:

Result Completed **RESTRICTED**
Result Reported **RESTRICTED**

Specimen Taken **RESTRICTED**
Specimen Received **RESTRICTED**
Specimen Identification Number **CLASSIFIED**
Specimen **COC CONFIRMED/PROTOCOL AZ**

Subject Age **RESTRICTED**
Subject Gender
DNA Result presence of human X-chromosome, **FEMALE**
DNA Result presence of human Y-chromosome, **MALE**
DNA Result presence of uncatalogued species most closely cross-references to RSI library specimen *Cyprinus carpio*, gender determination incomplete (CONFIRMED, see results)

Subject Race **RESTRICTED**

Method
Proprietary

RESULT

Determinations

D1. Cross-species genetic material present; contamination ruled out as genetic signature reproducible at cellular level across library of specimens (blood, tissue spectrum)
D2. Genetic byproduct analysis consistent with mature human female hormone expression; mature male human hormone production potential exists but is unexpressed (byproducts undetectable in blood/serum samples)
D3. Genetic byproduct analysis deferred for uncatalogued species, genomic similarity to *Cyprinus carpio* ≈ 93%.

Conclusions

C1. Human female and male DNA present; organism expression of mature female genetic hormonal byproducts (genotype female, possible phenotypes female and male due to intact dormant male genetic hormonal byproduct potential)

C2. Uncatalogued species suggests novel DNA consistent with new organism most closely related to common carp species, specifically *nishikigoi*, the brocaded carp, disambiguation, decorative **koi**, assigned new RSI library identifier, genetic byproduct analysis to be initiated **

C3. Unidentified genetic material found in sample, supernumerary unexplained STR segments present with unidentified chemical bases/unknown chemical bond structure

C4. Lead project science team believes genetic material originated from a single bio-organism_(CONFIRMED)

C5. Positive identification of cross-species/superhuman chimera; **<u>INDEX DNA EVENT</u>** labeled control specimen alpha (will be added to library catalogue as exemplar for RSI Taskforce AZ Priority/Defense Project

** Material characterization project commenced as of report date [classified]

Addendum posted to genetic profile of cross-species superhuman chimera alpha as of XX/XX/XXXX [date classified]:

Second specimen presented as alpha-1 exhibits confirmatory match to control specimen alpha, with the following genotypic/phenotypic exceptions:

RESULT

Determinations (as differ from specimen alpha)

D2. Genetic byproduct analysis consistent with mature human **MALE** hormone expression; mature female human hormone production potential exists but is unexpressed (byproducts undetectable in blood/serum samples) . . .

Conclusions

C1. Human female and male DNA present; organism expression of mature **MALE** genetic hormonal byproducts (genotype MALE, possible phenotypes female and male due to intact dormant female genetic hormonal byproduct potential) . . .

C6. Female and male phenotypic expression CONFIRMED . . .

Such a small sound would not otherwise have aroused Amaoke; indeed, under other circumstances, the guardian instincts that he had honed over centuries would have considered it, discarded it as a threat, and gone back to whatever state of repose his primitive brain was currently inhabiting. If it had proven otherwise, his many other gifts would have served to rectify the mistake.

But given the very strangeness of the past several days, and the fact that Aleta lay defenseless, fast asleep mere inches away, meant any unexplained event had to be investigated; she remained a target of the Morningstar. His nose brought to him the barest hints of something watery and almost fish-like, not a scent he had ever encountered in this landlocked subdivision. It was accompanied by a sulfurous signature that he could only identify with the Morningstar.

Convincing Aleta to sleep had not been easy. He had accomplished as much by promising to remain with her. She had saved him from the aftereffects of his altercation with Weston; her presence had cured him of despair and her compassion and empathy had triggered the reversal of his arrested change. She was bone-weary but understandably reluctant to rest at all, still significantly affected by her encounter with the Monster weeks before. Ironically, if not for Weston, she would have fallen victim to an unimaginable fate, and Amaoke was completely responsible for exposing her to peril yet again. Her sister had gone out of town, and she had called him, hating herself for having moments of weakness where she could not overcome her paranoia and fear, needing not to be alone.

"You have to get some sleep," he told her gently, alarmed by the depth and darkness of the hollows beneath her usually bright eyes. It was as if she had not slept since their last conversation in his backyard, nearly a week before. "Is there anything you typically do to relax?"

She shook her head mutely, still afraid to give in to her exhaustion, and admit to her worst fear, the loss of her precious independence. Soon enough, he could see, her body would betray her. That inevitability increased her fear. She didn't like surrender.

"I won't abandon you," he said, putting a reassuring hand on the small of her back, and feeling slightly guilty about how it affected him to touch her. It was the closest thing to a promise he could make, but he refused to lie and make assurances that he could absolutely ensure her safety. She was smart enough not to believe them anyway.

"I'll take some Tylenol," she whispered, something in her voice giving in to the idea of sleep. Aleta could see that Amaoke did not understand this, so she explained herself. "For some odd reason, when I have a headache and I take it, it makes me sleepy. I don't know why, perhaps it is a placebo effect, maybe it gives me an excuse to allow myself to take a nap, or it could even be because it is the strongest substance I ever ingest." In a weak attempt at humor she added, "It would probably knock *you* out for days."

"I don't know," he replied mischievously, following her lead. "I am a Native American male. I have burned the *ayuq* and *tarvaq* in ritual many times, and I might have inhaled." He didn't even try to keep a straight face as he said the last, and she was unable to deny her own amusement.

"That's enough NPR for you, mister," she told him, sounding a bit more like herself. "You're letting the modern world corrupt you."

He stood to help her to her feet, and she clung to him, this time reluctant to let go. He sensed this and swung her gently into his arms. She didn't protest, but seemed relieved when he bent down and captured her crutches in his fingers to show her that he wasn't going to leave her vulnerable without them. He took her to her bedroom and set her on her feet, returning the crutches so that she could ready herself for bed. He turned to leave, wanting her to have her privacy and regain some autonomy.

"Please don't leave," she said in a small voice. Her tone threatened tears, which he knew would cost her too much dignity.

"I won't," he promised, taking her chin in his hand carefully, but not forcing her to look at him. "I will be just outside the room."

But he could see she was still struggling, so he turned away from her to remove his boots before stretching out atop the duvet on her bed, on the side where her scent was most faint. Only then did she move on, into the bathroom, closing the door behind herself to attend to her nighttime ritual.

When she emerged, she had renewed purpose, coming straight to the bed and sliding between the sheets on the opposite side. Amaoke did not move to help her, indeed, did not move a muscle. She turned toward him and curled up on her side; in seconds, he could hear her breathing change as she finally succumbed to rest. He switched off the light and was asleep himself within minutes.

But something woke him. The sound he could have imagined; the fishy scent persisted. Although he loathed to endanger Aleta further by bringing the fight to himself, he hated to imagine leaving her alone and vulnerable while he investigated a nebulous suspicion. She was still deeply asleep, her exhaustion and shock contributing to a near complete shutdown of her consciousness. Amaoke moved only long enough to sit up on the side of the bed and slide his feet into his boots, then stretched out again next to her, lying back on top of the soft coverlet. He put his hands behind his head and crossed his legs, hoping Aleta would forgive him putting those dusty boots on her blanket. He'd already replaced it once, he was reasonably certain that she would frown upon the need for another, but that couldn't be helped.

His calmness belied his concentrated alertness; he used a hunter's stillness as he had since his adolescence and waited for his prey to come to him.

He was old enough, and experienced enough, that he was able to confuse other predators as to the true threat he represented. At least most of the ones he had previously encountered. He still felt strangely lethargic, as if he wasn't fully awake, as if he were somehow dreaming all of this. It was a strange sort of inertia, and instinctually he knew he should be alarmed, rather than comforted.

He forced himself to focus on a particular spot on the ceiling above, and soon realized it appeared to be moving. So he concentrated, suspecting that his stupor was influenced, and recognized the pattern on the ceiling to be similar to the necklace that Aleta now wore, mimicking the Mobius loop at her throat, except that it was in motion, and the creature which slowly coalesced from the undulating pattern was unlike anything he had yet seen in his long centuries of existence.

As blue as the summer sky, its serpent-like body had iridescent scales that caught the faint glow from the streetlights outside and the soft light emanating from a nightlight in the adjacent bathroom. Its limbs were small, vestigial in scale but clearly functional, ending in three-toed foreclaws and split-toed hind claws that did not appear to make purchase on the ceiling; rather, it hovered in the repeating loop, probably as a means to lull its prey.

Its head was large, akin to but fuller than that of a crocodile, with a mouth full of long, needle-like teeth and a questing, forked tongue. There were complicated fringed feelers around its muzzle that made him think of a catfish, and its eyes were large and intelligent, set beneath ridged brows on the sides of its face. It was crowned by a pair of complex horns and gauzy fin-like projections ran along its back and tail, reminding Amaoke of fancy fish he had seen in ornamental ponds. This probably explained its scent, but it had an overwhelming lizard-like quality as well, though its overall form betrayed it as clearly neither of those.

Without altering his relaxed posture, he opened his mouth, bared his teeth, and growled a warning, not wanting to wake Aleta yet needing to make his intentions clear. But Aleta did not stir, and he suspected there was some nefarious magic at work upon her to keep her docile. He listened carefully to confirm she was still breathing but did not take his attention from the unwelcome intruder.

In response to his challenge, it returned a throaty laugh, a woman's hum of amusement, breaking its patterned flight and straightening out like a ribbon, floating to a corner of the ceiling farthest from Amaoke. It seemed to collapse on itself, one moment a mass of writhing scales and graceful fins, the next, a statuesque young woman emerged, perched at the top of the intersection of the two walls.

She was nude, impossibly tall, with a stature that appeared to match his own, long-limbed and androgynous. Her inky hair was cut in a blunt cascade that mimicked the fins she displayed in her other form, and her eyes betrayed an Asian origin. She was inhumanly gorgeous, almost frighteningly so, and deceptively fragile; Amaoke imagined she manipulated these assets to deadly effect. Her eyes flashed with intelligence, aggression, and her own challenge, clearly in response to his. She briefly made eye contact with him before glancing at Aleta, so he said calmly, "I don't have to go to the fridge for my midnight snack. I was thinking leftover chicken, but sushi will do."

"Dog," she replied derisively, which signaled that she knew what he was and was using the term as a derogation. "If I wanted *her*, she would be done already. Pureflesh always make for tasty blood meals. Beautiful only adds to the pleasure."

Amaoke felt the change threatening, but the creature's response could only mean that she had come for him. It would have been easier to engage him in her other form, so his curiosity was peaked, and he hesitated. But his earlier guess had been right, her perceived fragility was a trap, and he detected the surge in her aggression by her scent. His hands and feet began the change as he called the Beast, but suddenly the air was charged with something, and Weston appeared between them, as if from thin air.

Weston's expression was surprised; he must have been asleep, as he was in dark warm-ups and a long-sleeved t-shirt. The grogginess of sleep had incompletely cleared, and he stumbled, catching himself awkwardly. Amaoke could see that he was without his spectacles. The woman sensed easier prey, turning her attention to Weston.

"Threat, Brother, threat!" Amaoke shouted, the timbre of his voice dropping into a snarl that he could not control, and he knew the Beast was coming. He was relieved to see that his warning had registered, and noted with satisfaction that Weston held his heavy crucifix in his hand. The priest would have to be quick; Amaoke's change would delay him a moment too long, and the creature was ready to pounce.

But the sharp smell of ozone heralded a third guest, who appeared in silhouette by the window. Another young woman, again unknown to Amaoke, with a strangely familiar scent. She, too, was tall and imperious. Her hair initially appeared to be an enormous halo that he quickly realized was some sort of ceremonial headdress made of the mane of a lion. Her breasts were bare, as were her long legs, but there were bands of gold encircling her upper arms and her ankles, and she wore an elaborate stiff armored skirt that smelled of an aviary and was covered in enormous feathers. The spear she carried was very old, indeed ancient, and somewhat rudimentary, but he could feel its power, and hers, greater than and unlike anything he'd yet experienced.

Whoever she was, she'd come prepared, and her eyes showed only concern and concentration. She took in Aleta's still-sleeping form, glanced at Amaoke in the Beast's skin, betrayed a small smile, and then her eyes moved on, touching on Weston briefly, and passing over him in favor of the greatest threat.

She locked eyes with the intruder, who appeared confused for the first time, and who now, Amaoke noted, smelled of fear.

"Oh, no, you don't," the spear-bearer spoke directly to the other woman, but in a strange musical language that was oddly familiar to Amaoke, and he suspected that everyone in the room understood her. She crouched down, oddly catlike, and pricked her own finger on the end of the spear. "No more mischief."

Then she stepped forward and placed her hand on Amaoke's arm, which dispatched the Beast immediately, returning him to his naked human form. Before he had time to register this shocking event, without letting go of him, she whispered, "*Home.*"

The air was alive with energy, crackling with electricity, Amaoke's long hair stood out like a cat's, and then he was thrown backward by some untold force. He scrambled to his feet ready to fight, but the other three were gone as suddenly as they had come, and the night was quiet once more, Aleta slumbering peacefully on.

Acknowledgements

Without the help of my sister-in-law, Yuko, this book would be less rich, less historically authentic, and less imaginative. When composing fiction, having that kind of expertise is invaluable.

With her characteristic enthusiasm, having very little idea of how much what she shared with me about the Japanese mythology of demons and heroes was fueling my already overactive imagination, she walked me through the history and the status of women in feudal 17th century Japan. She told me the legend of *Momotoro*, the 'peach boy', and happily answered what had to be some very confusing questions that were completely out of context of our relationship at the time (**north** was not yet written) without hesitation. I'm sure she thought my brother's *Ane* was finally unraveling mentally, asking about Japanese demons and deities on a family trip, and perhaps thought I needed some professional help, but was kind enough to treat my inquiries as if I always spend summer evenings grilling her for this type of information. I needed her intimate knowledge to supplement my tourist's observations. That husband of hers, my dear *Otōto*, was also extremely helpful, as a conduit to his wife and an impromptu research assistant at the eleventh hour.

I have taken my liberties this time with the history of the Tokugawa Shogunate (during Japan's Edo Period), the last line of ruling shoguns in Japan. Azuma's father was loosely based upon (and referred to as) Ietsune, fourth shogun in the succession. While he *was* the elder of two sons, the historical Ietsune (Ietsuna) was indeed first to ascend to power rather than his brother, although it was at age ten that he did so, supported by regent advisors. Ietsune was rumored to have fathered an illegitimate daughter at age twenty-five and he was succeeded as shogun by his younger brother upon his death (unlike the fate of the unfortunate fictional Tsunayoshi). It is true that Ietsuna's father, Iemitsu, was the shogun responsible for cleansing Japan of foreigners, specifically Christian (Catholic) missionaries, during his tenure following the Shimabara Rebellion. Since Ietsune's lifetime encompassed the aftermath of the Rebellion (1637-38) and followed the turbulent and violent events that accompanied the introduction of Christianity to the country, this created a likely background around which to build this story. While I do have to acknowledge the blurred historicity, in my opinion most fiction is enriched by using the stories important to human history to anchor an otherwise wholly invented timeline.   Finally, unlike in other books, I have avoided all but the most indirect parallels with any existing Japanese mythology in creating my own. Japan has many intricate and beautiful mythologies, but their tradition and observance is so steeped in local history and so rich in variation that I knew from the outset I would be unable to honor them properly, so I opted to create a fictional mythology which borrows from many different cultural legends.

Dr. Alexander Bennet's translation of the *Hagakure* was an invaluable resource regarding the philosophy and worldview of the samurai. *Prime Japan: The Beautiful Foolishness of Things* tied modern Japan to its rich past and attempted to help the outsider understand the enduring philosophies of this incredible country and its significant contributions to our own Western traditions.

I also must warmly thank Rabbi Jason Fleischer for his friendship and his patience. His knowledge of Israel, Judaism, faith, and human nature was imparted with wisdom and good humor.

Again, although my books occasionally mention real persons, some of them still living, they should be viewed entirely as works of fiction.

Glossary of Terms

Amateratsu – *Goddess (kami) of the sun, ruler of the Takama no Hara, the High Celestial Plane, which is the domain of the kami. Her name is derived from Amateru, which means 'shining in heaven'*

Akai hogo-sha – *The term generally means 'red guard' or 'red guardian(s)'*

Akenomyosei – *literally, Star of Morning; the Morningstar's formal address in this novel*

Ane – *Elder sister*

Bushido – *the code of honor and morals developed by the Japanese samurai*

Chiwosuu akuma – *a bloodthirsty demon*

Daimyo – *a great lord of feudal Japan; a vassal of the Shogun*

Do – *a part of the samurai's armor that consisted of a breastplate or coat that was frequently fashioned from leather plus armor plates covered in lacquer*

Fūjin – *God (kami) of the Wind, a strong elemental force. Also known as* **kami-no-kaze**, *from which the term* **kamikaze** *(literally 'the great wind or typhoon which protects Japan') is derived, as it was a typhoon which foiled the attempts of Kublai Khan's forces from reaching the islands in the early thirteenth century. Thus, kamikaze, long associated in the west with suicidal combat missions, is an honorific*

Imōto – *Younger sister*

Izanagi – *The Exalted Male, the initial great creator kami. Along with his wife, Izanami, created and/or gave birth to many of the greater islands of Japan. Izanagi also created some of the most powerful kami following his wife's death and capture within the underworld, plucking the sun goddess, Amateratsu, from his right eye and the moon god from his left, etc.*

Izanami – *wife and sister of Izanagi, the Exalted Female, mother of Japan*

Jinja – *Shinto shrine; each shrine is usually dedicated to a unique kami, the oldest, in Honshu, is the Ise shrine dedicated to the worship of Amateratsu.*

Kami – *a deity, whether minor or major, god/goddess*

Kanzashi – *the wooden sticks used to secure a hairstyle, although used prior to the Edo period, they became more ubiquitous during this time due to an increase in the types of elaborate hairstyles worn by Kabuki performers, Geisha, and noblewomen*

Karategi – *The loose clothing worn by practitioners of the martial arts, specifically karate, from which the outfit takes its name; more generally or disambiguated the word becomes 'gi,' the term most familiar to Westerners*

Kitsune bakuchi – *(and Chō han) One of two popular Japanese dice games, the term's literal translation is 'fox gambling'*

Kobakama – *The loose outer pantaloons of a samurai's battle dress*

Komoamatsukami – *The gods who were present at the creation of the universe, from which first the islands of Japan were brought forth, followed by the great kami of nature*

Kyuketsuke – *a blood sucking demon in the Eastern European tradition; a vampire*

Nekekube – *a special monster of Japanese legend; its head and neck detach from its body to fly about seeking human prey at night*

nodo Botoke – *the direct translation is 'throat Buddha' and it is the Japanese term for the Adam's apple*

Onigashima – *an island of legend, a place of monsters, that can appear or disappear at the whims of the dark gods; those who seek it might never find it, those who find it might never escape it*

Otōto – *Younger brother.*

Ouban – *Imperial guards or distinguished personal guard of the Shogun; this term was used most frequently during the Heian period*

Ryū – *Japanese dragon*

San'ninshō – *third-born*

Sashimono – *a battle standard that indicated the affiliation or allegiance of a samurai, often this was a small flag made of paper or cloth and carrying a design specific to that warrior's family or clan*

Shikibuton – *traditional Japanese floor mattress/futon*

Shinobi – *a ninja, a clandestine assassin, can also refer to the traditional garb the ninja wears*

Sōtō – *The medieval traditional burial ceremonies associated with Zen Buddhism that were practiced in feudal Japan; included cremation, prayer, and grave ceremonies, and an observance of mourning to the forty-ninth day following death*

Tatsuo Tomo – *The name of the human manifestation of the Ungalek/Forcas/Nyoka and Azuma's early advisor in this book, it is no accident* *that the name later attaches to the twin brother of Azuma; this combination was chosen ironically and for its utility — Tatsuo refers to a masculine dragon and Tomo means twin*

Teki — *Enemy*

Yokai — *a class of supernatural monsters, spirits, and demons in Japanese folklore*

Yomi-no-kuni — *The Land of the Dead*

About the Author

LJ Farrow's childhood fear of the dark was probably the result of an overzealous older brother who would leap out at her from behind doors, boxes, and furniture in the basement, coupled with an unnatural curiosity about scary things. She wholeheartedly endorses the modernization of classic monsters and their expanded role in popular culture. A Colorado native, she now lives and writes in rural Indiana. She remains afraid of the dark.

If you enjoyed **east**, look for **west**, the fourth and final book in the Morningstar series!

Weston, priest exemplar on special Vatican assignment. He operates outside of clerical hierarchy, answerable only to the Pope. For Father Weston is not just any priest. He is the half-demon offspring of a revivalist minister corrupted by the Morningstar, and his ability to attract demons is useful to Rome.

west is the fourth novel in the Morningstar series, which follows the lives of four supernatural beings, each of whom must overcome a specific challenge to their humanity as part of a personal journey toward redemption. The prevention of an apocalyptic war planned by the Morningstar will only be possible if they work together to harness the unique powers that each possesses.